ONE

R hys Evans looked over his shoulder to see two shadows following him. Fear prickled his scalp. His damp hands shook and he wiped them on his jeans. He ducked into a dimly lit doorway, aware of his shallow breathing and bunched fists. Everything smelt of fear, the scent of his own acrid sweat.

The only sound louder than his heartbeat was the music of the pizzeria next door.

A fist came out of nowhere. The first punch split his lip and forced him back against the door. Two shadows loomed over him. He tasted the metal of his own blood. His right hand hit a rough patch of ground as he fell. Stopping had been a mistake. He screamed as a black boot stamped, smashing the bones in his fingers. He was hauled to his feet. He should have made a run for it when he could. The hood of his assailant fell back, revealing a familiar grinning face.

''Ello, Rhys.'

With wide open eyes he stared at the man.

'You?' Blood sprayed as he spoke. 'Why?'

A second punch to the mouth. Pain exploded in his face. He spat a broken tooth. Blows rained down. Dazed. Confused. He lost the wit and strength to defend himself. A heavy door was dragged open and he was propelled into the poorly lit stairwell. Overcome by the beckoning darkness, he collapsed against the wall as the final blow fell. His last thoughts were of his mother. The mother he had never met.

***

The grey-haired man across the road watched through narrowed eyes as the body was dragged further into the stairwell and away from the prying eyes of the street. A commotion broke out about a hundred yards away. The man shifted to get a better look: just some drunken students on a pub crawl. As they clattered down the street, the man returned to the shadow, his attention back on the assault in the alley. One of the assailants silently touched the other's arm and nodded. Having done what they were sent to do, they melted away into the evening, the burlier of the two maintaining a tight grip on the objects he'd retrieved from the man's rucksack.

The man waited and watched from a safe distance, ramming the black baseball cap further over his hooded eyes. The boy's death was unfortunate, but the man couldn't afford to be exposed and the boy had been asking too many questions. He was now very close to achieving his goal. He had waited over forty years and it was finally within his grasp. Nothing and nobody was going to stop him. He smiled and turned away.

Payback time.

***

TUESDAY EVENING, 29TH MAY

DCI Jim Carruthers zipped up his brown holdall. All ready for leaving the following morning. He was looking forward to spending the next five days in Glencoe in his newly-purchased and top-of-the-range tent. His only companions were to be a bottle of Talisker and Ian Fleming's *Casino Royale*. He had decided to re-read all the Bond books. He stooped to pick up an old newspaper from the carpet. Just as he was about to chuck it in the recycling box the phone rang. He hesitated. As he threw the newspaper into the box he knew with a sinking heart that it would be the station calling. He answered.

'Jim, sorry to do this to you,' said Superintendent Bingham. 'We've got a suspicious death. You're needed back here in Castletown.'

'Is there nobody else who could take this one?'

'No,' replied Bingham. 'Get yourself over to 39, Bell Street.'

'Who's the victim?' Carruthers asked, his innate curiosity kicking in.

'All we know is, he's young and male. Details are sketchy.'

'OK,' said Carruthers, 'I'll be there in twenty.'

'I'm sending Fletcher and Harris over,' continued Bingham. 'Fletcher's as keen as mustard, and Harris, well, it'll stop him cramming his face with any more doughnuts. Bloody man's practically finished the entire bag.'

Carruthers smiled. Harris wasn't the only one with a fondness for doughnuts.

Car keys in hand, he left his cottage and locked up. He could hear the sound of water lapping the harbour. Despite the lateness of the hour, there were still one or two people by the quay finishing their fish suppers from Anstruther Fish Bar. It was a warm evening. A group of giggling teenage girls walked past. They were wearing short skirts and had flat midriffs on display. Carruthers tried not to stare, but it was difficult. He was just a man in his late thirties after all. One of the girls had her belly button pierced. As obesity levels soared, seeing a group of teenagers with flat stomachs was, sadly, an increasing rarity. Why was it that girls were either bordering on anorexia, or morbidly obese? What happened to nice healthy curves? He must be getting old wondering whether there were any normal and well-adjusted teens around. Perhaps they were just all at home getting ready for bed.

As he drove towards Castletown, he was aware of an enormous and dizzying expanse of sky stretched beyond him. Fife was so unlike the west coast of Scotland where he grew up, and although he loved the west with its majestic but moody mountains and heather-clad landscape, the Fife countryside already held a special place in his heart.

Today had been a beautiful day and the sky was still a hazy blue. Carruthers loved the drive to work in the summer. He was reminded of the colours on an artist's palette, as overgrown verges full of patches of cow parsley, clumps of bluebell and the occasional scarlet poppy flashed past.

Tana Collins

As he approached Castletown, leaving behind the undulating green and golden fields, he drew in a breath. For all the tourists and students, there was something otherworldly about the historic town.

There the town stood, nestled by the coast, at one time only easily reachable by sea. The spires of its cathedral and castle ruins glinted in the evening sun, as they had done for at least six hundred years. Lives tumbled upon lives, from the red-gowned student population that had shaped the town since the 1400s, to the gothic Victorians and beyond.

As he drove into Castletown, the town looked as it would on any other weekday evening. The fine weather meant that it was busy in the centre. Patrons from the Earl of Fife bar spilled out on to the cobbled street clutching their glasses. Carruthers, who had wound down his window to enjoy the fresh evening air, could hear the babble of chatter as he drove past. He saw a couple with a toddler and a baby in pushchair. They didn't look like tourists. Most likely locals or RAF. His parents would never have allowed him up this late at that age but, he shrugged, things changed. And what would he know about modern parenting?

Driving into Market Street he spotted a couple of young women in their twenties walking down the pavement arm in arm. Carruthers could imagine that they were confiding secrets or making easy small talk, the way good female friends do, or so he was told. As he turned into Bell Street, the women, who had also turned, stopped abruptly when they noticed the commotion ahead. A small crowd had gathered behind police tape. One of the girls stopped and pointed and the other followed the line of her arm.

The scene of crime boys were already busy. As Carruthers drew closer he saw most of the activity was confined within the stairwell of number thirty-nine. His senses came to full alert with the familiar quickening of pulse that always accompanied him to the scene of a suspicious death. As usual, he experienced a momentary apprehension for what he might find, just as he had the first time he'd seen a dead body.

Heart still thumping, he found a space and parked. Jumping out of his car he ran across the street, pushing through the throng of onlookers. He was aware of Detective Sergeant Harris pushing his way through the crowd in the opposite direction. He wondered briefly where the man was going. However, he put thoughts of Harris aside as he prepared himself for what lay ahead. Flashing his police badge, DCI Carruthers ducked under the tape. He nodded at the SOCO who handed him a coverall kit then pulled on the suit and latex gloves and shoes, and went through the partially open front door. The hastily erected mobile lighting lent an eerie cast to the stairwell, making it all extremes of dark and light.

Carruthers surveyed the scene, his keen blue eyes missing nothing. The flat itself was next to a pizzeria. There was a pungent smell of dough. Every so often he'd hear a blast of loud music. He guessed the stairwell led to student flats. Either that or the proprietor lived above the premises. He focused on the bulky frame topped by white hair. Dr Mackie was talking with Liu, the police photographer.

'What have we got?' Carruthers asked.

'Young male. Badly beaten,' responded Dr Mackie.

'Cause of death was a blow then?'

Mackie wagged a finger at him. 'You know me better than that, Jim. You'll have to wait for the lab results. He did receive a massive blow to the side of the head, though. It is a possible cause of death.'

Carruthers bent down to get a closer look. The victim was lying angled in the hallway, blood from the head wound covering his face and soaking his green T-shirt. Somebody had done a number on him.

Carruthers turned to Mackie. 'Do we know what he was hit with and whether he was killed here?'

'One question at a time if you don't mind, young man,' said the world-weary doctor, whose dishevelled appearance and five o'clock shadow belied an acute mind. 'To answer the first, a blunt instrument's been used. Whether that was what killed him, we'll just have to wait see. First impressions are he was killed here, or more likely,' he raised a hand towards the door, 'just over there and dragged in here to be better hidden.'

'Can you give me a time of death?'

'Always a difficult one, that. Not been dead long. I won't be pushed on a time yet though.'

Too soon for anyone to have reported him missing, thought Carruthers, but more than likely he'll be missed by someone. Soon enough there could be a parent or sibling, maybe a girlfriend or wife whose lives would be changed forever. *The boy only looks early twenties,* he thought. *Bloody shame.*

'There's something you should know,' continued Mackie. 'There's also significant old bruising here. In all likelihood, this man's been in a bad fight recently, but not as recently as tonight. Poor sod. Clearly wasn't having a good time of it. Guess his luck finally ran out.' The doctor lifted the T-shirt, revealing a welt of old greenish bruising across the chest.

Carruthers frowned. 'There was a bad fight between some of the townies and RAF boys about a week ago. That's worth following up.' He turned at the sound of footsteps to see the diminutive DS Andrea Fletcher approaching. She nodded at her boss as she stopped and wrote neatly in her black notebook.

As usual she was the picture of professionalism. She'd slipped a SOCO suit over a tailored short-sleeved white cotton blouse with black trousers and slim fitting lace up boots she'd been wearing on duty earlier. Her dark hair had been tied in a ponytail and she had used a grip to keep her fringe from falling into her eyes. Although younger and much less experienced than himself, her presence assured Carruthers the job would be well done. She was already a fine detective.

'So we've no idea who he is?' Carruthers said to Dr Mackie.

'That's your job, Jim, not mine, but I'll give you one clue, laddie,' said Mackie, his highland accent still discernible after more than thirty years in Fife. 'Look at this.' Mackie pointed at the man's upper arm.

Carruthers stared at the tattoo of a bluebird.

'Cardiff City fan?' said Fletcher leaning over the corpse. Her clear-cut English accent penetrated Carruthers' thoughts. 'That's their emblem,' she continued. 'Nice to know my passion for football can come in useful.'

As Carruthers peered at the prostrate man, trying to ignore the congealed blood and pulped bone, he was aware of the buzzcut beneath the broken flesh. A military haircut. There was an RAF base just six miles from Castletown.

Unlikely to be a local if he supports Cardiff, though stranger things have happened, Carruthers thought. He'd once met a Glaswegian who was a fervent Aberdeen fan. That took some beating in a city where there were only two dominant teams split by religious differences. Perhaps that had been the point.

'Victim looks like a squaddie tae me,' said the sweaty, overweight Detective Sergeant Dougie Harris suddenly appearing and leaning over Fletcher's shoulder.

'Who found him?' Carruthers asked.

'Student returning to the flat above,' said Fletcher. 'Already taken a statement from him. Victim's open rucksack was found a few feet from the body,' she added, 'but still within the stairwell. It appears to have been rifled through. No wallet or mobile.' She looked around her. 'No obvious sign of any weapon. Looks like a straightforward robbery gone wrong.'

'What about staff and customers next door at the pizzeria?' asked Carruthers, turning to Harris. 'Somebody may have seen or heard something. I want statements taken from everybody. Nobody's to leave until they've given one.'

'What, all of them?' grumbled Harris. 'There must be about thirty people in there. With our luck, there's probably a two-for-one special offer on.'

Lazy bastard. 'Well, you'd better get cracking then, hadn't you? And when you've finished those, talk to everyone behind the police tape. They may have seen something. Then you and Andrea can start conducting a door-to-door. Off you go, chop

chop.' Carruthers wasn't oblivious to the filthy look Harris shot him but, as ever, he just ignored it. Thinking about Dougie Harris, he suddenly frowned.

'By the way,' said Carruthers, 'where've you been for the last fifteen minutes? There's work to be done. I hope you weren't taking a piss in an alleyway. I've told you about that before. You should use a public toilet like the rest of us.'

'I wisnae taking a piss,' said Harris, looking offended.

'Well, what were you doing then?' demanded Carruthers.

'I was over by your car checking out your slow puncture.'

Carruthers sighed. It looked as if it was going to be a long night in Castletown. He wished he were in Glencoe, already ensconced in his new tent with two fingers of whisky and some old-fashioned espionage.

***

The man joined the crowd. Eyes narrowed, he watched the police. Inhaling his cigarette deeply he felt the nicotine hit him. It tasted good. He pushed past a couple of open-mouthed holidaymakers and jostled to get as close to the front of the crowd as he dared without making his presence too obvious. Deep inhalation made short work of the rest of the fag. He flicked the butt to the ground. Watched as the sparks hit the pavement before he ground it underfoot. He took a silver lighter from his trouser pocket and lit another. He stayed and observed for some time, slipping away just before they started to interview the crowd.

***

Glancing at her watch, dark-haired Siobhan Mathews stared out of the window again. Siobhan wrapped her shawl around her slender frame and turned to Tomoko. 'Tomoko,' she said, 'he's never been this late before. Where is he?'

Tomoko pushed her owlish glasses back up on to the bridge of her nose. 'Why don't you try his mobile again?'

'I keep trying but there's no response. I've already phoned the base, so I know he left Edenside on time. The guy I spoke to saw Rhys speaking with Dave Roberts just as he was leaving.'

'Have you still got Dave's number?' asked Tomoko.

Siobhan blushed, thinking of her one-night stand with Dave before she started seeing Rhys. She didn't like to dwell on it. It had been a mistake. 'Yes,' she said.

'Seriously Siobhan, if you're this worried, swallow your pride and give him a ring.'

Siobhan sighed. 'You're right. It makes sense. I'll do it now, before I lose my nerve.'

'Honestly, what's the worst that can happen? He's rude to you. At best, you'll find out what's keeping Rhys.'

Siobhan smiled at Tomoko. 'Ever sensible.'

Just as she was about to pick up the phone, Siobhan hesitated. She'd thought of another reason why Rhys may not have turned up. It made her feel sick to even think about it. *Maybe he's left me,* she thought. *Maybe he's got fed up with me and doesn't know how to tell me, so he's taken the coward's way out and just not turned up.* Siobhan knew she was being irrational, but she couldn't stop the thoughts crowding her head. It was all Roy's fault. Her ex had taken the coward's way out and just stopped seeing her without a word; now she suspected it whenever Rhys was just a little – OK, a lot – late.

'Siobhan, are you all right?' asked Tomoko. 'It's just you've gone awfully white and you're shaking.'

She wasn't going to let these feelings spiral. She now knew from counselling that she could control her feelings with a mixture of deep breathing exercises and meditation. She tried the deep breathing now. It seemed to help. She started to feel calmer. She was regaining control. Slowly she became aware that she wasn't actually alone.

'I'm fine, Tomoko, honestly. Just felt a bit faint for a few seconds but it's gone now. Probably tiredness and hunger. I'm just going to make that call.'

She composed herself and dialled Dave's number.

'Yes?'

'Dave, it's Siobhan Mathews here.'

'Yes?' This time the voice was slightly more impatient. There seemed to be a lot of background noise. She could hear music and another noise but she couldn't work out what it was.

She took a deep breath. 'Sorry to bother you. Just wondered if you'd seen or heard from Rhys?'

'No. Not since I saw him leaving the base to meet you.'

There was a muffled noise, then what sounded like panting. Siobhan strained to listen. Dave sounded like he was running for a bus. *Oh God, I hope he's running for a bus and not having a shag. How embarrassing.* She reasoned he wouldn't answer the phone if he was mid-thrust, so steeled herself and carried on regardless.

'I was expecting him several hours ago. He's not turned up.'

'Well, I haven't seen him and I'm busy.' He sounded really annoyed and he was panting. She heard something else in the background. To her mortification it was woman's voice.

'Dave, do you want me to go lower?' The voice belonged to a young woman. Siobhan blushed. *Why would he answer the phone in the middle of sex? No wonder he was cross.* However, embarrassed as she was, Siobhan pushed on, reminding herself that this was more important than Dave getting his leg over.

'You haven't heard from him at all?' That question was greeted by silence. 'OK, well, if you hear from him, can you contact me straight away? This isn't like him. I'm actually thinking of phoning the police.'

'Christ, don't do that.' Apparently, she now had Dave's full attention. 'Get off me you stupid cow,' she heard him muttering to his companion and then a thud as if something or someone had just fallen on to the floor.

'Look, Siobhan, Rhys has probably gone drinking with some mates and forgotten the time. He'll turn up when he's ready, and he won't thank you for getting the police involved. And yes, I'll phone you if I hear anything, OK, now I have to go.' Slightly away from the phone she heard him say, 'Of course I want you to go lower, you dirty little bitch.' Siobhan heard a giggle. Then the phone went dead.

'Oh shit, how embarrassing,' said Siobhan, her cheeks flaming. 'He had a woman with him. I don't know why I'm surprised. After all, I know what he's like.' She glanced at Tomoko who was trying to stifle a yawn. 'Look, you've been brilliant, Tomoko, but if you want to go to bed early – don't let me stop you. You look done in.'

'OK, do you mind?' She was already heading to her room. 'I'm exhausted and I really need to get this paper completed tomorrow. I've already had one extension. Come and get me if there's any news. No doubt if he comes in late, I'll hear the doorbell. And Siobhan, try not to worry.'

'Good night, Tomoko, and thanks.'

Knowing sleep would be impossible Siobhan made herself a milky coffee. She sat with it in the living room. Idly flicking through a magazine, she tried not to worry. But time passed. She glanced at her watch. More than two hours later Rhys still hadn't arrived or contacted her. Siobhan sighed and picked up the phone. She hoped that whatever she had interrupted earlier had long since finished. If not it was the longest blow job in the history of blow jobs.

'Hi Dave, it's me again, Siobhan. Sorry about earlier. I know you had company.'

'If you wanted to join us, you should have said. It's been a while since I had a threesome.'

She decided to ignore his remark. 'Look, I know it's late, but Rhys still hasn't turned up. I just wanted to check with you one final time before phoning the police. I know what you said about my being a laughing stock if I ring them this early, but I have to do something. This is just to let you know I'm going to give them a call.'

'If you're that set on phoning them, Siobhan, I'll ring them for you. OK? It's very macho down at the station and it's more than likely to be a male copper that answers the phone. If a bloke rings them to have a chat about a missing mate this time of night, they may take the conversation more seriously than if it's just the neurotic little girlfriend.'

Siobhan bristled at being called 'just the neurotic little girlfriend,' but exhaustion on top of anxiety had robbed her of her urge to fight. She just wanted to find Rhys, so she ignored Dave's condescension.

'Thanks Dave, are you sure? Can you ring me back as soon as you've spoken to them?'

'OK, Siobhan. If it gets you off my back. Look, seriously, try not to worry. It's unlikely they'll have any news of Rhys. He's probably had a skinful and is sleeping it off on a mate's floor somewhere. I'll ring the police now. Speak later. Bye.'

Though talking to Dave had got her no positive news of Rhys, Siobhan felt she was at least doing something. She lay down, still fully clothed, on the living room couch and shut her eyes. *I'll just have forty winks before Dave rings back,* she thought. She soon drifted off into chaotic and frightening dreams. She awoke with a start four hours later, stiff and cold but perspiring. Her first thought was that Rhys still hadn't been in touch. She checked her phone. Dave hadn't rung her back either.

***

WEDNESDAY MORNING, 30TH MAY

The man knelt down and inspected the contents of the bag. He slipped on a pair of gloves. He stroked the explosive lovingly. It hadn't been easy to come by but he'd been lucky. Still had some old contacts that owed him a few favours. It had cost him. Semtex wasn't cheap. But he reckoned these men were as loyal to him as he'd been to them. They believed in what he was doing.

He didn't have to worry about being grassed up. The only thing he wouldn't tell them was who or where the target was. Didn't want them to get in there first and spoil his fun. He could imagine there'd be hordes of people wanting to line up to take a potshot when they knew the target. He laid everything out on the old wooden kitchen table in the farmhouse. The last items out of the bag were a couple of photographs. One showed a man in his sixties. The man spat on the photograph. He then wiped the spit away with his gloved hand. His face softened as he picked up the second photograph. It was faded and old. It was of a young woman. Tenderly he laid it on the table.

**

'That's the last of the statements collated, sir,' said DS Andrea Fletcher the following morning. She stood in Carruthers' office at the police station in Castletown, like him drinking coffee. 'Nobody claims to have seen or heard anything.'

'What, nothing at all?' asked Carruthers. He put his glasses on his prematurely grey head and stared out of the window, noting the bustle of Castletown, even on the outskirts where the station sat. He couldn't believe that, in a busy university and tourist town, nobody had seen anything. He wondered what the hell had happened to get a young man killed in such a brutal fashion.

'No boss, but Italian restaurants can be noisy places. I used to work in one. I'm not surprised they didn't hear anything. Dougie was right: there was a two-for-one special on last night. That's why it was still so busy when we got there. Staff said they were run off their feet. Door-to-door hasn't yielded anything either, I'm afraid.'

'Call's just come in, boss,' panted Harris, entering the room with an air of purpose that, for Carruthers, seemed out of keeping with the man's generally lazy demeanour. That alone made Carruthers sit up and take note.

'Student fae the university reported her boyfriend missing. Apparently, he didnae turn up at her flat last night. She's worried sick. Says it's out of character. Want to know the best bit?' Harris didn't wait for an answer. 'He's based at RAF Edenside, aircraftman Rhys Evans. Reckon that's our man.'

'We don't want to jump to conclusions,' said Carruthers.

'Nae doubt with a name like Evans,' said Harris. 'It's hardly Scottish, is it? I love it when it's handed on a plate to us like this.'

'What's the girlfriend's name and address?' said Carruthers.

Harris read from his notebook. 'Siobhan Mathews, 56 Edgecliffe. Back in a sec,' he said, then was gone.

'Edgecliffe are student flats just down from the caravan site on the way out of town, boss,' said Fletcher. 'If our man was coming from the RAF base, what was he doing at Bell Street? It's nowhere near Edgecliffe.'

'What indeed?' said Carruthers. It hadn't taken him long to get his bearings in Castletown. Whilst quaint and full of character the centre was grid like and compact. Edgecliffe was a fifteen-minute walk from the centre of town. He knew where it was. He smiled. Fletcher clearly felt she needed to remind him. After a stint down south and coming from the West coast, he didn't know Fife too well, although it was where his estranged wife grew up. He turned to Fletcher. 'Did you say you'd studied here in Castletown, Andrea?'

'I did, for my sins. I have a BA from the University of East of Scotland. And like many students from England, much to the consternation of some of the Scots, I never left.'

Carruthers looked thoughtful. He'd only moved back to Scotland himself a couple of months ago from London, in the vain hope of saving his marriage. It hadn't helped. He pushed all thoughts of his failed marriage out of his head.

'And boss,' said Fletcher. 'I know I keep asking, but can you call me Andie? Much prefer it. Do you want me to go over to Edgecliffe, and talk to Siobhan Mathews?'

'We'll both go over to talk to her,' said Carruthers leading the way out of his office. 'I think she'll probably appreciate another woman's presence. And I've told you before, Andie. Don't call me boss. It's Jim. I like to keep things informal. Dougie can stay here. I want him to pull the report on that fight here in Castletown.' He glanced into the main office, it was empty. 'By the way, where's Dougie gone?'

'The gents?'

'Has that man got a bladder problem, or does he just go there to read his girlie magazines? Because if so, I'll have him on a charge. Oh, there you are, Dougie,' said Carruthers frowning as the man himself appeared.

'Christ, you're no' clocking how long I spend having a pee now are ye, guv?' said Dougie Harris, still doing his flies up. 'And dinnae tell me it's another one of those useless time and motion studies.'

'What, how much time it takes you to pass a motion you mean?' said Fletcher, trying not to laugh.

'Well, whatever it is, it's an infringement of my personal liberties,' said Harris.

'Look, Dougie, stop trying to sound like Arthur Daley and just get on with it, will you?' said Carruthers. 'Andie and I are going to pay this Siobhan Mathews a visit. I want you to stay here and go through every detail of who was involved in that street fight. I have a feeling the two events may be connected. If our man was involved, last night may have been a payback. Before you do that, though, I want you to phone RAF Edenside. Find out if they have any personnel matching our dead man's description. And don't take all day about it. We now have a suspicious death and a report of a missing airman. We need to find out if it's the same person.'

TWO

As Inspector Carruthers drove towards Edgecliffe Halls of Residence, DS Fletcher quiet by his side, he heard his own stomach growl.

'Did you have time for breakfast, Andie?' he asked.

She shook her head. 'I'm not very hungry.'

'Well, I am,' he said. 'Let's stop and get something to eat first.' They stopped for coffee and bacon sandwiches from a little café on Market Street, ate them in the car park overlooking East Castle Beach. Or at least Carruthers ate his. He could see that Fletcher was struggling with hers.

'You OK?' he asked.

'Bacon's making me feel a bit queasy,' she said, crumpling up the paper bag with most of the sandwich still in it. She placed the bag by her feet.

Carruthers looked at her, wondered if she was sickening for something. There seemed to be a summer bug doing the rounds.

It was half ten in the morning and the tide was out, exposing a vast expanse of silvery stretch of sand. The rays of sun were dancing, mischievously catching the shallow pools of water, making the scene a landscape photographer's delight. Carruthers finished his breakfast while Andie waited, then they were back on their way.

The flats at Edgecliffe consisted of a drab, ugly maze of pebble-dash concrete and brick buildings, set behind the imposing glass and brick Scottish Oceans Institute.

'Not much to look at, is it?' DS Fletcher's comment broke into Carruthers' thoughts as they clambered out of the car and shut the doors. 'Looks like a holding centre for illegal immigrants, I always think.'

'I certainly wouldn't want to be incarcerated in here, that's for sure,' said Carruthers, thinking of his cosy little fishing cottage over in Anstruther.

'When I was a student here, I got out of halls as quickly as possible and moved into a flat in Market Street.'

'Good move?'

'Much better. Closer to town too. Only problem was it didn't have central heating. I was so cold I got chilblains the first winter. They used to give me serious grief when I went hill walking.'

'Hill walking? I know you're a runner, but I didn't realise you like to get out on hills. You're a regular action girl aren't you? So how many winters did you survive in that flat?'

'Just the one.'

'What did you do about the fact there was no central heating?'

'Me and the other girls used to switch the gas fire on and huddle round it when Scott wasn't around.'

'Scott?'

'Friend and landlord. Didn't like the gas fire being on. Cost too much. But he was out a lot so he never really knew. Well, till the bills came in of course.' She laughed, but Carruthers noticed the smile didn't quite reach her eyes. Now he looked at her a little more closely, she looked tired and strained. It wasn't the first time he'd thought this over the past few weeks. In fact, she looked plain unhappy which wasn't like her. She was usually so bubbly. He wondered if she was having problems on the home front.

'Everything OK between you and Mark?'

Fletcher frowned. 'Yes. Why wouldn't they be?'

Prickly, thought Carruthers. *Clearly everything isn't OK but she doesn't want to talk about it.*

'I take it you've got central heating now? In your flat with Mark?' he asked, happy to get back to a safe subject.

'First thing I checked when I was looking for a place,' Fletcher's freckles stood out in her drawn face, every feature exposed since her shoulder-length brown hair was pulled up in a ponytail. She looked younger than her twenty-nine years. She took in the buildings in front of them. 'They might lack character and imagination but at least they're warm.'

'Hmm,' said Carruthers. He looked at them critically. From the outside, they were devoid of any soul. *Not the sort of place to stay if you were looking to be inspired. If these buildings were people,* Carruthers thought, *they were the shell that is left behind by advanced Alzheimer's.* The lights were on, but no one was home. At least not the person you'd know. His father's mother had had Alzheimer's. He felt sad when he thought of her last few years. 'Think I'd rather stay in a flat with no central heating,' he said. 'OK, where's number 56, then?'

They entered the maze of accommodation. It was surprisingly quiet. No loud music; no student voices; no students in evidence anywhere, in fact. The only noise above the babble of a nearby burn was an occasional seagull, banging door, or squeak of an opening window. He looked up at the lifeless structures, with their huge dark gaping square windows.

Having finally found number 56, Fletcher stepped forward and pressed the doorbell. Carruthers was surprised to see the door opened by a serious looking Japanese girl, whose round glasses magnified her already worried expression.

'DCI Jim Carruthers, and DS Andrea Fletcher. We're looking for Siobhan Mathews,' said Carruthers, showing the girl his police ID. Fletcher followed suit.

'What's happened? You have news of her boyfriend?' the girl replied, her eyes fixated on Fletcher's highly polished black boots.

'We're not sure. Is she here?' Fletcher asked.

'Please, follow me. I'll show you. I am her flatmate, Tomoko Kawase.'

Carruthers entered the kitchen to see a girl sitting at the kitchen table, her bobbed dark hair framing her face. She was dressed in snug-fitting black jeans and a white T-shirt.

'Siobhan Mathews?' he asked gently.

She looked up at him, and the dark circles under her eyes spoke of a poor night's sleep, yet he still found her strikingly, inappropriately attractive. For a moment she reminded him of his former wife, with the same dark hair and hauntingly beautiful green eyes, and he took a sharp intake of breath. How unfair it was that after nearly a year of separation, unguarded thoughts of his wife could accost him when he least expected them.

'It's bad news, isn't it?' she said. 'I've had a bad feeling all night about Rhys not turning up. It's not like him. He would have phoned me. Just tell me one thing. Is he dead?'

Carruthers hated these moments. 'A body of a young man has been discovered,' he said. 'There was no ID on the man. We're still trying to establish his identity. It may not be Rhys.'

The girl buried her face in her hands and wept. Fletcher went over to her and gave her a tissue from her pocket.

'Have you got a recent photograph of Rhys, Siobhan? He's in the RAF isn't he?' said Fletcher. There was no response from the sobbing girl.

'I'm sorry but we're going to have to ask some difficult questions,' said Carruthers. 'We need to find out who the victim is. Remember, it may not be your boyfriend.'

Siobhan dabbed her eyes with the tissue and blew her nose. 'Yes, he is. In the RAF, I mean. An aircraftman based at RAF Edenside.'

Fletcher got her notebook out and started scribbling.

'We've only been seeing each other about six months. That's how long he's been at the base. I've got a photo of us in my bedroom. Just give me a second. I'll go get it.'

'RAF personnel move around a lot. Where's he from originally, Siobhan?' asked Carruthers as Siobhan was leaving the room, his tone a little sharper than intended. Carruthers found he was holding his breath as they waited for Siobhan to answer the question.

Siobhan turned round and looked puzzled. 'Cardiff. Why?'

'What are you studying?' asked Carruthers, quick to change the subject until they'd seen the photograph.

'An MPhil in Philosophy,' she called from the bedroom.

Carruthers felt a fleeting moment of pain and swallowed. His ex-wife had been a philosophy lecturer. How uncanny.

'Can we see that photograph now, Siobhan?' Carruthers asked. Siobhan handed him a black and white photograph. Carruthers looked at it. The photograph showed two people with their arms round each other. Both were laughing. The girl's hair had been whipped up by the wind and partially obscured her face. They looked happy. He passed it to Fletcher.

'Did Rhys have any identifying marks? A tattoo maybe?' asked Fletcher.

Carruthers could see that the sudden question threw Siobhan for a moment, but the penny dropped quickly enough for her and she visibly paled. Her flatmate came over to her and put her arm round her. 'Yes,' she said, 'he's a big Cardiff City fan. Has a tattoo on his right forearm of a bluebird. I hate it.'

Carruthers and Fletcher exchanged glances. There was a telling silence. 'The man you found in Bell Street has a tattoo doesn't he? That's why you asked me.'

'What is Rhys? Five foot eight? Five foot nine? asked Carruthers.

'Five foot nine,' said Siobhan.

'How did he die?' asked Siobhan, starting to weep again. 'Was it quick?'

'I'm afraid we're unable to release details at this stage,' said Carruthers. 'We need to formally confirm the identification before we can say anything more.'

'Rhys would never hurt anyone. Why would someone do this?' The question remained unanswered. She looked from Carruthers to Fletcher. 'Do you want me to see the body?'

'Don't worry,' said Carruthers. 'You're not expected to do that. I'm afraid I'm going to have to keep the photo for the time being. You'll get it back, though.'

Siobhan nodded.

'If it is Rhys, someone from the RAF base or his next of kin needs to identify him. I'm afraid a girlfriend doesn't qualify. I do want to stress, however, that it still may not be Rhys.'

'But if it's Rhys, I want to see him. And he has no other family. His parents are both dead so I'm as good as next of kin.'

'Let's find out whether it's him first,' said Carruthers. 'We'll be in touch. It's very important we find the victim's identity out as quickly as we can. We may well be looking at a murder investigation, in which case every minute is vital.'

Suddenly Carruthers' mobile rang interrupting them. 'Excuse me,' he said to the room in general as he answered. 'Jim Carruthers,' he said. 'When? Right, OK, thanks.' With that he rang off.

Carruthers could see Fletcher looking at him questioningly. His attention was on Siobhan Mathews.

'Just tell me, inspector,' Siobhan said quietly.

'Rhys Evans' ID has been found and handed in to the police station by a member of the public. It was found in a gutter at the end of Bell Street.'

'Then it really is him,' sobbed Siobhan.

'It puts him or his ID in or near Bell Street, Siobhan, that's all,' said Fletcher. 'I agree it's not looking good, but like DCI Carruthers said, let's not assume anything at this stage. Castletown is a tourist destination. It's possible Rhys dropped his wallet during a drinking session and hasn't recovered enough to get in touch with you yet. We may find it's someone just passing through.'

Siobhan Mathews sighed, and Carruthers' heart went out to the girl. The sigh was weightier than words and spoke volumes. There wasn't much doubt in his mind that the body was that of the missing aircraft technician Rhys Evans although at this stage he wasn't going to share his thoughts with Siobhan. She was on an imminent and inescapable collision course with the pain and loss that a sudden and violent death always brings.

'What I don't understand is why the information Rhys was missing wasn't acted on earlier,' said Siobhan angrily, snapping Carruthers from his private thoughts.

Carruthers frowned. 'What do you mean?'

'What I mean is that I got Rhys's colleague, Dave Roberts, to phone the station late last night to report him missing. I don't understand this ridiculous need to wait twenty-four hours before the police will act on a missing person report. I assume that's what you told Dave.'

'All we wait for is reasonable evidence that the person is missing,' said Carruthers. 'Wait a minute,' he said, his brain going into overdrive, 'you're telling me Rhys was first reported missing last night?'

'That's right. When I couldn't get hold of Rhys, I rang one of his colleagues.'

Carruthers glanced across at Fletcher but she was already scribbling the information down.

'Dave Roberts. He's in the same squadron as Rhys,' continued Siobhan. 'They've known each other for years, well before they both joined the RAF. I don't like him but I couldn't think who else to call, apart from the police. Dave also saw Rhys leave the base. Anyway, it was Dave who ended up phoning the police for me.'

'Why didn't you phone the police yourself?' said Fletcher, looking up from her notebook.

'Dave told me to wait a few more hours. Said the police wouldn't thank me for wasting their time.'

'Then what happened?' prompted Fletcher.

Siobhan Mathews shrugged. 'Just over a couple of hours had gone by. Rhys still hadn't turned up. I was at the end of my tether. I rang Dave to say I was finally going to ring the police.'

'What time was this?' asked Carruthers, digging into his black trouser pocket and bringing out his own black notebook.

'I think the second time I rang Dave was just before midnight. He persuaded me the police might take a mate ringing from the RAF more seriously than a girlfriend. Offered to make the call. I was too tired to argue, and frankly relieved he was going to phone them. Anyway, he would've already had a name.'

'How's that?' asked Fletcher.

'He was interviewed by the police a couple of weeks ago. About a fight.'

Carruthers shot Fletcher a look. He was remembering what Mackie had said about the old bruising on the body. 'Get on your mobile, Andie. Phone the station. Check it out.'

'Was Rhys involved in this fight?' asked Carruthers, as Fletcher busied herself fishing out her mobile and punching in the number of the station.

'He was there, yes. Stepped in to try to break it up. Got punched a couple of times for his trouble. He would never hurt anyone. Like I said, he was a peacemaker.'

Fletcher ducked out of the living room and went into the hall. A couple of minutes later she reappeared snapping shut her mobile phone and shaking her head.

'I spoke to DS Harris,' she said. 'The only logged call about Rhys Evans' being missing was from Siobhan Mathews.'

'I don't understand,' said Siobhan. 'Why would Dave lie?'

'I don't know,' said Carruthers. 'But I think we need to speak to him.' He said his goodbyes to Siobhan and Tomoko. Fletcher followed suit. As they left the flats he turned to Fletcher. 'Sounds like Roberts might have been the last person to see Rhys before he left the base. Ring Dougie back. Get him to speak to all the staff on duty last night. I don't care if he's got to get them out of bed. I want to make doubly sure nobody took a call from Roberts.'

***

WEDNESDAY LUNCHTIME 30TH MAY

Jim Carruthers had seen a good number of corpses in his time, and however dispassionate he tried to be, the experience never failed to move him. When he looked at a dead body he always felt something. Of course, he felt more for the innocent than the hardened criminal, but he knew that even the hardened criminal had been innocent once. As for children, he didn't know of any police officer that wasn't affected by the death of a child. For him, having lost an older brother to a hit and run, dealing with the death of a child was the most difficult thing imaginable.

But most of all, he felt for the bereaved, for those whose loved ones had been taken from them, often in the cruellest of circumstances. He sighed and thought of Siobhan Mathews. He had just come out of the mortuary. Rhys Evans' commanding officer had positively identified the body.

Carruthers sat in his car listening to his voicemail. Nothing urgent. He called Fletcher and organised for her to pick up Siobhan Mathews to bring her to the mortuary the other side of Castletown. She was still insisting on viewing her boyfriend's body. This wasn't exactly procedure, but with no family confirmed by the RAF, Siobhan was the closest they had, and she might have information useful to the investigation. He had to chance it. Seeing Fletcher's distinctive green Beetle pull up, Jim opened the car door and got out. As he and Fletcher led the crying girlfriend across the car park he thought about the grieving process that had only just begun for her.

Shaking these thoughts off, he looked over at Siobhan. 'Are you ready, Siobhan?'

She looked up at him through almond-shaped green eyes. 'Will you come in with me? I don't want to be on my own.'

'Yes, of course,'

She smiled at him, although the smile didn't reach her eyes. He placed a hand on her shoulder and guided her into the building. They were met by a young woman he hadn't seen previously that morning. Perhaps she'd been on her break.

'DCI Jim Carruthers and DS Andrea Fletcher,' he said. 'This is Siobhan Mathews. Siobhan's boyfriend was Rhys Evans. She's asked to view the body. Is Mackie here?'

'Just popped outside for a cigarette.'

The woman who stood in front of him only looked to be in her late twenties. She had a surprisingly deep and seductive voice, at odds with her appearance. Her black hair was tied in a severe ponytail, and her glasses were too big for her face, giving her the look of the academic. Carruthers privately thought she would look much more attractive if she wore contact lenses and sported a fringe. She had nice eyebrows, he noticed. *Very sexy.* He then chastised himself for having inappropriate thoughts at a particularly inappropriate time.

'I didn't think he still smoked,' said Carruthers.

'He's been trying to give up. Did well. Lasted six months this time.'

Carruthers looked down at Siobhan Mathews' face. She'd managed to stop crying but it had left her face blotchy and red.

At that moment, the door opened and in walked Dr Mackie, flicking his cigarette butt on to the ground behind him. Carruthers frowned.

'I know what you're thinking, laddie. Shouldn't be smoking. Every fag I have I keep saying it'll be my last. Hard habit to break in my job. I see you've met my new assistant, Jodie Pettigrew.'

Carruthers hadn't been thinking about Dr Mackie's health at all, but rather about the way the pathologist had thoughtlessly disposed of his cigarette butt. He wasn't going to admit that, though. He looked again at Mackie's assistant. If smoking was Mackie's vice he couldn't help but wonder, with her prim academic look and sexy eyebrows, what Jodie Pettigrew's was.

Mackie motioned for Carruthers and Siobhan to follow him through some glass doors.

'Jodie, why don't you take your lunch now?' Jodie nodded and turned away. 'Nice girl, very intelligent. Got a first from Oxford,' Mackie said as Jodie disappeared, giving Carruthers an appraising backwards glance as she left. Carruthers didn't doubt her intelligence for a minute. He could easily imagine her captaining a team on University Challenge. Naturally she would be on the winning side.

Carruthers noticed Fletcher had her hand on Siobhan's shoulder. He turned to Siobhan. 'Right, are you ready?'

'Yes,' she said.

Mackie led them to the viewing area and then disappeared through a door.

Carruthers glanced at Siobhan. He wondered if actually viewing her boyfriend's body would trigger anything that might be helpful to their investigation. Through the Perspex, there in the centre of the room was the trolley. The shape of a body covered by a white sheet was lying on it. There had been a strong smell of disinfectant earlier masking the stench of death and Carruthers was grateful that for once he was on this side of the glass. Again, he looked over anxiously at Siobhan. Her chest was rising and falling with great rapidity; her hands clenched into fists. He could see from the determined look on her face she was trying to steel herself. She looked a bundle of nerves. Carruthers couldn't blame her.

Siobhan stepped closer to the glass wiping her hands on her jeans. Carruthers could see her bravado was fast evaporating.

Carefully Mackie lifted back the sheet just enough so that the head and shoulders of the young man were exposed. There was a sharp intake of breath as Siobhan peered at the corpse's face. Carruthers was grateful the rest of the body was covered.

Siobhan, hand over mouth, could only nod. She then turned away from Carruthers. Wordlessly, she almost stumbled out of the viewing area.

'I'll go after her,' said Fletcher. Carruthers nodded. As Fletcher left the room, Dr Mackie started to cover the face of the dead airman.

Carruthers rapped on the glass. 'Wait,' he called out. He studied the swollen and discoloured features of the deceased. *What had got him killed. Had it been a botched robbery or were the motives more sinister?* Only when he nodded did Mackie cover Rhys' face and step to meet him outside the room. 'Are you able to give me anything yet?' Carruthers said.

'No laddie. Too soon. You know that. I'll contact you as soon as I have anything concrete. It would just be conjecture at this stage, and you know how we pathologists hate to do that.'

'Not even a time or cause of death?'

'Persistent bugger, aren't you? I'm not being drawn on an exact time. You know how difficult these things are, although I would say, if he was found at 9pm, he hadn't been dead more than a couple of hours. This is unofficial, though, but that's all you're getting for now.'

'Can I nip in and just have another look at him?' said Carruthers. Mackie nodded. They entered the room after Carruthers had donned the obligatory white coat. Carruthers lifted off the sheet. His gaze travelled down the right arm and misshapen and bloodied hand of the deceased. Several bones broken in the right hand, thought Carruthers. 'Someone stamped on his hand?'

'Looks that way,' Mackie reluctantly confirmed. 'Some of the bruising suggests impact with a ridged object. Possible indentation of a thick tread.'

Carruthers frowned. 'A booted foot?'

'Again, I'm not ready to confirm anything just yet, but it's possible.'

Carruthers' gaze travelled up the torso to the face. He remembered Mackie telling him that the young man was also missing a front tooth. He'd clearly taken several hard punches to the face and body.

'I can't give you any more at this stage,' said Mackie, breaking into Carruthers' thoughts.

Carruthers shook his head, thinking not for the first time about the wanton waste of life.

'Now off you go, laddie,' said Mackie chuckling. 'Go and rescue your damsel in distress. Leave me to get on with the post-mortem. I'll be in touch.' He patted his lab coat pocket, no doubt looking for his cigarettes. Carruthers couldn't blame him for wanting another. He suddenly felt like smoking too. He'd given it up during his marriage, but there was no one to complain he tasted like an ashtray now.

He thought of Siobhan Mathews, and how she would have to come to terms with her boyfriend's death. Wondered if the relationship had been serious. He hoped she would be able to find a way to put all of it behind her and continue with her studies.

He knew, though, only too well, how the sudden death of someone, especially this young, would cast ripples, and would have far-reaching consequences for those left behind. He thought of his own family. The death of his fourteen-year-old brother when he was ten had meant that he had to grow up with an overprotective mother and a father who lost himself in drink. Sighing, he thanked Mackie and gratefully went outside to find Fletcher and Siobhan.

He didn't know how people like Mackie and Jodie Pettigrew did their jobs – the blood, gore and stench – an ever-present reminder of sometimes violent death. No wonder Mackie had trouble giving up smoking. He wondered how he slept.

Once outside, he took some deep breaths and looked around for the two women. He saw Siobhan, not far from his parked car, leaning up against a rather puny oak tree. A small pool of vomit lay close by. Fletcher was by her side.

'Sorry,' Siobhan said embarrassed, wiping her hand over her mouth. 'I could do with something to rinse my mouth. Have you got any water?'

'I've got a bottle in the car,' he said as he approached. 'Hang on.' With long lean strides, Carruthers walked to the car, opened the back door and retrieved the bottle. Undoing the screw top he gave it to Siobhan. 'Sorry, it's a bit warm,' he said.

She rinsed her mouth out and offered the bottle back. He told her to keep it.

'It didn't look like him,' she said.

Carruthers looked up sharply.

'I mean, of course it was him, but it just looked like a shell.'

Carruthers nodded. 'It's difficult to ask questions right now, but I have to ask them, Siobhan. You're sure you have no idea who'd want to hurt him?'

'No, none.'

'Looks as if the motive was robbery,' said Fletcher. 'Rhys' wallet and phone were missing, but at this stage we can't rule anything out.'

Carruthers frowned. Siobhan had reminded him of the fight between the RAF boys and some of the townies recently. He knew, of course, that Rhys had been present. According to Siobhan, he'd been trying to break it up.

'Siobhan, would you excuse me. I need to make a quick call to the station. Stay with her, will you?' he mouthed to Fletcher. She nodded.

Walking a discreet distance away, Carruthers punched in Dougie Harris's number. He looked back at Siobhan as he spoke. 'Dougie, I'm at the mortuary with Siobhan Mathews. Have you managed to pull that file on the fight? We know Evans and Roberts from the RAF base were involved, but who were the townies? Was it the usual suspects?'

Carruthers listened carefully.

'Callum Russell and Lewis Adamson were the main perpetrators,' Dougie Harris said. 'In their statement, they both say that they were having a quiet drink in The Earl of Fife wi' their pals. Three lads fae the RAF came over to them. Started to flash the cash. Insults were exchanged and then it all started kicking off over a girl. Russell and Adamson claim they were defending themselves, and that Dave Roberts threw the first punch.'

'I bet those two have never had a quiet drink in their lives.' In the couple of months Carruthers had been at the station the names of Callum Russell and Lewis Adamson had already cropped up half a dozen times. They seemed to be a two-man crime wave. 'Why is it trouble seems to follow them around like a bad smell? That's not their usual stomping ground, though. I would've thought The Earl of Fife was a bit too up-market for them.'

'Maybe they were feeling lucky that night? Thought they might pick up a couple of students,' said Harris.

'What did the RAF boys say in their statement? Don't tell me? Russell and Adamson started the fight and threw the first punch?'

'Aye. Pretty much got it in one.'

'OK, so what did the witnesses say?' said Carruthers.

'Pushing and shoving on both sides. One witness, one of the bar staff, claims it was one of the RAF boys who threw the first punch. Apparently, according to her, another one of their lot tried to break it up. Got assaulted for his trouble.'

'That could have been Evans,' said Carruthers. 'Did she have any trouble telling the townies apart from the RAF?'

'Naw. All three of the RAF had Welsh accents. And, of course, plenty of money.'

'All three?' said Carruthers. 'I wonder who the third was? How many Welshmen are up at Edenside anyway?'

'Third lad was a Sean Coombe.'

Looking over at Siobhan talking to Fletcher, Carruthers said, 'What are you up to now? Whatever it is, I want you to drop it.' Out of the corner of his eye he could see that Siobhan had left Fletcher's side and was walking towards him. 'Whilst I'm at the RAF base,' he said to Harris, 'I want you to track down the two slime balls, and interview them. I'll get Andie to drop Siobhan back at the student flats. You'll need to talk to Andie about where you're going to meet. Also interview the barmaid who was working in The Earl of Fife that night. Whilst you're out and about see if you can find the girl who this fight was over. I want a further statement from her as well. That should keep you out of trouble for a while.'

'Right you are, boss.'

'And Dougie – we need to move fast. We don't want to let the grass grow under our feet on this one.' Carruthers broke the connection and pocketed his mobile.

'I couldn't help but overhear the end of the call,' said Siobhan. 'Can I ask you to take me back instead? I'd like to talk to you about Rhys.'

Carruthers knew from the way he was starting to feel about Siobhan that he shouldn't be alone with this young woman, but he was curious as to what she wanted to tell him and why she'd want to confide in him rather than in a female cop. He trusted his instinct though he glanced over at Fletcher who had listened to the conversation. She gave him a quizzical look.

'I'll give Dougie a call and organise where we're going to meet,' Fletcher said, punching in his number. Carruthers shepherded Siobhan over to his car, opening the passenger door for her. She climbed in. He shut the door and in a few economical steps was round to the driver side. He sat beside her and waited for her to begin talking about Rhys Evans.

THREE

As Carruthers drove towards Edgecliffe, he tried to concentrate on anything but the woman sitting quietly at his side. *The case. Think of the case.*

Whenever there was any trouble in Castletown, especially trouble involving a fight, Carruthers could lay odds that it would involve Callum Russell and Lewis Adamson. In the short time he'd been here he'd had cause to read their files enough times to know they had both been teenage tearaways, and were now in their twenties. Both had collected convictions for theft and Adamson one for assault. Carruthers frowned. Street fighting and breaking and entering were their specialities. Would they go as far as murder? It seemed unlikely.

Christ, thought Carruthers, remembering Siobhan viewing the body of her boyfriend, *I hate days like these.* Sometimes he really wished for a different profession. He wondered how different his life could have been. If he'd had a less stressful job, with more time for his wife and family life, would that have saved his marriage? He knew Mairi had wanted children but she always complained that as a dad he just wouldn't have been around for his kids, and that as a husband he was married to the job. He remembered their final argument as if it had been yesterday.

Had their marriage really been that bad? He hadn't been a big drinker, unlike a lot of his colleagues. Had never had an affair, although there were times he'd wondered about his wife. However, he knew he could be moody and introverted, especially when investigating a tough case. As much as he'd loved his wife, he was, without doubt, a loner at heart. His hobbies of fishing and hill walking were an expression of that separation; they were passions his wife had never shared. She used to joke with friends that between them they had bagged two hundred Munros. He had climbed one hundred and ninety-nine; and she had climbed one. That had been in the days when she still had a sense of humour about their relationship.

One Munro had been more than enough for her. After a six hour slog up Ben Sgulaird, locally known as 'The Bastard', she had never gone up another mountain. That had been early in their courting days. He still regretted the choice of hill for her first Munro. Despite the fine views of the hills of Mull, the walk was steep and demanding. The nickname gave it away, really. The wry thought crossed his mind that Fletcher would have loved it. Maybe his wife had been right: maybe he was selfish. Selfish to do the job that he did, selfish in the way he spent his free time. He probably should never have married. He sighed. Better not to think about it.

'Would you mind pulling over?'

It was the first time Siobhan had spoken, so Carruthers quietly pulled over to the side of the road. It wasn't a pretty view, but this might be his chance to get information from Siobhan. Turning off his engine Carruthers turned to Siobhan Mathews. 'What do you want to do?'

Siobhan was silent. Her head was turned away from him, so he could only see the back of her head. By rights, his job was done. He should just drive her straight home. This stop was not his best idea. Somehow, though, he felt responsible for her, though he didn't know why. She turned to him. Her expression was bleak. Eyes empty of hope. He couldn't fully read her expression but he had a pretty good idea how she was feeling.

'I don't know what to do,' she said.

'Why don't I get you home?'

'No, I didn't mean that. I meant I don't know what to do now that Rhys has gone. I know we weren't together very long, but I had hopes the relationship might really go somewhere.' She hung her head and her shoulders sagged forwards.

Carruthers knew dejection when he saw it, and despair. It was a feeling he was all too familiar with. Siobhan looked up at him with her almond-shaped green eyes. Carruthers felt her sorrow but he had to press. 'You said you wanted to talk to me about Rhys.'

'Look,' she said, 'you might as well know. Rhys had put in for a transfer. It was something we'd talked about. If he'd got it, I told him I would consider leaving university and moving with him.'

Carruthers was surprised. Her masters was only a twelve-month course. Siobhan came across as a dedicated student. 'You'd consider leaving in the middle of your course? Couldn't you have joined him later?' The words were out before he could stop them. He shouldn't have asked. Really, it was none of his business.

'I didn't want to lose him,' she said simply.

***

Fletcher found out that the girl at the centre of the fight was named Charlene Todd. She lived in Crosshaven, an old mining village fifteen miles outside Castletown.

'Come on, Dougie. Let's get going.'

Harris, predictably, had his face in a bag of doughnuts.

'You're going to end up with a heart attack if you carry on like this.'

'My choice, doll.' A jet of strawberry jam shot out of the doughnut and Dougie scooped it up greedily with his fingers. 'I hope she's got a great pair of tits, this Charlene,' he said, licking the sugar and jam off his chubby fingers. 'I like them big myself. In fact, the bigger the better.'

'I'm sure you do,' replied Fletcher, rolling her eyes towards heaven.

'Have you ever thought of getting a breast enlargement?' he asked Fletcher.

She saw him glancing at her 32B chest. 'No, I bloody well haven't.'

'Well, I'd think about it if I were you. Your face is bonny. Imagine how much better you'd look if you had big tits. It's incredible what advancements have been made in surgery.'

'Pity they haven't managed to advance as far for a male brain enlargement,' retorted Fletcher, 'although I'm not sure it would be available on the NHS and I don't think you've got the money to go private.' She propelled him out of the door. 'Come on. Let's get going.'

Charlene Todd lived in a restored miner's cottage in the lower part of Crosshaven, close to the Docks. Having parked up, Fletcher strode over to the door and knocked irritably. Her head was full of the fact that she still hadn't managed to have a proper talk with Mark. He had hardly said two words about her pregnancy since she had told him. He was hardly ever home these days and when he was, he just wanted to watch TV or sleep. She was starting to wonder if he was avoiding her. How many games of football can a man play in a week? As the weeks carried on she was growing more and more anxious. She also needed to talk to Jim, too. She was lucky that she had such a good relationship with him. He would support her. She sighed. To say her private life was in turmoil was an understatement. She was now fourteen weeks pregnant. The pregnancy hadn't been planned and she had no idea whether she was going to keep the baby. She wondered what her tits, as Dougie called them, would look like after breastfeeding. She grimaced.

As she knocked, Fletcher looked around her. The place was a war zone. There was graffiti on the houses; litter blowing in the streets; broken glass on the road and pavement, dog mess everywhere. A couple of malnourished youths, wearing baseball caps, were hanging around near the corner shop. No children were playing.

She contemplated what it might have looked like forty years before. Despite the poverty, she imagined the neighbours with their doors open; the high street being the life of the mining community. Everyone looking out for each other. Children playing in the street.

Long before their parents had become too paranoid to let them outside, before anyone had heard the term 'paedophile'. Despite the obvious concerns of parents, the chances of kids being taken off by a paedophile, were a lot slimmer than kids' chances of becoming obese through a sedentary lifestyle. Most of the time, as Fletcher knew only too well, paedophiles turned out to be family or friends of family anyway. No getting away from them. Fletcher thought of the catalogue of health problems that these kids were storing up for themselves. She imagined what her own child might look like out playing. Then pushed the thought out of her head.

She wondered if it was harder to bring children up nowadays than fifty years ago. She had only a rough idea of what bringing up a child today would cost. That was another thing to consider. Not to mention who would look after the child when she returned to work. She sighed. But she knew, whether she had Mark's support or not, at least she wouldn't end up destitute. Down the street a small child, crossing the road with its mother, stumbled and fell. The mother scooped the crying child up in her arms. It had a look of anguish on its face. For some reason her thoughts turned to a picture she had seen recently of a mother and child refugee in Turkey. She shuddered. There but for the grace of God...

She smiled bleakly, trying to push all thoughts of the desperate scenes of drowning children out of her mind.

'Are ye gonnae chap the door again, or are we gonnae stand here all day like a pair of farts?' said Harris.

She raised her hand once more to the door. On this second knock, a girl wearing a black boob tube and leopard skin print leggings answered. Harris' eyes nearly came out on stalks. She had the most enormous pair of breasts Fletcher had ever seen outside a porn mag. She sighed inwardly. Harris was in for a treat. She just hoped he would behave himself.

'Charlene Todd?' she said.

'Aye,' she said, chewing on her gum, as she flicked back her dyed blond hair. Fletcher noticed she looked bored with the conversation already. 'Whatever you're selling, I'm busy.'

'We're not selling anything,' said Fletcher. 'We're police officers.' They flashed their ID cards. 'Detective Sergeant Andrea Fletcher, and this is Detective Sergeant Dougie Harris. We'd like to ask you a few questions about the recent fight in Castletown.'

The girl sighed. 'I've already given a statement.' She studied her long manicured nails.

'Can we come in please, Charlene?' said Fletcher. Charlene Todd rolled her eyes and with a sigh opened the door. She took them into the front room.

'S'pose you'd better sit down,' said Charlene. Whilst Harris sat in a large armchair facing Charlene, Fletcher took a seat on a small couch draped with a white long-haired Afghan rug. Immediately she heard a yelp from beside her. Startled she looked down to see a tiny curly haired poodle that had its front legs wrapped round a grey cuddly toy.

'Mind Mr Pickles,' said Charlene.

Fletcher inched further away from Mr Pickles who threw her a look of disdain. 'The fight was between some locals and some airmen from the base.'

Charlene just shrugged.

'One of the airmen, a Rhys Evans, has been found dead in suspicious circumstances,' Fletcher said. She noticed a rise of Charlene's left eyebrow.

'Has he? Nothing tae do with me.'

'You were the only girl present in the altercation,' said Fletcher. 'What was the fight about?'

'Me.' She looked smug as she blew a bubble with the gum.

'Care to elaborate?' said Fletcher thinking that women's lib had obviously bypassed this generation.

'I'm wi' Davey now. Callum couldnae stand it.'

'Callum?'

'Callum Russell. My ex.'

'And Davey would be?' said Fletcher, reaching for the black notebook in her pocket.

'Dave Roberts. He's in the RAF. We've been seeing each other a couple of months now.'

Fletcher held the black biro poised mid-air. 'You're having a relationship with Dave Roberts?' Fletcher and Harris exchanged glances. 'So you threw Russell over for Roberts? How did he take it?'

'No' well, obviously. I mean, they were fighting, weren't they? I've never been fought over before. It was braw.'

'Why did you dump Russell?'

'Well, me and Davey got it together one evening when I was with a group of my pals. I didnae go looking for it or anything. But sometimes it just happens, eh?

'So what was it about Dave Roberts?' asked Harris. 'Does he have a bigger cock?'

'Dougie,' admonished Fletcher.

'Aye, he does as it happens. And a bigger pay packet as well. He knows how to treat a girl. He was buying me mojitos all night. Callum only ever bought me buckie or lager. I dinnae think he would ken what a mojito was.'

'With his form, I would suspect he knows more about molotov cocktails than mojitos,' said Fletcher.

'Oooh, I don't think I've ever heard of them. Are they nice?' asked Charlene. 'Are those the ones with a twist of lime in them?'

Fletcher worked hard not to roll her eyes. 'Do you know where Roberts is now?' asked Fletcher.

'Naw. But we dinnae live in each other's pockets. He told me no' to worry if I couldnae get hold of him. Said he would be out on manoeuvres or something.'

Fletcher had heard it called a lot of things in her time but manoeuvres were a first.

'When did you last see or hear from Roberts?' asked Harris. Fletcher frowned. Harris' eyes were not on Charlene's face.

'You men. You're all the same,' said Charlene. 'And you're old enough to be my dad. Stop staring at my tits.'

'Just answer the question,' said Fletcher wondering, not for the first time, how Dougie's wife put up with him. From station talk she'd gathered that his wife was disabled and that he was her carer. His wife obviously saw a side to him that she hadn't seen at the station.

'Come tae think of it, I havenae seen him for a few days. But like I said, we dinnae live in each other's pockets.' Charlene resumed studying her nails.

'So you weren't with him last night?' persisted Fletcher.

'That's whit I said, isn't it? He wisnae seeing another girl if that's what you're implying. We're exclusive.'

'Did he tell you that?'

'Well, no, but why would he go out for burger when he could have steak at home.'

Clearly Charlene had never had a decent steak in her life. Fletcher chided herself for the bitchy reaction. Thank God she'd only thought it.

'OK, so who started the fight?' asked Harris.

'Well, me and Dave and a couple of his pals were having a quiet drink and in walked Callum and Lewis. They were looking for trouble.'

'How do you know that they weren't coming in for a quiet drink, too?'

'In The Earl of Fife? Are you kidding? They'd never usually drink there. Can't afford the prices,' scoffed Charlene. 'It's six fifty for a glass of wine.'

Fletcher didn't but the prices didn't surprise her.

'Daylight robbery,' agreed Harris.

'So there you were drinking your mojito, and in walks Callum Russell and Lewis Adamson. What happened next?' prompted Fletcher.

'Like I said, in walks Callum and Lewis. They were already steamin'. He comes over to me, Callum that is, and takes out the twizzler and cocktail stick, chucks 'em on the floor and stands on them.'

'Big gesture,' said Fletcher.

'That's what I thought.'

'Anyway, Davey sees this and wants to know who the guy is. I tell him it's my ex. Davey is no' happy and they face each other off.'

'Like in a western.'

'Aye, just like a western. Anyway, there's some pushing and shoving and the next thing…'

'Who pushed who first?'

'What?'

'I said, who pushed who first?'

Charlene looked a bit confused. 'Dunno, think it was Davey. Got fed up with Callum eyeballing him. I mean, it was Callum's fault. He was nose tae nose wi' Davey at this point. Davey hates anyone in his space. Makes him mad, see.'

'Carry on. What happened next?'

'Well, they both sort of pushed each other out of the pub. The next thing I know, we're all in the street.' Charlene's eyes lit up as she retold the story. 'Then the punches started flying in. It was a fair old stramash.'

'Who threw the first punch?'

'Callum.'

'Thought you said it was Davey?'

'Naw, I said Davey pushed Callum first. Callum threw the first punch.'

'You sure about that?' asked Harris.

'Oh aye, quite sure.' Charlene stood examining her nails again as she said that. For the first time, Fletcher noticed a fine gold charm bracelet on her wrist. As Charlene picked at a nail she appreciatively glanced at the bracelet.

'New purchase?' asked Fletcher.

'Davey bought it for me. Eighteen carat gold.' She blew another bubble.

'So, as you were saying, Callum was the aggressor?' said Fletcher.

'I already said that, didn't I?'

'Did Dave throw any punches?' asked Harris.

'Well, he had to defend himself.'

'Is that a yes, then?' said Fletcher.

'Aye, he might have thrown one or two. To be honest it was all a bit of a free-for-all.'

'What part did Rhys Evans play in this fight?' asked Harris.

'He tried to break it up. He shouldnae have bothered.'

'What do you mean?'

'Well, first he got smacked by Callum.' Fletcher nodded. 'And then he got smacked by Davey.' Charlene laughed.

'Wait a minute,' said Fletcher. 'You're telling us Dave Roberts punched Rhys Evans?' Fletcher's eyebrows knitted together. 'I don't remember reading that in your original statement.'

'I must have forgotten tae mention it. I cannae see that it's important. He probably just got in the way.'

'First, let us be the judge of what's important,' said Fletcher. 'Is that what happened? Rhys Evans got in the way?'

'Must have.'

'So it was an accident?' said Harris.

'Guess so.'

'So, how did Roberts feel about the fact Evans was trying to break up the fight?' said Fletcher.

Charlene shrugged. 'No' very happy. I mean, Davey wanted to show Callum who was boss. He was fighting for my honour.'

Fletcher doubted it was about fighting for Charlene's honour and more about the fact that Roberts was clearly a thug who wanted to throw his weight around, but she didn't voice her opinion. She wondered if Roberts had also wanted to show Evans who was boss.

'So the punch was deliberate?' said Fletcher.

'I never said that.'

'Well, was it deliberate or not?'

'Looking back, aye, I suppose it might have been.'

Roberts, the alpha male, thought Fletcher, *wanting to show everyone on both sides just who was kingpin.*

'You do know withholding information is an offence?' asked Harris.

'I didnae do it deliberately. I just forgot. That's all. I mean, everything happened so quickly.'

'OK, moving on. What did you think of Rhys Evans?' said Fletcher.

'He was hot. Pity he's dead. Had a nice bod. I didnae like his girlfriend though.'

'Siobhan Mathews?'

'Aye, stuck-up cow.'

'Did you see much of them?'

'Naw, usually it was just me and Davey or a couple of his RAF pals. We dinnae always go out either, if you ken whit I mean.'

'You said there was a third airman on the night of the fight in the pub with you,' Fletcher prompted. 'Who was he?

'Did I?'

'Yes, you said you were out with Roberts and a couple of his pals. Obviously one of them was Rhys Evans. In your statement you mentioned a third person. Can you give me his name?'

'Well, you've obviously read the statement. Why do you need to ask me again?'

'With all due respect,' said Fletcher, 'you've told us things today that you never put in your statement. I just want to double-check, that's all.'

'Answer the question, Charlene,' said Harris.

Charlene rolled her eyes. 'OK, it was Sean.'

Fletcher referred to her little black notebook. 'Sean? Do you mean Sean Coombe?'

'Well, I dinnae ken his surname, do I? But if you say his surname is Coombe, then it must be.'

'Where is he from, this Sean Coombe?'

'He's Welsh. Cardiff.'

Bloody hell, is there anyone in the RAF stationed at Edenside not from Cardiff? thought Fletcher. 'What's he like, this Sean Coombe?' she said.

'Quiet. Never says much. Pretty boring actually.'

'What was the relationship like between Roberts and Evans?' said Fletcher. 'I understand they'd known each other before joining the RAF?'

'It doesnae mean they have to be pals though, does it? I mean, I went to school with Tracey Lovett who lives three doors away from me and she's a right minger. Not that Davey had anything to do with Rhys' death,' Charlene added quickly.

'You sure about that, are you?' said Harris.

'Well, why would he have? Look, can you go now? I cannae see how I can be of any more help.'

Fletcher started to put her notebook away. 'OK, but just one more question. Is Dave Roberts aggressive?'

'I wouldnae say any more than anyone else.'

Fletcher shoved the notebook into her shoulder bag. 'It's just that you said earlier somebody invading his space made him mad.'

'Well, I suppose he doesnae like other people touching his possessions.' Her eyes lit up. 'There was one time we were oot and somebody picked up his lighter. Dave took it back and set their shirt on fire. The boy wisnae badly hurt though. Just first degree burns. He never pressed charges, or nothing.'

Probably too frightened, thought Fletcher. *Dave Roberts is starting to sound rather psychotic.* 'Is Dave quick to anger?' she asked, wondering if Charlene had become another one of his possessions, until he tired of her.

Charlene shrugged. 'Look, are ye done? I'm needing away for my messages.'

Fletcher sensed that they weren't going to get any more out of her. She stood up. Harris followed suit.

Fletcher gave Charlene a quick false smile. 'Thanks, Charlene. We'll be in touch if we need to be.' She headed for the front door.

'Davey willnae get into any trouble because of whit I've said, will he?'

Fletcher opened the front door. She walked out into the street leaving the question hanging in the air.

'Your thoughts, Dougie?'

'Interesting to find out Roberts punched Evans. They don't sound best pals.'

'That's what I thought. Roberts has got a temper on him. Clearly possessive. I'm wondering what the relationship was really like between him and Rhys Evans. C'mon, Dougie, we've got interviews to conduct,' said Fletcher, stepping over an enormous pile of dog mess.

FOUR

Carruthers was silent, mulling Siobhan Mathew's words over in his head. *She's insecure,* he realised. However, was she insecure solely over her relationship with Evans, or was it deeper rooted than that? He knew not to ask. He was already on dangerous ground. And really, why did he care? He changed the subject. 'Why had he put in a request for a transfer? Was he unhappy at Edenside?'

'He seemed happy when I first met him, but then he changed.'

'In what way?'

'He became withdrawn, quiet, moody. I asked him what was wrong. He wouldn't tell me. Whatever was bothering him, he was very tight-lipped about it.'

'So you have no idea at all?'

'None.'

Strange that she hadn't mentioned this earlier. But then she's had a shock. Carruthers knew that sometimes information trickled out over time. The big question was who, or what, was Rhys Evans trying to get away from? Whatever the reason, it must have been sufficiently serious for him to be prepared to turn his whole life upside down, even risk losing the girl he was having a relationship with. Carruthers wondered if Rhys Evans had loved Siobhan Mathews as much as she appeared to have loved him.

His thoughts drifted back to his own situation and the relationship he'd had with his ex-wife. Hadn't he been willing to move the length of the country for her? Not only willing, he'd actually done it. He'd put in a request for a transfer, and here he was back in Scotland. His boss in London had thought he was mad. He'd been told he had a bright future with the Met. He'd enjoyed living in London. However, he had been so blinkered and so desperate, that he had refused to see what everyone else must have seen – that his marriage was over and he was uprooting himself for nothing.

Had his situation been so different to Siobhan's? Who was he to judge her anyway? Mairi had told him, while they were still in London, that she didn't love him anymore. But he hadn't believed her. Or if he had, he'd believed he could win her back. He'd left a good job with great prospects, friends and a life, for what? To move back up to Scotland. He swallowed. She didn't love him. She'd said those words in the last conversation they'd had. It still hurt.

He wondered how she was. When she'd left him, she'd moved back in with her parents in Cupar. He knew she was now in her own flat in Ceres. Leaving her job in London as a part-time lecturer at Hackney College to focus, she said, on writing a short layman's guide to the history of philosophy before resuming her lecturing career. She had laughed and said she was on a quest to make philosophy accessible to the masses.

It had also seemed that she had been on another quest – a quest to shake off her past life, and eradicate anything that reminded her of him. Over the subsequent months, she'd become more and more distant and unresponsive, refusing to take his calls. In the end, to his utter mortification and anger, she'd gone and changed her phone number, becoming ex-directory. For him, that had been the last nail in the coffin. All the time he'd been in contact with her, he'd felt that there was at least a chance of getting back together. Once she'd cut all ties, he knew there was no hope. *It had hurt*, he thought bitterly. Once they had been so close he couldn't ever have imagined life without her. *Oh yes, it certainly hurt.*

'Penny for them,' said Siobhan. 'You were miles away.'

'Sorry.'

'Jim?'

The use of his first name startled him.

'Can you take me home now please?'

The drive across Castletown to the Edgecliffe Halls of Residence took twenty minutes. There was little said; each was lost in their own thoughts. Carruthers pulled up in the car park.

'Thank you for being there for me today.'

He tried to smile. 'All part of the job.'

'Thank you. I appreciated it. I don't know how I would've got through that if you hadn't been with me.'

'You would have found a way to cope. Will you be OK?'

'I have to be. I'm going in now.'

Carruthers started to unbuckle his seat belt. The least he could do was see her to the door.

'I think I need to be on my own for a bit. I might lie down. I'm done in.'

Carruthers hesitated, unsure whether to see her to the door or not. He wondered why he suddenly felt so unsure of himself. He was usually so professional and in control. He was beginning to realise he didn't feel so professional around Siobhan Mathews. He didn't know whether it was because she had reminded him of his former wife, but he realised he needed to get a grip on this unusual feeling of connection. Regaining his composure he said, 'I'm not surprised. You've had a hell of a couple of days. You've got my number. If you think of anything that might be helpful to the investigation, call me.'

'I will.'

'We'll find the person who did this, Siobhan, I promise.'

Siobhan looked across at Carruthers her eyes welling up. She bit her top lip. As she looked down to undo her belt Carruthers saw a single tear fall on to her cheek. Without looking up she opened the car door, got out, shut the door and walked over to her student flats, front door key already in her hand. She didn't look back.

After she was gone, Carruthers sat in his car for a few moments drumming his fingers against the steering wheel thinking once again about the wanton waste of human life.

***

Tana Collins

The man rammed his baseball cap down over his face, sat back in his car and watched the girl get out of the detective's car. He rubbed a callused hand over his stubble. Heard the rasping noise it made. Wondered how much she knew. How much had she been told by Rhys Evans? Thinking of the girl he softened slightly. Something about Siobhan Mathews reminded him of his sister. He waited until the detective had driven off in his old Vauxhall Vectra. Saw a light go on in the upstairs bedroom of her flat. Waited a few minutes. Then started the ignition and drove away. Back to the farmhouse.

The farmhouse. Renting this place had been ideal. Right in the middle of nowhere. Nobody for miles. Owner abroad. He flicked his cigarette butt, ground it into the earth. Walking over to the 4x4, he lifted the car boot, looked around him and, satisfied he was alone, brought out the shotgun, handgun and silencers. The others would be arriving soon. They'd already had their orders from him. But it didn't hurt to go over the plan a fourth, fifth or sixth time. Almost laughed out loud at the thought of who he'd enlisted the help of. And from his own home town too. And with the boy's expertise in bomb disposal, he'd be invaluable. He fished out his new pay-as-you-go phone and called his latest recruit.

***

Fletcher glimpsed the docks in Crosshaven from the passenger seat of Harris' car, and that one glance was enough to trigger a powerful and long-forgotten memory.

I must have been about five years old. She remembered a country walk on quiet roads, holding her mother's hand. The memory of the walk itself was all a bit vague and hazy, but she remembered the feeling of being overwhelmed and amazed when, after a steep climb of the lane, they had reached the top, to be greeted by the sight of the River Humber nestled down in the valley.

The river, with its enormous sandbanks, had seemed huge to her and the famous Humber Bridge was awe-inspiring to her five year old self. She remembered a wooden bench where she and her

48

mother used to sit to admire the view. Her mother in silence, lost in her thoughts. Even at that young age she remembered having a strong sense of belonging – to the area, the people, being part of the fabric of the landscape. It had been a comforting feeling.

Her great grandfather on her father's side had been into shipping and at one time had part-managed the biggest shipyard in the area. That had been during the Second World War when her grandmother had been small. She remembered her mother telling her that grandmother had been sent off to boarding school to escape the bombing of Hull. For the first few years of her life she had grown up in the area that her mother and her grandparents had grown up in.

Within a year they had moved the length of England from the tiny village of Welton in East Yorkshire to the South East Coast of Sussex. For a long time, she had felt like a displaced person. She'd later found out that her mother's brother had moved South and her grandmother, not wanting the family to be so far away, had persuaded her mother that they should all move too. She thought of her mother now. How on earth was she going to tell her parents about her pregnancy? She rubbed her tired eyes. Drew some deep breaths. She was so worried about finding herself pregnant she wasn't sleeping properly. That and Dougie's appallingly erratic driving was making her feel travelsick. Or was it her morning sickness kicking in? She sighed.

As if on cue Harris suddenly braked, as a large hairy mongrel came running out into the street, bringing Fletcher out of her reverie.

'Christ alive,' said Harris.

Fletcher drew in a sharp intake of breath at this sudden jolt. 'Right. Where we heading? Callum Russell's flat first?' asked Fletcher, as she unwrapped the seat belt from its precarious position round her neck.

'I thought we'd kill two birds with one stone,' answered Harris smugly. 'It's nearly lunchtime and knowing those two, they'll be off somewhere for a liquid lunch.'

Fletcher raised her eyebrows. 'So where we going?'

'The Saltire. Does a great pint of Belhaven Best. And their steak pie is better than a poke of chips.'

'I hope you're not suggesting we have a drink. We're on duty. Anyway, you know Jim wants us to interview them separately, so they can't corroborate each other's story.'

Harris snorted. 'They're both as thick as mince so the interview will be a piece of piss. Whether we interview them separately or together, it willnae make a difference. I'll get the truth out of those two wee scrotes, even if I have to flush their heids down the shitter. If they're responsible for killing that Taff, I'll find out. Anyway, I've been looking for an excuse to have a pop at Russell for ages. Ever since I found out he's been banging my sister's kid.' Harris rubbed his hands in glee as he pulled into a car parking space.

'I think you should rein yourself in, Dougie. Just follow my lead.'

'No' on your wee English nelly. I'm looking forward to this. Dinnae tell me he doesnae have it coming to him.'

'Well, just bear in mind there's such a thing as enjoying your job too much. And just to be clear, if you step out of line and get reported I'm not risking my career by covering your fat arse.'

'At least I get results,' scoffed Harris.

'At what cost?'

Harris fell silent.

The Saltire was Castletown's roughest pub. It was also one of the oldest. Most self-respecting locals drank in the New Inn. Those down on their luck, and looking for a cheap drink, ran the gauntlet and drank in the Saltire.

In order to gain entry Harris and Fletcher had to step over a large chained-up mastiff bulldog. It was snoozing, its face in a pool of its own drool.

'Ya beauty. We're in luck. They're inside. That's Adamson's dug.' Harris opened the door and strode straight over to the bar. 'Pint of Belhaven Best,' he said to the gangly, ginger haired publican who was busy cleaning the top of the bar.

'We don't want any trouble,' said the publican.

Fletcher thought the man looked as if he could smell the police a mile off. She watched him nervously pick at his rather angry acne. *Might be worth running a check on him.*

'Well, don't cause any then,' replied Harris, turning to Fletcher and giving her a wink. 'What you having, doll?'

'Look, don't call me doll. I'll have an orange juice.'

'Christ. You're so uptight. Live dangerously. Put a vodka in it.'

Ignoring Harris, Fletcher spoke directly to the barman. 'Just an orange juice, thanks.'

'Right,' said Harris, 'look after the drinks. I'm away for a pish.'

'That will be four-forty,' said the publican to Harris' fast retreating back.

'I'll get these, shall I?' said Fletcher with a sigh and shake of the head, as she took her shiny black handbag off her shoulder and unzipped it. Not only would she be paying for the drinks, she would also be driving.

A pimply-faced youth with big cauliflower ears thrust two empty glasses on to the bar. 'Gizza another couple of pints, and some water for the dug outside?'

Fletcher looked at him with curiosity. 'Lewis Adamson?'

'Who's asking?' Adamson looked around him.

'Detective Sergeant Andrea Fletcher.' She showed him her warrant card. 'I've got a few questions for you.'

'About?'

'It's about your involvement in a recent fight. Won't take long. Shall we sit down? Where's your mate?'

'Having a piss.'

'That might turn out to be a very unfortunate decision,' said Fletcher, nervously wondering how long to give Dougie Harris in the gents' before going in, all guns blazing, to rescue Callum Russell.

***

'Well, well, well, what do we have here?'

'What the?' Callum Russell was urinating and still in mid flow when Harris walked into the gents'. Russell swung round so quickly some of the urine went over his trainers.

'Shite. What you doing here? What do you want? Me and Shirl split up. I already told ye that,' he replied, rapidly tucking himself in and zipping up his jeans.

In a flash Harris had grabbed hold of the boy's neck, yanked his head back. Russell started to struggle. Manoeuvring out of the policeman's grip, Russell managed to turn round and lashed out at Harris with a fist. Harris, seeing it coming, side-stepped leaving Russell to overbalance and fall on to a wash basin. Blood spurted from his nose.

'Aw fuck, look what you've done. You've broken my nose. Yer aff yer heid.'

Harris shook his head. 'That's no way to speak to the polis, is it? Mind yer manners, ya wee prick. Anyway, ye fuckin' fell.'

Harris grabbed hold of Russell's left arm and hauled him into one of the cubicles. He slammed the door shut with his foot, and forced the man's head down the toilet. Dunked him a couple of times. Blood stained water fast disappeared down the hole.

'You'll be sorry for doing this. I'm wearing a Ralph Lauren shirt and you've fuckin' ruined it. I'm going to report you,' Russell spat when Harris pulled him back up by his hair. Water was streaming down his light blue T-shirt soaking it, turning it dark blue.

'The way I see it, I've only been defending myself. After all, you came at me first.'

'I never.'

'Ye tried to punch me, remember?'

Still gripping the youth's hair Harris forced his head back with one hand, and got him in a half nelson with the other. Russell nodded dumbly.

'Right. Let's get down to business,' said Harris with an arm up the back and still gripping Russell by the hair. 'Where were you yesterday afternoon?'

'At my Gran's funeral.'

'Pull the other one. Do you think I was born yesterday?'

'I swear I'm telling the truth! Ask anybody. What am I supposed to have done?'

'Remember the fight with the Riff-Raf? One of their boys has turned up dead, that's all.'

'I had nothing tae do with it.'

'What time was the funeral?' demanded Harris.

'I bet you'll find they turned on each other. One of them was a real psycho.'

'What time was?'

'Three at the crem. Then we went on tae the wake. I was with my family until ten that evening. Ask anyone. Le' go of me. You're hurtin'.'

Harris made a swift calculation. Russell couldn't have killed Evans if his story was true. Evans had been seen at the RAF base, still alive, late afternoon, to be found dead at around 9pm.

Harris loosened his grip on the boy. 'What was the fight about?'

'Just some cow. The Welsh boys were flashing the cash. The birds were all over them. It was enough to make you sick.'

'That's no way to talk about your ex-girlfriend, is it? So you thought you'd teach them a lesson?'

'She's no' my girlfriend, any more. Like I said, she's just some wee cow. We just wanted a piece of the action. It's no' fair. Us local boys don't get a look in with the RAF so close.'

Harris yanked Russell out of the cubicle and kneed him in the balls. The boy bent double and sank to his knees.

'Well, it might help if you got a job and did something about your acne.'

***

'Where were you between 5pm and 9pm Friday evening?' Andie Fletcher was perched, knees crossed, on a faded tartan chair. She sipped her orange juice as she watched Adamson. He was sitting on the edge of his seat and his right leg was shaking uncontrollably.

'Over in Dundee. Darts tournament. I was playing for the Saltire. Ask anyone.'

'Was Russell with you?'

'Naw, his gran died. He was at her funeral.'

'We'll be checking your alibis so you'd better be telling the truth. What are you doing for work nowadays?'

He leered at her. 'A bit of this and a bit of that. Ye ken how it is.'

'No, I don't know how it is. And you're wearing an expensive shirt. I'm wondering where you got the money to buy it, that's all.'

'We both do odd jobs.'

'What sort?'

'All sorts. Gardening. Labouring. Whatever's going. Times are hard. Especially if ye havenae got a qualification.'

'Well, maybe you should have stayed on at school.'

'I never liked school.'

There was a sudden noise from the gents', as if someone very drunk had had a collision with the door that he had forgotten to open.

'What's going on in there?' the landlord shouted over. 'If it's one of your lot beating up one of my customers, there'll be trouble.'

Suddenly the door opened. Out came Harris looking very pleased with himself.

'Where's Russell?' asked Fletcher, her heart sinking.

'Just touching up his make up,' smirked Harris. 'Won't be long. He's got an alibi, by the way.'

A few seconds later, the door opened for a second time and Callum Russell appeared. He was soaking wet, and was dabbing a very blood stained wad of tissues to a still bleeding nose.

'What the—' exclaimed Adamson. 'What have ye done to him? Looks like you've broken his fuckin' nose.'

'It's police brutality. He's an animal, that one. I'm away home.' With that, Russell made a dash for the door.

Adamson wriggled out of his seat and was off after Russell like a shot, leaving their drinks on the scarred wooden table.

'Christ. What have you done?' said Fletcher. 'We'd both better be going too.' Dougie picked up his glass.

'Leave it,' said Fletcher. 'We need to get back to the station. Let Jim know they both claim to have alibis. If their alibis do check out we'll have to look further afield.'

'I know who my money's on,' answered Harris with a knowing look. 'By the way, I'm no' going anywhere. It's lunchtime and I've worked up an appetite.'

Harris took a slug of drink.

Fletcher rounded on him. 'Answer my question first. What happened back there? Looks like you've broken his nose.'

Harris shook his head. 'He tripped.'

'Tripped? Really? You'll have to do better than that. So why's he soaking wet?'

Harris was silent. He carried on drinking.

'What you going to do if he makes a complaint?' asked Fletcher.

Finally Harris put his glass down. 'I'm telling you he tripped. Now you gonna leave a man in peace to finish his pint?'

'What about Jim and the statements?'

'Screw Carruthers. We'll phone him. That's what these are for,' he said, brandishing his mobile in her face. He took another swig of his pint and wiped the back of his hand over his frothy moustache. He settled resolutely back into his chair, lifted a bum cheek and promptly broke wind.

Fletcher glanced down at her half-drunk orange juice wishing, despite her pregnancy, that the publican had indeed put vodka in it.

FIVE

'How was your day?' asked Carruthers.

Fletcher looked up from her report to see Carruthers standing at her desk. She saw his careworn face and knew that he would have had a bitch of a morning at the mortuary. The jacket in his hand made her wonder if he was coming in or going out.

'Better than yours by the looks of it,' she said. 'How was it?'

Carruthers shrugged. 'As expected. How did the interviews go?'

Fletcher knew that she should say something about Harris' altercation in the gents' toilet, but she wasn't one to grass up a colleague. And she believed him when he said Russell had tripped – although how he'd got wet through was another matter. But still, Harris might be old school but she just couldn't see him physically beat up a suspect. Even he wouldn't be that stupid. She felt a pang, but as long as it wasn't reported by Russell, Carruthers would be none the wiser. Anyway, both boys had been scared. She thought it unlikely either would report it. However, she couldn't help but wonder how many more secrets she was going to have to keep from Jim.

Instead she said, 'Yeah, they went OK. Both claim alibis. Russell swears he was at his gran's funeral. Adamson insists he was playing in a darts match in Dundee. Both swear blind they never left their venues. They claim at least a dozen people can vouch to their whereabouts.'

Carruthers rubbed a hand over his short hair. 'Well, in Russell's case, it's all family members. Knowing that bunch of outlaws, they'll be more than happy to close ranks. OK, can you chase the alibis up?'

Fletcher nodded. 'Leave it with me.'

'Anything else?'

Fletcher tapped her black ballpoint pen against her front teeth. 'The really interesting thing is that Russell's ex, Charlene Todd, is now going out with Dave Roberts.'

Carruthers' brows rose indicating his interest in this idea. 'Well, well, well. Is she now? She certainly gets around. So that's what the fight was about. I don't remember reading she was seeing Roberts in her original statement. Don't tell me, Russell's jealous and wants her back?' He picked up a file and started leafing through.

'I don't get the feeling he wants her back, but I do think it's a case of jealousy. The RAF boys have more success with the women. And a lot more money. Adamson linked the two and I've no reason to doubt him on that point. That's not the most interesting thing though. During the course of the fight, according to Charlene Todd, Dave Roberts was pretty free and easy with his fists. Not only did he punch Russell, he also punched Evans.'

Carruthers looked up from the file. 'Roberts punched Evans? Now, that's interesting. Do we know why?'

Fletcher shook her head slowly. 'I'm not entirely sure. Roberts is obviously quick to anger. Didn't like Evans trying to break up the fight. Thought he was interfering. Wonder if it's more than that, though. Is it possible Evans made a pass at Charlene and Roberts found out?'

Carruthers rubbed his eyes. 'Well, he was already seeing Siobhan Mathews. If he was into her as much as she was into him, then I would say it was unlikely.'

'It's a possibility though, isn't it?'

'Anything's possible,' said Carruthers. 'I learnt from Siobhan Mathews that Evans had put in for a transfer. The question is why? Mathews didn't seem to know. Evans was really tight-lipped about it. So it begs the question, does his transfer request have anything to do with Roberts? And does Roberts have anything to do with his death?' Carruthers started to pull on his jacket. 'I'm going over to the base now. Hopefully we'll get some answers. Perhaps Roberts was bullying Evans. That's why Evans had put in for a transfer.'

Fletcher pushed a lock of dark hair out of her face. 'Do you want me to come with you?'

Carruthers paused, considering it but only for a moment. 'It's OK. You stay and write up your interviews.'

Fletcher saluted. 'Yes, sir.'

'Andie,' he paused before heading out, 'I was meaning to ask. Do you still go hill walking?'

'Not for a while. Living in Fife isn't the easiest for getting away to the hills, but every so often I go out with the Perth Mountaineering Club. Why do you ask?'

'No reason.'

'Oh boss, I was meaning to…'

But he had already left. She heard his desk phone start ringing in the next office. After about six rings it stopped. No rest for the wicked. She wondered when she would have a chance to have a proper chat with him. She needed to talk to him about the pregnancy. She sighed. *Damn, another opportunity gone.*

She made herself a cup of tea and then sat and re-read the statements. She was feeling tired so grabbed a sugar lump from the communal sugar jar, thinking it might pep her up. Absentmindedly she stirred her mug with a spoon. Back at her desk once more she flipped open her notebook. Fifteen minutes later she had picked up the phone.

'Good afternoon. This is Detective Sergeant Andrea Fletcher from Castletown Police Station. I believe you had a pub darts team playing in a tournament in Dundee yesterday. I need to find out where the tournament was being held. I also need to know the names of the members of your darts team. There's one individual in particular I'm interested in. His name's—'

From her peripheral vision she could see Harris striding up to her desk. 'What have you said to Carruthers, ya wee clype?'

'What do you want?' Fletcher said, covering up the mouthpiece as she answered Harris. 'Can't you see that I'm on the phone?' She heard a voice down the phone. Put the phone back to her ear. She tried to shoo Harris away.

'Oh yes, that's right. I need to know which pub in Dundee the tournament was taking place. No. It's urgent. I need it today. It's in relation to an ongoing investigation. I also need to know if a Lewis Adamson played for the Saltire.'

Harris grabbed the phone out of Fletcher's hand. 'You told Carruthers I assaulted Russell, didn't you? I know it was you, so dinnae try to deny it.'

'Give me the bloody phone, Dougie. I'm in the middle of an important call.'

'Well, what did you say to him? Am I going to be up on charge? I need to know.'

'Dougie,' said Fletcher making a successful lunge for the phone. 'Did anyone ever tell you that there are two gs in bugger off? Now do one.' She glared at Harris as she returned the phone to her ear. 'Yes, sorry, I'm still here. No, I'm not telling you to bugger off.' Fletcher felt her face burning in mortification. 'Just having a bit of station banter with a colleague.' She scowled at Harris, who finally tutted and stomped out. 'No, the person I need to check is a Lewis Adamson. I believe he was playing for your pub. I want to check the time the tournament started, where it was played and how far the Saltire got in the tournament. Yes, if you can get that information to me as soon as possible that would be great.' Fletcher gave him her number, thanked him and hung up.

Fletcher wondered if she had time to check Russell's alibi before Harris interrupted her again. She had worked with him long enough to know that he didn't easily let things go. She should have expected Harris would assume it was her that had grassed him up.

Harris walked back into the office, shirtsleeves rolled up. Fletcher's heart sank.

'Well?' he said.

'Well, what?'

'I want to know what you said to Boy Wonder.'

'I haven't said anything.' Fletcher stood up. Even though she was only five foot two she would rather face a belligerent Harris standing up than sitting down. Harris had moved to her side of the desk and now he stood right in front of her, invading her personal space. Fletcher took a step backwards and immediately regretted it. She didn't want Harris to know that she felt intimidated. He would love to know she was feeling uncomfortable. She felt tears prick her eyes. She wasn't usually given to displays of emotion but recently her moods had been all over the place.

'Look, believe what you bloody well like, Dougie, but like I said, I haven't told Jim anything. He just asked me how the interview went. I told him everything was fine. I didn't mention what happened in the pub.'

Harris was looking at her, hands on hips, one eyebrow raised.

'Well, if it wisnae you, who was it? If I find out you are lying to me, I'll–'

'Oh wind your neck in, will you? For the last time, I haven't said anything. I might not agree with your tactics for getting information from suspects, but I'm not going to grass you up, either.' She reached over for her now cold cup of tea. 'By the way, I hear the station's running an anger management course. I suggest you go on it. That temper of yours will be the end of your career one of these days.'

Harris swore and left the room. Fletcher sighed. She wondered how Jim had found out and so quickly. She supposed she could be wrong. Perhaps Adamson or Russell had been on the phone after all. Then she remembered Jim's phone had been ringing when he left the office. Callum Russell? Taking a deep breath she steepled her hands in front of her face. The knock-on effect, of course, was that she wasn't exactly going to be popular with Jim when he found out she'd been keeping things from him. Some coppers would take that as a personal affront. She hoped he wasn't one of them. She bit her lip. She wished she'd managed to tell him of her pregnancy before the Adamson and Russell interviews.

She dug out the number of the Crematorium and made the call. It was as Callum Russell had told Dougie. The funeral of Ethel Annie Russell had taken place at 3pm.

As she hung up, she wondered how Dougie had written up his interview notes, seeing as the interview had been conducted in the gents' toilet. Nosiness got the better of her. She went over to his desk. How he managed to find anything on it was beyond her. The place was a midden. Cups of cold coffee; sticky orange stains of what she suspected were Irn-Bru; and underneath his police manual, a copy of Playboy. *He really is a throwback to the 1970s,* she thought with disgust. She couldn't find any paperwork on the interviews so she went back to her own desk and sat, deep in thought.

Fletcher now needed to find the information on where the wake had been held. She flipped through her black notebook again. Whitecraigs Golf Club. Apparently the family had hired it from 4pm onwards. Of course, Fletcher was aware that while Russell might have been at the wake, that didn't preclude him from having ducked out for a couple of hours. This was only one step on the road to alibi corroboration. It was such a large dysfunctional family and all the members had the tendency to drink a lot and close ranks when questioned. Jim was right: was it really much of an alibi?

***

Carruthers bunched his fists. He could feel the heat of the flush spreading up his neck into his face. The phone call he'd taken had been a complaint from the pub landlord of the Saltire. The landlord wanted to report DS Dougie Harris for assaulting one of his customers – none other than Callum Russell.

His anger was directed towards both Harris and Fletcher. He was disappointed in Harris, but not surprised. But he couldn't help but feel resentful of Fletcher for not having told him. He knew he'd feel differently once he'd calmed down. If he'd been in Fletcher's position he would have been tempted to do exactly the same thing and keep quiet. Squealing on a fellow cop was just not done. It certainly wouldn't win you any friends. In fact, it would make life very difficult. Fletcher was ambitious. She wouldn't want to rock the boat. He would deal with Harris later. He turned his attention to Dave Roberts.

Carruthers hadn't yet got an angle on why Roberts had lied to Siobhan about reporting Evans missing to the police, if he had indeed lied. He knew stress did strange things to people. There was a chance Siobhan had remembered events wrongly. Even so, he was keen to get Roberts' version. There was a possibility Siobhan had lied, but it wasn't a thought he wanted to entertain. Of course, as a policeman he was used to people lying to him; but his gut instinct told him Siobhan wouldn't deliberately lie. He wanted to be proved right. Right now, he was keener than ever to meet and interview Roberts, who seemed to be at the centre of so much.

***

'You can't interview Roberts,' said the RAF policeman who had been phoned from the sentry gates.

'Why not?' said Carruthers, looking at the man's close-set eyes and boozy unsmiling face. Carruthers disliked him on sight. 'This may be a murder investigation. We're wasting valuable time.'

'You can't interview Roberts because he's gone AWOL.'

Carruthers was flabbergasted. 'AWOL?'

'Absent without leave. He didn't turn up for guard duty today.'

'I know what AWOL means. I'm just finding it difficult to believe Roberts has disappeared – that's all. We have one dead lad from the base on our hands as it is. Now a second's gone AWOL. You have to admit, it looks bad, especially given Roberts may have been the last person to see Evans alive. According to Evans' girlfriend, Roberts claims he reported Evans missing to us. However, there's no evidence that that call was ever made.'

'I wouldn't give that too much significance,' said the RAF policeman. 'One of your lot probably just forgot to pass on the message.'

Carruthers' face reddened. 'Well, given the seriousness of the situation, can I at least see Evans' room? Or interview this third man, Sean Coombe?'

'No on both counts,' responded the man with a sneer. 'Not without a warrant.'

'Can I see Roberts' room?' persisted Carruthers.

'I'm not in the habit of repeating myself. Not without a search warrant. I'd like you to leave now.'

'You realise you're being obstructive, don't you?' said Carruthers, his temper finally starting to fray. 'I want to see your superior.'

'And I'm sure he would like to see you. After all, you're trespassing.' He picked up the phone.

'No, I'm not.'

'I asked you to leave. And you're still here.'

Carruthers' heart sank.

There was an uncomfortable few minutes whilst both men awaited the arrival of the group captain. Carruthers decided to brazen it out rather than beat a hasty retreat. He hoped he had made the right decision. He ran his finger around the inside of his collar and felt the sweat on his neck.

'Does Superintendent Bingham know you're here?' Group Captain Philips, head of RAF Police, was a balding pug-faced individual. He came striding towards Carruthers.

'Bingham? What's he got to do with anything?' said Carruthers, a sense of foreboding already creeping in.

'Maybe I'll give him a call. We were at school together, at Winchester, and I'll lay odds he doesn't know anything about your visit here today. Well, does he?' persisted Philips.

Carruthers remained silent. Trust the old boy's network to be flourishing, even in Fife. If he had his way he would do away with all public schools.

'Well, are you going to leave, or am I going to have to get you escorted off the premises? The RAF Police will be taking the lead in this enquiry. If I need your help I'll ask for it.' said Philips.

Carruthers put his hands up. 'Alright, alright,' said Carruthers. 'I'm leaving.'

'See that you do.'

Carruthers turned to go but shot over his shoulder, 'Just to give you the heads-up I'll be back with a search warrant. Rhys Evans was killed off base. It's our investigation, not yours.'

Carruthers allowed himself a self-satisfied smile when he saw the man's face reddening. He stepped outside as he heard the group captain shout at a couple of loitering uniforms to escort 'the inspector' off the base. The sneer in the man's voice was unmistakeable. Swearing under his breath, he began to walk away.

'Inspector?'

Startled, Carruthers turned round. This was not one of the men Philips had been shouting at. This man had materialised from another direction altogether. A nondescript man with mousey hair and a weedy light brown moustache had fallen in step beside him. He reminded Carruthers of a ferret. A nervous ferret wearing an RAF uniform.

'I'm Sean Coombe,' he said. 'The man you want to talk to.'

Carruthers wondered how Coombe could possibly have known who he was. 'Coombe? You know Evans and Roberts?'

The man glanced around him. 'Listen, we have to make this short. I can't be seen talking to you.' He looked over his shoulder. 'I know Dave's gone AWOL. It's all over the base. Is it true Rhys has been murdered?'

'It's looking that way. What do you know about it?'

'Like I said, I can't be seen talking to you. It's too dangerous.'

'Dangerous?' Carruthers halted abruptly and turned to face Coombe. 'If you know something you have to tell me.'

'Keep walking,' said Coombe.

'Who are you afraid of?'

'Evans was a nice guy. Roberts isn't. I don't know who killed Evans but I'd imagine it's the men Roberts is working for.'

'You mean the RAF?' said Carruthers, confused.

Coombe laughed mirthlessly. 'No, not the RAF. His other paymasters. Look, I don't know anything for sure. All I can tell you is that Roberts has got himself involved with people he shouldn't. Dangerous people. I've said enough. Don't contact me again. And if anyone asks, this conversation never happened.'

With that Coombe took a sharp left and walked smartly into the NAAFE, leaving Carruthers looking quizzically at his retreating back.

***

The man with the binoculars pretended to be looking at a road map when the policeman passed him. He recognised the steel-haired cop with the athletic gait from Bell Street and Edgecliffe. Wondered if he would be a menace. Did he need to be disposed of? Wasn't interested in going on a killing spree but had no qualms about killing a policeman.

Had seen Sean Coombe talk to the cop through the binoculars. Wondered just what had been said. Had been told Coombe might be a liability. But Coombe would soon be out of the picture and, as far as he was concerned, Coombe didn't know enough to jeopardise his plans. Taking one last drag on his cigarette, he flicked it out of the window. Taking out his mobile he made the call. Organised a rendezvous to shift the Semtex.

***

'I need a search warrant. Fast tracked,' said Carruthers back at the station. He was facing a pile of paperwork.

'For RAF Edenside?' questioned Fletcher, putting down her mug of tea. 'At this time of day? It probably won't come through till tomorrow.' She looked at her watch.

'Something's going on at the base. I spoke with Sean Coombe. He was shit scared.'

'What about? Evans' death?'

'And Roberts' disappearance,' said Carruthers.

'So they're linked?'

'He seems to think so. Thinks Roberts is involved in something dangerous.'

'What?'

'Didn't say. But Coombe obviously knew more than he's letting on. Talked about Roberts having another paymaster besides the RAF.'

'What did he mean?'

'No idea,' said Carruthers.

'Is he allowed to have a second job?'

'I don't think it's legit. Look, I've got somewhere else to be now but I've made up my mind. Tomorrow morning I'm going back to the base to interview Coombe. Set it up for me, will you? Through the official channels. Don't want my balls squeezed by Bingham any more than they're already going to be.'

'What if Coombe's too scared to talk?' said Fletcher.

'We could offer him police protection?'

'Whilst he's in the RAF? How would that work?'

'Could be done. We'd need the cooperation from the RAF of course.' *I haven't made a good start,* he thought ruefully. *Good luck with that one.* 'I'm heading off.'

Fletcher looked up surprised. 'Bit early, isn't it?'

He tried to ignore her sniffing, it was discreet, but he spotted it. Wondered if she could smell the aftershave he'd freshly applied. 'I'll be on the mobile.'

'Business or pleasure,' she called after him.

'Business,' he replied and left the room.

***

Carruthers got behind the wheel of his car, hesitated for a fraction of a second then turned the ignition on. He knew that he shouldn't be going alone but he wanted to make sure Siobhan Mathews was OK. He wondered if she'd remembered anything else that might be useful to the investigation. He wasn't sure why she felt more comfortable talking to him than Fletcher but he felt the last conversation had proved fruitful. Siobhan was starting to trust him and open up. But still, he shouldn't be going alone and if anyone at the station found out he could be in serious trouble. He sat in his car weighing up the risks. A couple of minutes went by. Finally, he took the handbrake off and cruised out of the car park.

After approximately a mile Carruthers realised he was being followed, for a second his heart ramped up. A green Beetle was following him. It was keeping its distance two cars behind, but not covert enough to be unseen. There was only one person he knew who drove such a car. What the hell was Fletcher doing following him? He took a sharp left and momentarily the green Beetle was out of sight. However, when the road straightened up there it was again. He drove another mile or so, then pulled off the road sharply when it was safe to do so. He waited for the Beetle to catch him up.

Both of them got out of their cars. Carruthers slammed his door just a little bit too forcibly. He marched up to her. 'What the hell are you doing tailing me, Andie?'

He could tell she was embarrassed: she was avoiding eye contact with him. 'I was worried about you. You're going to see Siobhan Mathews, aren't you?'

Carruthers tried to keep his expression unreadable. 'I'm going to see her for work reasons.'

'It isn't my place to say this, but I think you're making a mistake.'

Carruthers bunched his fists. 'What I'm going to Edgecliffe for is none of your business.'

'You're not going for work reasons though, are you? You're wearing aftershave.'

'Oh for Christ's sake. Are you my bloody mother? If you must know, I'm going to interview her about Evans' relationship to Sean Coombe. Wearing aftershave isn't a crime. I've been working all day. Anyway, what the hell am I doing justifying myself to you?'

'Well then, let me do the interview. After all, it isn't really a job for a DCI, is it? You've got to trust me some time, you know. I'll do a good job. Scout's honour.'

He turned on her, couldn't help himself. 'I don't think I'm the one with the trust issues, do you? Although God knows I should be.'

'What do you mean by that?' But he could see it from her sheepish face she already knew.

'What do you think I mean by it? I know about this morning's interviews. What the hell were you thinking letting Harris beat Callum Russell up and then not telling me?'

'Has Russell made a complaint?'

'The publican has,' said Carruthers.

'Shit.' Her eyes were downcast. 'Jim, I'm sorry. You know how hard it is to rein Dougie in.'

'You should have said something.'

'I know.' Fletcher let out a long sigh. 'Would you have said anything in my position?'

'I can understand why you didn't. But you have to trust me. And more important, I have to trust you.'

'You can trust me.'

'Can I?'

'Yes. I made a mistake. I'm sorry. What about the interview with Siobhan Mathews, Jim?'

'Go on then. You conduct it. I could do with an early night.' He opened his door. 'Be in tomorrow at 8am.' He got into the car and slammed the door.

'Jim?'

He opened the car window and put his head out. 'What is it?'

'I'm sorry. About earlier. The interviews. I was in a difficult position. Nobody likes a snitch.'

Carruthers eyeballed her. 'I realise that. But *you* have to understand where your loyalties lie. They are with me.' He started the ignition.

Fletcher nodded and got back into her car.

***

As he drove home, he gripped the steering wheel tightly and thought about Fletcher. He let out a huge frustrated sigh. Then, of course, there was Harris to deal with. He let himself into his cottage, went straight to the kitchen and selected a bottle of merlot from the wooden wine rack. He foraged in the freezer for something to eat. Finding a steak and kidney pie that his mother had brought over for him a while back, he took it out. He didn't know how long it had been there but he was pretty sure it wasn't more than a couple of months old. Putting the oven on, he opened the wine, poured himself a glass. He hunted for his mobile phone, decided to switch it to silent whilst he ate and plugged it in to recharge.

He sat down in the living room nursing the glass. Bottle at his feet. Thinking of his mother he wondered how she was getting on in Rhodes. His phone had been unusually silent whilst she'd been away. They were close but he really wished she didn't phone him quite so often. He listened to the silence. A wave of loneliness swept over him. He felt in the mood for some folk music. He leapt up and put on a CD. He shut his eyes as he listened to the soothing sound of Gillian Welch.

By the time the pie was ready he had already drunk half the bottle and was feeling the effects. It had done the trick; taken the edge off and kept the loneliness at bay.

He settled back into his brown leather chair with his food, stretching out his long legs in front of him. Having finished the meal and the wine he got himself a whisky and put some music on. One finger of whisky turned into two and soon enough he fell asleep in his chair with the packaging of his empty dinner for one forlornly beside him. As he was drifting off an image of beauty came into his head. The woman was standing with her back to him. She was tall, slim and elegant. It was Mairi. The woman turned round. She had green eyes, dark well-defined eyebrows and black shoulder length hair. He had been mistaken. It wasn't Mairi at all. It was Siobhan.

At some point he thought he heard the house phone ringing. It was too much effort to drag himself from his drunken stupor to answer it. In the end the ringing stopped and his dreams continued.

***

THURSDAY MORNING, 31st MAY

Jim rolled his shoulders and stretched his neck; he might have slept like the dead but a night in a chair had left him aching and uncomfortable. He pretended this was the worst of his discomfort but he knew his aborted visit to Siobhan was a colossal mistake. So did Fletcher. He also knew pride and superior rank would stop him from thanking her for saving his hide. He wasn't sure what was going to stop his neck bleeding, though.

He dabbed another piece of toilet roll on to the shaving nick and tried to ignore his haggard features, the red veined bleariness of his eyes. The cut had bled on to his collar in the car so he changed his shirt for the spare he kept at the office. He had no way to iron the thing so it wasn't as crisp as he would have liked and he shifted uncomfortably as he tried to smooth the creases out.

Just as he was wondering how to greet Fletcher, in she walked, looking as immaculate as ever. She was wearing a pristine white shirt and a navy knee-length skirt. Carruthers could barely summon the energy to greet her. He had a ferocious hangover and his aching muscles weren't feeling any better. He couldn't remember what time he'd awoken with a mouth like a bear pit, but it must have been four or five in the morning. As the birds had started their dawn chorus he'd climbed the stairs and crawled into bed. He felt like he'd barely closed his eyes before the alarm had gone off.

After a cursory 'good morning', he said, 'What did you find out last night?'

'Very little. Mathews says she only met Sean Coombe once. Didn't hear Evans talking about him much. Didn't know who else Roberts might be working for.'

He massaged his neck. 'Oh well, it was a long shot. I'm just completing some paperwork then I'm heading back to the RAF base to interview Coombe. I take it the documentation's come through OK?'

Fletcher stared at him, hands on her hips.

'What?' he asked.

'Didn't you get any of my messages last night?'

'What messages?'

'The messages I left on your mobile and house phone.'

Surprised, Carruthers took his mobile out of his pocket. It was on silent. Five missed calls. Shit! As for the house phone, he'd thought he'd heard it through his alcohol haze, but imagined it had been part of his dream.

He looked up at Fletcher. 'I went to bed early. Out like a light. What did you want?'

'Coombe's left the RAF base. Apparently he'd put in a request for a transfer a few months ago.'

'Shit. Not another one,' he said. 'What the hell's going on at that RAF base? Where's he gone? Not far I hope.'

'Falkland Islands.'

Carruthers muttered an expletive. What a bloody fool he'd been. Distracted by a woman he hardly knew, then drinking himself into oblivion.

He stood up. 'We need to stop Coombe boarding his flight,' he said. 'We'll insist he be brought back here. We need him for questioning – that sort of thing. I'll talk to Bingham.'

'No point. I've checked. Flight's already left.'

'Oh Christ,' Carruthers groaned and gingerly touched the side of his head that was throbbing.

'I'll get you a coffee. You look as if you could use it.'

Carruthers nodded, utterly shamefaced. He stood up, left his office and walked into the gent's toilet. It was unoccupied. He walked over to the wall and punched it. Cursed. Then nursed his now sore hand. At the sink he splashed water on his face.

Whatever possessed him to get drunk? He hadn't set out to get pissed and yet he still had. It reminded him of the early days of Mairi's departure where he had spent too many nights in an alcohol induced haze. He wasn't an alcoholic but he knew he'd almost got to the point of becoming dependent a few months ago. He was determined to learn a valuable lesson from this. He wouldn't turn into his father. He was buggered if he was going to make another costly error. He walked back to his desk, gingerly flexing the fingers of his damaged hand.

Fletcher came back into his office carrying a black coffee. Setting it down with two painkillers she looked at him but said nothing. He felt she was expecting him to speak.

'It was a one-off,' he finally said.

'My stepfather used to say that. He was an alcoholic.'

***

The man ground the cigarette into the pavement with his foot and looked at his watch. It was 1:05pm. Ten minutes to go. He watched a teenage girl with long red hair walk past with a Scottie dog. The dog stopped and sniffed the ground. It then cocked a leg. The owner pulled on the lead but the dog started walking further into the car park taking the lead with it. The man cursed. The man found he was holding his breath. Glanced at his watch again. Rubbed his damp hands down the side of his jeans. He hadn't expected to feel nervous, but he did. Fumbled the cigarette packet with nicotine-stained fingers. The dog trotted up to the first car. Sniffed the front tyre. The red headed girl was once again pulling at the dog. 1:10pm. Five minutes to go. At 1:13pm the girl finally managed to drag the dog out of the car park. The man's eyes shifted from dog and girl to the front door of the university department. The professor was nowhere in sight. The car park was empty. 1:14pm. He cursed. Where was he? He should be coming out of the front door now. He found he was holding his breath.

The hands of his watch said 1:15pm. Suddenly there was a blinding flash, an ear-splitting explosion and the sound of breaking glass. A plume of fire barrelled into the sky. A woman inside the building screamed.

***

Carruthers was leaning over Fletcher's desk. A loud crumpling noise sounded somewhere outside.

'Jesus,' said Fletcher. 'What the fuck was that?'
Instinctively Carruthers leapt to his feet knocking some of his paperwork to the floor. 'Explosion.'

Carruthers raced through to Bingham's office. The door was open so he just walked straight in to find the super on the phone. Putting his hand over the mouthpiece Bingham said, 'Can't talk now. Got the chief super on the phone. Get over to the politics department of the university. Take all available manpower. Looks like a bomb.'

SIX

A thick plume of acrid black smoke filled the air. As Carruthers drew closer he could see several cars on fire and one completely destroyed. Twisted, blackened metal and broken glass littered the car park. The windows of the ground floor had been blown in by the explosion and the building's fire alarms were going off. The intensity of the suffocating heat kept the knot of onlookers back.

Carruthers dispatched Harris to shepherd them back further behind the police tape that Fletcher was hastily erecting. A deafening noise hurt his ears as the flames ignited a petrol tank. A shower of sparks and debris rained down on them. Someone screamed.

'Jesus, what's keeping the fire brigade?' he shouted to Fletcher. 'Take cover in case there's another explosion. And get these people well behind the tape.'

A plump bespectacled middle-aged man, casually dressed in brown corduroy trousers and a crumpled shirt, approached Carruthers. He appeared to be ducking under the police tape until Carruthers put his hand out to prevent him.

'No closer, sir. It's unsafe to cross the tape.'

'Good God. Is it a gas explosion?' The man was visibly shaken and immensely pale.

'We don't know what's caused the explosion at this point,' said Carruthers. He wondered who could have planted a bomb. He could taste the bile in his mouth. He wondered about the conversation between Bingham and the chief super. How had they known so quickly where the explosion had occurred?

'Only I know whose car has exploded. That is— was the car of Professor Nicholas Holdaway.' The man gestured towards the burning vehicle. 'Christ, could it be a bomb? I wonder if he was the target. I knew his views were controversial, but I had no idea anyone would go this far.'

The man had started to babble. *Must be a nervous reaction,* thought Carruthers. 'Controversial?' asked Carruthers. He heard a wail of sirens and out of the corner of his eye he could see the fire brigade approaching.

'He'd been getting hate mail. I told him to report it to the police but he seemed reluctant.'

'And you are?'

'Oh sorry,' he shouted over the noise of the inferno and the siren of the approaching fire brigade. 'Professor Edward Sadler. I have the office next to Holdaway.'

'OK, Professor Sadler, how many people are still in your building?'

'There shouldn't be anyone. We're all out the back. It's a miracle nobody's hurt. There's broken glass everywhere.

'Is anyone missing?' asked Carruthers.

'I don't know. Barbara Fairbairn, our secretary's going through the register at the moment. What d'you think's caused the explosion?'

Carruthers placed a hand on his arm. 'Can you find out for us if everybody's accounted for? Make sure they're right away from the building and this car park. We'll need to take a statement from you all, so make sure nobody from the department leaves the vicinity until they've spoken with us.' Before Sadler had the chance to ask another question Carruthers turned away from him to address Fletcher.

'I'm going to fill the firemen in on what we know, which is precious little,' he shouted, striding towards the first of the vans. 'Just make sure nobody gets into the cordoned off area. He surveyed the gaggle of onlookers behind the police tape before turning to Harris. 'And Dougie?'

'Aye, boss.'

'Get on to the station and ask them to check up on Nicholas Holdaway, professor of politics. See if there's anything on file about him receiving hate mail.'

'You've done a good job securing the area and setting up the exclusion zone but we need to make it much wider,' said one of the firemen, a thin-faced man in his thirties with receding reddish blond hair. 'Christ, we would've been here a lot sooner but we've just got back from a hoax. Some wee scrote's had us out on a wild goose chase. Told us there was a fire over in Methil. We'll take over from here,' he shouted.

Carruthers nodded.

'Looks like the fire started in bay five and spread to surrounding bays,' said the firefighter over his shoulder to Carruthers.

A breathless Professor Sadler ran up to Carruthers. 'I've spoken to Babs, our secretary. She's taken the register. The only person missing is Professor Holdaway. He was in the department this morning. Nobody remembers seeing him leave.' He stared over at the inferno still raging in Bay 5. 'Oh my God. You don't think...' he left the question hanging in the air.

'Dinnae see anyone burning in the front seat, do you?' said a sweating Harris, the buttons of his shirt straining over his hairy belly.

'Can you give us your statement now, sir?' Carruthers looked over at Fletcher who was talking to one of the fire officers. 'Andie, take a statement from Professor Sadler, will you?'

'Yes, of course.' Fletcher went over to Professor Sadler, taking him by his arm and guiding him away from the blazing car.

'Boss,' said Harris. 'The super wants you back at the station, pronto.'

'What, now?' said Carruthers surprised.

'Got the feeling it's something to do with the explosion. Of course, I'm just a lowly DS so he's no' gonnae to tell me, is he?'

Carruthers pulled the car keys out of his pocket and strode past the cordoned off area. A small crowd had gathered. His last sight was of the firefighters ordering the public to leave the area.

***

The man melted into the crowd of horrified onlookers but not before pulling his baseball cap well over his face. He wondered where Holdaway was and how he'd managed to escape. How had his recruit so right royally managed to fuck things up? Yes, the explosion had been on a timer but it had been the younger man's responsibility to make sure Holdaway was at his car by just after one. The recruit would have to be dealt with. However, part of him was enjoying this game, he thought, feeling in the inside of his jacket pocket for his gun.

Holdaway deserved to feel fear and to have his death drawn out. He reminded himself he was doing this for his sister. Pushed the image of his sister out of his head. *Focus.* Whenever he thought of her he didn't see her in the wheelchair. Refused to see her confined to that God awful metal contraption. In his dreams she was laughing, walking, wearing one of her long hippy dresses. Her long blonde hair framing her face. But then the dream changed as it always did. He would hear gunshots and screaming. He would turn to see his sister lying on the ground covered in blood. That's when he thought of Holdaway.

***

'I've heard the car that blew up belongs to a Professor Holdaway. What do we know about him?' Grim-faced Bingham came straight to the point. Instead of sitting behind his desk he was pacing up and down his office. Carruthers wondered how he'd got that information so quickly.

'Apparently,' said Carruthers, 'according to one of his colleagues, a Professor Sadler, Holdaway had been receiving hate mail.'

Bingham stopped pacing and faced Carruthers. 'Is this on file?'

Carruthers shook his head. 'He didn't report it. What's going on, sir?'

'We've had the *Castletown Citizen* on the phone. They've taken a call from a group calling themselves "Bryn Glas 1402." They're claiming responsibility for the explosion.'

Carruthers was aghast. 'That's what you were talking to the chief super about?'

Bingham nodded. 'We haven't heard back from the fire brigade yet to confirm it's a bomb,' continued Bingham, 'so it's not been verified. Don't think it's in any doubt though. Have you heard of this group, Bryn Glas 1402, Jim? I hadn't.' Bingham sat down behind his big mahogany table and rolled up his sleeves.

Carruthers searched his memory and drew a blank. 'No.'

'Well, we need to find out who they are,' said Bingham, 'and, if they've targeted this Professor Holdaway, why on earth him? I've managed to get the *Citizen* to keep quiet about this for the moment.'

'What evidence is there they're targeting Holdaway? I take it they didn't name him in their call to the paper?'

'No, they didn't. But I've just had the Fire Chief on the phone. The fire started in a car in bay five. I learned that—'

'That bay is Holdaway's,' said Carruthers.

'Exactly. What else do we know about him?'

'Very little, other than he's a politics lecturer. And allegedly receiving hate mail. I left Fletcher interviewing Professor Sadler. Apparently their offices are next door to each other in the department.'

'Good. Where's Holdaway, now?'

'I don't know. Sadler hadn't seen him. According to the fire register he's the only one missing. Can't be far if his car was in the car park, though.'

Bingham picked up his phone. 'Find him, Carruthers. Send someone to his home. See if he's made it back there. Speak with Fletcher. Get a debrief of her interview with Sadler. Report back to me when you know more. Be quick about it. Can't let the grass grow under our feet on this one.'

'You don't think it could be Islamic State…?' said Carruthers.

Bingham put the phone back down. 'Let's not speculate, although it might be worth checking whether Holdaway has any Middle Eastern connections. There is one other thing that might be helpful. The journalist that took the call says he's pretty sure the man had a Welsh accent.'

Before Carruthers had a chance to pass comment Bingham once again picked up the phone. 'I've got some calls to make,' he said, waving Carruthers away with his free hand. 'Close the door on your way out, will you? And Jim?'

'Sir?'

'Keep this to yourself for now. And don't go too far. I may need to speak to you again shortly.'

***

Carruthers went back into his own office. Shut the door to make the call from his mobile.

He punched in Fletcher's number. 'What's happening?' he said. 'Has the fire brigade contained the fire?' He strained to hear her over the shouting in the background.

'Yes, it's under control, although it's wrecked a total of five cars. But nobody's been hurt – which is a miracle.'

Carruthers let out a long breath. He'd been dreading the news that they'd found a body. 'Does anybody know where Holdaway is?'

'Not yet,' said Fletcher.

'OK, find out Holdaway's home address and get someone over there, will you?'

'Right, boss.'

'OK. What have you learnt from Sadler? Anything useful?'

'Bit of personal info on Holdaway. Mid-sixties. Been lecturing for thirty years. Published three books – the most recent on the failings of Welsh nationalism. Apparently he's got some quite outspoken views.'

'Jesus Christ.' Carruthers strode over to his computer and googled the words, 'Bryn Glas 1402.' The results confirmed his growing dread. Momentarily he placed the mobile phone down on his desk.

'Look, what's going on, Jim?' demanded Fletcher.

'Andie, I need to talk to Bingham. Keep speaking to people. Find out as much as you can about Holdaway, especially this new book he's bought out. Has the fire brigade said anything official to you or Dougie about the cause of the explosion yet?'

'No, sir. You don't think the book—'

'He needs to be found, Andie. Make it a priority. If he lives within walking distance, perhaps he popped home over lunch and is unaware of the explosion.'

'I would think the whole town heard it. Would have been loud enough.'

'I need to go. Keep in touch.' With that, Carruthers finished the call and went to find Bingham.

He put his head round Bingham's door. Rapped on the inside of it. 'Sir, I've found something out about Holdaway that you need to know.'

'This is a bad business, Jim, a very bad business,' said the superintendent ushering Carruthers into his roomy office.

'Sit down,' said Bingham, offering up one of his brown leather chairs. The room had a smell of stale tobacco smoke, and Carruthers often wondered if, despite the smoking ban, Bingham still smoked his pipe in his office late at night when the rest of the station had gone home.

In his agitation, Bingham had pursed his thin lips so tight they had turned white, his frown was so pronounced it appeared that he only had one eyebrow. With his naturally pallid complexion, it gave him the appearance of a horror movie character. That twitching of the eye was a nervous tic that Carruthers knew only surfaced when he was extremely stressed or angered. He hoped this was stress.

Bingham took off his jacket, and laid it thoughtfully and deliberately over the back of one of the leather chairs. He paused, as if composing in his mind what he was going to say next. His white shirt was crumpled, and pools of sweat were staining the armpits. He turned and faced Carruthers.

'We've just had a call from the fire brigade. They've confirmed the explosion was caused by a bomb.'

Carruthers frowned. Even with an explosion and the call to the paper he just couldn't fathom the prospect of a lone bomber, let alone terrorists. It had been nearly a decade since the ramming attack at Glasgow Airport.

'Has Holdaway been found yet?' said Bingham.

'No sir, not yet, but I've discovered something about him that you're not going to like.'

'Go on, man.'

'Apparently Holdaway has some pretty outspoken views about Welsh nationalism and how it's failed. He's just published a book about it. There's something else. I looked up Bryn Glas and found a reference to a battle between the English and Welsh in 1402. We could be looking at a new terrorist group.'

'Yes, I've found the same information. Christ. If this lot are a new terrorist group… I never thought I would live to see the day Welsh extremists targeted individuals in Scotland. The IRA never did and amongst republican extremists, there's always been an unwritten rule you don't target your own. We have a lot of unanswered questions, Jim. Why has a professor of politics at a Scottish university been targeted, if indeed he was the target? And why now? If he's been receiving hate mail, why hasn't he reported it? Has the hate mail been sent by the same people who phoned the *Castletown Citizen*?'

Bingham let out a long sigh. 'We need to find out what is it about this particular man at this particular time that has made him a target. Surely to God there must be plenty of individuals to target closer to home. What are Welsh terrorists doing travelling this far north? Why are they on our damn patch? Just doesn't make sense.'

Carruthers nodded. He couldn't understand it either. 'Unless it's a cover to distract us from finding the truth,' he said.

'We've got to move quickly,' said Bingham. 'I've already made a call. I'm bringing in Superintendent Alistair McGhee from London to work on this one.'

Carruthers stiffened. *Christ, not McGhee.*

'With his background in explosives and counterterrorism both in London and Wales he's an excellent man to have on board. We're lucky he was available. He's travelling up overnight from Scotland Yard. I want him to take the lead on the investigation into the explosion. You'll be assisting him. But clearly, you're lead investigator into Evans' death.'

Carruthers saw Bingham was watching closely for his reaction.

'I've heard you two don't always see eye-to-eye, but you're going to have to make an effort. We need results and quickly. I don't have to tell you what a bombing campaign in Scotland would mean for public confidence, or indeed how much money is generated by tourism in Castletown. Christ, man, we've got the Dunhill Cup here in October.'

Carruthers was quietly fuming. Superintendent Alistair McGhee certainly had a background in explosives. McGhee particularly excelled at creating explosive situations. The last time he'd seen McGhee, which was over a year ago, Carruthers had punched him after he'd made a pass at Mairi. He wondered idly what he looked like with a broken nose, and hoped that it had ruined his so called-good looks.

It was a moment before he realised that the Superintendent was still talking.

'It goes without saying, all leave's cancelled until we catch these people. I'm going to cancel my trip to Morocco. No doubt Irene will go spare when I tell her. What a week. A suspicious death, a disappearance, and now a bomb.'

'Do you think they could be linked, sir?' asked Carruthers dragging himself back to the conversation.

'Linked? In what way?'

'Well, they're all Welsh – both the dead and missing aircraftmen. Now the possibility of a Welsh terrorist group, if they really are behind the explosion. Just seems too much of a coincidence otherwise.'

'I don't see what the link would be. If you're implying Evans and Roberts could be members of this terrorist organisation, what on earth would they be doing in the RAF? Doesn't make any sense. Think you're barking up the wrong tree there. To all intents and purposes, looks like Evans was just a botched robbery. It happens. I want that wrapped up quickly. As for Roberts' disappearance, probably homesick for the valleys. Leave it to the RAF to deal with. We've more than enough on our plates.'

'It would be a good smokescreen though, wouldn't it, sir? Joining the RAF whilst in a paramilitary organisation? And by the way, just for the record, Roberts is from Cardiff, not the valleys.'

'Just for the record, you wouldn't get past the security checks to get into the armed forces whilst in a paramilitary organisation, as well you know.'

'Unless you were recruited from within,' said Carruthers.

Bingham banged his fist on the table. 'Leave it, Carruthers. That's an order.'

Calling me by my surname again. Bugger, thought Carruthers. *That only happens when he's really pissed off with me.*

'You're already treading on very thin ice,' said Bingham. 'I've had a phone call from Group Captain Philips from RAF Edenside. Remember him? I certainly do. We were at school together. He was an annoying little bugger even then. He's made a complaint against you about the belligerent way you were trying to gain entry to the rooms of those RAF boys. Why didn't you tell me you were visiting the base? There are procedures to be followed. Not just by the lower ranks either. They're there for you as well. Got it?

'Sometimes procedure gets in the way of results, sir. You know that. I just thought—'

'I don't care what you thought. We all need to follow procedure. Christ, you know that. Now out. I'm sick of telling you this, but go through the proper channels next time.'

As Carruthers was leaving the room, Bingham called after him once more. 'I know you've had your differences, but Superintendent McGhee says he's looking forward to working with you again. I don't know what went on between you two, but he's obviously willing to put the past behind him. I suggest you do the same.

I'll see you in the incident room at 9am tomorrow morning. Tell the rest of them, will you? And I want a full quota of staff.'

As Carruthers walked away, his face was impassive but his knuckles were clenched. So Alistair McGhee was coming, was he? Would he never be free of that man? And what the hell had McGhee said to Bingham? He could neither forgive nor forget. Bad enough the man had made a pass at Mairi, but the context in which he had done it was unforgivable.

He had first met fellow Glaswegian Alistair McGhee when working on a case in London about the murder of an illegal immigrant. McGhee was already working in counter-surveillance. Their paths had crossed when McGhee's people-trafficking investigation had led him to look into the suspicious death of the same illegal immigrant. There had been connections between the traffickers and a terrorist organisation with links to Al Qaeda. The work McGhee had been engaged in had been both sensitive in nature, and exhausting in the long hours it demanded. Carruthers had given McGhee all the help he could, and for a while there, they had been close, sharing drinks and confidences about their respective lives.

Looking back, Carruthers had realised that McGhee had been pumping him for information about the state of his marriage, under the guise of a friendly and supportive shoulder. He had been left feeling used and manipulated. He was almost as angry at himself as he had been with McGhee.

Mairi had told Carruthers she had rejected McGhee's pass at the police charity ball, but there had always been that little seed of doubt at the back of his mind. It had been like a maggot eating away at him. Carruthers' constant badgering of Mairi over McGhee had ultimately been the final straw. On top of all their other problems, the whole relationship had disintegrated like a pack of cards. Mairi accused him of suspicion and jealousy, had told him that she could no longer live with him. Carruthers had pleaded with her not to leave him. He loved her that much. They managed to patch things up for a few months but the relationship had never been the same. Finally, she left him.

SEVEN

FRIDAY MORNING, 1ST JUNE

At 9am the next morning, they all assembled in the incident room back at the police station – Carruthers, Fletcher, Harris, McGhee, Superintendent Bingham and the rest of CID. There'd been some discussion about setting up an incident room close to the politics department but with the police station being in the same town, albeit on the outskirts, Bingham had deemed it an unnecessary waste of resources. They'd decided on a mobile unit outside the politics department car park instead, manned by two officers, as the first point of contact for the public.

Despite the early hour, the air was charged with a sense of anxious anticipation. Carruthers glanced round the room noting that for once Harris wasn't reading *The Racing Post*. The man's eyes were on McGhee. Carruthers also caught Fletcher looking McGhee over. They were sizing him up. As the last man assembled, a hush descended, the tension mounting, as the station members waited for the super to speak.

Andie looks decidedly peaky. Carruthers worried about her as he studiously avoided making eye contact with McGhee. Less than a moment later Fletcher put her hand over her mouth and dashed for the door. Carruthers watched McGhee study Fletcher's retreating back, appraising her as if she were a piece of meat. He could feel his blood pressure rise even if the man so much as breathed. As if aware of Carruthers' steely blue eyes boring into him, McGhee turned round.

'Sorry sir, something I ate,' apologised Fletcher returning a couple of minutes later. 'I'm fine now,' she added quickly.

'Good,' said the chief superintendent. 'This investigation won't wait.'

'First things first. Has Holdaway been found?'

'We sent a uniform to his home, sir,' said Fletcher. 'He's not there.'

'I take it someone went inside?'

'No, sir. Sorry. Uniform made an error. Thought a search warrant was needed. I've only just been informed.'

'He's not a suspect. Get back there as soon as you can. See if you can find anything in the house to suggest where he might be. He needs to be found.'

'Yes, sir,' said Fletcher.

'Right. I've just heard back from the fire brigade,' continued Bingham. 'They've confirmed the explosion yesterday was indeed caused by a bomb. The damage at the scene is characteristic of plastic explosive, though we're waiting on residue analysis to confirm exactly what the explosive was. We've also had a call from the *Castletown Citizen* to say a group calling themselves Bryn Glas 1402, are claiming responsibility. Thankfully, we've been able to persuade the press to keep quiet about this, at least for now, whilst the investigation is in its earliest and most crucial stage. Just to warn you, this may well be a fast-moving investigation so you need to be on your toes. We've got a very serious situation on our hands. Thankfully, there were no casualties, but the intended target may have been Professor Holdaway. He's a controversial figure, I understand, who in his time has had a lot of damning things to say about Scottish and Welsh Nationalism.'

'Why now, sir?' asked Fletcher clearly trying to redeem herself. 'I mean, he's been lecturing for thirty years, and has always been outspoken. Why has he been targeted now, unless it's got something to do with the result of the Scottish Referendum?'

Superintendent Bingham cleared his throat. He looked tired but was more smartly dressed than the last time Carruthers had seen him. He looked like he was once more in total control.

'That's a good question, DS Fletcher,' said Bingham. 'There's a few theories in circulation. First, as some of you already know, the group claiming responsibility, as I said, is Bryn Glas 1402. We all need to bring ourselves up to speed with who these people are. Nine months ago, Holdaway took part in a discussion on BBC Radio Wales, which tackled various political issues until they got side-tracked into a conversation about the English buying second homes across the border. What seems to have kick-started the discussion is that Holdaway admitted he was thinking of buying a second home there himself. As you know there's been a lot of trouble in the past with English holiday homes being fire-bombed by Welsh militant groups.'

'That was years ago, though,' said Fletcher. 'I believe the last fire-bombing took place back in the mid-90s. Didn't most of the main players get sent to prison? I think Welsh politics has moved on. It's more about Westminster rule and the failure of the Assembly to gain more money-raising powers now.'

'Quite so,' said Bingham. 'To be honest at the moment we don't have much to go on. We're currently looking at every avenue.'

He took off his jacket and laid it on the back of his chair. 'Now the question with regard to the professor, assuming the bomb *was* planted by a new strain of Welsh terrorist, is were they trying to kill him, or was it just a warning? Is it a one-off, or the start of a campaign in Scotland? Are they working on their own, or are they linking up with Scottish extremists?'

'To be honest, sir, I just can't see Scottish extremists linking up,' said Fletcher.

'Still cannae believe it was a "no" vote,' groaned Harris, slapping his notebook down on his desk. 'We could have been finally free of Westminster and the fucking Tories.'

'Extremists are not always governed by logic,' said Bingham. 'And let's be honest: we don't yet know what their agenda is, if it is them. We've brought in Superintendent Alistair McGhee,' he indicated the man with a look and slight smile, which McGhee acknowledged with a small nod, 'a leading expert on home-grown terrorists. He was a major player for the security forces in the Glasgow airport bombing, even has experience of counterterrorism in Wales. We shall be relying heavily on him and the explosive ordinance disposal boys from Edenside and further afield. Alistair will be leading the investigation. I want you to give him your full cooperation. Over to you, Superintendent McGhee.'

Alistair McGhee stood up, drew himself to his full five foot ten, and purposefully strode to the front of the room clutching a sheaf of papers. The grey-suited Glaswegian exuded an air of confidence and efficiency. Carruthers studied him. It rankled that despite the broken nose he'd landed on McGhee, there was still enough symmetry to mark the man as classically attractive. Mairi had always said that McGhee's looks and personality were magnetic. He'd never really agreed with his wife's assessment but had to give it some credence: even he could see what the ladies saw in the man.

'Good morning. I've just spoken to the fire brigade so I'm going to start with what we know about the bomb,' said McGhee briskly. His Glaswegian accent was still broad, even after his years in London and Cardiff.

'The Forensics Science Lab at Dundee is going to be responsible for all further examination and testing. I've called in a few favours and they're going to give it top priority. In fact, they've been working through the night.'

He just has to get that bit in about calling in favours, thought Carruthers. *A friend to everyone, trusted by none – if they had any sense.*

'What I can tell you,' continued McGhee, 'is that the bomb was small, no more than a pound, but, as you saw, plastic explosives can still pack a helluva punch. And can still kill.'

'What can you tell us about the bomb itself?' asked Chief Superintendent Bingham.

'I've just had it confirmed from Dundee that they used Semtex.'

'Just like the IRA,' said Harris.

'Aye, Semtex was the IRA's preferred choice of incendiary. Now I must stress that, despite the fact there are strong similarities in the bomb-making equipment, the intelligence we've so far gathered, suggests it's highly unlikely that Bryn Glas 1402, or anyone else for that matter, has hooked up with the IRA.'

'Could this be the start of a bombing campaign by Islamic State?' asked Harris.

'Despite this Welsh group claiming responsibility, we still need to keep an open mind; although it's highly unlikely to be an extremist Muslim faction,' said McGhee. 'For obvious reasons I can't tell you why I've come to that conclusion, so you'll just have to trust my information.'

'How did they set the bomb off?' asked Harris. 'Was it by remote control?'

'Dougie, isn't it? There are only three types of bomb. The first is the time bomb, which is pretty self-explanatory. The second is the command control device, which is detonated by wire or radio signal, or even nowadays by mobile phones. Mobiles have quite often been favoured by terrorist groups like Al Qaeda. The third and final type is the victim-operated or booby trap. Thankfully we can rule out the third, as there was nobody near the bomb when it exploded. The experts' belief is that this device was on a timer. We don't at this stage know if the primary aim was to kill the professor, but the fact there was no prior warning suggests that those responsible do not care about casualties.' He looked across at Fletcher. She held his gaze. 'What worries me most,' said McGhee 'is the fact they used Semtex. It's not easy to get hold of, or cheap. These people must either have money, or – most likely – links to some very influential people or organisations. Due to the seriousness of this case, we're going to be liaising with both the Scottish Crime and Drug Enforcement Agency – you know them better as SCDEA – and the Serious and Organised Crime Agency, or SOCA, which is based in England. Some of their number will be arriving shortly. I'll expect full co-operation from you all in the days ahead. Be aware that this could be just the first of a series of incidents, although so far there is no evidence that this is the start of a bombing campaign. We think the aim is to frighten and not to kill, but we can't afford to be complacent.'

McGhee played with his signet ring on his right hand. 'We need to speak to the university about tightening up security. I would be much happier if we could persuade the professor to leave Scotland for a while, once he's been found. It's outside the university's term-time, so perhaps he can take his holidays now. Easier than for us to try to find the manpower to put him into protective custody.'

Carruthers saw Bingham nodding. Wondered what Bingham was doing letting McGhee tell him how to do his job. Surely protective custody would make much more sense.

McGhee continued speaking. 'My job down south is to track the movements of home-grown extremists across the UK, from the BNP to those with links to Islamic State and Al Qaeda. As for the Welsh militants, in previous years they have conducted a pretty ruthless arson campaign against English-owned properties in Wales, and were even active over the border in England. However,' he shrugged, 'with a lack of sustained interest from the majority of the population in independence, that type of militant nationalism has flagged. Having said that, there are one or two people we're keeping an eye on... but I'll go on to that in a minute. Suffice to say, if Welsh militants are responsible then this will be the first time they've targeted Scotland. And they certainly haven't used Semtex before. Their bombs were pretty primitive. If it *is* them, this will represent a major change in both tactics and location. But the most interesting thing of all is the timing. Why now?'

'Alistair,' said Bingham, 'perhaps you can give us a brief outline of the Welsh terror groups. I think that would be very helpful.'

Carruthers glanced round the room. Everyone was paying rapt attention to McGhee. Personally, he wondered if this history lesson was strictly necessary. Then again how did the saying go? Those who choose to ignore history are doomed to repeat it. Perhaps there would be something useful that came out of it after all, but only if the bomb had been set off by Welsh extremists.

'There have been a surprising number of Welsh terrorist groups,' continued McGhee. 'Cymru 1400 and the Keepers of Wales are two groups that you may have heard of. Four of the leaders of the Keepers of Wales are currently in prison so we're not too worried about them. There are, however, certain outfits we're keeping a closer eye on. In particular, the REAL Sons of Glendower, and this fairly recent group, Bryn Glas 1402, who've claimed responsibility.'

'Do we know who they are, sir?' asked Fletcher.

'Both groups are Welsh Militants,' said McGhee. 'The REAL Sons of Glendower, who, incidentally, split from the Sons of Glendower, are better known than Bryn Glas 1402 who appear to be a smaller unit.'

'Sons of Glendower?' repeated Carruthers frowning. 'Name's familiar. Isn't that the main group who'd previously stepped up an arson campaign against English-owned property in Wales?'

'The one and the same,' said McGhee. 'The group have previously favoured violence to fight what many Welsh still oppose – the increased immigration of the English into Wales. In certain areas there is still a strong undercurrent of nationalism. The English influx is still blamed by some for diluting the Welsh language and culture and inflating house prices beyond reach of the local people.'

'But that's like anywhere,' said Fletcher. 'Look at Cornwall. Surely this is out of date. No longer relevant.'

McGhee glowered at Fletcher. He spoke slowly and carefully. 'There have been a few recent incidences of threatening letters to English people and vandalism to properties. Also a couple of nasty assaults, which we believe were racially motivated. We know at least two of the people behind it: Mal Thomas and John Edwards. Incidentally, we discovered recently that they're both members of Bryn Glas. However, we just didn't have enough evidence at that point to bring them in.'

'So who are Bryn Glas 1402?' Carruthers asked. 'And why would they be operating in Scotland?'

'Bryn Glas 1402 have been disowned by the REAL Sons of Glendower, and they look to be resurrecting the philosophy and tactics of the Welsh Republican Movement. You've heard of the Welsh Republican Movement, of course?'

'Was that the Welsh version of the IRA, sir?' asked Fletcher.

'Spot on. Back in the 1950s, M15 feared that a group of extreme Welsh republicans was setting up its own version of the IRA to win home rule. M15 believed the would-be Welsh terrorists were in close contact with their Scottish counterparts.'

'Given that was back in the 50s,' said Fletcher, 'most of the major players will be very elderly or dead by now. What's happened since? I don't remember reading an awful lot on the Welsh republican movement.'

'That's just it. Interest in them appears to have declined in the absence of any terrorist atrocity.'

'So the Welsh republican movement petered out in the 60s, and this new group, Bryn Glas 1402, has started to become active. What do we really know about them? And why on earth would they be operating up in Scotland? Surely there's individuals to target down in England or Wales?' asked Fletcher.

'Bryn Glas 1402 have connections to the Sons of Glendower, at least in name,' said McGhee. 'Bryn Glas was a famous battle fought on 22 June 1402 near the town of Knighton and Presteigne in Powys. A great victory against the English for the Welsh rebels under the command of one Owain Glyndwr,' said McGhee.

'Gyndwr? Sons of Glendower?' said Fletcher.

'Exactly,' said McGhee. 'The Sons of Glendower took their name from the leader of the battle of Bryn Glas.' He strode over to the incident board and pinned on two photos.

'Mal Thomas and John Edwards. Both have recently become members of Bryn Glas 1402. Both on the radar of South Wales Police over a couple of racially motivated assaults. Both from an area of Cardiff where there's high unemployment.

'Why did they join?' asked Fletcher.

'This man,' said McGhee, producing a third photograph and pinning it to the incident board. 'Ewan Williams. He fronts a series of successful businesses – nightclubs, massage parlours, lap-dancing clubs. All the businesses operate just within the boundaries of the law. Edwards is an old business associate of Williams.'

Fletcher studied the photograph. It showed a man in his mid- to late-sixties with a greying crew cut and strong, uncompromising features.

'Has Williams got a criminal record?' asked Fletcher.

'He's been charged twice with possession, but never convicted. That was in his younger days. He doesn't have a criminal record, but the suspicion is that that has more to do with having the most expensive lawyer money can buy. There's no shortage of that.' McGhee paused for effect.

'A major player then?' asked Bingham glumly.

'Aye. A really nasty piece of work. Although never proven, he was even implicated in the suspicious death of a couple of his drug-dealing rivals.'

'So, he's a hard line criminal, but how did he get involved in terrorism?' asked Fletcher.

'Quirk of fate. Whilst his criminal dealings appear to be purely business, his interest in terrorism is definitely personal. For many years, counterterrorism knew he was on the periphery of other militant nationalist groups. In the past he's turned up to secret meetings of the Sons of Glendower and the Keepers of Wales. Then we started hearing chatter about this new group, Bryn Glas 1402. But we didn't know who was fronting it. That's the thing with terrorists, though. Individuals and groups remain covert, Bryn Glas 1402 only came to our attention just a few months ago, and whilst we knew, or at least had some inkling of the minor players, we had no idea who the leader was. He kept his identity well hidden. We have been, however, keeping a very close eye on Ewan Williams. There was just something that didn't add up.'

'What?' asked Fletcher, intrigued.

'Unlike other successful criminals, Williams isn't showy. He doesn't drive a big car or hide behind electric gates in a mansion in the country. He still lives in Ely, a poor working class suburb of Cardiff in a very modest semi-detached bungalow. Yet, by our calculations, he must have made a lot of money from his businesses. So what did he do with the cash? Ewan Williams is no fool. He isn't a gambler, and although he probably deals in drugs, we have no evidence to suggest that he uses them himself. He doesn't seem to have any expensive tastes, at least that we could see, and yet, his annual turnover for the combined businesses could have given him a very opulent lifestyle. We kept asking the same question – what did he do with the money?'

'Not only does he front Bryn Glas 1402, it's likely he funds the organisation from his own pocket,' Fletcher said.

'It's certainly looking that way. And anyone investing that amount of money makes it a very personal cause.'

'Which is?' asked Fletcher.

'It didn't take much digging to find out. It appears his interest in nationalism isn't confined to Wales.'

Another over-dramatic pause.

Get on with it, thought Carruthers, impatient for the information.

'In 1971 Williams' sister moved over to Belfast. She took up with a man by the name of Liam McDaid. As far as we know, up until that time, none of them had any links with the IRA. However, both Williams' sister and her boyfriend attended the Bloody Sunday March in 1972. She got shot. Her husband, like many other people that day, subsequently became a member of the IRA. Ewan Williams suddenly seems to become interested in Irish politics around that time and we believe he became an IRA sympathiser due to his sister's shooting. Williams more than likely donated to IRA funds over the decades.'

'Did she die? His sister?' asked Fletcher.

'Ended up in a wheelchair.'

'Why has Holdaway been targeted?' said Fletcher. 'I mean, surely there's plenty of people to target closer to home?'

'No idea,' said McGhee. 'It's your job to find that out. One thing we know for a fact though. Ewan Williams is currently in Scotland. We believe the other two men are too.' There was a low murmur around the room.

'How do you know?' asked Carruthers.

'You don't need to know the details. Let's just say we found evidence from searching his property in Cardiff that he's north of the border.'

Carruthers wondered exactly what activities McGhee had been engaged in to make him so unwilling to provide them with any details.

'You think he's up here to get Holdaway?' said Bingham.

'Put it like this,' said McGhee, 'I'll lay a bet he's not up here on holiday.'

'If the explosion has indeed been caused by this outfit, Bryn Glas 1402, how did they get their hands on the explosives they used?' asked Fletcher.

'Williams may well have used his old contacts in the IRA,' said Carruthers.

There was a silence whilst everyone in the room digested this.

'Despite what happened to Williams' sister, we've found no connection between Bryn Glas 1402 and nationalist Irish groups,' said McGhee. 'Even though Williams has a personal connection to the Irish through his sister, it's highly unlikely Bryn Glas 1402 have hooked up with Irish dissident groups like the Real IRA. Although...' he paused, 'it's thought the Real IRA has access to explosives and detonators which once belonged to the Provisionals. It's possible Williams got his hands on some leftover explosives. However, as Williams is currently operating in Scotland, it's worth considering whether they've managed to get the explosives from their Scottish counterparts. There's currently some pretty angry and disappointed nationalists.'

'Christ. If the Welsh nationalists have linked up with the Scots, that's all we need,' remarked Bingham.

'Better than them linking up with the Irish, is it no'?' said Harris.

There were murmurs of agreement.

'It's a line of enquiry we'll be following,' said McGhee.

'But the Scottish bombing Scotland? With all due respect, I just don't see that happening,' said Carruthers.'

McGhee just raised his eyebrows at Carruthers. 'It's true to say the Glasgow Airport attack was the first terrorist attack to take place in Scotland since the Lockerbie bombing in '88, and the first attack ever to target Scotland,' said McGhee. 'However, what you've got to remember is that University of East of Scotland is seen by some to be a very English university. Perhaps they see it as a legitimate target. Let's face it, every year there's a huge influx of snotty English students to UES, disappointed that they didn't get into Oxford or Cambridge.'

'I think that's a bit unfair,' said Fletcher, colouring.

'Graduate of UES, are you?' asked McGhee, arching one eyebrow.

Fletcher turned puce. 'That's irrelevant. No, I don't see this at all. I don't see the Scots getting involved in any bombing campaign. They won't have the stomach for it, not in our current political climate.' She shook her head.

'How far will home grown terrorists go?' asked Harris.

'What you've got to keep in mind is that terrorists are, by their nature, fanatics,' said McGhee. 'And they'll go as far as they need to go. In January 2008, two of the main players in the SNLA, were convicted in Manchester of sending miniature bottles of vodka contaminated by caustic soda, and threatening to kill English people. They were going to do this by poisoning the country's water supply. They were both sentenced to six years for these offences. In June 2009, the son of the founder of the SNLA, was jailed for six years for sending packages containing shotgun cartridges and threatening notes to Glasgow City Council amongst others.'

'Anything more recent?' asked Carruthers.

'There's a public perception that hardcore Welsh nationalism has all but died out. However, there has been a recent increase in physical threats made towards non-Welsh residents on certain nationalist blogs by a minority of people which we are taking seriously.'

'Whoever this group is, do they intend to kill?' said Harris.

'Million-dollar question, isn't it?' said McGhee. 'They've never killed before, and whilst it's true their tactics have changed, if – and I stress if – it is the Welsh, I still think the primary objective is one of publicity, and fear, of course. I think they want to show us what they're capable of.'

'But I still don't get what the motive is,' said Fletcher. 'This doesn't make any sense. It can't possibly be because Holdaway is thinking of buying a holiday home. Trying to bomb him, in Scotland of all places, seems a bit extreme.'

'Certainly the SNLA operated a policy of fear,' said McGhee. 'A Welsh nationalist group operating in Scotland may seem perverse, but it sends a very clear message, doesn't it. That they're prepared to travel the length of the country, and they have the capability and clout to link up with other home-grown terrorist organisations, be they Scots or Irish.'

Fletcher waved her notebook in the air. 'I'm not sure targeting an Englishman up in Scotland would have the same impact as targeting someone down south. A lot of English people have no interest in what happens up in Scotland. A good number have been genuinely baffled as to why Scotland would even want to separate. And a sizeable minority in the South East, from talking to my stepfather's friends, would have been happy to see the Scots go.'

'Do we know whether Holdaway has actually gone ahead and already bought a holiday home in Wales?' Carruthers looked over at Fletcher who shook her head.

'I don't think he's actually gone ahead and bought a home yet,' she said. 'Of course, as we already know, he's gone and published a book on what he sees as the failings of Welsh nationalism. In it he ironically argues Welsh Nationalism fails to make an impact purely because there has not been a powerful enough sign these people mean business. In other words, what he argues is that the lack of a serious terrorist outrage has reduced their potency.'

Carruthers was impressed. He wasn't the only one: all the eyes in the incident room were on DS Fletcher.

'I did a bit of reading up last night,' admitted Fletcher.

McGhee looked round the room. 'Right, any other questions?' Silence.

McGhee collected his mobile and file from the table in front of him. 'I'll leave you to it now as I have a telephone briefing with the Secretary of State in,' he glanced at his watch – Carruthers resisted the urge to sneer when he noticed it was a Rolex – 'twenty minutes.'

Carruthers controlled his facial expression as he watched how McGhee stole a glance at Andie before he turned smartly on his heel and strode away. *Damn arrogant man.*

'Over to you, Jim,' said Chief Inspector Bingham. 'I'll be in my office if you need me. Brief me later on any developments.'

EIGHT

'Right,' said Carruthers, 'there's a lot of ground to cover so pin your ears back. We'll start with the university.' Jim looked towards the bald-headed man centre right. 'Kiely, you've done that recent course in security, so it makes sense for you to arrange a meeting for university staff. The aim is to make them more vigilant without paranoia. Can you handle that?'

'Of course, guv,' came the pleased response.

'Andie, I want you to work alongside me to locate Holdaway. Let's assume for the moment he is the target. Whilst he's out there and we don't know where he is, he's vulnerable to another attack. I want someone to get on to the taxi firms to see if they've picked him up. McGhee's team are arriving later this afternoon. Let's get as much ground covered as possible. I don't want McGhee to think we're a bunch of slow-witted hicks. Dougie, I want you to find out as much as you can about Holdaway. Use the internet, talk to his colleagues, read his book if you have to. I take it you can read?'

Dougie Harris rolled his eyes then gave Carruthers the finger. Several people laughed.

Carruthers was relieved it was all taken in the right spirit. The last thing he needed on a big case was colleagues too stressed to do their jobs.

'As you know, the superintendent wants Holdaway to leave Scotland for his own safety whilst these maniacs are still at large, so we need to get that arranged. Although, frankly, I think putting him in protective custody would make much more sense.' Fletcher nodded.

'Now, whilst it's vitally important we catch these lunatics as quickly as possible, let's not forget we also have Evans' death to deal with. We're in charge of that one. Whatever Superintendent Bingham thinks, I'm not convinced it was a botched robbery. We're still waiting on Mackie's lab results. Also, Andie, can you confirm whether a call was logged at the station about Rhys Evans's disappearance the night of his death?'

'Nothing's been logged, Jim,' said Fletcher 'I've already spoken to the night staff.'

'Then it looks as if Roberts was lying,' said Carruthers.

'Or Mathews,' said Fletcher.

Carruthers' phone rang. 'Excuse me,' he said looking at the caller ID. 'This is Mackie.' He accepted the call. 'What've you got for me?' Carruthers visualized Mackie on the phone, glasses perched on the bridge of his sharp nose, that shock of unruly white hair framing his face. It wasn't just his intelligence that had earned him the nickname of Einstein.

'Death was caused, as suspected, by the blow to the back of the head. You'll be looking for some sort of blunt instrument. I've also found fibres of wool in the wound. Whatever was used to kill him was wrapped up in a garment, maybe a sock. Not my place to say it, but I've been in this job a long time. If the motive was robbery then, in my opinion, excessive force was used.'

'Are you saying killing him was intentional?'

Mackie cleared his throat. 'Hear me out. There's bad news on the fingerprints front. Only partial have been found. All smudged. I believe the stairwell was used by students and staff from the pizzeria so unfortunately there's been lots of human traffic.'

'Yes,' said Carruthers. 'Doorway from the second floor leads to a store room for the restaurant.'

'I've found strands of wool under Evans' fingernails. Looks like the assailant or assailants might have been wearing gloves, and seeing as it's summer, that in itself makes the casual robbery theory look pretty iffy. Of course, I don't need to tell you that. That's your job, but I thought you might like my opinion.'

'As ever.'

'Toxicology will take longer to come back, so you'll just have to be patient. Not your strong point, I know, laddie, but they do say that it's a virtue. That's pretty much it.'

'OK, thanks. Can you email this over to us and get back in touch as soon as you find out anything else?'

'Will do.'

Breaking the connection Carruthers turned to his staff. 'Right, listen up. We've got one dead man. Killed by a blow to the back of the head. No useful fingerprints. Doc thinks assailant or assailants were wearing gloves.'

'What killed him?' asked Fletcher.

'Mackie says blunt instrument wrapped up in some sort of woollen material. This is starting to sound premeditated, so we may well be looking at murder instead of manslaughter. Nobody claims to have seen or heard anything. Door-to-door has yielded nothing helpful. Empty wallet, ID and keys of the deceased were found two hundred metres away from the body. The last person to have seen him alive, Dave Roberts, has in all likelihood lied to Evans' girlfriend about reporting his disappearance to the police. He's now gone missing himself. This is fast becoming a mess and I don't want this team looking like a bunch of idiots over it.'

'What about CCTV, sir?' asked Fletcher.

'I'm getting Brown and Kiely, to trawl through it. It's yielded nothing significant yet though.' At the mention of Brown's name Carruthers visualised the ardent SNP supporter. Brown had been at the station almost as long as Harris. The man with the Bobby Charlton comb-over was almost as lazy. Another dinosaur.

'What's your gut feeling, boss?' asked Fletcher.

Carruthers stroked the bristles on his chin. 'Roberts' disappearance is in some way linked to Evans' death. Perhaps Roberts killed Evans. So he's done a runner.'

'How does this fit in with the explosion over by the politics department?' asked Fletcher.

Carruthers shook his head. 'Your guess is as good as mine. It may not. There's no evidence as yet to suggest any link at all.'

'For what it's worth,' said Fletcher, I just don't buy into a Welsh terror group bombing an English professor in Scotland because he's brought out a controversial book and is looking to buy a holiday home. It makes no sense to me. It's gotta be something more personal that also involves Rhys Evans.'

'We need to keep an open mind. We also need to look more closely at the relationship between Evans and Roberts. Talk to those who were close to both of them. That's our starting point.'

'Back to the RAF base then, Jim?' said Fletcher.

'Yes, at some stage. However, I've been warned off by Bingham for not having a proper warrant. We'll go back to the base, but we also need to pay Siobhan Mathews another visit. However, first, we need to locate Holdaway. You've got his home address, Andie?'

'He's not in Castletown. He's out near Strathburn. The Lodge, Hillside Road, Strathburn.'

'That's only a few miles outside Castletown. Right then, that's where we will begin our search.'

***

Carruthers and Fletcher drove silently towards Strathburn in Fletcher's green Beetle. A few miles away Fletcher knew that the Firth of Forth would look like smoky blue-green glass, smooth with the occasional ripple.

'By the way, I didn't ask how badly Dougie beat up Russell,' said Carruthers.

Fletcher imagined Jim must have had all the gory details from the landlord. Perhaps he wanted to see if her story stacked up. Fletcher shifted the gear and smoothly overtook a tractor.

Without looking at her boss she said, 'Broken nose. But, like I said, Harris told me Russell tripped and fell. I believe him.' *How he tripped and fell and ended up soaking wet was another matter, though,* thought Fletcher.

Carruthers groaned. 'Think Russell will make a complaint?'

She glanced over at him. 'Don't think so. He's too scared. Jim, I'm really sorry I didn't say anything. You know how it is. If word had got out I'd grassed Harris up, things would've been really tough for me. He already thinks it was me that told you.'

'Is Dougie giving you grief?

'I can handle it.'

'You shouldn't have to. There are laws against discrimination and we need to remove bad apples from the cart. I am still disappointed in the pair of you. Dougie for what he did, you for what you didn't do. But I do understand. If Dougie, or anyone else tries to make trouble for you over this, then you let me know. We can't have that in the team.'

'Dougie Harris has been in the force a long time,' said Fletcher. 'He's not going to change now.' Feeling the heat, she wound down her window.

'Honestly, when are you going to get a car with air con?' he asked.

'You can talk. You're still driving a Vauxhall Vectra. Anyway, I like my old car,' she said. 'There's something else you should know. The thing is – I reckon it was personal. Russell had a sexual relationship with Dougie's niece. She's only sixteen. That's why he went off on one.'

'Oh Christ,' said Carruthers. Fletcher glanced at him as he ran his hands through his short greying hair. 'This is all we need,' said Carruthers. 'Now I understand why people call Fife "bandit country". Talk about incestuous.'

'Well, in villages and small towns everyone knows each other,' said Fletcher. 'Happens up and down the country. Have you never watched *Midsomer Murders*?'

Carruthers also wound down his window a couple of inches. 'Dougie still can't behave like this, Andie, using his professional standing to wage personal revenge. He's not some renegade cop taking the law into his own hands.'

'I know, but he won't see it like that. He's old school. He'll see it as taking the initiative and doing the world a favour. Anyway, let's face it; you're a bit of a renegade yourself at times. I bet you've already given Bingham countless sleepless nights, and you've only been here a couple of months.'

'I've never beaten anyone up in a toilet. Well, the matter will have to be dealt with. Dougie'll have to be disciplined. Anyway, not your problem.'

They lapsed into silence.

'You like her, don't you?' she said.

'Who?'

'Siobhan Mathews.'

'Why on earth would you say that?' asked Carruthers, with his brows knitting together in a frown.

'I don't know, just something about the way you looked at her, I suppose. I'm sure you won't want advice from me, but I think you should tread carefully.'

Carruthers took a sideways glance at Fletcher. 'You're right. I don't want advice.' There was an awkward silence. 'Look, Andie, I know you mean well. Truth is, it's bloody irritating being mothered by a girl nearly ten years your junior.'

Fletcher kept her silence.

'If I was staring at her for a little bit too long it's because she reminds me of someone, if you must know,' Carruthers said eventually.

'Well, it's another woman so I reckon it's got to be your ex-wife. She's a philosophy lecturer, isn't she?'

'How on earth would you know about my ex-wife?'

'So you *are* talking about your ex-wife?'

Another silence.

'Oh God, it's worse than I thought.'

'What is?'

'Well, by the time most people split up they can't stand each other. But you're still in love with her, aren't you? You're still in love with your ex-wife and now you've met a woman who reminds you of her. Bloody hell. No wonder you needed a drink. I'm right about you liking Siobhan Mathews, though, aren't I?'

'OK, if you really want to know – I do like her. I don't know why. And perhaps she does remind me of my wife. And yes, I still have feelings for Mairi. We were together for ten years and you don't just switch emotions off. At least, I can't. I'm acutely aware of the fact this is a murder investigation and Siobhan Mathews is the victim's girlfriend. I am a professional, Andie. All I want to do is find the person or persons responsible for her boyfriend's murder – to try to find out why they did what they did, and help her get some sort of closure.'

It was Fletcher's turn to fall silent. Now, while they were in a confessional mood, would be a good time to tell him about her pregnancy. She couldn't keep hiding it. She could kid herself all she liked that the reason she hadn't told him was that she hadn't found the right time. The truth was that she didn't want to tell him because she didn't want it to be true. That point was too tender, so she switched back to thinking about Jim.

'Is that the reason you got drunk?' There was no answer. Fletcher looked across at him. 'Look you can talk to me, you know. We do work together. I might not have been married but I still know how painful a break up can be.'

'Thank you. I'll bear that in mind. Now I've got a question for you. How on earth do you know all this stuff about me?'

She smiled. 'I Googled you, boss.'

'You *what*?'

She looked across at him. 'I Googled you.'

'Why on earth would you do that?'

'Well, I was bored one day and I knew we had a new DCI coming to the station. I wanted to know what your background was. And then I asked Harris.'

'Did you now?' said Carruthers.

'You don't like Superintendent McGhee much, do you?' said Fletcher changing tack.

Carruthers sniffed. 'Not much.'

'Does it have anything to do with your wife?' asked Fletcher. 'Sorry, forget I just said that. I'm not usually so nosey about personal matters. The only reason I asked is, well, how can I put this nicely? He's a bit of a sleaze, isn't he?'

'Did you get all this from Dougie, too?' said Carruthers, smiling.

'Well there's been station talk. Apparently your fall out with McGhee is legendary. What happened, if you don't mind me asking?'

'I've only been at this station two months. How on earth do folk know about my fall out with McGhee?'

'Well, apparently, Kiely told Harris that his dad knows your ex-wife's mother. Fife can be a small place. So what happened?'

'You're doing it again, Andie.'

'What's that?'

'Being nosey. And I do mind you asking. It's private.'

Fletcher felt her cheeks go red. She could have kicked herself for going too far again.

Some minutes passed before Carruthers finally spoke. 'So you noticed he was a sleaze then?'

'Are you kidding? Don't think I didn't notice the way he was looking me up and down and to be honest although he's good-looking and all that – there's something... not attractive about him. I wouldn't go within a mile of him.'

'Good,' said Carruthers.

'Anyway, I very much doubt he'd be interested in me in my condition,' continued Fletcher. *It was now or never*, she thought.

'Condition? What condition?' asked Carruthers.

'Look, I know this is really bad timing, but I've been trying to find a way to tell you. The thing is,' she had to push the words out, 'I'm pregnant.'

She looked across anxiously at him but at the same time a weight felt as if it had already been lifted. She expelled a deep sigh of relief. She'd finally managed to share her burden with someone. Unfortunately, she knew that whilst she might be starting to feel better, Carruthers might not be. She threw a glance at him wondering if he would say anything. Hoping he'd say something. Was he taking this as a bombshell, a bad thing? Had she just damaged their working relationship?

Knowing him and how conscientious he was, she figured he'd be thinking about staffing levels and the extra work her absence would cause.

A few long moments went by. Finally, he opened his mouth but whatever he was about to say was halted by the shrill ring of his mobile.

He answered. Barked his name. After a few terse sentences he snapped the phone shut. 'We need to get a speed on. That was Bingham.'

'What's he want?'

'If we can't locate Holdaway, we're to double back and bring in Edward Sadler. Bingham thinks he'll be useful in giving background on Holdaway.'

'I've already taken a statement from Sadler,' said Fletcher.

'A few more probing questions needed, I think. Right, come on. No lunch for us today. If you're OK with that given—'

'I'm fine. I'm not that hungry at the moment.'

'OK, so put a spurt on then.'

She drove in silence. Fletcher was disappointed and frustrated at the timing of Bingham's call. She'd obviously blindsided Carruthers. She needed his support. Wanted him to say something about her news. *Anything.*

They took a left on to a straight road. On the brow of the hill stood a solitary old stone building.

'Christ, I think that's it,' she said. 'Talk about living in splendid isolation.'

'Sorry,' he said at last as if he had read her thoughts. 'I know I should say something. I just don't know what. Is "congratulations" appropriate? You don't seem exactly thrilled.'

She decided honestly was the best policy. 'It wasn't planned.'

'How far along are you?'

'Fourteen weeks. And just for the record you're the first person I've told – other than Mark.'

Once more they lapsed into silence. She sat there, her stomach full of knots. This was so much harder than she had imagined.

'Look, Andie,' he said as she pulled into a gravelly drive, 'we'll find time to sit down and have a proper chat. OK? We need to find Holdaway first, though.'

She nodded.

They parked up. Stepping from the car they walked up to the front door. A deafening roar made her jump, the low flying aircraft reminding her of the RAF base over at Edenside. Carruthers knocked. They waited. He knocked again. Still silence. They walked round the side of the house and Fletcher spotted a kitchen window that was ajar. 'Looks like we won't need to force entry after all. I'm pretty sure I can get in through that space.'

Before Carruthers was able to say anything Fletcher called out, 'Come on. Give me a bunk up. And don't say anything about my being pregnant. If I don't think I'll be able to manage it, I'll say.'

As she squeezed her way through the window, Fletcher had to ignore the look of concern etched into Carruthers' brow. It could be he was worried about her; it could be the weight of the case. Once on her feet, she turned, offered a smile she wasn't quite feeling. 'Won't be able to do that in a few months,' she said ruefully. 'When we find him we'll have to talk to Holdaway about his security. I'll meet you at the front door.'

Fletcher walked through the hall to the front door and picked up the post lying on the mat. She opened the door. Carruthers wasn't there yet, having to come the long way round.

'Anything interesting in there?' he asked as he stepped up to the door.

'Precious little, just a couple of bills and junk mail.'

Carruthers stepped in and took the post from her, placed it on a small hallway table.

'C'mon, let's start the search,' said Carruthers having a good look around the hall. 'Anything to give us an idea of where he might have gone.' The hall smelt of pine wax and was spacious with various rooms off to the side and an enormous varnished spiral staircase at the end of it.

They searched each room in turn, starting with those downstairs first. They found nothing in the sitting room, or utility room. They got to the downstairs bathroom, which was next on the left before the kitchen. A moment or two later, Fletcher heard a rattle and turned to see Carruthers before the open stainless steel cupboard. He was holding a bottle of prescription sleeping pills. Frowning he held the bottle for Fletcher to see. She saw that they were made out to an N Holdaway.

'He has trouble sleeping,' was all he said.

They walked into the next room, which was the kitchen. The remains of Holdaway's last meal of toast and cereal were still sitting on the breakfast table. The milk had been left out. Carruthers picked it up and smelt it. 'Sour.'

A couple of bluebottles buzzed around. Fletcher opened the fridge door. 'A lot of perishables in here and a lot of ready meals,' she called out. 'Wife must do the cooking. Don't think he'd planned to be away.'

Carruthers turned away from Fletcher. She followed his gaze to the floor noting the number of empty wine bottles in the recycling box.

'He's either forgotten to put the recycling out for a while or he's a big drinker,' he said.

'Or he's had a few friends round,' said Fletcher.

'Or he's had a few friends round,' he repeated. 'Wonder what sort of man the professor is. Outgoing, or more of a loner?'

They walked to the foot of the stairs and entered a large dining room to the left of the stairwell. After having a good root around and finding nothing Carruthers opened the door to a small study, which was dominated by an enormous writing desk in the middle of the room. Fletcher looked around her.

'Crikey, I've never seen so many books,' said Fletcher, gazing at the wall-to-wall bookcases.

'Well, he *is* an academic. See if you can find a diary on his desk. And play those messages.'

For a moment Fletcher was floored, then she spotted a flashing answer machine on the desk; couldn't fault Carruthers' powers of observation. She played the messages as Carruthers scanned the bookshelves. There were two calls from Holdaway's wife, asking him to give her a ring in Spain. The first was from the previous day. In the second message, left earlier that morning, she sounded irritated. Probably thought her messages were being ignored. Also a message from a library to inform him the book he wanted was in. Fletcher made a note of the number on her pad. Carruthers held his hand out for it. In response to Fletcher's curious stare he responded, 'I've got to phone the library anyway.'

She copied the number a second time and tore out the page for him. He folded the sheet and tucked it into his jacket pocket.

'He's well read,' Carruthers said as Fletcher continued to hunt for a diary. 'There's everything from Plato to Pushkin. Disappointingly, no sign of the books the professor wrote.'

'They must all be in his office at the university,' Fletcher ventured as she slid open another drawer of the writing desk and rummaged through.

'Bingo,' she said.

'What have you got?'

She held up a passport. 'Well, at least we know he's not planning on going too far afield.'

'No sign of a diary?' asked Carruthers.

'Nope.'

'But what have we really found out about the professor?' said Carruthers. 'His wife clearly doesn't know where he is. He likes his wine, hasn't put the recycling out for a while, has an impressive library in his study, doesn't sleep well and doesn't have his passport with him. None of this was any help in telling us where Holdaway might have gone.'

With nothing of value to add, Fletcher didn't respond.

'I don't think we're going to find anything else downstairs,' said Carruthers. 'Let's go upstairs.'

They climbed the spiral staircase. There was a bathroom at the top of the stairs. 'Grief, he's got a copper bath. Haven't seen one of those for years,' said Fletcher. After searching the bathroom and finding nothing of interest Carruthers put his nose round the doors of the three other rooms. 'A master bedroom and two guest bedrooms. Looks like Holdaway's been sleeping in one of the guest bedrooms.' He pointed to the dishevelled and unmade bed and a half-drunk cup of cold coffee on the bedside table. He lay down on his front on the floor and looked under the bed. 'Nothing except a pair of slippers.'

Fletcher shrugged. 'Perhaps the mattress is better in here? One thing's for sure though. When he left the house he expected to come back.'

'Except that he hasn't,' said Carruthers, walking into the main bedroom. He opened the hanging wardrobe and started going through Holdaway's clothes, feeling in the shirt and trouser pockets. Fletcher assumed it was for any scraps of paper, something that might give them a clue as to the professor's whereabouts. Carruthers withdrew his hand from the empty front pocket of a pair of dress trousers. 'Nothing. So where the hell is he?' The question was left hanging in the air. 'OK. I don't think we're going to find anything else here. Next job on the list. Have you got an address for Sadler?'

***

'How do we play this?' asked Fletcher. They were standing on Sadler's doorstep. 'How much do we tell him?'

'As little as possible,' said Carruthers. 'However, I want us to leave no stone unturned. We need to find out everything we can about Nicholas Holdaway, and I mean everything.'

'Professor Sadler, sorry for disturbing you,' Carruthers said, as the door was opened. 'We don't want to intrude, but we have a few more questions.' The large man was wearing mustard-coloured cords and a white dress shirt.

'Look, come in. I was just going to have an early lunch.' Sadler gestured for them to follow him through the hall into a spacious bright front room with a large bay window. He gestured for them to take a seat at a large pine table; it was set for one though there were six chairs.

'I'm sorry, I rather tend to forget about food, but my housekeeper spoils me, she also nags me if I don't eat what she puts before me. Truth is, without Mrs Carter, I'd stick my nose in a book and completely forget about food. I can't cook a jot and since my wife died, Mrs Carter has become a lifesaver. I'd have faded away without her.' He gave an embarrassed laugh.

Carruthers looked at Professor Sadler, and tried not to stare at the man's protruding belly. In his mid-sixties, Sadler was very well covered, denoting a man of some means who did indeed get looked after rather well and was clearly used to the finer things in life. Carruthers reckoned that, if by some change of fortune he ever lost the cooking skills of Mrs Carter, he might take some considerable time to fade away to nothing.

Sadler smiled at them. 'Can I offer you a sandwich? She always makes too many.'

'No, no. Thank you. We won't be staying long,' said Carruthers. Just at that moment Fletcher's tummy rumbled. The officers studiously avoided looking at each other.

'Are you sure? You would be most welcome.'

'Well, perhaps just the one then,' said Carruthers gesturing for Fletcher to take a sandwich. Carruthers figured they could do the interview just as well in the man's house as at the station; and he didn't want a pregnant DS keeling over on him. *Christ. Pregnant.* He knew he hadn't handled her announcement well. The truth was that he felt awkward and embarrassed. Perhaps a little disappointed, too, if he was being honest. He'd hoped she would have confided in him sooner than fourteen weeks.

He noticed Fletcher had been staring longingly at a dainty white sandwich. Its crusts had been cut off and it was bursting at the seams with a deliciously fresh looking egg mayonnaise.

She selected the sandwich next to it that looked to be cheese and tomato. Carruthers picked up the egg mayonnaise. No wonder she had been looking exhausted and strained. He could only imagine what emotions were going through her mind. He wondered how Mark had taken the news about the forthcoming baby.

'Sit down, sit down,' said Sadler. 'Have you found Nicholas yet?'

'No. We've just come from his house in Strathburn. Doesn't appear to be anyone at home. Any idea where he would have gone?'

'After a scare like that? Hard to say. If it had been my car it would have utterly terrified me, I don't mind saying. Perhaps he's gone into hiding.'

'Why would you say that, sir?' asked Fletcher.

'Well, stands to reason. If somebody had deliberately blown up my car, I wouldn't stick around long enough for them to finish the job and kill me. Would you? By the way, is there any news yet from the fire brigade? Do we know the cause of the explosion? Was it a bomb?'

Carruthers and Fletcher exchanged looks. News had a way of getting out. 'We're still investigating the exact cause of the explosion,' said Carruthers carefully. 'You said he'd been receiving hate mail,' he continued. 'Are you aware of the contents of his letters?

'No,' said Sadler helping himself to a plate. 'He never revealed what was in the letters. I just knew he'd received a few from time to time, but I have no idea what the specific threats were, if indeed they were specific.'

'Did he ever say he knew who these letters were from?' said Carruthers.

'They were anonymous.' He glanced over at Fletcher. 'But I told your colleague here that yesterday.'

'Yes,' said Carruthers, 'sorry if it appears we're going over old ground. I'm just trying to build up a picture of the professor and his movements. We have to work out, if he's gone into hiding, where exactly he would be.'

Sadler reached over and placed a napkin on his lap. Helped himself to a sandwich. 'I can't answer that, I'm afraid. I really don't know what he thought when he heard that explosion. I can only assume he also thought it was a bomb. We all made that assumption, I'm afraid. Too many bomb stories on the news these days. He must have known it was his car destroyed; why else would he take off the way he did?'

Why indeed? thought Carruthers.

Sadler pulled a face. 'We aren't that close. Aside from departmental functions, which are few and far between, we don't tend to socialise outside work. But I would've thought with Castletown being the size it is, there can't be too many places for him to hide out.' The sound of a house phone ringing interrupted the interview. Sadler excused himself and left the room.

'He's right, Jim,' said Fletcher. 'Unless he's left Castletown. Of course, he's got no means of transport, so if he wanted to go further afield he would have to get public transport.'

'Or a taxi.'

'That information has already been checked. None of the taxi companies have picked up a man answering his description.' Fletcher whipped out her little black notebook and scribbled in it.

Sadler re-entered the room and took his seat. 'Bloody cold call,' he said.

Carruthers turned to him. 'You wouldn't know who Holdaway's friends are, would you?'

'No, sorry. Like I said, we're not close.' He stood up. 'I don't feel as if I have been much help.' He looked crestfallen. 'I don't know his friends. He never showed me the letters. I don't even know how many of them there were, or when the last one was received. He seemed very reticent to discuss them. I'm assuming he didn't report the letters to you?'

'No, he didn't,' said Fletcher.

'I wonder why ever not?'

'Perhaps he thought we wouldn't take him seriously?' said Carruthers.

'I really can't answer that. Maybe he didn't take them seriously himself.'

'Do you know how long he'd been at the university?' said Fletcher.

'Longer than me, my dear, and I joined in 96. I think he started quite a while before that, though I don't know the year. Sorry.'

'So you wouldn't know what he did before he joined the academic staff.'

Sadler considered the question for a moment. 'Do you know, I haven't got a clue. Isn't that strange? You don't think of anyone having a life before they join the faculty but I suppose he must have done. I would assume he would have been at another university.'

'How did he get on with his students?' asked Carruthers.

'I think it's fair to say he tolerated them. It's true he was more interested in pursuing his own academic research than teaching, but he realised it was the teaching that paid the bills.'

A large cafetière arrived carried by the broad-shouldered housekeeper, Mrs Carter.

'Ah, Mrs Carter. Wonderful,' the academic beamed. 'What would I do without you?'

'Away with you,' she replied shyly setting the tray down on the table. As she left Carruthers could see that she looked rather pleased with the compliment.

'Thinks of everything.' He gestured to the three cups and saucers that had accompanied the cafetière, sugar pot and milk jug. 'Shall I be Mummy?' he asked.

'Yes, please,' said Carruthers. 'You said Holdaway was more interested in pursuing his own academic research. He'd written a book, hadn't he, on the failings of Welsh nationalism? Do you think that in itself would be enough to make him a target of Welsh extremists?'

'To be honest, I have no idea. I don't know much about Welsh extremism. That was Holdaway's bag. I'm much more mainstream, I'm afraid.'

'What do you teach?' asked Fletcher.

'The history of British politics and the Scottish political system. Going back to his book, I dare say it would have caused a lot of anger amongst certain sections of the Welsh. Notwithstanding the recent purchase of his holiday home in Wales. I understand a sizeable minority of the Welsh have previously been against that sort of thing, haven't they? A bit like the Cornish. Do you know that for all the tourism Rick Stein has brought into Padstow, there are still those who resent him? You'd think they'd be grateful, wouldn't you, to have some decent eateries down there, but there's still a fair amount of resentment towards him because he's not Cornish…'

'Wait a minute,' said Carruthers, 'did you say Holdaway has gone ahead and has actually bought a second home for himself? In Wales?'

'Yes, that's right. Apparently his family used to holiday in Wales when he was a child. He always loved the Welsh countryside. His mother died recently I understand. I'm no psychologist but perhaps buying this holiday home is a way of feeling close to her and to his childhood.'

There was a pause whilst Carruthers exchanged glances with Fletcher.

'Do you know where his holiday home is in Wales?' asked Fletcher.

'I'm afraid not, no. All I know is that it's close to the English border.'

'You mentioned he enjoyed academic research more than teaching,' said Carruthers.

Sadler nodded. 'That's right. Like I said, he tolerated his students, but he hardly had an "open door" policy. He didn't encourage students to drop by his office for a chat, for example.'

'So you wouldn't say he was particularly approachable?'

Sadler laughed. 'I don't think lecturers or students found him particularly approachable. Oh, I don't mean he had a problem with other lecturers. He seemed to get on well enough with them most of the time. I just mean he didn't come across as a people person. His students didn't find him particularly approachable. I've also heard lecturers complain that he wasn't especially interested in hearing about their work. Of course, let him talk about his own work and you couldn't shut him up. I probably shouldn't say this but I think he also has a bit of a drink problem.'

'A drink problem?' said Carruthers, thinking of the empty bottles of wine in the recycling box. 'You mean he's an alcoholic?'

'No, I don't think he's an alcoholic but he's notorious for getting a bit worse for wear at the few drinks functions he does attend. There have been a couple of times he's had to be taken home. That kind of thing. Perhaps he just doesn't tolerate alcohol very well.'

'Have you ever seen him drink at work?'

'No, no, I haven't. But I think he hits the bottle pretty heavily at home.'

'Why do you say that?'

'I've smelt the drink on him the next day. Fairly regularly, actually.'

'You said he got on with the other lecturers most of the time,' said Fletcher enquiringly. 'What did you mean by *most* of the time?'

'Well,' laughed Sadler seemingly a bit embarrassed, 'there's been one or two run-ins over the years. That's to be expected, though.'

'What sort of run-ins?' said Carruthers.

'Nothing really. Just silly. Department got refurbished a few years ago in order to create more space. It needed doing, anyway. We had a couple of visiting professors from the US and nowhere to put them. Holdaway made a bit of a stink about trying to get a bigger room, that's all.'

'Did he succeed?'

'No. In fact he was ousted from the room he was in and actually given a smaller office. He didn't like that, I can tell you.'

'Hardly a reason to destroy his car,' said Carruthers.

'Good Lord, no.'

'Did he have any problem students over the years?' asked Fletcher.

'We all have problem students from time to time,' Sadler laughed. 'Students who don't turn up for lectures or who don't hand their work in on time. Students who are lazy, who could work harder, but still expect a top-notch grade. The Americans are particularly bad for that. Going on about their GPAs and so on. That sort of thing.'

'GPAs?' asked Fletcher.

'Grade Point Averages,' explained Sadler. 'Then of course, they have a litany of excuses for their poor timekeeping and shoddy work.'

'Did Holdaway have any trouble with any particular students over and above the normal?' asked Carruthers.

'Now you come to mention it, there was one student about five years ago. I did hear about it. In fact, it was Holdaway who told me.'

'What happened?'

'Holdaway had to fail him. We try not to fail people but it happens. The boy got rather nasty about it.'

'Nasty? You mean he threatened him?' said Fletcher.

'Yes, I suppose you could say that. But Holdaway took it as an idle threat. As far as I know he didn't report it to the police. And it was five years ago.'

'Can you remember the name of the student?'

'No, I can't. It would be easy enough to find out though. Just ask the departmental secretary, Mrs Fairbanks. She never forgets a name.'

'Thank you, sir,' said Fletcher making another note.

'You won't be able to speak to the student about it, though.'

'Oh?' said Carruthers.

'I may not know his name but I do know he got killed several months after moving back home. Hit and run.'

Carruthers digested this piece of information. He wondered if the student's parents had blamed Holdaway in any way for the death of their son. After all, if the professor hadn't failed the boy, presumably he wouldn't have been back home at the time of his death. Grief, as he knew, did strange things to people.

'Is there anything else you can tell me about Holdaway?' asked Carruthers. 'Anything at all? Any personal problems he's had over the last few years?'

'He did have to have time off work several years ago. Some kind of stress. I'm not sure what.'

'Do you remember when?'

Sadler cast his eyes upwards. 'This would have been about 2002.'

'How long was he off for?'

'About four months. Nobody really knew why.'

'He hadn't had a bereavement? That kind of thing?' asked Fletcher.

'No, I don't think so. Actually, it was all a bit strange.'

'In what way?'

'Nobody seemed to know the reason he had to take time off work. But then if it's for a personal problem you don't want to pry, do you?'

'How did he appear when he came back to work?' said Fletcher.

'Distant. And jumpy. Definitely jumpy. I'm sorry. I wish I could be more help.'

Sadler lapsed into morose silence that seemed to stretch forever but when he looked up again his face had brightened considerably.

'There is one thing that may help, however.' The professor got up from the table, smoothed his crumpled cords, brushing a few crumbs away and went over to an enormous wooden bookcase. There his gnarled hands searched amongst the contents for something.

'Damn. Can't see without my glasses. Where are they?' He went over to the table and tugged at his brown linen jacket, which was hanging on the back on his chair. Felt around in the inside pocket. Victoriously brought out his glasses, which he flourished in front of them. Placing them over the bridge of his nose he went back and resumed his search of the book cupboard.

'Ah, I was looking on the wrong shelf. There we go. Knew it was here somewhere.' Professor Sadler selected a large hard backed book. Carruthers could see Fletcher peering over at the cover questioningly.

'This might help,' said Sadler. 'It's Nicholas's book. I couldn't remember the title of it. I'm ashamed to say I haven't read it. He gave me a copy. I just stuck it in the bookshelf. I thought it was called *The Failings of Welsh Terrorism*. But it's not. It's actually entitled *The Death of Welsh Terrorism*.' He handed it over to Carruthers. 'Ironic really. If the explosion has indeed been caused by a bomb, and Welsh terrorists are behind it, I would say Welsh terrorism must be very much alive. Wouldn't you?'

***

'What have you discovered?' said Bingham, cracking his knuckles. He was sitting behind his desk in his office.

'We've searched the house at Strathburn,' said Carruthers. 'No clue as to where Holdaway's gone. He seems to have just disappeared into thin air. His wife's currently in Spain. He's not made contact with her. She's been on the phone looking for him. Left two messages asking him to call her.'

'You must have found something out?'

Not a hell of a lot, Carruthers wanted to say. Instead he said, 'He appears to be a big drinker and he's on sleeping pills. And he had to take some time off work for stress in 2002. We don't know why. That's about it.'

'OK, Jim, what are you doing the rest of the afternoon?'

'I've got a few phone calls to make.'

'Keep me up to date.'

Carruthers checked his watch as he left Bingham's office. It was already after four. He walked back to his own office, picked up the phone and started with the call to Holdaway's library. The book Nicholas Holdaway had requested was ready for pick up. Carruthers almost dropped the phone when he was given the title. *Bloody Sunday – Truth, Lies and the Saville Enquiry* by Douglas Murray. What the hell was Holdaway's connection with Northern Ireland? Not just Northern Ireland but Bloody Sunday? Making a quick decision Carruthers gathered up his mobile and keys. He put his head round the open plan office to see Andie was still hard at work.

'I need to head out,' he said. 'I'll be on the mobile if you need me.'

'Where you heading?' she asked.

'I've got a lead. Need to go to the library here in Castletown before it closes.'

He debated telling Fletcher about his find but instead leapt into his car. Within fifteen minutes he was leaving Castletown's library clutching the book Holdaway had ordered. Perhaps it would give him the answers he needed. He decided to head home so he could read it in peace.

He sat in his living room devouring each page. From the very first it made for uncomfortable reading. But all the time his thoughts strayed. Where was Nicholas Holdaway? Where could the man have gone? His car had been parked at the politics department. It was now a lump of incinerated metal. The man hadn't gone home. That much was clear. He didn't seem to have any friends. He hadn't made contact with his wife. Where the hell was he? His eyes felt scratchy so Carruthers decided to have a quick break. He stood up, took off his work shirt and trousers and pulled on a T-shirt and a pair of jeans. With a sigh, he began the task of picking up his hill walking gear from his living room floor and putting it back into a cupboard. He knew he wouldn't be getting away to the hills anytime soon. He slammed a chicken jalfrezi ready meal for one into the oven and opened a bottle of IPA. He took the first thirst-quenching swig of the golden liquid. As he waited for his supper to cook he picked up the book on Northern Ireland and continued reading. He was still reading as the light faded.

NINE

'That interview with Sadler wasn't very informative,' said Carruthers. He was standing with Fletcher at the coffee machine. 'It left too many loose ends.'

'Instead of narrowing the search, it seems to have widened it.' She took a sip of coffee. 'What about that lead you were chasing?'

'I found out the book Holdaway ordered from his local library is on the enquiry into Bloody Sunday.'

'Jesus, what's Holdaway's connection with Bloody Sunday?'

'I have no idea.'

'Perhaps he's thinking of writing another book… maybe he's unearthed something about Ewan Williams … something that threatens the Welshman. What about his sister?'

Carruthers considered and dismissed it. 'Already a matter of public record. We need to find Holdaway.' *If he's still alive.*

'Look,' said Carruthers lowering his voice, 'about your pregnancy, how are you feeling about it?'

'I don't really know to be honest. I'm still in shock.' She sighed. 'If you really want to know… I'm terrified. I've never had any maternal feelings. Suddenly I'm going to be responsible for a new life. If I go through with it, that is. All I've ever wanted is to be a police officer. I don't want this to get in the way.'

Carruthers' mobile rang.

He took the call then put his phone away. 'Holdaway's here. He's just walked into the station. Bingham wants me to interview him.'

'What happened to McGhee leading the bomb investigation?'

Carruthers shrugged. 'All I know is McGhee's not in the station right now.'

Fletcher put her cup down. 'What about Mathews? Want me to go talk to her instead?'

'That'll have to wait. This is the priority. And I'd like you with me. I'll pass on the coffee. I need a quick word with Bingham.'

Carruthers put his head round Bingham's office door. The man was sitting behind his imposing desk, glasses perched on the end of his nose. Carruthers rapped on the door.

Superintendent Bingham looked up. He motioned for Carruthers to enter. 'Two things, Jim,' he said. 'The first is, Holdaway's asking for police protection. I've made it clear we don't have the manpower for a twenty-four hour guard. I'm going to suggest he flies over and joins his wife in Spain until these lunatics are caught.'

Carruthers remained silent.

'The man's an idiot,' continued Bingham. 'Not only did he not report the threats he received, he's waited until they've been acted upon, and now he wants police protection. I haven't read his book from cover to cover but I've glanced at it. Pretty inflammatory stuff. Did he not think when he wrote it that he might become a target of the more lunatic fringes? I'm damned if I'm going to waste taxpayer's money on him. Who does he think he is? Salman bloody Rushdie? Not only has he put himself at risk, he's also put the residents of Castletown at risk.'

'Where has he been the last forty-eight hours?' asked Carruthers, thinking Bingham was being a bit harsh.

'That's the second thing. Says he can't remember,' snorted Bingham. 'I've put him in interview room two to make him sweat. Don't let him leave until you get some answers.'

'He would be much more comfortable in an office,' said Carruthers. 'Why don't I see if there's one free?'

'Leave him where he is,' snapped Bingham.

'He's not a suspect. Don't you think he's been through enough? Besides, if he's relaxed he might open up more.'

'Leave him. That's an order.'

Carruthers left Bingham drumming his fingers on his desk, picked up his notes from his office then made his way down to interview room two. He hadn't said anything to Bingham about the library book Holdaway had requested. Wanted to see what the man had to say first. He collected Fletcher from the break room and headed to the interview room.

The academic stood up as they entered. 'Professor Nicholas Holdaway? DCI Carruthers and DS Fletcher. Apologies for putting you in one of our interview rooms. All private offices have been commandeered for this investigation. Please sit down, sir.' Carruthers and Fletcher sat down opposite Holdaway in identical plastic chairs. Carruthers leant forward across the scuffed table and stared intently at the politics lecturer.

The last forty-eight hours had not been kind to Nicholas Holdaway. He was dishevelled and clearly exhausted, with great bags under his eyes. There was grey stubble on his face and his white hair looked like it hadn't seen a comb for a couple of days. His pink shirt was half tucked in, half hanging out of his brown corduroy trousers, which were stained with grass and mud. He looked like a haunted man who'd been sleeping rough. He had his head bowed.

Carruthers felt guilty about lying to Holdaway about the reasons for the choice of room. He hated all interview rooms but this one in particular. For a start it was the smallest and Carruthers hated small rooms. It was also in need of a good lick of paint. It had originally been painted grey. Now it just looked dirty. There was little natural light as it was a room with only one small window. Orders from Bingham, who clearly wanted Holdaway rattled and at a disadvantage during the interview, were not to be disobeyed though.

In the short time he'd been at the station, Carruthers had become adept at being selective in the orders he chose to bend or break. He hadn't had much of a chance to decide how to proceed with the interview. He was going to ask the man where he'd been but in light of the recent revelation of the library book he jumped straight in with the most obvious question first.

'Why would you want a book on the events of Bloody Sunday?'
Holdaway frowned. 'Northern Ireland interests me,' he muttered.
'Is that all it is?'

The question was greeted with silence. Carruthers couldn't
decide whether Holdaway was simply exhausted or being evasive.
He changed tack. 'We've had confirmation that the explosion was
caused by a bomb. A Welsh extremist organisation known as Bryn
Glas 1402 are claiming responsibility.'

Holdaway jerked his head up. He made eye contact with
Carruthers briefly then looked away. In that moment, the police
officer saw a mixture of emotion; fear, alarm, wariness even, but
interestingly, not surprise.

'The group's led by a man named Ewan Williams. Have you
ever heard of him?'

Holdaway shook his head. Carruthers wasn't sure whether to
believe him. After all, the man was supposed to be the Welsh
terrorism expert. Then again, if people like McGhee had only just
made the link between Bryn Glas and Williams...

'Ewan Williams' sister married an Irishman.' Carruthers
watched Holdaway's face. A mere flicker of the eyelid. 'She moved
over to Northern Ireland in the early 1970s. She was involved in
the march you've just requested a library book on. She was shot
on that march.'

Holdaway remained silent but his face drained of colour.

'Pretty big coincidence, don't you think?' *What is going on?*
thought Carruthers. 'I'm going to ask you again. What is your
connection with Northern Ireland?'

Holdaway bit his lip. 'I'm thinking of writing a book on
Northern Ireland and Bloody Sunday,' he said.

*Was there any truth in Fletcher's suggestion that the professor had
some information about the circumstances of the shooting of Williams'
sister?* Carruthers wondered.

The professor then remained silent. *A nut can be cracked without
a sledgehammer,* thought Carruthers. However, he was getting
increasingly irritated especially as they were here to help Holdaway.

'I understand that you've received threatening letters?' said Carruthers, watching Holdaway closely. 'Can you tell me about that? How long had it been going on?'

'About four months. I received a number of anonymous letters in the post.'

'So you didn't know at that stage who'd written the letters?'

'No. Like I said, they were anonymous.'

'Have you kept them?'

'No. I've thrown them away,' Holdaway admitted.

Carruthers sighed. 'They may have contained vital forensic evidence. Why did you never report these threats to the police?'

'The same reason I threw the letters away. I decided not to take them seriously. To be honest I've had a fair few threats from crackpots over the years. If I'd taken every one of them seriously I would never have ventured outside my front door.'

'Can you describe the letters? What about postmark?'

Holdaway thought for a few moments. 'I couldn't make out the postmark on any of them. Address was typed,' he said carefully. 'Inside, the letters had been cut out of a magazine or newspaper, and stuck on a page to form words. I can't really tell you much more.'

'How many did you receive in total?'

'Four.'

'So approximately one a month?'

'Yes, I suppose so. There would be a gap of three or four weeks then I would receive another one.'

'Do you remember what these letters said?'

'The usual.'

'What's the usual?'

'English Scum.'

'That all?' *Insulting but hardly threatening*, thought Carruthers. 'For the first one.'

'Short and to the point. Was it signed?'

'None of them were. No.'

'What did the others say?'

'My wife threw the second out. I never saw but apparently it said, "We are watching you."'

'What about the last two?'

'"We know all about your past. You have been warned," was the third.'

'What did that mean? We know about your past?'

'I'm thirsty. Can I have a glass of water?'

Carruthers looked across at Fletcher. 'Andie, can you get us a jug of water and three glasses.'

'What did that mean? We know about your past?' repeated Carruthers as Fletcher left the room. Holdaway shook his head. He looked away from Carruthers as he spoke. 'I have no idea.'

Carruthers wondered why Holdaway was being evasive. There was a lot more going on than just fatigue. *What had got him so afraid that he couldn't help the police in their investigation? What was the information he was withholding? What was his* real *interest in the Bloody Sunday enquiry?* Carruthers wasn't sure if he believed that Holdaway was writing a book. He studied Holdaway intently. The man clearly knew more than he had admitted.

'If you want us to help you, you have to tell us everything. Tell me about the last letter. What did it say?'

'You will pay for what you did.'

'What did you think they meant by that?' Carruthers wondered about blackmail.

Holdaway didn't look up and he didn't answer.

'Professor Holdaway, have you received any demands for money?'

'No.'

So they're not trying to blackmail him, thought Carruthers. *OK, professor. Now, the million-dollar question:* 'Where have you been since the explosion?'

'In hiding.'

'In hiding,' Carruthers repeated. He sat back in his chair. Scratched his chin. Something wasn't adding up. The professor could have had no way of knowing that it was a car bomb at that time or that it was his car that had been targeted. He had to keep probing but first he was going to change tack.

'We understand you've just brought out a book on the failings of Welsh nationalism. I presume I'm right in thinking that would make you pretty unpopular with the Welsh nationalists?'

The door opened and Fletcher walked into the room carrying a tray loaded with a jug of water and three plastic glasses. She set them down on the table and took her seat.

'I suppose so.'

'I haven't read it,' said Carruthers, pouring three glasses of water and offering one to Holdaway, who accepted the glass without acknowledgment. 'But I understand that in it you argue Welsh nationalism has failed because it never posed a serious enough threat to the security of UK citizens. Am I right?'

Holdaway lifted the glass to his lips. 'Well, I didn't exactly say that.'

Carruthers felt the need to push on. He watched Holdaway take a thirsty gulp. 'Would you agree, though, that the publication of your book would put you at serious threat from one or two of the more, shall we say, extreme elements? Perhaps a splinter group?'

'It's looking that way, isn't it?'

Carruthers made eye contact with Holdaway. 'You think it's the Welsh?'

'To be honest, I have no idea who planted the bomb. I can only think the likelihood is it's Welsh terrorists who don't like the fact I've brought this book out.'

'Clearly they wouldn't be too happy that you've bought a second home there either? Professor Sadler told us.'

Holdaway bristled. 'That busybody.'

'I don't want to call into question your judgment, but did it not occur to you that buying a holiday home in Wales so close to your book being published might not be the brightest idea? I take it you do know there've been various arson attacks by the Welsh on holiday homes of the English in the past?' Even as he said the words Carruthers didn't believe this was the reason Holdaway had been targeted. After all, it was twenty odd years ago. His mind was still trying to find connections between the professor's choice of library book and the shooting of Ewan Williams' sister.

'Of course I do. I've written the book, remember? I've come across these groups in my research. But life's moved on since then. The last one was a long time ago.'

So Holdaway doesn't believe it's Welsh Nationalists any more than I do, thought Carruthers. *Interesting.*

'It didn't deter you from either writing the book, or from buying a holiday home though, did it?'

'I believe in freedom of speech, inspector. Both freedom of speech and freedom of movement.'

Carruthers drew in a long breath and exhaled it sharply. 'Very noble. Do you still believe in freedom of speech, even when your right to free speech may jeopardise your own safety? Or other people's safety?'

Holdaway stood up shakily. 'Look, I didn't come into the police station to be insulted. I would also like to remind you that I'm not a suspect.'

'Sit down, please.' Carruthers felt a sharp burst of irritation. 'We haven't finished here yet. You didn't think you might become a target, even when you started to receive anonymous letters?'

'I live in Scotland. I didn't think they would bother targeting someone as far north as this. Like I said, I didn't take them seriously.'

'Didn't take them seriously? Isn't that the exact problem you were touting in the book? Welsh Nationalism wasn't taken seriously because they weren't violent enough. How is that not an open invitation to Professor Holdaway hunting season?'

Holdaway's left eye started to twitch. Carruthers studied him.

'Did you have any reason to believe, when you received the letters, that they might be from Bryn Glas 1402?'

'No, I didn't. Like I said, I didn't take them seriously. Is there any chance you might be mistaken? That they're not from Bryn

Glas 1402, I mean, but rather a group or individual setting out to try to discredit them?'

'It is a line of enquiry we're considering,' he admitted. He supposed it would make Holdaway feel better to believe that Bryn Glas 1402 were the target, and he was merely an unlucky pawn. '

'Do you know a man by the name of Rhys Evans?' he asked.

Holdaway shook his head.

'Dave Roberts?'

Another shake of head.

'No. Who are they?'

'Rhys Evans was the man murdered in Castletown earlier this week,' said Carruthers.

'The man from the RAF? Are you saying there's some connection between his death and the car bomb?'

The room was warm. Carruthers was starting to get a headache. He could smell sweat. Wasn't sure if it was Holdaway's or his own. He picked up his own glass of water and drained it. Poured himself another and topped up Holdaway's. 'I don't know,' he admitted. He studied the older man. 'Would there be any reason Bryn Glas 1402, rather than another terrorist group, would target you?'

'None, except that they're currently active, unlike the Welsh Republican Army. But like I said, I've never felt under threat from a specific group, despite receiving those letters. Perhaps you're right. Perhaps it was foolish of me. No Welsh terrorist group has operated in Scotland before. Mostly their activities have been confined to the Welsh border.'

'Have Welsh terrorists ever attacked individuals before rather than holiday homes?'

'They have tried to target individuals in the past but not been successful. And they've attacked more than just holiday homes. For example, the Conservative Party Offices in London were attacked in the late 1980s, as were a number of estate agencies that handled Welsh property transactions to the English.'

Carruthers lifted his eyebrows in surprise. 'I don't remember reading about that.'

'Oh yes, these businesses were widely dispersed. Think one was in Birmingham. In fact, as far as holiday homes are concerned, between 1979 and 1994 they've claimed responsibility for three hundred arson attacks on English-owned properties. However,' Holdaway continued, 'what you've got to remember is that, realistically, the number is a lot lower. You can't rule out insurance claims, that sort of thing.'

A minimum of twenty years ago, thought Carruthers. His intuition was telling him they were starting to get off track. Like Fletcher he just couldn't buy into the theory that it was a Welsh terrorist group in operation. The peak of Welsh terrorism was just too long ago. So who were Bryn Glas, really? And why had they claimed responsibility?

Carruthers frowned. 'There's a possibility that whoever's planted the bomb is linking up with their Scottish counterparts. It's something we're currently investigating. As you'll be aware, a lot of these groups have connections with terrorist organisations in other countries.'

Holdaway shuddered, but nodded. 'I know there is a sizeable number of folk bitterly unhappy about the results of the Scottish Referendum. And the timing would certainly make sense. Is that something you are looking in to?'

'It's certainly a line of enquiry,' said Carruthers.

Carruthers shuffled his notes. 'Now, we have been led to believe that you always take your lunch break at 1pm. The car exploded at precisely 1:15. You were incredibly lucky not to be in or close to the car when it exploded. Talk me through the events that occurred just prior to you leaving the building.'

'I got a phone call,' said Holdaway, whose hands shook slightly.

'From the bomber?' Carruthers was surprised. He riffled through his notes again. As far as he'd been aware there'd been no warning given.

Holdaway made a visible effort to stop the tremor in his hands by placing one on top of the other. When this didn't work he placed both of them on his lap palms down.

What did they say? In this phone call?' Carruthers prompted.

'Well, that's just it. I picked up the phone and the person rang off without speaking.'

'What did you say when you picked up the phone?'

'What do you mean?'

'Did you say hello or good afternoon? Did you mention your name? How would you normally answer the phone?'

'Professor Holdaway. That's how I answered the phone. It's how I always answer the phone.'

'I'm just trying to establish whether it might have been the bombers who rang you. Can you remember what time you took the phone call? It's very important.'

'Yes, it was exactly 1pm.'

'How do you know?'

'I looked over at the clock on the wall. I'm a creature of habit, Inspector Carruthers. As you have already pointed out I always take my lunch at 1pm.'

'And you're in the department every day?'

'Yes, well, at least on week days.'

'The bombers would have known that. They would make it their business to find that out. They like people whose movements are habitual. OK, what happened next?'

'Well, I gathered up my car keys, briefcase and left the office.'

'How long did it take you to get ready?'

'A few minutes.'

'So you would have actually left the office at approximately 1:05? Yet you never made it to the car park?'

'No, that's just it, though. On a normal day I would have been in the car by about 1:05.'

'Where do you usually drive to?'

'I like to get out of the building. I always take the car and go for a little drive. Park up somewhere. Don't you see? They meant to kill me. I'm sure of it. If it hadn't been for that student waylaying me on the stairs…' Holdaway left the rest of the sentence hanging in the air. He was clearly rattled. His shakes seemed to have got worse.

Carruthers' ears pricked up at the mention of someone on the staircase.

'What student?' he asked.

'I got halfway down the first flight of stairs and this bloody student accosted me.'

'What did he want?'

'To ask me questions about a particular course I teach. Told him to go through the proper channels; that I was on my lunch break. He seemed most insistent. Wouldn't take no for an answer. He was a bloody nuisance to be honest but now it looks as if I owe him my life.'

'What did he look like?' said Carruthers sharply.

'Well, now you mention it. I did think it rather odd at the time. He didn't really look like a typical student.'

'In what way? asked Carruthers.'

'Older for a start. Mid-twenties.'

'He could have been a mature student,' said Carruthers. 'Was he enquiring about an undergraduate course?'

'Yes, nationhood and nationality. It's very popular.'

'I'm sure it is. What else can you tell me? How would you describe him physically?'

'Let's see. Quite short, about five feet seven inches, stocky, short cropped black hair.'

'Accent?'

'English.'

'Regional dialect?'

'Don't think he had one.'

So in all likelihood the Home Counties, thought Carruthers, wondering how important this new piece of information was. Could this man be connected to the bombers? He had an English accent, though, so maybe it was an innocent enquiry after all.

'Oh come off it. You don't think he was connected to the bombers do you?' Holdaway asked.

'I really don't know. You said yourself he didn't look like a student. What was he wearing?'

'Nothing out of the ordinary. Blue jeans, sweatshirt.'

'Logo?'

'No logo. At least none I could see. He was carrying a rucksack. I remember that. Kept fiddling with the strap.'

'Colour and make?' prompted Carruthers.

'Black. Yes, definitely black. Not sure of the make.'

'This might be nothing but we'll get you to work with putting a likeness together. We need to eliminate this man from our enquiries.'

'You mean a police artist?'

'We're now using computer based facial composite systems.' Carruthers looked across at Fletcher. 'Andie, can you get this set up?' Fletcher stood up. 'Can you also get the professor some sandwiches?'

Fletcher nodded and left the room.

'Right, we'll see if we can get a likeness put together straight after this interview. You look like you might function better after eating. Now, what were you doing when the bomb actually exploded? Were you still talking to our would-be student?'

'Yes, yes I was. He opened the rucksack to get out, well, I thought it was a bottle of water. Then the explosion happened. It was deafening. A few seconds went by and then there was chaos. We both ran downstairs. I knew instantly it was a bomb.'

'You said he was carrying the rucksack. Did he have it on his back or on one shoulder?'

Holdaway thought about it and spoke carefully. 'I think it was on his shoulder because when he unzipped it he just swung the bag round. I don't remember him having to take his arms out of it before opening it.'

'You said he'd been fidgeting with the straps. Did he appear nervous?' Once again Carruthers felt he was missing something. Something important. Something Holdaway had said perhaps. What was it?

'Nervous? A bit perhaps. Excitable, definitely.'

'Which shoulder did he carry the rucksack on?' asked Carruthers.

'The right, I think.'

'Did you manage to see inside the bag when he unzipped it?'

'No, not really. I mean, I wasn't really looking at his bag. Just noticed he had one and that he unzipped it.' Holdaway raked his shaking hands through his hair.

'After the bomb exploded, nobody saw you, professor. Where did you go and how did you leave the building without being seen?'

'I came down the stairs. The front door was open. I could see Barbara Fairbanks, our secretary, standing in the doorway. She had her back to me. Her office is on the ground floor. I heard her say, "Oh my God." Like I said, I knew it was a bomb. It was Northern Ireland all over again. I just panicked and fled out the back door. I realised it was me they were after. Thought there might be a sniper out the front to finish me off.'

'You served in Northern Ireland?' asked Carruthers astonished. And then it came back to him. He'd moved on too swiftly in the interview. Hadn't given proper thought to all the man's answers. Holdaway had said he'd known it was a bomb. How could he have known that? Unless of course he'd heard bombs explode before. That's why he'd wanted the bloody book from the library. Now he thought about it, Holdaway had stood up when Carruthers had entered the room. That was often the sign of a military man. It wasn't much but still, he should have taken more notice. It was all falling into place.

'Yes. Parachute Regiment. 1971–1974.'

Carruthers looked at Holdaway. 'Why didn't you tell me this at the start of the interview when I asked you about the connection with Northern Ireland?'

Carruthers riffled through the notes Harris had gathered on Holdaway. Christ, there was no mention of Holdaway having been in the army, let alone serving in Northern Ireland. What the fuck had Harris been thinking to have omitted that vital piece of information? It was a rookie's mistake. 1971–1974. The dates fit. And Holdaway was over in Northern Ireland during the so-called peace march.

'So you served in Northern Ireland from 1971–1974?'

'I wasn't in Ireland all that time.'

'OK. Can you give me the dates you were in Northern Ireland.' Carruthers picked up a pen.'

'I was over there for six months from early 1972.'

Carruthers suddenly switched tack. 'You told Superintendent Bingham you couldn't remember what happened after the bomb exploded or where you went.'

'That's right,' admitted Holdaway looking rather shame-faced.

'Why did you leave the army?'

Holdaway looked rattled at another sudden shift of questioning and remained silent.

'Why did you leave the army? After all, you only served three years.'

In the silence that followed, Carruthers noisily exhaled his breath. 'You know that we could charge you with wasting police time, don't you? Not to mention withholding information. You've already given the bombers forty-eight hours head start on us. Now for the last time, why did you leave the army?'

'Medical discharge. Satisfied now? I was found to be suffering from a kind of, well, you would call it post-traumatic stress disorder nowadays. I've spent the last forty-odd years trying to put it behind me. The past never leaves you, though. All it took was that explosion and I was back there in Northern Ireland.'

'You experienced a flashback?'

'I must have done. Look Carruthers, I've been in hiding, sleeping rough. In truth I've never really been the same person since Northern Ireland. It took me a long time to get over what I witnessed. And what I did. I suppose that's why I like the safe environment of university life.'

Hardly a safe environment if you're going to be bringing out contentious books, thought Carruthers. *This man is full of contradictions.* 'You've just said it took you a long time to get over what you did. What did you do, professor?'

'I did a politics degree then masters and a PhD after I left the army.'

Carruthers wasn't sure if Holdaway was starting to ramble or if he had just misunderstood the question but he let him continue.

'I was always fascinated by politics, just not destined to be on the cutting edge, that's all. We aren't all cut out to be foot soldiers. I found a niche at university. I'm good at lecturing. OK, so the students get on my bloody nerves, but I guess you can't have everything.'

'You say you like the safe environment of university, professor, yet you court controversy with your academic opinions.'

There was a knock at the door of the interview room. Fletcher walked in holding a plate of sandwiches.

'Thanks Andie. Can you also get on to the press liaison office and get someone down here. I'd like to get a nationwide broadcast arranged: our bomber could be anywhere now.'

Fletcher placed the sandwiches on the table between them. 'Right you are,' she said and left the room.

Holdaway pounced on a sandwich and took a bite.

'Right. Back to 1972,' said Carruthers.

'It's not something I like to talk about,' Holdaway said with his mouth full.

'Do you want them to take another potshot at you?'

'Of course not.'

'You clearly saw action whilst you were over there.' He watched Holdaway take another sandwich. Who knew when the man had last eaten?

There was only one thing that made any sense and that was if Holdaway had actually been involved in the policing of the march. He thought about Bloody Sunday. *One of the most infamous days in Irish history and British politics.* The worst civilian massacre by the army since Peterloo in 1819.

He voiced his thoughts. 'Were you involved in the actual policing of the Bloody Sunday march?'

Holdaway nodded. He then put his head in his hands.

'Professor Holdaway, I need you to tell me everything that happened,' said Carruthers. 'Everything that Private Holdaway did on that fateful day.'

Holdaway nodded. Perhaps he was finally going to let Carruthers in. 'I was young,' he said. 'Just nineteen. Too young. "The Troubles" as they were called had started in 1969. By 1972 they'd worsened. Street patrols were the worst. You never knew when you'd come across a sniper or a car bomb. You couldn't let your guard down for a second. My God, I saw one poor chap... Blown up by a car bomb. Unrecognisable... They had to shovel him up, or at least shovel what was left of him up. Right in front of me. It was terrible.'

'Is that the incident to which you were referring? The reason you got medically discharged from the army?'

Holdaway shook his head. '30 January 1972, the Army deployed the Parachute Regiment to suppress rioting at a civil rights march in Derry.'

Bloody Sunday. Carruthers nodded, trying to encourage Holdaway to talk about the infamous day when troops had opened fire on demonstrators, killing thirteen and injuring another twelve.

'It was bloody.' Bitterness had crept into his voice. 'It was absolute mayhem. One minute it was peaceful then... well, all hell broke loose. We were terrified. I was terrified. I was nineteen, inspector, nineteen. What were you doing at nineteen?'

Carruthers thought about it for a moment. *Probably getting pissed in the student union bar.* 'You'd better tell me everything. And start at the beginning.'

Despite his hunger Holdaway pushed the plate of sandwiches away. 'It's more than forty years ago. My memory might still be vivid but I can no longer remember the detail.'

Carruthers nodded. 'Tell me what you remember.'

'We'd got wind before the march that an IRA sniper was operating in the area. At least that's what we were told. We were given permission by our commander to go in to arrest rioters.

It was an unlawful march, after all.' He swallowed. 'I remember running down Rossville Street and across wasteland with other soldiers.'

'Rossville Street?'

'That's how we entered the Bogside. I had a strong impression I was being shot at. I heard a crack of fire. A few moments later I heard a volley of shots. I looked around me to see other soldiers. They looked as if they were under fire.'

'How do you mean?'

'I could see it in their postures. They were crouching.'

Carruthers looked at Holdaway. The man was pretty spot on with certain details but then he'd probably relived the day thousands of times over the last forty years. How much of it was true Carruthers didn't know. Perhaps Holdaway no longer knew. He did know one thing, though. Memories are notoriously unreliable. He knew that every soldier and protestor witnessing the same event would have a different interpretation of that event. And consequently, a different memory. And a memory already over forty years old – now that was another matter altogether.

'Look, there is one thing I need to tell you,' said Holdaway, 'I'm an alcoholic, albeit a functioning one. I have been for a long time.' Carruthers wasn't surprised. It concurred with what Sadler had told him. The only surprise was Holdaway's admission. He wondered if the seeds of the alcoholism lay in the man's soldiering days… But he couldn't afford to be distracted

'Thank you for your honesty. Please continue.'

'I got separated from the other soldiers. I don't know how it happened. I remember my knees shaking. I thought they were going to buckle under me.'

Carruthers saw a fine sheen of perspiration on the man's face.

'I remember being down an alleyway chasing protesters. I was on my own. No backup. I can feel the fear now. I heard a shot behind me. It was loud and close. On instinct I turned, crouched and fired.'

'How many shots?'

'Three. Thought they had fired at me. The next thing I saw was a young woman falling. She'd been shot. I'd shot her.'
Dear God. Ewan Williams' sister. It has to be.
'And the shot behind you?'
'The noise had been another soldier shooting a protester.'
'Do you remember the name of the woman you shot?'
'A man shouted to her. He called her Meg. He shouted her name but it was the look on his face I'll never forget.'
'His face? Whose face?'
'The man with her who was cradling her head when she fell. I assume it was her husband. He stared right at me. It was a look of such intensity and hatred. I'll never forget it. Of course, I found out her name. I needed to find out. It was Margaret McDaid.'
Carruthers leant forward. Steepled his hands on the table.
'They've found me,' said Holdaway, pushing his water away from him. 'It's all over. We got promised anonymity during the enquiry,' he said bitterly. 'But that was never going to happen. It was bad enough when I got called back to give evidence during the Saville Enquiry.'
Perhaps that's why he wanted the book. To read up on the findings of the enquiry and perhaps get a feel for the public mood, as if he didn't already know. Carruthers had a brain wave. He opened his notebook, flicking it back until he came to the interview with Sadler. He made eye contact with Holdaway. 'You took a few months off work during 2002?'
Holdaway nodded. 'I got called to give evidence at the Saville Enquiry.' He shook his head. 'I couldn't handle it. I had a breakdown afterwards. Had to take some time off work.'
Now it was Carruthers' turn to nod.
'They're coming after us,' said Holdaway.
Carruthers frowned. 'Who are?'
'You must have heard that soldiers who took an active part in the shootings are being investigated for murder? Dear God, a sixty-six-year-old man – an ex-soldier is currently being held for murder. They're saying two-hundred and fifty men may be requisitioned.'

Carruthers had heard this. He also knew that families of those killed would welcome the news. There would, however, be those less happy with the news. Certain former military commanders for one. He'd skim read that in the book. He looked keenly at Holdaway, who was staring at Carruthers with haunted eyes.

'I can't get over the fact the man who fronts Bryn Glas 1402 is the brother of the woman I shot more than forty years ago. When I was researching and I found out…' For a moment the older man's voice and attention slipped away, he was shaking his head. You have to understand, inspector, we were trained soldiers of the Parachute Regiment. We had a job to do. Whether it was fitting that 1 Para should have been deployed into the Bogside in Derry at all, that was not my call to make. As a soldier you have to follow orders. And you have to make split second decisions. Sometimes we get those decisions wrong.'

In the silent moments that followed, Carruthers could see Holdaway was back on that terrible day, reliving the moment he shot an unarmed woman.

TEN

SATURDAY AFTERNOON, 2ND JUNE

'Holdaway thinks they were trying to kill him. He's terrified. He's also, by his own admission, a functioning alcoholic,' said Carruthers.

Bingham brought his mug of steaming coffee up to his lips. 'I wouldn't be too thrilled if somebody had just blown my car up either. Well, we need to get some confirmation of Williams' involvement before deciding whether he intended to kill Holdaway or not. We need to find the man on the stairs. Could be a critical witness. Clearly wasn't Williams. Too young. Williams will be well into his sixties now.'

'It's out of term time,' said Carruthers. 'All the undergraduates have gone home. So who was he? Didn't look like your typical student, according to Holdaway.'

'In what way?'

'For one, he was older.'

'Mature student?' wondered Bingham.

'Holdaway doesn't think so. Adamant he's not the bomber though. Pretty convinced the man saved his life.'

'Well, he's got to be one or the other, surely? Bomber or student?'

'He was nervous, according to Holdaway,' continued Carruthers. 'Fiddling with the strap of his rucksack.'

Bingham cracked his knuckles. 'Well, we now know the bomb was on a timer. If he was the bomber, it begs the question why did he need to be there at all? What went wrong? Did he change his mind, couldn't go through with it? Purposefully decided to delay Holdaway from getting to his car? Ideals are all well and good but perhaps once he'd come face-to-face with his victim, couldn't murder him in cold blood.'

'He's definitely suspect,' said Carruthers. 'Apart from everything else, he disappeared as soon as the explosion occurred.'

'We need to find him,' said Bingham.

'And we will, sir. Holdaway's currently building up a profile of the man as we speak. We'll get that circulated to the press as soon as possible. And we'll see if we can get anything useful from the car park CCTV. Luckily it wasn't damaged in the explosion.'

'Why didn't you know ahead of interviewing him that Holdaway had an army background? Parachute Regiment. Served in Northern Ireland in the early 70s for Christ's sake,' snapped Bingham.

'I wasn't in possession of the information,' Carruthers ignored Bingham's outburst – which he'd been expecting – and continued calmly. 'He was invalided out with mental health issues, what would today be diagnosed as post-traumatic stress disorder. He believes he suffered a flashback when the car bomb exploded.'

'Christ. There was nothing in his biog about him being in the army,' said Bingham.

'Well, I suppose you wouldn't want to publicise the fact you'd served in the Parachute Regiment in Northern Ireland around the time of Bloody Sunday,' said Carruthers.

'I'm not expecting his bloody memoirs. But… Christ Almighty. Make it your business to find out every detail of what happened. Don't leave it to Dougie Harris. Useless article. I presume he was the dunderhead that was supposed to give you the background information. Of course it wouldn't be Andrea Fletcher. She's too bright to make that kind of mistake. She'll go far. Pity she's a woman.' There was an embarrassing pause before Bingham coughed realising what he had just said.

'Don't let Andie hear you say that.'

'Good God. Of course not, man. Sensitive creatures, women. Likely to take it the wrong way. Probably end up at some tribunal or other.'

Carruthers groaned inwardly. Talk about foot in mouth. Bingham could give Prince Philip a run for his money sometimes.

'Let's hope to God the Irish aren't involved. This is way over our heads. I want you to find McGhee and brief him – without baiting him. Now, what about Holdaway's personal life? Did you find out anything useful there?'

Carruthers thought about the conversation he'd had with the professor after the lengthy talk about his short-lived military career. 'He's been with his wife for over thirty years. Says he's happily married and had never cheated.'

'You don't believe him?'

'Wife's on holiday without him.'

Bingham shrugged. 'Not uncommon for a couple to have separate interests and holiday apart.'

'With all due respect, sir, she's hardly gone potholing.'

'I know all the evidence is pointing towards Ewan Williams but there's one thing I don't understand,' said Bingham.

'Which is what?'

Bingham cracked his knuckles again. 'Why leave it this long to go after Holdaway?'

***

'Do you fancy the pictures tonight, Siobhan?' said Tomoko. 'I could do with a break from studying. It might take your mind off things for a while.'

Siobhan smiled weakly and wiped her eyes. 'No thanks. Don't think I can face being with people who are enjoying themselves. Not until they catch whoever killed Rhys. Besides, Castletown hardly feels safe at the moment, what with that explosion. I heard it was a car bomb and that one of the politics professors was the target.'

'It's really scary. We could always watch a DVD here instead. Let's both have a break and stick on the TV. There's due to be a news update soon. Perhaps there'll be news of an arrest.' Tomoko grabbed the remote control and pointed it at the TV in the corner of the sitting room.

'Breaking news. Police have issued an impression-fit of a man they want to question in connection with the car bomb in Castletown. The man is approximately five feet seven inches, stocky build, short cropped hair and an English accent,' the newsreader continued.

Siobhan's cup clattered noisily in its saucer as she stared open mouthed at the picture.

'Oh my God,' said Tomoko 'I know I only met him a couple of times but doesn't that just look like…? It can't be though. They said he has an English accent.'

'I'm phoning Inspector Carruthers. It's him, Tomoko, I'm sure it is. That's Dave Roberts.'

***

The day had ended up being hot, with a heat haze over most of Fife. The beach had been crowded with holidaymakers, mostly families sporting brightly coloured windbreakers as protection either against the cold easterly wind or occasionally strong sun. Many were still there.

Having phoned the police, Siobhan decided to go for a short walk to clear her head before her interview with Inspector Carruthers. She gathered her rucksack, putting in a bottle of water and her mobile phone. She set out through the maze of pebble-dashed accommodation to the gate that led to the beach. She gazed out to sea. The usually soothing motion of the tide didn't calm her today. Her head was buzzing with unanswered questions and an icy fear gripped her heart, as she contemplated the possibility that Dave may be linked to the bombers. If that was the case, what part then did Rhys' death play in the drama unfolding in this university town?

Rhys couldn't have got himself involved with terrorists, could he? No, it was unthinkable. Even the thought of Dave playing a part seemed ludicrous, despite his unsavoury views.

What turns people into terrorists? she wondered. *The really scary thing is how normal a lot of terrorists appeared. They are the people next door, they hold down jobs. One of the Glasgow bombers was a medic, for goodness sake. How many news reports are there of parents who hadn't known their own sons and daughters had been terrorists?* mused Siobhan. *Sometimes the bombers were even parents themselves.*

Siobhan couldn't clear her thoughts of all these unanswered questions. They seemed to be on a constant loop in her head. Before she knew what she was doing she'd left East Castle Beach behind her, and briskly walked past the packed children's play area and crazy golf course, climbing the steep path past the cathedral towards the West Castle Beach on the other side of town. The children's shouts started to recede into the distance. A moment's loneliness gripped her. She wondered how people could still be carrying on as if nothing had happened.

After a few minutes she stopped and gazed at the vast expanse of beach. That was more like it. That was a real walk. The tide was out. She started walking over the sand, kicking her way through the seaweed and shells. She walked further on the beach than she had ever walked before. Away in the distance beyond the late heat haze of the day were the lush evergreen trees of Pinetum Park Forest, punctuating the horizon like an oasis in the desert.

A strong breeze blew towards her. It was hard going walking into a headwind in sand. After a few minutes she stopped. Breathless, she scanned the panorama. Once she stopped, the heat hit her as if an oven door had been opened. To the right was the ebbing tide, and to the left the grassy banks of sand dunes. She brought out the bottle of water from her rucksack and thirstily drank from it. The still hot wind fanned her face as she continued walking. The noise of dogs barking and children shouting receded into the distance as she walked further away from the ancient town. She turned back to face it, admiring its spires glinting in the sun. She breathed in the sea air, the salt hitting the back of her throat as she swallowed. The wind brought a lock of her hair over her face. She brushed it out of her eyes and turned round so she now had her back to town, and continued walking.

She passed between a group of kite flyers on the landside, and in the water a few kayakers. As she edged closer to Pinetum Park Forest, the drone of an aircraft became apparent. One circled right overhead and Siobhan tilted her head back and watched it until she became dizzy.

She started to think about how well she'd known Rhys. He had been intelligent, good humoured, easy going. Well, that was at the beginning. The last couple of months he'd changed, becoming withdrawn, nervy and irritable, especially when Dave's name had been mentioned. She'd stupidly thought it was because he was having no success finding his birth mother. Now she realised it was so much more.

Something had changed in the nature of his relationship with Dave. She was certain of it. He seemed almost scared. *Yes, that's it.* She hadn't put her finger on it until now, but now she thought about it, she realised Rhys had been afraid of Dave. Suddenly, for Siobhan, it all fell into place. Rhys had been scared of Dave. The police were looking for Dave in connection to the car bomb, and Rhys had been murdered. He must have found out what Dave was planning and tried to stop him. That's why Dave hadn't reported his disappearance to the police. It was the only explanation that made any sense.

She turned away from the wide expanse of golden sand and, with head down, started the long walk back.

***

'Superintendent McGhee's looking for you, Jim,' Fletcher said as she rushed down the corridor at the station. Carruthers swung round from the water cooler.

'They've got a lead from the facial composite,' said Fletcher, eagerly. 'Taken several calls from the RAF base. It's possible the man in the picture's Dave Roberts.'

'I had the same call from Siobhan Mathews. I'm heading over to interview her now.'

'I'll come with you,' said Fletcher gathering her belongings.

'I'm going to go on my own.'

'You really need someone of the opposite sex with you,' said Fletcher.

'For some reason, she trusts me… stall McGhee for me, will you?'

'Yes, but Jim, McGhee wants you over at the RAF base with him. He's organised a meeting with some of the leading RAF personnel.'

Carruthers, pretending not to hear, was already out the door. The less time he spent with McGhee the better, and the idea of McGhee getting hands on with Fletcher made his skin crawl. But he trusted Fletcher to know better. Mind you, he'd also trusted Mairi.

***

If Carruthers had been a post-graduate like Siobhan Mathews, he hoped he would have been in better housing than Edgecliffe.

This time it was Siobhan who opened the door. As she led him into the living room he noticed a vase of freshly-cut flowers. He found himself wondering why people always bought flowers for the bereaved and where that tradition had come from. He always found the cutting of flowers for the dead rather distasteful. He particularly hated seeing flowers in their cellophane packaging laid at the site of a car accident or murder. It reminded him of the flowers at the side of the road where his brother had died. His mother had taken him to look at them, and the cards. As she had walked away with him, holding his hand so tightly it had hurt, he had wrenched his hand out of hers, ran back and bulldozed into the flowers kicking them high into the air. The counsellor had told his mother he was suffering from grief. Grief and guilt. After all, his brother had been knocked down going after the football Jim had accidentally kicked into the road. Carruthers forced his mind away from these terrible memories.

He knew he'd get a bollocking when he returned to the station, but McGhee could wait. He instinctively knew he would uncover more personal information about Roberts from Siobhan Mathews than talking to the personnel at the base. He was sure the two crimes, the probable murder of Evans and the car bomb, were linked. And even though there was no concrete evidence linking Roberts to either case yet, Carruthers was convinced he had to be the man on the stairs. The question was, why had he been on the stairs?

He was feeling weary and it wasn't yet 6pm. It had been a long day. Hell, it had been a long three days and he was keen to go back to his cottage and unwind. He thought about a home-cooked supper. He enjoyed cooking. Perhaps a tomato-based pasta dish with a nice bottle of red wine. *Dream on.* By the time he got home it would probably have to be a takeaway, Indian if it was still open. So be it. As long as he could end the night with a much-needed bath and a finger or two of Talisker while listening to some Neil Young, he would be happy. He hoped the investigation wouldn't take yet another unexpected turn to rob him of those little pleasures, too.

***

'Andrea, where the hell's Carruthers?' demanded Superintendent Bingham who was standing at Fletcher's desk beside a very disgruntled looking Alistair McGhee.

McGhee's face bore a scowl the like of which Fletcher had never seen. She studied his usually lively features intensely. *Talk about being able to curdle milk.* She'd heard his moods could be mercurial and wondered how he had managed to get promoted to a senior rank with an unpredictable temperament. She decided she wouldn't cross him. Not for the first time she wondered if there was any truth in the rumour that he'd slept with Carruthers' ex-wife.

'Said he had to go over to the far side of Castletown, sir. I don't think he'll be long,' she answered Bingham.

'What the hell is he doing over there? He's needed over here with Superintendent McGhee. We're in the middle of a potential terrorist investigation, or doesn't he realise that? What the hell does he think he's doing?'

'What about Superintendent McGhee's men? Thought they were on their way?' asked Fletcher making an attempt to change the subject.

'Been delayed. Going to be another couple of hours. And don't think I don't know what you're doing changing the subject. I admire your loyalty, Andrea, but make sure it's not misplaced.'

'I'll go, sir. I'll go over to the RAF base with Superintendent McGhee. I have nothing that can't wait.'

'In light of Carruthers' absence, you'll have to do. Is that OK with you, Alistair?'

'I'm sure I'll be able to find a use for her. No doubt it will make the men's day. Much better looking than Carruthers. Hopefully a bit more approachable too.'

The last bit he said under his breath to Fletcher, whilst carefully appraising her. Even Bingham looked a little uncomfortable. She knew she was looking good, though, wearing a pair of low cut cream cotton trousers with a slight flare at the ankle, and a figure hugging cherry red sweatshirt. Thankfully she still had a figure to hug, though that wouldn't last long.

'Well, as long as you can handle it, Andrea,' said Bingham.

Fletcher didn't know if he meant the interviews, or McGhee's attitude. 'I can handle it just fine, sir,' said Fletcher looking McGhee straight in the eye with what she hoped was a no-nonsense expression.

She waited for Bingham to walk away. 'More approachable than Carruthers? Why would you think that? Just because I'm female? Doesn't make me any more available to the RAF lads than I am to you.'

'Bite me,' said McGhee looking like he would rather enjoy the experience.

'Only after a full set of inoculations.'

McGhee threw his head back and roared with laughter. The laugh completely transformed his face. Not exactly the response Fletcher was expecting. 'OK, let's go then,' he smiled.

'I'll just get my bag,' said Fletcher standing up. 'I'll meet you at the front door.'

'That's right, mustn't forget your lipstick and tampons,' said McGhee walking away.

So much for the charming man, thought Fletcher. *He's just plain obnoxious.*

She retrieved her bag and met McGhee at the front door. As she was walking out of the building with him she managed to catch her bag on the door handle, spilling personal items onto the floor. McGhee turned round. Both knelt down to pick up her belongings. She tried to stuff a magazine about pregnancy back in the bag before McGhee had a chance to see it, but it was too late. He picked it up and as he did so he looked at the front cover. Silently he gave her the magazine with a conspiratorial wink.

Fletcher swore under her breath.

***

The man's eyes narrowed as he watched Dave Roberts struggle against the ropes that bound him to the chair in the farmhouse cottage. He noted the swollen and closing eye, the blood dripping from a cut on his face.

The man lit a cigarette. Took a drag. Blew the smoke into Roberts' face. Roberts coughed.

'You're about to find out what happens to people who disobey my orders,' he said. 'Ever had a cigarette burn?' he asked the bare-chested Welshman. Held the cigarette about an inch off the younger man's chest then stubbed it out just below his left nipple. He watched Roberts grit his teeth. The smell of burning flesh filled the air.

Dropping the butt to the ground, he lit another. 'I went to a lot of trouble to get that Semtex. And what do you do? Decide to double-cross me by not finishing the job. Why?' He stubbed the second cigarette viciously into the man's chest. The smell grew more pungent. Roberts remained silent but the man was rewarded by seeing beads of sweat on the younger man's forehead. 'What went wrong, Davey boy? Why wasn't Holdaway in his car when it exploded? That was the one job you had to do, apart from set the bomb. Make sure he got to his car on time. What happened? Did you lose your bottle?'

'I couldn't do it. Couldn't go through with it. Couldn't kill someone in cold blood.'

'Interesting. Not strictly true though, is it? You killed Rhys Evans in cold blood.'

As he watched Roberts he curled his lip. The man was a thug. He'd watched the way he'd killed Evans. With an excess of violence. Even malice. He thought about the girlfriend who had come out of the mortuary crying.

With hands tied tightly behind his back Roberts tried to twist in the seat. He jerked so violently the seat toppled over. He must have trapped and broken a couple of his fingers, and his cry of pain filled the air.

'Everything was so carefully planned… until you ruined it.' The man walked around Roberts. 'You really are as thick as horseshit, aren't you?' He kicked Roberts in the stomach. Roberts yelped like a pup. 'Even smiling up at the CCTV as you planted the bomb. They'll be playing that back at the station. You do realise the police have had an artist draw up your likeness. It's even out on fucking telly. Would only have been a matter of time before you got picked up. I bet you would have spilt your guts too. Sang like a canary. Luckily we got to you first. Get him up, boys.' Two men stepped out of the shadows. They walked over and hoisted the chair and its occupant to an upright position. 'Cut him free,' said the older man.

The man saw the look of relief in Robert's face.

'Oh no, not done with you yet,' he said. He turned to his accomplices. 'I want him tied by his hands to that beam. Take his shoes and socks off.'

Roberts started to struggle wildly and screamed in terror.

'You can scream all you fucking like, boy. You're at a farm in the middle of nowhere. Nobody around to hear you.'

As Roberts, sweating heavily, was trussed up to the beam of the farmyard cottage, the man turned away and, picking up his gun, loaded it.

ELEVEN

'Siobhan, the station's taken several calls from the RAF base identifying the man on the stairs as Dave Roberts,' said Carruthers a short while later.

Siobhan nodded. *She looks so fragile,* thought Carruthers. *Fragile but beautiful.* She had her hair in a short ponytail. One dark tendril had escaped and had been tucked behind her right ear. She leant forward to sip her tea and the tendril fell across her face. Carruthers had an overwhelming desire to lean forward and wrap his fingers round it, and gently push it back for her. That would probably be seen as a pass, something he was in no position to make. However, what he felt for Siobhan, he realised, was less about sex and more about wanting to protect her. There was no denying it, though. He was deeply attracted. All the same, he knew he would never cross that line.

'How are you feeling now?' he asked her.

'Empty,' she responded honestly. 'Tell me, have you ever lost someone you loved?' she asked him quietly.

'Yes, I have.' Once more his brother came into his mind.

'Do you ever get over it?'

'I don't think you ever get over it, especially when it's a violent death, or someone you love dies young.' He swallowed the golf ball in his throat. 'You hope to come to terms with it. The pain does fade, but it's always with you.'

Siobhan sighed and Carruthers he knew how to comfort her. She asked him no more questions for which he was grateful. He knew that it wasn't wise to get too emotionally close to a murder victim's girlfriend and he felt instinctively that there was a growing bond between them. He wished he had met her under different circumstances.

'I don't know about you, inspector, but I could do with a proper drink. I know it's a bit early but would you like a glass of wine?'

Carruthers couldn't think of anything he would like more than a glass of wine, except perhaps a glass of wine over a meal, with the rest of the evening spent in the company of Siobhan Mathews. He also knew that was never going to happen.

'Call me Jim, please, and I'm both on duty and driving, so I'll have to say no, but thanks.'

'Tomoko's got some really good Japanese beer in the fridge,' Siobhan persisted. 'Sorry, I don't mean to be pushy, but I just thought you looked like you could use a drink, too. She wouldn't mind.'

The last thing he needed was a conviction for drink driving. It just wasn't worth the risk. 'No, I'd better have a soft drink. Have you got a coke?' He had already crossed the line coming over without another officer being present. *Damn Fletcher for being right. Bless her too.*

He studied her form as she walked to the fridge. She was wearing a green shift dress over blue jeans, with a long blue-green beaded necklace. He was reminded of the similarity between her and his former wife, both slight of form, both dark haired and green eyed. However, his wife's taste in clothes was very different.

'So, tell me everything you can about Dave Roberts,' said Carruthers, when Siobhan had come back from the fridge. He'd taken a seat on the sofa at the far end of the one room that comprised the flat's communal area. 'Your impressions of him; what sort of man he is; how he interacts with other people.' He had refused a glass, and brought the can of coke to his lips, never once losing eye contact with Siobhan.

'I didn't like him.'

Carruthers took a swig, put the can down. 'Go on.'

'I know this sounds awful but as I got to know him I realised he wasn't particularly intelligent, and I couldn't stomach a lot of his views.'

'What sort of views?'

'He was a racist, pure and simple, always going on about blacks and pakis and how they should be sent back to their own countries. I have black friends myself and to be honest I found his views really pretty repulsive. Christ, and don't even get him started on Muslims. I got the feeling he didn't like anyone very much.'

'Did you ever hear him talk about Welsh nationalism?' Carruthers found himself holding his breath.

'Well, he made a few jokes about driving the English out of Wales but that's what I thought they were. Just jokes. It was hard to tell with him, though. When he was joking, I mean, and when he was being serious.'

'Did Rhys ever show any pro-nationalist feelings?'

Siobhan spoke slowly whilst she thought about it. 'I think Rhys was sympathetic to the concerns about the English buying second homes, and effectively pushing Welsh people out of the housing market, but he wasn't a nationalist. As he was adopted and didn't know who his birth parents were, I think he realised that for all he knew they could be English.'

Carruthers put his can down and leant forward. 'Wait. Rhys was adopted? Why didn't you tell me this before?'

'I didn't think it was relevant. Anyway, I had other things on my mind.'

Carruthers felt chastised. 'Yes, of course. Sorry. Wasn't thinking. Did Dave know Rhys was adopted?' Carruthers was trying to work out what, if any relevance, this may have to the case.

'Yes, I'm sure he did. Communities are close-knit in Wales, even in a city like Cardiff and they knew each other from schooldays. Rhys wasn't so much adopted as abandoned on a doorstep of the couple who eventually took him in.'

'That's very unusual.'

Siobhan looked at him.

'Unusual being taken in and adopted by the people who found him, I mean. Tell me more about his being abandoned.'

'It caused quite a scandal at the time, even in the 1990s. It got into the local papers. Well, I guess it would, wouldn't it? Baby abandoned on doorstep makes for a good news headline. The middle-aged couple that took him in gave him their name. The Evanses both died in a car crash six months ago. They were devoted parents according to Rhys. It was very sad.'

Carruthers was trying to take in all this information. 'It was a big undertaking on their part. Any idea who his birth mother and father were?' he finally asked.

Siobhan shook her head. 'His birth mother was young. That's all Rhys knew. He was trying to find her. He'd decided to try to trace his birth parents. I got the feeling last time I spoke to him he'd made some sort of breakthrough.'

'In what way?'

She smiled sadly. 'I don't know. He never got the chance to tell me. But I know he was on his way to see me with some information he'd found out in the last couple of days. He said something about bringing a folder. Any chance I could get that back?'

'There's been no folder found yet but we'll keep you posted.' Carruthers took another sip of his coke. 'What was the relationship like between Rhys and Dave? They'd obviously known each other a long time. Were they friends?'

'I was thinking about this earlier, about their relationship, and to tell you the truth I think Rhys was afraid of Dave. I think back in Cardiff Rhys tried to distance himself from Dave. From what Rhys told me, Dave was always in and out of trouble, although he never gave me any specific details. Back home he had some pretty unsavoury friends, had got in with a bad crowd. I don't think he had a criminal record or anything, but Rhys' view was that if Dave hadn't joined the RAF, then he really might have gone off the rails. I got the feeling recently Rhys was trying to avoid Dave. Given Dave's extreme views and the fact Rhys knew that I didn't like him, I'm not surprised. Rhys was more intelligent, quick to learn, eager to get on. Dave, on the other hand, could be aggressive. He was a bully and had a cruel streak.'

'Did you ever see him get aggressive?' asked Carruthers thoughtfully.

'Yes, when he'd had a drink,' responded Siobhan. 'Although come to think of it he could be aggressive even without a drink.'

'It doesn't sound as if Dave Roberts is a very nice person. Did he have any redeeming qualities?'

'Well, I suppose he could be quite entertaining when he wasn't too full of drink.'

'In what way?'

'He was a good mimic. Very good with accents.'

There was a silence, whilst Carruthers digested this latest piece of news. 'Did you ever hear him doing an English accent?'

'As a matter of fact, I did. Just the once. A Scouse accent.'

'Two more questions. Do you think Dave Roberts is capable of being involved with a terrorist organisation?'

'I've asked myself the same question. I don't want to believe it, but how well do we ever know someone? I suppose it's possible, yes. He did seem full of hate a lot of the time. Was he so full of hate he'd go to those extremes? I just don't know. I could understand him joining a far-right organisation, like the BNP, but the Welsh nationalists?' she shrugged. 'However, like I said, how well do you ever know someone?'

'Final question, Siobhan. Is it possible that if Dave Roberts was a member of a terrorist organisation, Rhys found out and Dave killed him?'

Siobhan spoke slowly. There were tears in her eyes. 'If you are asking me do I think Roberts could be capable of murder, then the answer is, yes. I think he was pretty much capable of anything.'

***

'Look, I don't think we got off to the best of starts,' said Fletcher, thinking that despite her growing dislike of McGhee, she'd better make an effort, if they were to work together. She held the keys tight in her hand whilst they walked to one of the pool cars. She was prepared to make an effort, but she didn't want him in her

Beetle. She unlocked the door and climbed into the driver's seat. McGhee followed suit, climbing into the passenger seat. She started the ignition.

'Don't you?' McGhee turned to her as he put his seatbelt on, a smile playing on his lips. He looked amused, and as she looked up at him, she could see the challenge in his eyes, as he tilted his head coquettishly to one side.

My, but he's a player, and a dangerous one at that. He held her with his gaze. She was the first to look away. Regretting it, she looked back at him almost immediately, assessing what Carruthers' ex-wife might have seen in him. His eyelashes were long and dark, his brows almost black, making his eyes even more arresting. She had never seen eyes that colour. They were of the most unusual light brown. She had to admit that she could see why some women would find him attractive. She started the engine up and pulled out of the station car park.

'How pregnant are you?' he asked.

'I don't think that's any of your business,' she said.

'Do Carruthers and Bingham know?'

She stayed silent.

'I take it that's a no. You'll have to tell them. How do you get on with Carruthers?' he asked.

'He's a good boss. We get on well.'

'How well?' asked McGhee, the playfulness back in his eyes, his gaze lingering on her still slim belly.

'Not that well,' she said starchily.

'Is this your first big case?' said McGhee.

'We're a bit of a backwater out here,' said Fletcher, steeling herself to be professional and grateful to be moving the subject on. 'Our usual problems involve drink-related disturbances involving the usual suspects.'

McGhee raised his eyebrows.

'Mostly locals and students, locals and RAF, or students and RAF. Well, if you're talking about Castletown. Fridays and Saturday nights are the worst.'

McGhee smiled.

'We also get our fair share of drug related problems here in Fife,' she continued. 'We had a spate of break-ins a few months back. Related to drugs. Also had three drug-related deaths linked to a tampered batch of heroin. Very sad. Of course, like anywhere, we get the occasional murder.'

'So you've worked on a murder case before? I hear you're working on a suspicious death at the moment.'

'Yes we are. Jim thinks the case is related to the car bomb, although Bingham disagrees.'

'Jim? On first name terms, eh?'

Fletcher willed herself not to redden but remained silent.

'What do you think?' said McGhee.

'I don't believe in coincidences, so I agree with Jim. I just haven't worked out what the connection is yet. Seems too much of a coincidence that the airman killed was Welsh.'

'I agree.'

'What do you think's going on? Do you think it's a terrorist attack?' asked Fletcher.

'Whoever's behind this is clearly not targeting the Scottish population as a whole. Why would they? On the other hand, though, if they have linked up with a group of Scottish extremists, it could get messy. My personal view? I think Holdaway's been targeted by Williams and his associates for the sole reason of payback for the shooting of Williams' sister,' said McGhee. 'His motive is personal. As such, it's more than likely a one off. Hopefully Williams hasn't hooked up with any other militant groups.'

'Why have Bryn Glas 1402 claimed responsibility then? Why didn't Williams just operate on his own? It would be much easier. Surely the more people involved, the more can go wrong,' said Fletcher.

McGhee shrugged. 'Perhaps Williams couldn't operate on his own. He may have needed help.'

'So you don't think Williams has linked up with the Real IRA or another faction? Bit more likely than linking up with the Scots, isn't it?'

'No,' said McGhee. 'There's been no chatter over the internet about Bryn Glas 1402 linking up with any other terror group. You really are like a terrier, aren't you? Get your teeth into something and you don't let go. I'll admit previously if the Welsh thought their cause could be furthered by hooking up with the Irish, they wouldn't hesitate. But this was back in the 60s.'

'Tell me what happened?'

'There was evidence to strongly suggest the Free Wales Army, another terrorist outfit, acquired a consignment of old IRA weapons. We're not sure if they bought them or were given them. A cache of weapons was discovered on a coastal path in Pembrokeshire in the 1980s, reasonably close to Fishguard.'

'Fishguard? That would be significant because it's the port at which the Irish ferries dock?' Fletcher spoke slowly, working things out in her head as she said them.

'Yes, exactly,' he said. 'Like I said that discovery was a long time ago now. The chances of both the Irish and Welsh extremists linking up to plant a car bomb in Scotland are very unlikely. Don't you worry your pretty head.'

Fletcher clenched her jaw as he continued speaking.

'We haven't received any information to alert us to a possible alliance between two of those groups.'

'Well, have you received any information on how Bryn Glas 1402 managed to get their hands on Semtex? That was the preferred choice of explosive of the IRA, was it not?' said Fletcher. 'Ewan Williams must have tapped his old colleagues in the IRA. Perhaps they owed him for all the party funds he'd given them over the years. So there must be some link between Williams and the IRA.'

'I don't need you to tell me now to do my job.' McGhee suddenly looked furious. 'What I've forgotten about the complexities of terrorism is more than you'll ever know.'

'I didn't mean to imply–' the ring of McGhee's mobile cut the rest of her sentence off.

'We're on our way.' McGhee's face was set as he stared straight ahead, studiously looking at the road. Studiously not looking at her. She had fallen out of favour it seemed. She was starting to wish she'd never made herself available for the trip to the RAF base.

***

SATURDAY EVENING, 2ND JUNE

Carruthers was still digesting the conversation he'd had with Siobhan Mathews as he made his way back to the station. He arrived some twenty minutes later and parked up.

'Where the hell have you been, Carruthers?' asked a red-faced Bingham. 'You don't get paid to go walkabout. You were needed over here with Alistair McGhee. I had to send DS Fletcher. I'm seriously disappointed in you. You seem to want to thwart me at every turn.'

Carruthers ignored the comment. 'Is Fletcher alright?' he asked.

'Of course she is. Why wouldn't she be? Unless you're talking about her pregnancy. McGhee told me. Accidentally, I might add. I take it you knew?'

'She told me yesterday. And with all due respect, sir, it wasn't McGhee's place to say anything, accidentally or otherwise.'

'You're right. It wasn't McGhee's place to tell me. It was yours.'

'I don't agree. It was Fletcher's place to tell you.'

'I don't appreciate finding out information like that from someone outside the station.'

'Like I said, she only told me yesterday. In confidence,' answered Carruthers. Trust McGhee to have found out and told the superintendent before Carruthers had had the chance. Instinctively he knew that if Fletcher had told McGhee it would probably have been to halt his advances.

'Bloody inconvenient. She's a good copper,' said Bingham.

'And will remain so,' replied Carruthers.

'Hmm. We've got more important things to worry about than Andie Fletcher being in the family way. We need to find Dave Roberts and fast. The RAF Police are on to it as well of course. I've had a tricky time of it I can tell you, smoothing the way for McGhee's lot. The RAF want to investigate Roberts' disappearance and Evans' death themselves. They've been insisting on taking the lead. It's not their call, though. Any death outside the military base, even of military personnel, is the responsibility of civilian police. Now there's a possible connection with bombers of course, it's a no-brainer. It's now become part of a bigger investigation. They've been forced to understand the need to bring in more expert advice.'

Carruthers bunched his hands into fists but kept his face neutral.

'Anyway, back to Dave Roberts,' said Bingham. 'They're pretty sure the description matches him. Apparently, speaking with his colleagues, he's pretty good with accents. This better turn out to be innocent. The alternative doesn't bear thinking about, that an extremist organisation has infiltrated one of Britain's armed forces. What have you been doing anyway, Carruthers? It had better be connected to the case.'

'I was interviewing Siobhan Mathews, sir. Not only was she our dead man's girlfriend, but her boyfriend knew Dave Roberts way before they joined the RAF. They were at school together. She was able to give me quite a profile on Roberts. It doesn't make for pleasant reading. If you've got time I'll fill you in.'

'You still think the two are linked then? This Evans' boy's death and the explosion?' said Bingham.

'Well sir, Dave Roberts seems to be the missing link in both cases. He's been placed over by the university in suspicious circumstances, just before the bomb was detonated. There is also the matter of his lying to Mathews about informing the police of Evans' disappearance shortly before he went AWOL. Why would he lie to her? Apart from the fact he fits the description, his extremist views have been mentioned both by Mathews and at the base. We now know he's good with accents. Mathews told me the same thing. It all fits.'

'The boy's got no links to Bryn Glas, though,' said Bingham.

'Not that we've found,' said Carruthers. 'Yet.'

'We're having a station meeting here at eight tomorrow morning,' said Bingham. 'Pity Holdaway went into hiding. We would've had vital information we needed at least forty-eight hours earlier. Go home and get something to eat, man. You look done in.'

***

As he left the station the sun was beginning to set. The sky was a fragile bird's egg blue broken up by diagonal lines of white and grey clouds. The huge orange sun cast its warm glow as it dipped across the fields.

It wasn't long before Carruthers was settled down with an Indian takeaway and a bottle of Caledonian IPA in front of the TV. Although not lavishly decorated, his cottage had a nice homely feel to it. He had a good-sized living room with a wood burning stove as the focal point. The ceilings were sloping, and the décor was understated. He had painted the walls cream, which gave the room a light open feel. His one comfy brown leather armchair, in which he relaxed to eat his dinner off his lap, was old and a little shabby, but still serviceable. Sometimes that's how he felt, despite not yet having turned forty. Old and a little shabby.

He finished his meal. He knew he should be running a bath and getting an early night, but, despite his tiredness, he was too wired. He decided to go for a walk and get some air. He grabbed his house keys and locked up his cottage. He loved the fact he was so close to the sea. And being just nine miles from Castletown, Anstruther or Ainster as locals called it, wasn't too far from work. This evening tourists and locals alike were strolling along the cobbled harbour front. There was a smell of salt sea air and the lingering aroma of fish and chips.

This charming fishing village, fronted by its attractive harbour already felt like home. He'd read that in its heyday it had been one of the busiest fishing ports in the East Neuk of Fife. He knew it was also a mecca for tourists, due to its being on the Fife Coastal Path, and he was already looking forward to walking along the coast when he had a bit more time.

James II of Scotland had once famously described The East Neuk as a fringe of gold on a beggar's mantle. Carruthers loved that description.

He settled himself on one of the benches overlooking the harbour. To the west, the sunset was full of colour. Red, orange and purple streaked the sky, beautiful to look at but as ever, short lived. The colours were already fading. He smiled suddenly but the smile was tinged with sadness. Mairi had loved sunsets. He supposed that she still did. She had always said that a sunset was best appreciated when watched with somebody else. He wondered if, somewhere, she too was watching this sunset, and, although he knew he was being uncharitable, hoped that she was on her own. He wasn't ready for her to be happy with somebody else. Not yet.

He watched the first stars twinkle. He thought about his previous life with Mairi in London. It was as if it was already another lifetime. He looked up at the sky again. The air was so clear here, he thought. It was almost as if someone had thrown the stars randomly into the sky. He remembered Fletcher telling him how she'd once seen the Northern Lights over Castletown.

Later, when the light had finally faded, he settled back in the bath with *Casino Royale* in one hand, and a beer in the other. Strains of Neil Young's 'Old Man' filtered through the open door from the CD player in the living room. He jolted as he started to fall asleep in the bath.

TWELVE

SUNDAY MORNING, 3rd JUNE

'We've heard back from the Forensics Explosives Lab. They've established that the bomb was on a timer,' said McGhee in the morning briefing. What have you got for us, Jim?'

Carruthers hated McGhee calling him by his first name but let it slide. 'Still no sighting of Dave Roberts,' he said. 'He may have left Scotland, so we're linking up with other forces, including South Wales Police. His room's been searched by the RAF Police. Nothing found linking him to Welsh extremists. However, a large amount of racist material has been discovered. No surprise considering what we now know about him. Harris is currently running a check with the SID to see if he's an active member of the BNP, or some similar organisation. The RAF are conducting their own interviews of his closest colleagues.' Carruthers wondered what the Scottish Intelligence Database would turn up, if anything.

'This may be a long shot,' said Superintendent Bingham, 'but is there any known connection between members of British far right extremist groups and members of Nationalist groups in the UK or Ireland, Alistair? If there is a strong connection somewhere, perhaps we'll have found the link to Roberts. It's currently proving elusive.'

McGhee faced Superintendent Bingham in response to his question.

'That's a good question,' he said. 'Well, as I've said before, certain nationalist groups, most notably Cymru 1400 in Wales, have previously stated their willingness to cooperate with any source to gain their ends. Presumably that would include the far right. Naturally though, there's a stronger link between the Scots, Irish and Welsh, rather than the BNP. One of the Welsh splinter groups has got a link to the BNP on their website, although when questioned, they denied they were anti-English or anti-black. Also, certain high profile figures in British far right groups, such as Mark Dobson have expressed their admiration for Welsh nationalist groups, such as the Sons of Glendower.'

'Interesting, so a connection is feasible,' said Bingham.

'Well of course the BNP has now morphed into Britain First, which is the fastest growing right wing organisation in the United Kingdom.'

'What do you think of the possibility that Bryn Glas 1402 could have linked up with the Irish, rather than the Scots?' asked Fletcher.

McGhee scowled at Fletcher. 'We've already had this conversation. I told you it was extremely unlikely, even given what we now know. The IRA has embraced the peace process. It would no longer be in their interest. As for the Real IRA, like I said in my previous meeting, there's been no intelligence to suggest an alliance between those two groups.'

'Yes, but surely it's still worth pursuing,' said Fletcher, 'given the fact that Holdaway served over in Northern Ireland. Not only that, he shot the sister of the leader of Bryn Glas. Then there's the Semtex. We still don't know where or who Ewan Williams got it from.'

'We're working on it,' said McGhee. 'To put your mind at rest, Andie, we're not ruling out a possible link between Bryn Glas 1402 and the Real IRA for that very reason. But leave it to the experts, eh?'

Duly chastised, for once Fletcher fell silent.

'What explosives have the Welsh previously used?' asked Carruthers. McGhee's shortening of Fletcher's name had not escaped him. He realised he didn't like it. Didn't want the man to be overfamiliar with his team. Or him.

'Mostly industrial explosives from the many quarries or coal mines that were still active at the time,' said McGhee. 'Others are believed to have made do with the enriched fertiliser type used by the Provisional IRA in their early days.'

'Jim, I want you and Andrea to go over to the RAF base,' said Bingham. He turned to the rest of the team. 'The meeting between Alistair and senior RAF Personnel was most fruitful.' Looking directly at Carruthers he then said, 'it's impressive the results you can get when you go through the right channels. Procurator Fiscal's also been very helpful. Pity you weren't there. I've got permission from Group Captain Philips for you to conduct your own search of Roberts' room.'

Carruthers nodded, ignoring Bingham's swipe.

'The RAF understand the importance of our teams working together, with us taking the lead, thanks to Alistair,' continued Bingham. 'The military police were ordered to leave his room exactly as they found it. You may not turn up anything new, but who knows. Given the seriousness of the situation, it's worth a look.'

'Can we take a look at Evans' room as well, sir?' said Fletcher, finding her voice again. Carruthers nodded his agreement.

'No point. I already asked. The room is bare. Personal effects already gone back to his family.'

What family? thought Carruthers.

Carruthers watched Fletcher frown. 'Why would they have done that?' she said. 'They know we're conducting what could be a murder investigation.'

'I'm not happy about it either, Andrea. Group Captain Philips is making enquiries and getting back to me. Looks like the room may have been cleaned due to a misunderstanding. Philips said he gave strict instructions for it to be left untouched, whilst the investigation's still on-going.'

***

'What are we looking for, boss?' asked Fletcher a couple of hours later, after they had been shown into Dave Roberts' room at RAF Edenside. Carruthers watched her put on a pair of latex gloves. He'd already put on his own.

'I'm not sure,' said Carruthers, wrestling with the coat hangers in the tightly packed wardrobe. 'Hoping I'll know when I find it. Anything out of the ordinary. Something that doesn't fit.'

He stepped back, took a look round Roberts' room. It was small and untidy, devoid of anything personal. There were no photos up on the desk, no pictures on the walls. There was, however, a faint odour of old trainers and stale sweat. He knelt to look under the bed.

'Do you think we'll really find anything contentious that's not already been found by the RAF Police?' asked Fletcher wrinkling up her nose.

'It may be something quite innocuous. Something overlooked by the RAF Police. Don't expect to find anything really obvious. After all, if he is a member of a far right or terrorist organisation, I doubt even he would be stupid enough to leave details of his membership lying around.'

'What's the position of RAF Personnel being members of the BNP, Jim? I know membership's banned in the police and prison services.'

'My understanding is that whilst not explicitly banned, they are barred from political activity or demonstration.'

'So I'm assuming political activity would also include active recruitment of others?'

'I would say so, yes,' said Carruthers.

'I don't get the link, though.'

'What link?' said Carruthers looking up from his place on the floor. He had seen nothing but a pair of smelly trainers and a used condom. He could think of better ways of spending his Sunday.

'The link between the RAF, the BNP and Bryn Glas 1402.'

'That's why we're here Andie, to find it.' He sat back on his knees. 'Now are you going to help or am I going to be doing it on my own? You start by going through the books and magazines. I'll look through his desk drawers and wardrobe.'

'Oh goody, *Air Craft Monthly*. Just what I've always wanted to read,' said Fletcher with a grin. Carruthers had already caught sight of a pile of aircraft magazines stacked up in a bookcase. His eyes flitted over the titles of some of the books on the shelf. Most of them, like the magazines, were about aircraft. No surprise there.

He looked over at her and frowned. 'Don't just stare at them, Andie. Start thumbing through. We don't want to be here all day.'

'Sorry boss,' said Fletcher, selecting a hard-backed book on the Tornado F1. They worked in silence, Fletcher having thumbed through half a dozen books, until she picked up a copy of *Men's Health*.

'You know Mark reads *Men's Health*. I can never see what the fascination is. Every issue's pretty much identical. There's always an article on how to lose your belly and how to have better sex.'

Carruthers laughed. As she thumbed through, Carruthers noticed something falling from the pages to the floor. It was a photograph. Fletcher picked it up. He saw from the look on her face it was something important.

'Oh shit,' she said. 'I think you should take a look at this.' He took the photo she handed him with a frown. Studied it. His eyes widened in shock, then narrowed into a steely glint. His frown deepened and his mouth became grim set.

'Christ,' he said. 'This could change everything.'

'I know,' Fletcher answered.

The photograph was of two people kissing each other passionately. The girl was standing in her blouse and panties, with her blouse unbuttoned. She wasn't wearing a bra. Her arms were wrapped around the man's neck. She was standing on tiptoe to reach him. The man's hands were possessively cupping the girl's bottom. From the intimate nature of the photo and the lack of self-consciousness of the two people, Carruthers hazarded a guess that they had put the camera on to self-timer. There was no mistaking that they were in this very room. And there was certainly no mistaking the two people in the photograph. Dave Roberts and Siobhan Mathews.

'Mathews lied to us,' said Fletcher.

Carruthers got up from the crouching position. 'Yes, she did. At least about how well she knows Dave Roberts. Clearly they've slept together at some point. No mistaking that. But the question is, when was the photograph taken, and why did she feel it necessary to lie?'

'She didn't want to appear to be cheap?' said Fletcher. 'You know this gives Roberts a motive for Evans' murder. Jealousy.'

'Yes, but it also means Mathews may be more involved in her own boyfriend's death than we first thought.'

'In what way?'

'I don't know, Andie, but it now makes Siobhan Mathews a suspect. We need to invite her in for questioning. She's lied to us. She's has had a sexual relationship with a suspect wanted in connection to a possible murder and a car bomb attack. It also begs the question that if she's lied about how well she knows Dave Roberts, what else has she lied about? Get on your mobile. Ring the station. Get them to run a check on Mathews. Let's get her brought in. She may not be the innocent student we all took her to be.'

'Perhaps they were in it together, sir. Maybe they planned Evans' murder together.'

'Yes, but what was their motive? And does that mean Mathews is connected to the explosion?' Carruthers was staring at the photograph. He was frowning. 'Andie,' he said, 'take another look at this photo.' He handed it to her. 'What do you see in the background?'

'Not much. Too many bodies in the way. A book shelf, books, poster above the bed.'

'Exactly. Take a closer look at the poster. What does it say?'

'Really hard to make it out.' She pulled the photo closer, twisting it to give the best light. 'The lettering is rather small for a poster. I can see a few letters and numbers. There's an R and an

N and the numbers 40. Looks like the first number or numbers are obscured.'

'Could it be 1402? As in Bryn Glas 1402?'

'Shit. Maybe.'

Carruthers slipped the photo carefully into an evidence bag he unearthed from his trouser pocket and tucked it into his jacket pocket. He then took Fletcher by the arm. 'Come on. Let's get out of here.'

'Are we going straight back, sir?'

'No. Change of plan. We're going to Edgecliffe. I want to bring Mathews in myself.'

****

Twenty minutes later they were at 56 Edgecliffe. They pressed the doorbell but there was no answer. Carruthers looked up towards the window of the living room, but it was in darkness. He phoned Siobhan on the mobile number she had given him, but it just went to voicemail. He didn't leave a message.

'Let's get back to the station,' he said. 'We'll pick up some sandwiches on the way.'

'I know a really good new deli opened up just off Market Street,' said Fletcher. 'They do Panini's as well as baguettes. Why don't we swing round there? We could park up and eat them in the car.'

***

'I'd better warn you that the whole station probably knows about your pregnancy. McGhee told Bingham. Bingham wanted to know why I hadn't said anything,' said Carruthers taking his Panini out of its wrapping. They were sitting in the car still in Market Street. It was more private than back at the station. 'I'm surprised you said anything to McGhee,' he said.

Fletcher sighed. 'First, I hope you told Bingham it's still early days. And secondly, I didn't tell him. To be fair, it's more what I didn't say.' She daintily wiped a spot of avocado from the corner of her mouth. 'My shoulder bag spilled open. He picked up a magazine on pregnancy that had fallen out. Put two and two together. I didn't deny it. Can't believe he told Bingham though. What a creep.'

'You OK about the news coming out like that?'

Fletcher grimaced. 'I'm going to have to be.' She sighed again. 'Keeping the news to myself for much longer would have been a strain anyway. I'm almost glad it's out there now.'

Carruthers wondered how she'd cope if she decided on a termination now the whole station probably knew about her pregnancy. It was a question he wasn't going to ask. There was silence as they both ate.

'This is really good,' she said, looking at the rest of her chorizo, avocado and salad Panini. 'I would never have thought of putting chorizo with avocado but it works. How's yours?'

'Better washed down with a pint of Dark Island,' Carruthers responded, referring to the real beer from Orkney he liked so much. He loved both the real beer and whisky from the islands. Thought about how much Talisker he had left. His mind went back to Fletcher. He wondered if changing the subject had been deliberate. 'No, it's pretty good,' he said, wolfing the rest of his chicken and prosciutto baguette. 'I wish you'd told me about the pregnancy sooner though.'

'It's still early days, Jim. I wanted to, but I didn't know the best way of telling you, then we found ourselves in the middle of a murder investigation. It never seemed like the right time. And if I'm completely honest I wanted to make a decision first about whether I'm going to keep the baby. I'm not sure I feel ready to become a mother. I don't know what I'm going to do so—'

'Have you had a proper talk with Mark?'

Fletcher shook her head. 'We keep missing each other.'

Missing each other, thought Carruthers. *Or avoiding each other? Not my place to ask.* 'You're going to have to make some pretty tough decisions.'

'I know. But the fact is that if I don't think about it I can almost pretend it's not happening.'

'That won't work for long. And certainly not now it's getting round the station.'

'I know. And I will sit down and have a good talk with Mark. I just need a bit more thinking time. I don't feel ready to make a decision yet.'

'How did your visit to the RAF base with McGhee go?' asked Carruthers, feeling a little awkward and deliberately switching subjects.

'You mean did McGhee try anything on? I'm sure he would have done if he hadn't found out I'm pregnant. I think he was a bit disappointed he wouldn't get the chance.'

'Just watch him. I wouldn't put it past him to still try it on.'

Fletcher looked up, eyes wide.

'Think about it,' said Carruthers. 'It's the one time he's guaranteed not to get a woman pregnant.'

'Hadn't thought of that. But don't worry, I've got his card marked.'

'Good, but actually that wasn't what I meant. Did you discover anything?'

'Unfortunately, the visit didn't really turn up anything new. Either that, or the RAF are closing ranks. Anyway,' said Fletcher scrunching up her paper bag, 'I guess we'd better be making tracks.'

***

As they walked into the station they were aware of a very noticeable sense of heightened activity.

'DCI Carruthers!'

Carruthers turned to the desk sergeant. 'What's going on?' He needed a pee so he hoped the sergeant wouldn't keep him long.

'Body's been found. Male. Pinetum Park Forest. Looks like he's been shot.' said Brown. 'That's all I know. Call's just come through. You're wanted by the Super. Good timing you getting back when you did. He'd just asked me to phone you.'

Carruthers changed direction and strode towards Superintendent Bingham's Office. His bladder would have to wait.

THIRTEEN

SUNDAY AFTERNOON, 3ʳᴰ JUNE

Carruthers put his ear to the door and heard voices from within Bingham's office. Hesitated a moment then knocked twice and entered. McGhee was with Bingham. They were standing close together, talking in murmurs. Both fell silent and looked up when Carruthers entered.

'Take it you've heard?' said Bingham.

'That a man's been shot?' said Carruthers. 'Yes. Do we know who it is?'

'Not yet. I want you to go straight over to Pinetum Park Forest. Take Fletcher with you. SOCOs have been sent for. We also need a statement taken from the woman who found the body. Anything on just now?'

'I'm inviting Siobhan Mathews in for questioning. Found out she's had a sexual relationship with Dave Roberts. We've also found possible evidence to connect Roberts to Bryn Glas 1402. A poster on his wall.'

'Christ. OK. Keep me informed.'

'Jim,' said Superintendent McGhee catching Carruthers up as they left Bingham's office. 'Can I have a word?'

'What is it?' said Carruthers still walking.

'I haven't had a chance to say this. I'm sorry to hear about you and Mairi.'

'No, you're not,' responded Carruthers, glancing at McGhee contemptuously.

'I never slept with her, you know,' said McGhee.

Carruthers didn't stop walking but said over his shoulder, 'No, but you wanted to.'

'Well, of course I did. She's an attractive woman. I must admit I never did work out what she saw in you,' answered McGhee.

Carruthers stopped and turned to face McGhee. He took in a deep breath. Held it. Started counting to ten in his head. His former wife was his one weakness, his Achilles heel. He couldn't bear anyone talking about her.

'I admit,' said McGhee, 'I tried it on. Couldn't help myself. Call it a defective gene.'

Carruthers gritted his teeth. Bunched his fists until he could feel the nails dig into the flesh of his hands.

'But we both know,' McGhee said, lowering his voice, 'I could have had her any time I wanted.'

Carruthers saw red. His right fist shot out catching McGhee squarely on the nose. Blood spurted. Pain exploded in his hand. McGhee cried, swore. Lashed out at Carruthers, catching him with a right hook to his left eye. Carruthers staggered back from the force of the punch, the corner of his eye already bleeding, caught by McGhee's signet ring. McGhee launched himself at Carruthers and pinned him back against the wall, holding him by the throat.

'For fuck's sake,' said McGhee, nursing his nose with one hand and holding Carruthers against the wall with the other. 'Nothing happened. I already told you that.'

For all that he was the shorter man, McGhee was incredibly strong. Naturally stocky and full of muscle and coming from the tough east end of Glasgow, he had the advantage over Carruthers.

The skirmish had brought Bingham out of his office at the same time as Brown and Fletcher came running round the corner to find out what the commotion was.

'Right, you two,' roared Bingham. 'What in God's name's going on? McGhee, take your hand off Carruthers' throat this instant. That's an order.'

McGhee increased his grip round Carruthers' throat. Pinned back, Carruthers was still struggling for release. He also started to make some alarming choking noises.

'Jesus,' said McGhee, 'just move on, you loser. You lost her. Deal with it.' Without releasing his hold on Carruthers' throat he said, 'I could report you for this. From what I hear you're not exactly flavour of the month right now, are you?'

Bingham motioned to Brown, then the two men pulled Carruthers and McGhee apart. Bingham held on to Carruthers, Brown onto McGhee.

Carruthers looked down at his bleeding knuckles. 'That wasn't for Mairi. That was for me. You manipulative fuck. And keep away from Fletcher.'

'Christ, you're not setting yourself up as a champion of women's causes are you? Or is it that you fancy Andie yourself? What am I supposed to have done to her, anyway?' said McGhee struggling against Brown. Carruthers was also struggling to be free of Bingham.

'That's enough,' roared Bingham.

'Oh, just leave it,' said Carruthers thinking it was pointless telling McGhee he should have kept his mouth shut about Fletcher's pregnancy.

'We've still got to work together,' said McGhee sounding aggrieved, nursing his nose with some Kleenex he'd found in his trouser pocket. 'Jesus, I'm bleeding all over my shirt.'

'I don't know where it came from, to be honest.' Carruthers offered an insincere smile. 'Call it a defective gene.'

McGhee scowled. Carruthers, who suddenly seemed to be aware of Bingham for the first time now that the red mist had evaporated, put up a hand as if in apology. He hastily tucked his shirt back into his trousers.

'Both of you. My office,' said Bingham, 'NOW!'

As soon as Bingham had marched both men into his office he shut the door and turned on them.

'Do you two mind telling me what the hell is going on here?' said Bingham. 'I will not have two officers fighting in my station. Start talking. Now!'

McGhee shrugged. 'It was nothing,' he said.

'It didn't look like nothing to me,' said Bingham. 'There is not to be a repeat of this. Do you hear me? Do you, superintendent?'

'There won't be, sir,' said McGhee.

'OK, dismissed. I want a word with Carruthers. Don't think this matter is finished with, Alistair. You may be a senior officer but this is still my station. I will not have thuggish schoolboy nonsense here.'

Bingham closed the office door after McGhee, and turned on Carruthers. 'Right, what have you got to say for yourself?'

Carruthers was silent.

'OK, I'll make this very clear for you, shall I?' said Bingham. 'When this case is over I want you to take some leave while I decide whether or not you have a future here. It's clear you have some unresolved personal issues, Carruthers, but I won't have one of my officers behave like you did today. If this happens again, you're out. Got it?'

'Yes, sir.'

'Dismissed.'

Carruthers nodded shamefaced.

'And Carruthers, before you leave the building, change your shirt, dammit.'

***

'Don't say anything,' said Carruthers as they left the building. He could feel his eye starting to close. He gently probed the tender area of throat where McGhee's hand had been.

'I wasn't going to,' said Fletcher. 'But… what on earth were you thinking?'

'I wasn't.'

'Well, that much is obvious.' Fletcher sighed. 'What are you going to do about that eye? It looks really bad. The cut's still bleeding. And the bruising's already coming out. I think you should go to hospital, get it stitched.'

'No time. We've got a corpse to check out, remember?'

'Well, at least let me look at it for you. Come over to my car. I have my first aid stuff in the boot. Anyway, I could use the practice.'

Fletcher wrenched open the boot of her Beetle. Whilst Carruthers stood there feeling foolish she took out the first aid box and brought out butterfly stitches and a clean cloth.

'What did Bingham say?' said Fletcher.

'Gave me a warning. Look, do you mind if we take two cars? I need some thinking time.'

What he actually wanted was to sit in brooding silence. Think over Bingham's words about whether he had a future at the station.

Fletcher gave him a momentary hard stare then shrugged. 'OK. Fine.'

Was it fine? thought Carruthers. Or was it the sort of *fine* women say when things are anything but? He had no idea.

Once Fletcher had wiped the wound and applied butterfly stitches, they took two cars and drove the short distance to Pinetum Park Forest. They parked up by the edge of the forest, where a uniformed officer directed them. Carruthers noticed the wind was picking up. Blackbirds chatted noisily to each other. Ears of green wheat swayed in the wind, changing colour swiftly as the sun danced over the fields.

'Do you know much about this area?' asked Carruthers, breathing in the sweet scent of pine.

'I haven't been in the forest since I was a child. It's a popular nature reserve. Great for bird watching. We used to come up here for family holidays,' Fletcher admitted, coming across to him from her car carrying overalls, latex gloves, face masks and paper shoes.

'Come on. We'd better rescue the poor dog walker,' he said.

Carruthers led the way. As they approached the crime scene, they saw the woman with her dog. She moved from side to side, full of nervous energy, but knowing she couldn't go anywhere. Her breathing was juddery, and the hand not on the dog lead shuddered as she fiddled with her headscarf. She appeared to be in her late forties. The dog, a Labrador, sat quietly by her side, but came to swift attention as the officers arrived.

'Have you touched anything?' asked Carruthers.

'No, of course not!' She looked quite offended by the suggestion. 'He's back that way.'

'Would you show us?'

'I would rather stay here if you don't mind,' she sniffed. 'I have no wish to see it a second time.' Her accent was well-to-do Edinburgh, perhaps Morningside.

'We'll need to get a statement from you, Mrs...?' said Fletcher, taking up her notebook.

'Mrs Henderson.'

'OK, Mrs Henderson. Sit tight and I'll be right back.'

Carruthers and Fletcher walked further into the forest, the fresh scent of pine in Carruthers' nostrils. With every step it grew darker. Twigs snapped underfoot sounding like starting pistols on sports day. His right hand throbbed. He wondered if he'd broken a bone.

The body, that of a bare-chested young man wearing blue jeans, was lying on its side in the undergrowth.

As Carruthers walked into the forest, the canopy of trees seemed to close in on him. The forest was so dense it shut out the sky. It was overcast but humid, and inside the forest was airless, oppressive and dark.

Fletcher threw a packet towards him. Threw it harder than strictly necessary. She started to put on her overalls.

Carruthers started to pull on his own overalls. Clearly he'd annoyed Fletcher, and as much as he resented his current position, she was right, it was time to start being professional again. He put his feet into the paper shoes.

'Shit,' said Fletcher, wrinkling her nose as they approached the corpse. The smell of death was overpowering. Even from a distance there was no mistaking the condition of the body. She reached into her pocket for the tape and started taping around the crime scene, marking the minimum exclusion zone.

'He's been tortured,' said Carruthers. 'See those rope marks on the wrists, cigarette burns on his chest.' He looked at the bloody concave mess of his scalp. 'He's also been shot in the head.

179

Perhaps that's what killed him but we'll have to wait to see what forensics say.'

The two approached the body cautiously from another angle. Remembering the photograph, Carruthers said. 'I think it's Dave Roberts. What do you think?'

'Looks like the same man to me,' said Fletcher. Then 'What's that smell?'

'I can't smell anything over the smell of the corpse,' said Carruthers. 'Decomposition will have already accelerated in this heat.'

'I can smell smoke,' she said.

'Perhaps someone's got a barbeque set out.'

Fletcher frowned. 'There are strict rules about firing up barbeque sets in forests. Look.' She pointed at a small clearing a few metres away, looked like a couple of trees had fallen in the winter and nature had yet to fill the gap in the skyline. As they gazed towards the gap a plume of smoke filled the scrap of sky. A sudden roaring noise erupted, and a huge jet of orange flame leapt into the air.

'Jesus Christ, it's a forest fire. And it's close. Quick, call the fire brigade,' said Carruthers. 'All it takes is if the wind changes, and we'll be in serious danger.'

Fletcher deftly got out her mobile phone and punched the number of the emergency services into it. 'They're on their way. We're in luck. There's a crew from Lochgelly training over at Edenside. They won't be more than a few minutes. They're also mobilising crews from Castletown and Cupar. They have Tayport on standby.' In answer to his raised eyebrows, Fletcher explained, 'The last forest fire here took ten hours to put out after reigniting, and had six fire crews in attendance.'

Carruthers' eyes widened before he said, 'We'd better be making tracks. I want you to rescue Mrs Henderson before her day gets any worse. We'll take the statement from her once we get her to safety.'

'Not before I do this,' said Fletcher taking photographs of the body and the area around the body at different angles with her mobile phone. 'I know it's not the same, but just in case the SOCOs don't arrive in time, it's better than nothing.'

Suddenly a faint cry could be heard from further inside the forest. 'Ssshhh. Did you hear that?' asked Carruthers. 'It sounds like someone crying for help.' They both listened.

'It sounded like an animal to me,' said Fletcher straining her ears.

'There it is again,' said Carruthers.

'That's definitely human.'

'Stay here, Andie. I'll go.'

Fletcher made a move to join Carruthers.

'I mean it. Now you're pregnant you have to put the baby first. I won't be long.'

'Be careful, Jim.'

Carruthers listened for the cry for help. It came again, this time a little fainter. He couldn't tell if it was a man or a woman, but it definitely wasn't animal, that was for sure. He started walking towards where the voice was coming from, hoping that it wouldn't lead him straight into the path of the fire. As he moved deftly, twigs broke underfoot. He brushed branches of pine trees out of the way as he hurried through the undergrowth. The normally sweet smell of pine was marred by the acrid smoke being carried on the wind. Carruthers was concerned. The smoke was becoming stronger, and the density of the forest, coupled with the smoke from the fire, meant visibility was becoming poor. He stepped over a fallen branch, but failed to see another half hidden by undergrowth, and catching his foot on its underside, tripped right over it and went sprawling.

'Fuck.' He sat up awkwardly. Gingerly tested his ankle. It was tender, but he was still able to walk on it. He brushed himself down. Kept walking. Suddenly he stumbled across one of the many cycle paths in the forest. 'Where are you?' he shouted.

'Over here,' came the response.

Carruthers looked over to where the voice had come from. A lycra-clad young man was lying in an awkward position on the ground, his electric blue mountain bike behind him at an angle. Carruthers limped over to him.

'Must've hit a hidden tree stump. Went over the handlebars. I've banged my head on a stone or something and my knee's a mess.' Carruthers saw a gash on the man's head. He then looked down at his legs. The man's left knee was bloody. He looked at Carruthers in his SOCO get up. 'Christ, you been to a fancy dress party?' He touched his lip with a dirty hand. 'Think I bit my lip when I fell,' he said tentatively probing his cut lip with his tongue.

'What's your name?'

'Michael.'

'Can you get into a seated position, Michael?'

Carruthers half-helped Michael into a sitting position. 'We need to get you to hospital, get them to take a look at that head wound,' he said. 'But first, we need to get you out of here. Not to alarm you, but there's a forest fire.'

'I know. I can smell the smoke.'

'How long have you been here?'

'I don't know. I think I blacked out.'

'OK,' said Carruthers. 'Look, this is going to hurt, but on the count of three I'm going to haul you up. Put your arm round my shoulder. We'll talk as we go but I want us to get moving.'

Carruthers winced as he took some of Michael's weight, his ankle tender and weak. They stumbled as Carruthers steered the injured cyclist through the dense undergrowth back to relative safety.

'Shit, I think the wind's picking up,' gasped Carruthers. There was a whooshing noise through the trees and his voice came out in jagged breaths. 'Let's hope it doesn't blow in this direction.'

'Thank God you found me. I don't think I could have managed on my own. My knee's throbbing. The other bloke I saw just ignored me.'

Carruthers looked at Michael intently. 'What other bloke? There was another man in the forest?'

'Don't know who he was. Looked like a vagrant. He had wild eyes. Like he was out of it. Seemed to see me, but not see me, if you know what I mean.'

'Can you describe him? What he was wearing? How old was he?'

'Why are you so interested? Are you a policeman or something?'

'Yes.'

They suddenly heard some shouts coming in their direction. 'There you are. I was getting worried. You've been ages,' said Fletcher. She stopped when she saw Michael.

'Who's this?' she asked.

'This young man's had an accident mountain biking. Can you call for an ambulance? He's had a nasty bump on the head and he's hurt his knee.'

Fletcher nodded. 'The SOCOs are already here,' she said. 'I've filled them in on the fire. Told them the fire brigade's on its way.'

'OK, that's good.' He turned to Michael. 'Can you stand unsupported?'

'Yes, I'll be fine.'

Carruthers limped towards Fletcher.

'I tripped. Don't ask. We need to get a move on.'

'You'd be surprised how quickly we can work,' interrupted Dr Mackie, striding towards them as the gowned-up officers in white worked silently and efficiently in the taped-off area. He looked Carruthers up and down, no doubt taking in Carruthers' dishevelled appearance and half-closed eye, but said nothing.

'What's going on?' asked Michael, straining to see over Carruthers' shoulder. Carruthers watched Dr Mackie, Liu the photographer and the SOCOs grimly going about their tasks.

'Who's this?' asked Mackie frowning. 'The public shouldn't be in this area.'

'Oh my God. Is that a body?' said Michael aghast. He pulled away sharply, turned his back and was noisily sick all over his own shoes.

'That's one reason for keeping members of the public away,' said Mackie. 'On top of everything else, I don't want to have to sidestep pools of vomit.'

'Sorry, never seen a body before.' Michael wiped away a dribble of vomit from his chin. He winced with the pain in his shoulder.

'Come on. We need to get you checked out. We also need to interview you about the man you've seen in the forest,' said Carruthers. In the distance he could hear the wail of the fire engines.

Fletcher's eyebrows shot up. 'When was this?'

'Only about five minutes before I saw him,' said Michael looking towards Carruthers.

Fletcher opened her mouth to say something but it was drowned out by shouts from the approaching firefighters ordering everyone to leave the area. Carrying hose reel jets, water backpacks and beaters they started making their way further in the forest.

'We need to get the body moved.' Carruthers addressed his comment to Mackie. If Mackie heard, he gave no sign of it. He was already kneeling by the body starting to take temperatures.

'As soon as I take the temperature. Then we'll move him.'

Carruthers looked away. He knew Mackie would be taking the rectal temperature. He wasn't particularly squeamish but he felt that everyone deserved a bit of dignity in death.

Fletcher scoured the ground. 'I don't see any tyre tracks,' she said to Carruthers, 'drag marks or footprints.'

'Andie, I want you to take Mrs Henderson to safety. Take her statement. I'll see you back at the station. Get a statement from the injured cyclist before the ambulance arrives.'

Fletcher nodded.

'Don't take any risks,' said Carruthers. 'You're no good to me dead. I'll see if the SOCOs need any help.'

'Right,' said Fletcher turning to Michael. 'Let's get going.' She called over to Carruthers. 'See you back at the station.'

Carruthers spent the next few minutes with the SOCOs, gleaning what information he could before they took the body away to the mortuary. Back at his car he called Fletcher for an update.

'The dog walker can't give us anything useful, I'm afraid,' said Fletcher.

Can't? Or doesn't want to get involved? Carruthers thought of the way the woman had reacted when she was asked if she'd touched the body.

'What about the cyclist?'

'Not much better really. I checked the description he gave with the local uniform boys and they say the guy is a known vagrant who has been living rough in the forest for a couple of months,' said Fletcher. 'What's the current situation on the fire? Are you still at the scene?'

'We're just leaving. They're still trying to contain it,' said Carruthers. He looked across to see a couple of fire-suited men with hedge beaters.

'Has it crossed your mind it might have been started deliberately to cover up the evidence?' said Fletcher.

'They could have just set fire to the body? Would have been a lot easier.'

'Perhaps they weren't expecting it to be found so soon. After all, it's pretty dense in that forest.'

'We won't know the facts about the fire until we speak to the firefighters and find the cause. If it was a fag, it may have been smouldering for a while. Of course, if the vagrant's been living in the forest, then it could've been his fire. If the cyclist saw him then he was in the area when the fire took hold.'

'Have you spoken to the SOCOs yet?' asked Fletcher.

'Yes, I have. And I've spoken with Mackie. He's being as tight-lipped as usual. Says he needs to do the PM before giving any information. Ten to one it's our man, Roberts, though we need a positive ID.'

'Do you think he was killed by Williams?' said Fletcher.

'Perhaps he'd outlived his usefulness. Maybe Williams thought if he got caught, he'd talk. His photofit's been on national news, after all. They would know it was only a matter of time before he got picked up.'

'Or maybe they killed him because he screwed up. Didn't kill Holdaway. Or perhaps he got greedy, or was trying to double cross them,' said Carruthers. 'Could be any number of motives.'

'Why torture him?' asked Fletcher.

'Why does anyone get tortured? Mostly it's because the torturer wants information, or is just plain sadistic. They probably wanted to know if he'd passed on any information to anyone else. They would make it their business to know who his friends were.'

Carruthers was distracted and lapsed into silence. Two of his own sentences kept ringing in his ears.

They probably wanted to know if he'd passed on any information to anyone else. They would make it their business to know who his friends were.

Or who he had slept with. If Siobhan Mathews was innocent, then she might well be in danger. It didn't excuse her lying, though. They needed to get her in for questioning.

'The SOCOs are pretty close to finishing,' said Carruthers. 'I'm heading back after I have a word with the firefighters. We've now got two dead bodies to deal with. Let's get Siobhan Mathews in and see what she's got to say for herself.'

FOURTEEN

SUNDAY EVENING, 3ᴿᴰ JUNE

Carruthers took a good look at the woman sitting opposite him in interview room one. He took a deep regret-filled breath as he pressed the record button on the machine. 'Why did you lie to us, Siobhan?'

'Lie to you? I don't know what you mean. Why have you brought me to the station? Am I being arrested?' She looked at him closer. 'What happened to your eye?'

'No. You're not being arrested.' He noticed her wide eyes and trembling bottom lip. 'You've been invited here to help us with our enquiries.' Carruthers then very slowly and deliberately slid the photograph across the table towards her. He searched Siobhan's face for her reaction. It didn't disappoint. All colour drained from her.

'Where did you get that?' she asked in a low voice, a mixture, Carruthers judged, of embarrassment, shame and fear.

Carruthers ignored the question. 'Why didn't you tell us you'd been intimate with Dave Roberts?'

Siobhan said nothing.

'When was the photograph taken, Siobhan? Must have been pretty recently. After all, you've only been at the university since September.'

'How long have you been in a relationship with Dave Roberts?' asked DS Fletcher. 'Why didn't you tell us about something so important? What are you hiding?'

Siobhan burst into tears. 'I'm not hiding anything. I didn't tell you because it's not important. It was a mistake, OK?'

'Not important?' bellowed Carruthers, his jaw practically dropping open. 'We're investigating the suspicious death of your supposed boyfriend. Rhys Evans, remember him? You didn't think to tell us that our prime suspect is your lover?'

'I can hardly deny I've been intimate with Dave, can I, given the evidence is staring right at me?' said Siobhan pushing the photograph away. 'But it wasn't a relationship,' she said turning away.

Carruthers pushed it back towards her. 'Take a good look at the photograph, Siobhan. Pick it up. I want to know what the poster is in the background. Do you remember what it said?'

Siobhan reluctantly picked up the photograph. She wiped her nose with her hand. 'All I remember is the words looked Welsh.'

'There's an R and an N and the numbers 402. Could it have said Bryn Glas 1402?' said Carruthers.

'I didn't pay much attention,' said Siobhan Mathews. 'I'd forgotten all about him having a poster in his room. It didn't mean anything to me and we didn't exactly talk about how he decided to decorate his bedroom.' She blushed.

'Bryn Glas 1402 is the name of the terrorist organisation fronted by the man who we think is behind the bomb blast in Castletown,' said Carruthers.

'Oh my God,' said Siobhan, starting to cry again.

'Start talking, Siobhan,' said Fletcher. 'It had better be good. For starters, we can charge you with withholding information in a murder enquiry.'

Carruthers noticed Siobhan's eyes widen with shock.

'When did you first meet Dave Roberts,' asked Fletcher, 'and when was the photograph taken?'

'We met the first week of university back in September,' said Siobhan. 'In Mothers.'

Carruthers nodded, he knew Mothers Bar, on Cliff Top Wynd. It was popular with students and RAF alike. 'I was with a group of students from my course. We were getting to know each other. Like I said it was the first week. I was desperate to make friends.

I'm not very good socially. I'm shy. Sometimes to compensate I have too much to drink.'

'Is that what happened that evening?' asked Fletcher

Siobhan nodded. 'A group of lads approached us. We got talking. They were from the RAF base. One was Dave.'

'Who were the others?' asked Carruthers. Fletcher had her black notebook in her hand, poised.

'One was Rhys,' she said, colouring. Fletcher and Carruthers exchanged a look not lost on Siobhan, as she went on to mention two other names.

'Now can you see why I didn't tell you? Look, I know what you're thinking, but I'm not a slut.'

'No one said you were,' said Carruthers. 'What happened next?'

'It got pretty late. I was drunk by then. Dave asked me back. It's not something I'm proud of but it happened.'

'You went back to the RAF base with him?' said Carruthers.

'How did you manage to gain entry on to the base?' interrupted Fletcher. 'There're strict rules.'

'Dave said he knew the guards on duty.'

Carruthers glanced at Fletcher and saw her raising an eyebrow. Either there had been a serious lapse of security or Siobhan was lying. But then they had the photographic evidence to prove she was there.

'Carry on,' said Carruthers.

'As I said I went back to the base with him. In the morning we larked about with the camera. I think I was still drunk to be honest.'

'Why do you say that?' said Fletcher.

'Being that uninhibited in front of the camera is completely out of character,' said Siobhan blushing. 'And, as I said, I don't generally sleep with a man on first meeting.'

'So you still felt drunk in the morning?' said Carruthers. 'Did you sleep with him then as well?'

'I don't have to answer that question,' cried Siobhan.

'Well, it seems to me you're blaming it entirely on the drink. You said you still felt drunk in the morning. At what point did you sober up?'

'The moment I saw his stash of *Searchlight*. It's a magazine of the far right.' She turned to Fletcher. 'Look, I made a mistake. I'm not into casual sex and when I realised how heavily he was involved in the far right, I knew I didn't want to have a relationship with him. He even started talking about how the Holocaust had never happened. It turned my stomach. He asked to see me again but I made my excuses and left.'

'So it was a one-night stand,' said Carruthers.

'Yes, like I said. Why don't you believe me?'

'Get off your high horse, Siobhan,' said Carruthers. 'You've lied to us, or at least failed to tell us the whole truth. For all we know you might be lying now. You and Dave might have planned Rhys's murder together.'

Siobhan stood up abruptly. Her chair scraped the floor. 'How can you even suggest I had something to do with Rhys' death? I loved him. Why would I want to kill him?'

'Sit down,' said Carruthers. 'You loved Rhys, but you never loved Dave. How do you think that made Dave feel knowing you preferred his mate to him? Knowing you were kissing Rhys, doing all the things in bed with Rhys that you had been doing with Dave? How soon after sleeping with Dave did you take Rhys to your bed by the way?'

Siobhan shook her head then sat back down slowly. 'You're horrible saying all this to me.' She bit her lip. 'Anyway, Dave was never in love with me. He's had countless women since me, if his bragging is to be believed.'

'Grow up Siobhan. We're talking about suspected murder,' said Carruthers. 'And if Roberts was never in love with you, why did he still have a photograph of you both in his room?'

'Maybe he took photos of all his conquests,' said Siobhan, sniffing.

'We didn't find any photographs of any other women, Siobhan, not even of his mother,' said Fletcher, handing her a tissue she fished out of her pocket. 'Just you. Maybe he was in love with you.'

'*Was* in love with me?' said Siobhan frowning.

'Who else would have known about you and Dave?' asked Carruthers.

Siobhan looked puzzled. 'Very few people in Castletown. But back at Edenside, knowing Dave, probably half the base or more,' answered Siobhan. 'Why do you ask? Look, what's going on?'

Carruthers and Fletcher exchanged another look. Carruthers nodded.

'There's been a development, Siobhan,' said Fletcher. 'We think we've found him.'

'Do you mean Dave?' said Siobhan, looking startled at the unexpected piece of news. 'Has he confessed? Was he behind the bombing?'

'I'm afraid we can't ask him that question,' said Fletcher.

'I don't understand. Why not?'

Carruthers leant across the table before answering. 'The man we've found is dead. His body dumped in Pinetum Park Forest. It's not very pleasant, I'm afraid.' Carruthers opened the buff file once more and took out photographs of the mutilated body of Roberts.

Siobhan had been pale before, now she turned white. Put a hand over her mouth. Carruthers wondered if she would be sick.

'The thing is, Siobhan,' continued Carruthers, 'if he was murdered by the bombers, which is looking increasingly likely, they may have tortured him because they were looking for information.'

Siobhan looked from Carruthers to Fletcher. She took her hand away from her mouth. 'Information? What sort of information?'

'We don't know yet,' admitted Carruthers. 'If they were looking for information, then anyone who got close to Roberts may also be in danger. You've been close to both Rhys Evans and Dave Roberts. Both are now dead. You may be in danger.' He noticed beads of sweat forming on Siobhan's upper lip and forehead.

'Why... I...'

Siobhan's eyes rolled as she fainted, slumping on top of the table before either Carruthers or Fletcher could stop her.

***

'What do you think, sir? Do you think she's legit?' asked Fletcher. They were standing outside the interview room watching Siobhan Mathews sip her water. Carruthers caught Fletcher looking at her watch. No doubt she was wondering when they would both get home.

'She's certainly coming across that way. Either that or she's a damn good actress.'

'What do we do now, Jim?'

'Get Siobhan Mathews back to Edgecliffe. I'll leave that job to you. We have no reason to hold her.'

'Do you think she'll be OK? I mean, do you think the bombers might go after her?' said Fletcher.

'Well, if she's telling the truth, if it was just a one-night stand back in September, I wouldn't imagine the bombers would think her that important.'

'What about pillow talk?'

'Reckon there'd be much time for pillow talk during a one-night stand?'

It was Fletcher's turn to go crimson.

'We'll keep an eye on her though. Just in case. Oh by the way, before I forget, I rang the hospital. The cyclist's going to be fine. They're keeping him in overnight for observation, because of his head injury.'

'Talking of injuries, how's your eye feel?' said Fletcher.

Carruthers probed it with his finger. 'Sore, but I'll survive.'

'And the ankle?'

'Think I was lucky. Definitely not sprained.'

'Well, I could have told you that. A bad sprain and you wouldn't be able to walk on it. Any news on the vagrant?'

'Hasn't been found yet. We're hoping he'll come forward. He may have vital information. Of course, living rough he hasn't got a TV, so can't see any of the police requests.'

'I would suspect if he has witnessed anything, he's even less likely to come forward. If it was me, I'd be terrified. I'd probably be lying low somewhere. By the way – the fire? Do we know how it started?'

'Discarded disposable barbeque set, just like the last one. There really are some thoughtless idiots out there.'

Harris approached looking smug and carrying a sheaf of paper, which he was waving around as if he had just won the football pools.

'I've just got the information from the SID, and other sources. Roberts was a paid-up member of the BNP,' he finished triumphantly.

Carruthers wondered if the lapse in security at the RAF station extended to more than the sentry box. Then again Roberts wouldn't be the first member of Britain's armed forces to join a far-right organisation while serving. 'No surprises there then,' he said. 'Nothing on him being a member of Bryn Glas 1402?'

''Fraid not.'

Carruthers' thoughts drifted back to Siobhan. After the business with McGhee he'd vowed he'd never be made a fool of by another woman, but several months later, Siobhan had managed it. *Well, that's what you get for putting your trust in an attractive woman.* He knew that he was always hard on himself. Wondered if he'd been too hard on her. Perhaps she had been telling the truth. And how many people have a poorly-judged one-night stand in their past?

***

The first thing Siobhan did when she got home was have a shower. Scrubbing to rid herself of the unpleasant smell of the interview room, the feeling of being dirty, remembering her mistake with Dave Roberts. Afterwards she couldn't settle, so she picked up her keys, mobile, a bottle of water and rucksack and went for a walk. Leaving the student accommodation, she took the path once again behind Edgecliffe that led her through the gate to East Castle beach. Rather than walk on the beach, she walked on the sandy coastal path by the crazy golf course. She started walking as in a daze, not really caring where her feet took her. Eventually she found herself at the end of the harbour.

She walked past all the lobster pots and took a left turn to the start of the pier. The pier was one of her favourite places. She always found taking a walk here calming. In her first week at the university, she had loved hearing about how visiting preachers to the religious centre of Castletown had arrived in town by boat to give their sermon. Before decent roads, travelling by sea had been common. Every Sunday the students had greeted the preacher by walking to the end of the pier and at the end of the sermon they would escort him back. Although the visiting preacher no longer came by boat, the town upheld the tradition of the pier walk. Every first Sunday of the month, the red-gowned students walked to the end of the pier and back again. Thinking about the town's history and traditions soothed her soul, helped put the troubles of her own life into perspective.

She turned away from the pier to the little harbour. Watched as a fisherman took his boats out. A small dark blue boat with the words 'Crusader Castletown' written on its side, chugged past her. It was flying the blue and white flag of Scotland, which furled with the ever-increasing wind round the flagpole.

Two elderly men wearing suits were sitting on a bench between the lobster pots, eating ice cream and talking about the changes Castletown had seen. The two men finished their ice creams and shuffled off. Siobhan took her rucksack off her shoulder laying it down by her feet. She sat down on the bench they had vacated, being careful not to sit on a dollop of melting ice cream.

She was shocked Dave Roberts had been found dead. Not only dead. Tortured. Was it the same people who had killed Rhys? The terrorists who'd planted the bomb? It must have been. She had known both men. She thought of Inspector Carruthers' words. Would they now come after her? She suddenly felt very vulnerable. Being outdoors, she was a sitting duck.

Suddenly she felt something hard and cold, pushed into the back of her neck. She started with shock. She hadn't been aware that anyone else had been even near.

'Stand up,' a young male voice hissed in her right ear. 'Don't make a sound. You're coming with us.'

Siobhan let out a squeak of terror. The man had a Welsh accent.

'I said, don't make a sound, or it'll be your last.'

She felt another prod, this time harder.

'This is a gun and I know how to use it.'

Siobhan tried to stand up, but her legs gave way beneath her. She was shaking. A hand roughly grabbed her elbow in a vice-like grip, and hauled her on to her feet.

'Start walking,' said the voice. 'And don't look round.'

The man guided her a few yards behind the lobster pots and bobbing fishing boats. The wind had picked up. Her hair was suddenly in her eyes. She tried to brush the stray lock away with her hand. Her eyes were watering.

'Keep your hands down.'

Siobhan looked round hopelessly for help. The nearest people were a group of students half-way down the pier, but they were too far away and strolling away from her.

A white van came towards them. Perhaps she had a chance after all. It came to a halt a few metres away, and a burly man wearing a black T-shirt and jeans jumped from the driving seat and opened the sliding doors. Siobhan opened her mouth, but before she had a chance to say anything the burly man spoke first.

'This her?' he asked of her assailant. The man grunted something and Siobhan felt a cloth clamped over her mouth. The sweet cloying smell was overpowering and made her feel sick. She was picked up and like a slab of butcher's meat she was hauled none too gently into the van. Her rucksack was thrown in after her. The man with the gun, who was slighter and shorter than his colleague, jumped in after her, threw the door shut, straddled her, and grabbing rope, started binding her wrists.

Siobhan moaned and tried to block out the nausea. Hearing the sound of the engine and the screech of tyres she knew they were on the move. The noise seemed to be a great distance off, though, as if coming through a funnel.

She felt her hair being stroked. She stiffened. Hot rank breath on her face. She felt her right breast being squeezed. It hurt. She managed a whimper. A large calloused hand over her mouth. A voice whispered in her ear telling her to be quiet. She nearly gagged on the smell of stale sweat coming from him. A crushing weight moved over her as the man straddled her. She felt him tearing at her clothes. She struggled. Tried to scream but he covered her mouth once again with the cloth silencing her until the world turned black.

FIFTEEN

MONDAY MORNING, 4th June

'Something's been bothering me. I now know what it is,' said Fletcher, putting her head round Carruthers' office door.

Carruthers looked up from under yet another report. His backlog of paperwork was building. Quite a lot had been bothering him recently, so he knew the feeling.

Fletcher was hanging on to the door frame. 'When we visited Dave Roberts' room, I knew there was something missing. I couldn't think what it was. Now I can't believe how I missed it. So obvious.'

'What was it?'

'Where was his stash of BNP magazines? There was a stash of far-right propaganda found in his room, according to the RAF. Siobhan Mathews also said she'd seen a load of magazines. The RAF people were told not to remove anything,' she continued. 'When we searched the room, the magazines weren't there. So who took them?'

Carruthers frowned. Put his glasses on the top of his head. 'Who else searched his room?' he asked.

'I didn't think anybody had apart from the RAF Police.' She turned to go. But hesitated. 'Jim? I've just had a thought. It's not about his magazines. They were clearly taken after his death. But just say he didn't keep all his things in his room at the base.'

'What do you mean?'

'If you were seeing someone there comes a time in a relationship when you start keeping some stuff at theirs. Don't you? Toothbrush? Spare shirt? I think we should get a search warrant out for Charlene Todd's place: she claims she's Dave

Roberts' girlfriend. Maybe Dave left stuff there. Whoever killed Rhys would have been covered with blood. What would they have done with their blood-stained clothes? Mackie told us we were looking for a blunt instrument covered with a sock. That's never turned up.'

The phone rang in Carruthers' office. As he picked it up he turned to Fletcher and said, 'I'll talk to Bingham about organising a search warrant. DCI Carruthers,' he answered. Fletcher turned and disappeared back out of his office.

'Hi Jim, John Mackie here. We've got information on the Pinetum Park Forest body. Just preliminary findings at this stage.'

'Fire away,' said Carruthers.

Mackie chuckled. 'Bad choice of words, considering our corpse could have been burnt to a cinder. Our man was definitely already dead when he was brought into the woods.'

'So he *was* killed elsewhere?'

'As you noticed there wasn't much blood or brain tissue at the scene from his head wound which is an indicator he was shot elsewhere. The body was then dumped in the forest.'

Carruthers had known at the site that there wasn't sufficient blood for Roberts to have died there, yet the entry wound was swollen and bloodied. *So he was still alive when he was shot.*

'The findings at this stage indicate he died most likely from a single shot to the head,' said Mackie.

'What else have you got for me?' said Carruthers.

'He'd been tortured. But you knew that. He had several cigarette burns to the chest. From the inflammatory response, I can confirm he was alive when these were inflicted.'

'Not much point after he was dead, although I guess you've got to stub your cigarettes out somewhere. Any idea how long he'd been dead?'

'Always a tricky one that, but rigor mortis had already set in. Approximately twenty-four to forty-eight hours is my reckoning. There's evidence of some insect activity. Of course, it's been pretty hot recently. One other thing. His hands had been tied tightly.

Useful for us. We've found fibres. The material used to bind his wrists was some type of braided rope.'

'Right, thanks,' said Carruthers, 'Nothing new on the Rhys Evans case?'

''Fraid not.'

'OK. I'm going to brief the Super. Get in touch when you have some more info for us.'

'Will do. We'll have the rest of the findings within twenty-four hours.'

A few moments later, Carruthers was tapping on Superintendent Bingham's door with some trepidation. Bingham finished the call he was on and replaced the receiver. After Carruthers had given him the update from the lab, Bingham had his own piece of news.

'The RAF police have been in touch. We now know the body's definitely that of Dave Roberts. One of his commanders has positively IDed it. There was never much doubt, to be honest. His parents are heading up from Cardiff.' Bingham sighed. 'Two dead men on our hands and we're no closer to catching the bombers. If Roberts did plant the bomb under Holdaway's car, getting rid of Roberts is one way of keeping him quiet. Silenced men can't talk.'

'I would like to interview the parents myself, if that's OK?' said Carruthers.

'That's fine. Make sure you keep McGhee abreast of any developments. You may have your differences, but I still want you to work together as part of a team. I also want you to apologise to Alistair, Carruthers. I don't want bad blood.'

Carruthers remained silent.

'Did you hear me?'

'Yes, sir. I'll do it.'

'Do we know yet if Roberts was a member of the BNP?' said Bingham.

'Yes, he was. But Fletcher made the point that there's been no discovery of any racist material in his room. Looks like it's all been taken. Question is by whom? And if someone has been in and taken that, what else have they taken? Perhaps the Bryn Glas poster that was most likely hanging on his wall.'

'Begs the question what was the motive for taking them?'

'Sir, I want to get a search warrant for Charlene Todd's home in Crosshaven. She had a relationship with Roberts and Fletcher thinks that Roberts may have left some of his stuff at Charlene's. We've drawn a blank with Evans' death. Roberts is the most likely candidate for the murder. If Evans found out what Roberts was up to, Roberts would certainly have had motive to kill him. It's worth a shot.'

Bingham nodded. 'I wonder if we could get this done under the Terrorism Act. I'll talk to McGhee and make a call. Give me the requisition form. I'll get it fast-tracked.'

***

Oh no, not again. For the last couple of hours Fletcher had been feeling sick again. The nausea was coming over her in waves. However, the last ten minutes she'd also started to get stomach pains, which seemed to be increasing in intensity. She kept her head down as McGhee walked in but not before she noticed him striding towards Carruthers, who had been walking towards her desk with a steaming coffee.

'Has there been a development for me to be summoned back so abruptly?' asked McGhee. 'I was in the middle of something over at Edenside.'

'You could say that,' said Carruthers. 'Do you know anything about magazines going missing from Roberts' room?'

'What you talking about? What magazines?'

'The BNP literature that was supposed to have been there.'

Fletcher tried to stand up. An agonizing pain gripped her stomach. Now she was really scared. She wanted to go to the bathroom but she was frightened of what would happen if she did. She could taste beads of perspiration on her top lip. Christ, why did she suddenly feel so hot? Her fear increased. Now she was struggling to breathe. She felt she was suffocating. There was a tingling in her head. She definitely had to go to the bathroom. She stood up, managed a few steps but her legs wanted to buckle.

'Jim?' she said, just as Bingham walked in.

'What is it, Andie?' asked Carruthers.

'I'm not feeling well. I think something's wrong,' said Fletcher suddenly collapsing against the nearest wall clutching her stomach. 'Can you drive me to hospital?'

'Is it the baby?' asked Carruthers, alarmed.

'I don't know what it is, but I'm in pain.'

'Shit, let's go.' Carruthers slammed his coffee down, heedless of the spilling liquid. He moved to Fletcher, the pain kept her from standing straight and she leaned heavily into him for support. McGhee stood impotent as Bingham sped ahead of the slow-moving pair, opened the doors for them.

'I'll give you a call from the hospital,' shouted Carruthers to Bingham.

'Just get her to hospital, Carruthers,' said Bingham. 'My people come first.'

SIXTEEN

MONDAY EVENING, 4ᵀᴴ JUNE

Carruthers snapped his phone shut. He'd just finished speaking to Andie Fletcher's boyfriend, Mark. The man was on his way to see Fletcher in hospital but there had been something odd in his reaction to the news. Carruthers couldn't put his finger on it. It was almost as if he was reluctant to visit her. He wondered what any man could consider so important it trumped a girlfriend's and baby's health.

Now he stood on the doorstep of Charlene Todd's flat in Crosshaven. He directed Dougie Harris to knock on Todd's door again.

'Not more police?' said Charlene Todd rolling her eyes when she saw Carruthers' police ID. 'What do you want this time?' Her eyes then fell on Dougie Harris. 'I ken you. You were the one perving at my tits.'

'We need to search your property,' said Carruthers.

'Why?'

'We have a search warrant. Would you mind standing aside.'

Carruthers motioned for Harris to head into the living room. As he disappeared behind the door a little white poodle shot out.

'I need to know if Dave Roberts kept anything here at your house,' said Carruthers.

'What sort of thing?' asked Charlene. 'There is some stuff of his here, yeah. I have his PlayStation and some DVDs.'

Carruthers wondered if Charlene Todd had been told about Roberts' death by the RAF. The police certainly hadn't told her. She wasn't behaving as if she was grief-stricken.

'Is there anything else of his?' asked Carruthers.

Harris came out of the living room. 'It's clean,' he said.

Charlene Todd looked from Harris to Carruthers. 'He came in with a bag of clothes recently. He said he was going to do up an old car and they were overalls he was going to change in to.'

'Where are they?' said Carruthers.

'Under the sink in the kitchen.'

'Show us.'

They walked into the kitchen. Harris strode over to the sink, and yanked the door of the cupboard under the sink open. He got down on his haunches and started to move bottles of cleaning fluid and disinfectant out of the way. There was a rustling noise and he brought out a black bin liner. It was tied at the top. Carruthers nodded. Harris ripped into the bag and pulled out a shirt and trousers. They were soaked in blood.

'Have the RAF Police been to see you, Charlene?' asked Carruthers.

'No, why should they?' Carruthers noticed she'd gone pale as she looked at the blood-stained clothes. 'What sort of bother is Davey in?'

Carruthers made his voice as gentle as he could. 'I'm afraid Dave Roberts is dead, Charlene. We found his body in Pinetum Park Forest yesterday afternoon.'

A loud wail pierced the air. Carruthers guided Charlene out of the kitchen to her living room and pushed her into a seat. The little white poodle jumped on her lap and she buried her face in his corkscrew fur.

'Is there anyone who can sit with you?' he asked. Only half his mind was on Charlene Todd and Dave Roberts. The other half was on his need to free up some time to ring the hospital and find out whether there was any news on Fletcher.

'My next door neighbour.'

'I'll go and chap the door.' said Harris. Carruthers nodded.

***

Back at the station processing paperwork, Carruthers breathed out a sigh of relief and sat back in his chair. He'd just phoned the hospital again. This time there had been some positive news. Fletcher was going to be OK. So was the baby. They were still running tests, but it looked as if she'd a bout of acute food poisoning. She was being kept in overnight for observation and would need a few days off work to recover.

As relieved as he was that she was going to be OK, why did she have to go and get food poisoning now? He needed her quick mind and attention to detail, and frankly, would miss having her to bounce ideas around with. Dougie Harris had already made several mistakes in an investigation that was proving to be as complex as it was time-consuming. There were so many twists and turns that even Bingham had admitted he was labouring. Carruthers began to think about the details of the case.

First, who had killed Evans, and why? Most likely suspect was Dave Roberts now the blood-stained shirt had been found at Charlene Todd's flat. But Carruthers knew he still needed the results back from forensics on the blood. Would it be a match for Rhys Evans? If Roberts had killed Evans, was it in a fit of straightforward jealousy over Siobhan Mathews? It seemed unlikely. What made more sense was the possibility that Evans had been killed because he'd found out something about the imminent operations of Bryn Glas and Roberts' involvement in it.

Carruthers certainly didn't buy into it being a random robbery. To his mind, it had been premeditated, and Evans had been followed.

His thoughts turned to the car bomb. Witnesses had seen Roberts in the vicinity at the time of the explosion. Had Roberts tried to recruit Evans? Had Evans refused but threatened to turn whistle blower? If so perhaps his murder had nothing to do with Siobhan Mathews.

So, what had got Dave Roberts killed? Had he known too much, or had he tried to blackmail the terrorists? Was it because he'd interfered with Holdaway's planned death? What had been the purpose of torturing him? Forensics were still trying to trace the bullet from the gun used to kill him. It would have been helpful to have the gun but it still hadn't been found.

Carruthers' eyes felt hot and gritty and he yawned. He needed a good home-cooked meal and some decent sleep. Pushing all thoughts of food and rest out of his head, he sat down at his computer and connected to the internet. He was searching for information on Bloody Sunday. Like everyone of his generation he had learned of the infamous day in school, but he'd never read the detail. Having read the book Holdaway had ordered about the Saville Enquiry he was keen to see if other reports matched the details.

As he read the reports about the mayhem that occurred on the march he wondered how his parents would have coped had he been involved. If it had been him shot in the back as he was trying to run away from the soldiers. Unarmed. Defenceless. Not much older than a boy. Or even worse, shot as he had come to the aid of a wounded friend. He swallowed a lump in his throat. He then read the pitiful attempt at first aid given to a dead man by a friend. The friend had taken the man's shoes off and had gently laid them out by the body. Asked why he had done that his response had been to prevent the man's feet from swelling. Perhaps it hadn't been so much about first aid but more about one final act of kindness and comfort even in death. This last detail was just too much to read. Hastily Carruthers took his glasses off, wiped his eyes with a hand and replaced them on the bridge of his nose.

Carruthers wondered how the families of those involved had felt when they had read the Widgery report published six weeks later, which laid the blame with the protestors. The soldiers had stated that the protestors had been armed and had fired first. The Saville Report had stated that the soldiers had been lying. Lord Widgery, who had conducted the initial report, had taken the side of the soldiers without interviewing witnesses.

Carruthers sat back and thought about it from another angle. How had the soldiers felt? Had the soldiers been under pressure to lie? And if so, how high up the chain of command had it gone? How would he have felt had he been one of the soldiers? Would he have been able to separate a rioter from a peaceful marcher in the heat of the moment? He knew that when the stress response was activated the more intelligent part of the brain was switched off. Would he more likely have been shit-scared and lost control, as accounts in the subsequent report indicated? After all, as a soldier, he might not have been much older than some of the protestors. But how would he have felt when asked to lie about events afterwards in the cold light of day?

He couldn't answer these questions. He hadn't been there. He thought about people like Holdaway. What he'd witnessed as a young soldier. What he had done. How had those soldiers who had killed innocent civilians felt in the weeks, months, years afterwards? Had they suffered nightmares? Been prone to depression or PTSD like Holdaway? One thing was certain; every member of the Paras that took part in that march must now be living in fear.

He could understand why more people had ended up hating the British Army after Bloody Sunday and why they might subsequently have joined the IRA. The anger, the frustration, having to live with the injustice of the hated Widgery report telling you your son was fair game because he'd had a gun and had started shooting first. All lies. Carruthers imagined the stigma and the shame. He read the last line in the report. 'A tragedy for the bereaved and the wounded and a catastrophe for the people of Northern Ireland.' He couldn't argue with that.

Carruthers wondered how many deaths would have been avoided on both sides had the march been allowed to be just a march. And what now? What purpose would it serve to charge these former soldiers with murder? Would it be a positive step towards justice or would Northern Ireland face the peril of dredging up the past, thus jeopardising their fragile peace? More questions he didn't know the answer to.

Switching off his computer, he took off his glasses, placed them on the top of his head and once more rubbed his eyes. He found it hard to switch off from what he'd just read. He sat back and his thoughts turned to Holdaway once more. The man Holdaway had become wasn't matching up to the soldier Holdaway had once been. Holdaway had *claimed* to be a man who had unsuccessfully attempted for forty-five years to put the past behind him. He had told Carruthers he liked the quiet life of academia. However, bringing out a controversial book on the death of Welsh nationalism and taking part in impassioned radio shows weren't the actions of a man wanting the quiet life. He frowned. Was it possible Holdaway wanted to be found out? That he was deliberately courting danger? There was a knock on the door. A young PC put her head round the door. 'That file you requested is in.' He thanked her as she handed over the buff file to him.

'Thanks, Louise.'

Before absorbing himself in the information from Welsh Intelligence on Ewan Williams he decided to get himself a strong coffee. Bringing the coffee back to his office, he sat down. He risked a sip. It was too hot to drink, so he placed it to the side as he found himself absorbed in the Williams' file. His mobile rang startling him. He was surprised to see that the caller ID was Fletcher.

'Andie?'

'Jim?'

'What the hell are you doing ringing me from the hospital? I take it that you're still there?'

'They're keeping me in for observation.'

'How are you feeling?'

'A lot better.'

'I hear the baby's going to be OK, too.'

'Yes, thank God.'

'So why are you ringing when you should be resting?'

'Well, I've got a bit of news,' she said. 'I've decided to keep the baby. This scare, it made me realise what I could have lost.'

'That's great news. It must be a huge relief to have made the decision.'

'Yes, it is. But Jim,' she said, 'I just want you to know that I'll be returning to work after the baby's born. I need to work. Will there still be a place for me?'

'Of course there will. We aren't allowed to get rid of officers because they get pregnant. You know that. But you'll be back at the office in a few days. Why are we talking about this now?'

'Just wanted to check. Also, while I'm on the phone I was wondering if there'd been any developments since I came in? Now I know we're both going to be OK, I feel I can relax.'

'You've only been in a few hours.'

'I know, but I just wanted to be brought up to speed.'

Carruthers found himself telling her all about the visit to Charlene Todd's. He heard a whoop when he told her about the blood-stained find under the sink.

'Have you got that information on Ewan Williams from the South Wales Police yet?' she asked.

Carruthers took a sip of his coffee. It still burnt his lips. 'I was just reading it through when you phoned.'

'What does it say?' asked Fletcher eagerly.

'Are you sure you're up to this?'

'Definitely.'

'Well, if you don't feel well, just let me know. I don't want you to set your recovery back.'

'The file? Do they know where Ewan Williams is at the moment?'

'Bingham's spoken to South Wales Police and corroborated what McGhee has told us. Ewan Williams, Mal Thomas and John Edwards are definitely not in Wales, but there's no record of them leaving the UK.'

'So they are most likely up in Scotland. What do we know of Williams himself?' said Fletcher.

'As expected, it's a pretty big file. So far it makes for pretty depressing reading.' As Carruthers skim-read the file himself, he read out salient bits to Fletcher. 'Says here Williams had come from a family of six kids. Looks like his father had been in and out of prison for various crimes, mostly burglary.' As Carruthers turned over the page he tutted. 'That's not good.'

'What?' said Fletcher.

'Says that his mother, an alcoholic, had died giving birth when Williams was just sixteen, to the last of Williams' five brothers. She had six children in total. Five boys and a girl.'

'Shit. How awful. Having six kids would've been a handful in itself.'

'And imagine not having a mother around and a dad in and out of prison. Must have been really tough on the kids. Poor little sods.'

'What else does the file say?'

'Williams left school at sixteen. No qualifications.'

'So he left school the same year his mother died?'

'Seems so. Looks like he was the oldest too. Most probably left to look after the other siblings. Not uncommon, though, I'd imagine. Lots of kids would have left school at sixteen back then. Different time, Andie.'

'Still a long way from becoming a terrorist, though,'

'True. He was picked up twice in 1967 for vandalism. In 1968 and 1969 he was arrested for theft.'

'How old would he have been then?' asked Fletcher.

'Late teens.'

'What happened after that?'

'Charges get more serious as he enters his twenties. He got charged with assault in January 1971 and again in July the same year. More serious charges were levied against him as the decade progresses. That's really strange.'

'What is?'

Carruthers frowned. 'Looks like some pages are missing. They've been ripped out of the file. We're missing information for the years 1971 to 1973. How odd.' Searched his desk in case they'd dropped out and he hadn't noticed. They weren't there. 'In

1975 Williams was arrested for stabbing a nightclub owner who was himself a known criminal. Hmm. That's odd.'

'What, what?'

'Looks like the charge was dropped.'

'In all that time he's never been given a prison sentence?'

'No. Looks like he never even went to court: all charges were dropped before legal proceedings.'

'All charges dropped?'

Carruthers flicked through the notes. 'Looks like.'

'I wonder why. So, it looks as if petty misdemeanours in Williams' teens led to a life of organised crime by the time he was in his mid-twenties,' said Fletcher.

Carruthers smiled to the empty office. Fletcher might not be in the office, but this chat was nearly as good. At least it assured him that she was already feeling better. 'Yes, and it only got worse by the looks of things from this file. His name had been linked to both money laundering and drugs by the time he was in his thirties. He's never had a charge brought against him, though.'

'Any evidence he was a drug user himself?'

Carruthers flicked through the file. Shook his head, then realised the stupidity of that during a phone conversation. 'No, nothing on file. Although saying that, he's been arrested twice for possession. Never charged.'

'So looks like he sold drugs but never used them. Never charged. How did he keep getting away with it?'

Carruthers shut the file before answering. 'I've no idea. He sounds very clever – and if he's that clever then he's dangerous. Definitely not to be underestimated.'

'So it looks as if his being a big-time criminal is a front for his terrorist activities?' said Fletcher.

'Yes and let's face it, if they're a terrorist outfit that needed access to bomb-making equipment, they would have to get their hands on a hell of a lot of money. More money than comes from mere donations and party subscriptions.'

'In that case both money laundering and dealing drugs would have been perfect. They wouldn't be the only terrorist outfit to be funded that way.'

Carruthers was just about to say something else when he heard Fletcher speaking to someone away from the phone.

'Sorry Jim, that's the nurse. She's asked me to finish the call and rest.'

'Well, you'd better listen to her. I wouldn't want you to get on the wrong side of the nursing staff.'

'What plans now?' said Fletcher. 'When are you interviewing Dave Roberts' parents?'

'Tomorrow morning. They've asked to see their son's room.'

Carruthers suddenly heard an argument breaking out on the other end of the phone. He took it as a good sign. If she was strong enough to carry on a conversation with him and start a row with the nurse, she must be feeling better. 'I take it that's your cue for departure, Andie?'

'Yes, I have to go. Apparently, the doctor's doing his rounds and wants to talk to me. Hopefully I'll be out of here soon.'

'Well, just make sure you listen to the medical staff. We don't want you coming out too soon and having a relapse.'

'You'll ring me if there are any significant developments, won't you Jim?'

'Yes, Andie, if it makes you feel better. Now talk to the doctor and then get some rest.'

Carruthers said his goodbyes and hung up. He resumed reading. Something caught his eye. In terms of personality traits, he read that Williams was considered to be a charmer, excellent at manipulation and ruthless. Also, the police had written that there was evidence to link him, but not implicate him, to the murders of at least two other known criminals.

There was no information on Williams having been a drug user. Carruthers was surprised by that. And what had happened to his brothers? Three of the brothers had gone on to a life of petty crime. Hardly surprising. One brother appeared to have no criminal record, and the only sister, Meg, had left home at nineteen. No further information had been given on her in the file. But, of course, Carruthers knew what had happened to her. She'd moved to Northern Ireland to be with her boyfriend. Being in the wrong place at the wrong time had changed her life forever – and the lives of those close to her.

As he was contemplating the Williams' family, Bingham walked in.

'Fletcher's going to be OK, sir. I've just heard from her at the hospital. Food poisoning. She'll need a few days off though.'

'Damn. Of course, it's good news she'll be OK,' replied Bingham quickly. 'Baby alright too?'

'Yes.'

'What else is going on?'

'We've got a bit of news,' said Carruthers. 'Harris and myself have been over to Charlene Todd's. We found a T-shirt in a bag under the sink soaked in blood. We've taken it away for forensic testing.'

'Good work, Jim. Looks like we might have Rhys Evans' killer. Keep me posted. Anything else?'

'I've been reading the Williams' file. It's all a bit odd.'

'What is?'

'He's never been charged with anything. Looks like the South Wales Police would have had enough to charge him on a number of occasions. A couple of times, he was initially charged, but those charges appear to have been dropped.'

'Hmm.'

'The other thing is, there's been a number of pages torn out of his file. Pages that relate to the years 1971 to 1973. Of course, we now know he was most likely in Northern Ireland in early '72. It's very odd. He was obviously on South Wales Police's radar. He seems to have been a very busy boy, especially in his youth, and there's got to be some incidents in those years.'

'Yes, it does look a bit odd –, but paperwork goes missing, especially over such a long period of time. It was over forty years ago,'

'I realise that, sir, but if paperwork was going to go missing, you would expect the whole file to be missing. Not individual pages deliberately torn out.'

'I can't answer that. You'd have to phone the South Wales Police. Don't expect them to be able to throw light on it though.' Bingham drew himself up to his five feet ten. 'Right, I've got a meeting with Superintendent McGhee. Am I right in thinking you're interviewing Roberts' parents tomorrow in Castletown?'

'Yes.'

'Good. Excellent. Keep me informed. What are you doing at the moment?'

'Just following up on a lead, then heading home, with a bit of luck.'

'Anything I should know about?'

'Not yet – and it might turn out to be nothing.'

'OK. It's good news about Fletcher.'

'Yes, it is.'

'What about you, Jim? Anyone special at the moment? You know, since you and,' Bingham coughed, 'Mairi, was it, split?'

Carruthers glanced at his watch. Wondered what excuse he could invent to end the awkward conversation. It was very unlike Superintendent Bingham to be showing an interest in his personal life. He wondered if McGhee had been gossiping about him.

'Nobody at the moment. No.'

'Good. I mean, probably for the best. Big case going on. Don't want to be distracted.'

'No,' said Carruthers feeling a moment's loneliness and thinking he'd quite like to be a bit distracted from time to time. There was only one person he'd recently met that he wouldn't have minded being distracted with: Siobhan Mathews. And she was off limits. He wondered if he'd been too harsh on her at the station. His gut instinct was that she was innocent of any involvement in Evans' murder. He also couldn't imagine her involved in any part in the car bomb. It was obvious she had just shown bad judgment in sleeping with Roberts then getting involved with Evans. Now that was messy, especially as there had seemed to be no love lost between those two men. His mind wandered to the photograph of Siobhan and Roberts. He'd felt all sorts of emotions when he'd first seen that photo. Jealousy and disappointment were just two of them. Stupid when he hardly knew her.

He thought of her now and wondered what she was doing. She'd seemed genuinely horrified at the news of Roberts' death, and terrified when he told her she might be in danger. He wasn't sure if Siobhan was in danger or not, but he wished he'd played it down and hoped that her flatmate was at home with her that evening.

SEVENTEEN

TUESDAY MORNING, 5ᵗʰ JUNE

Carruthers was in work at eight the next morning. The first thing he did was to fix himself a double espresso. Too much caffeine, but at least it wasn't alcohol. There hadn't been a repeat of that awful night where he'd passed out in his chair.

He decided to ring the South Wales Police before interviewing Mr and Mrs Roberts. The missing information was playing on his mind. However, first he would ring Dr Mackie. He knew Mackie was an early bird.

'No forensics back on the T-shirt yet, Jim. I know you're champing at the bit. I'll call you when they come in.'

Damn. Most likely won't have the forensics back before interviewing the Roberts'.

He set about ringing PC Rachael Turner of South Wales Police, and readied himself for a fight. 'PC Turner, I believe you forwarded the Ewan Williams file to me. There's a bit of a problem: some pages are missing. Particularly those relating to the years between 1971 and 1974. They've been ripped out. Any idea where they might be?'

'I couldn't tell you, sir. To be honest, I didn't notice anything when I had it sent over but then you were in such a hurry for the file I just bundled it into the post.'

'Could the pages be mislaid in someone else's file?'

'I'm afraid we don't have the manpower to spend our time looking through archived files.'

'We've got a very serious situation on our hands here. We know Ewan Williams is fronting the terrorist organisation

Bryn Glas 1402 and we believe he's currently operating here in Scotland. You might have seen on the news about a car bomb here in Castletown?' The inarticulate noise she made seemed to be agreement. 'We believe he was responsible. I want to know why those pages could have been ripped out of his file.'

'I'm sorry. I can't help you. We have nobody in the station who worked here forty years ago.'

Carruthers tersely thanked her and slammed down the phone. 'Christ, they're unhelpful in that bloody police station.'

'Which police station?'

Sergeant Brown was just passing Carruthers' office holding a can of Irn-Bru. He poked his head round.

'I've just been speaking to the police in South Wales. Pages are missing from Williams' file relating to his activities in the early 70s.'

'Early 70s did you say? That rings a bell... Oh aye, that'll be it. I had an Uncle through marriage who was in the Swansea Police Force sometime back. I remember him talking about the Cardiff lot. I'm not surprised they're no' forthcoming. Don't you remember? There was a massive police bribery and corruption case relating to the Cardiff Police around then. It was found that a couple of high-ranking officers were in the pockets of local gangsters. Several senior officers got pensioned off. If it had happened at your station, it's not something that you would want to be reminded of. Mind, it was a long time ago now. You'll probably find there's not enough staff, and not enough interest.'

Exactly as PC Turner had said, although he did wonder just how old Brown thought he was, expecting him to remember corruption charges in the 1970s. But this was a useful detail. 'So it's possible that detectives in Cardiff could have been in Williams' pocket in the early 70s?' said Carruthers.

Brown was standing leaning against the office door. 'Anything's possible. Did it actually happen? That's another question.' And with that, he left.

'Right, I had better get cracking too.' Carruthers said to nobody in particular. He checked his watch, hastily gulped back the black coffee and disposed of the paper cup in the bin. He picked up his notebook, car keys and jacket and left the office to set off for the bed and breakfast where he was to meet Dave Roberts' parents.

***

'Mr and Mrs Roberts, I'm Detective Chief Inspector Jim Carruthers. Can I just say how sorry I am about the death of your son?'

'Thank you,' said Mrs Roberts. She was a large woman with a kindly face. Carruthers looked at Mr Roberts and was reminded of an undertaker. The man was tall and thin with a gaunt face. He remained silent.

'I'm afraid I need to ask you a few questions about Dave.'

'What's the good of that? Why aren't you out there catching his killers?' Mr Roberts demanded.

'Oh, Tom. I'm sure they're doing their best.' Mrs Roberts laid a comforting hand on her husband's shoulders.

'I thought he'd turned his life around when he joined the RAF,' said Mr Roberts. 'He promised us that he'd put all that political nonsense behind him. But he hadn't, had he? And now he's wound up dead.'

'Political nonsense?' said Carruthers.

'Tom, we don't know that it's got anything to do with that.'

'Of course we do, woman. It all fits.'

'Mr and Mrs Roberts, can I ask you to start at the beginning.'

'I'm sorry, chief inspector,' said Mrs Roberts. 'Can I offer you a cup of tea? I must say it's very pleasant to have tea and coffee making facilities in the room. We don't travel much. Don't see the need. My hip plays up, which makes movement difficult. Doesn't it, Tom?'

Mr Roberts nodded.

Carruthers thought Mrs Roberts strangely calm and chatty for someone who'd just lost their son to a violent death. But then again, bereavement did strange things to people.

'Nothing for me, but thank you. So, what did your son do before he joined the RAF?'

'He worked in a garage when he first left school. Joined the Territorial Army too,' said Mrs Roberts.

Mr Roberts turned to his wife. 'No, he'd left the garage by the time he'd joined the TA. He was working for McDonald's when he joined them. There was that unpleasantness at the garage, and he was forced to leave.'

'Unpleasantness?' said Carruthers.

'Happiest day of his life when he joined the RAF. That's why he joined the TA, you see. Thought it might help him get into the RAF,' said Mrs Roberts.

'No, he thought it might help him get into the army. Then he changed his mind and decided he wanted to join the RAF instead.'

'That's right.'

'Why did he get asked to leave the garage?' said Carruthers.

'They took on another apprentice,' said Mr Roberts. 'Coloured feller. He and Dave didn't see eye to eye. There was some trouble. He made a complaint about Dave.'

'What was the complaint?' There was a moment's silence and Mr and Mrs Roberts exchanged glances. 'I need to know,' said Carruthers.

'Somebody daubed a swastika onto the back of the coloured boy's jacket. He accused Dave,' said Mr Roberts. 'He may have been a bit wayward, but he was never a bad lad.'

Carruthers raised his eyebrows.

'It was never proved. There were no witnesses, but as Dave was overheard calling him a nig-nog on a previous occasion the manager decided he had to let him go.'

Carruthers was silent.

'It was never proved,' Tom repeated, 'and calling someone a nig-nog doesn't mean anything, does it? It's like saying you're going out to get a chinky, or you're going down the Paki shop.'

Carruthers could feel his stomach tighten with irritation and distaste. He knew very well that ignorance played a big part, as did the custom of language, but he doubted there could be a person alive who didn't think that 'nig-nog' could be meant as anything other than a term of abuse. Apart from the Roberts, apparently.

'Well, it's not as if he called him a nigger, is it? Nig-nog's more friendly somehow. Anyway, it's no worse than calling a Scotsman Jock.'

The tightening in his stomach continued. 'Isn't it? Surely it depends on what their relationship was like.'

Mr and Mrs Roberts looked confused.

'Whether they were friends,' continued Carruthers. 'It sounds like the new apprentice started to suffer from a catalogue of racial abuse. It's unlikely it would have stopped at the two incidents you've mentioned. The kid did the right thing to report it. Nobody should have to put up with that sort of harassment at work.'

Both Mr and Mrs Roberts were silent.

'Do you remember the name of the young lad at the garage, and what the garage was called?' asked Carruthers.

'What on earth do you need to know that for? It was over four years ago,' said Mr Roberts.

'Just routine enquiries. I need all the background detail I can get. You never know, it might help to catch Dave's killers.'

'I don't see how, unless you think it was that nig– black apprentice at the garage,' said Mr Roberts.

Carruthers now knew where Dave Roberts' racist views came from.

'But if you really need to know…' Mr Roberts thought about it, 'what was the name of the garage again? Oh yes, Williams Garage. I don't remember the name of the boy, do you?'

'Yes, I do as it happens,' said Mrs Roberts. 'It was Eustace.' She turned to her husband. 'Don't you remember? Dave used to call him Useless.'

The irritation in Carruthers' stomach was giving way to an unpleasant acid curdling which was also finding its way into his mouth. He swallowed the bitter bile back down.

'Can't think of his surname though,' continued Mrs Roberts. 'No point in trying to contact him now though, inspector. He left the garage soon after. Well, didn't so much leave, as disappear into thin air. Left them right in the lurch. I heard all this from our neighbour. One day he was here and the next he never turned up for work.'

Carruthers made a note of all these details in his little black notebook. There was a sinking feeling in his stomach about the apprentice's disappearance. This was something that needed to be followed up. 'Do you know where he went?'

'No, but it would've been about the time Dave had the accident,' said Mr Roberts.

'No, he had the accident well before that, Tom. It was before he joined the garage. Don't you remember?'

'Accident?' Carruthers ears pricked up. 'When was this?'

'Just before he joined the garage. Would have been seventeen.'

'What happened?'

'Him and some other boys were larking about. Climbing trees. That sort of thing.'

Carruthers was thinking that at seventeen he was a bit old to be climbing trees, but he kept quiet. 'What happened?'

'Branch broke and he fell out. He landed on his head. Physically he recovered, but it seemed to change his personality.'

'In what way?'

'Well, he became moody and more aggressive. I don't know. I can't explain it. Got into more fights.'

'What did the doctors say? Was there any permanent injury?'

'Oh no, he wasn't brain damaged, inspector. Just seemed to change his personality a bit. That's all.'

'Where did Dave work after leaving the garage?' said Carruthers, wondering how Roberts had passed the RAF medical.

'McDonald's. By then he'd joined the TA. We encouraged him. Like Tom said, he was never a bad lad but he had started to keep bad company.'

'Who did he run around with?' asked Carruthers.

'There were three of them, weren't there? Tom Petty's lad, John. Billy Thomas and Dave.'

'Billy Thomas?' asked Carruthers. 'Any relation to a Mal Thomas?'

'Younger brother.'

Carruthers frowned. 'That wouldn't be the same Mal Thomas who is a member of Bryn Glas 1402?'

'I wouldn't know,' answered Mr Roberts.

Both he and his wife became silent but Carruthers caught the look that passed between them. He had a strong feeling that they knew more than they were saying.

'I take it you've heard of Bryn Glas 1402?' said Carruthers.

'Not until this week,' said Mr Roberts quickly. He looked away from Carruthers when he next spoke. 'You're barking up the wrong tree there, though. Dave was never a member. We would have known.'

'Could he have become a member after he left home to join the RAF?'

'I don't think he was that interested in Welsh nationalism. Certainly not enough to have become a member of an organisation like that.'

Carruthers looked from one to the other. Why didn't he believe them? There was something they weren't telling him.

'Mr and Mrs Roberts, you've said Dave had a problem with the coloured apprentice at the garage where he worked. Would it surprise you to know we've learnt that Dave was a paid-up member of the BNP?'

'I've voted Plaid Cymru all my life, and I'm proud of it,' said Mr Roberts. 'I won't deny Dave had some strong views, but the BNP is still a legitimate political party, inspector. If he wanted to join it, then that was his right.'

On the other hand, thought Carruthers, *Bryn Glas 1402 is not a legitimate political party. It's looking likely that it's a terrorist organisation fronted by an ex-con..*

'We've heard a man matching Dave's description was seen in the politics department at the university at the time of the car bomb,' said Mr Roberts. He leant over and took his wife's hand.

'We might not get out that often, but we watch the telly,' said Mrs Roberts.

'We want you to know that we've no idea why he'd have been there,' said Mr Roberts. 'But I can tell you one thing. There's no way Dave would have planted that car bomb unless he was forced to do it.'

'Why would he be forced into doing it?' asked Carruthers.

'Well, supposing it is Bryn Glas 1402 who planted that bomb. They'd be looking for someone with a knowledge of bomb disposal in the area, wouldn't they? They also happen to know Dave through one of his mates.'

'As far as I'm aware, Dave was an aircraftman working on the Tornado aircraft at RAF Edenside along with another Cardiff boy, Rhys Evans. You know that we're also currently investigating his death?'

Mr Roberts shook his head.

'He was found dead in a doorway of Bell Street in Castletown. He'd been beaten to death. I'm led to believe,' continued Carruthers, 'that Dave knew Rhys from his Cardiff days? How long had they known each other?'

'They were at school together,' said Mrs Roberts.

'But they didn't hang out together?'

'No.' Mrs Roberts turned to her husband. 'We knew of him but don't think we ever saw him at the house, did we?'

Mr Roberts shook his head again. Carruthers was starting to form an opinion that he was a man of few words.

Carruthers directed his next question to Mrs Roberts as she was the chattier of the two. 'They weren't friends?'

'Why are you asking us all these questions?' said Mr Roberts. 'What has this boy's death got to do with Dave?'

'We're not sure,' said Carruthers quickly. The forensic results from the T-shirt found at Charlene Todd's house still weren't yet in and he didn't want to give out too much information. He certainly didn't want to accuse their son of murder if it was subsequently found that the blood didn't belong to Evans.

Or Roberts, for that matter. He brought his mind back to the previous part of the conversation before he had started talking about Rhys Evans. There was an important question he needed to ask of them.

'How would Dave have knowledge of bombs?' he asked.

'I thought you would have known,' said Mr Roberts. 'Back in Cardiff when Dave was in the TA, he was in the bomb disposal unit.'

Carruthers was so dumbstruck that he nearly forgot to ask the final question he had for them. Forced himself to get back on track. 'What do you know of Ewan Williams, the front man of Bryn Glas, and his family?'

'Of course we've heard of him. Williams might be a popular name where we come from, inspector, but everybody's heard of Ewan Williams. We're from Ely, the same suburb of Cardiff as Ewan Williams. Our parents knew his parents.'

'They had five sons and one daughter. The daughter left home at nineteen. How much do you know about where she went and what happened to her after she moved out?'

'I remember the girl,' said Mrs Roberts. 'She was very close to Ewan. She moved to Belfast to be with her boyfriend. It was very sad what happened to her. She got injured in the Bloody Sunday march. 1972 wasn't it? Ended up in a wheelchair, until she died.'

'Sorry? You say she's dead? How recently did she die?'

'Two months ago. We heard from someone down my bingo club,' said Mrs Roberts. 'Although she'd moved away she became a bit of a local hero in Wales and in Northern Ireland in the 1970s. I remember my parents talking about her. She insisted, just after her shooting, that she didn't want any reprisals, see.'

Thinking what an incredible woman Meg McDaid must have been, Carruthers thanked the Roberts for their time, stood up and left.

EIGHTEEN

TUESDAY LUNCHTIME, 5ᵀᴴ JUNE

'That march fuelled nationalistic fervour, leading to many more individuals joining the IRA,' said Carruthers. 'This is a personal crusade for Ewan Williams. I believe we now know the reason he's waited so long to act. I found out Margaret McDaid died two months ago.'

'You think her death was the catalyst then?' said Bingham.

'Almost certainly. Apparently, after her shooting, she called on the community not to seek reprisals. We know Williams was close to his sister. Perhaps he made her a promise, which he kept during her lifetime, not to hunt down and kill the man who maimed her. However, with her death, he may feel freed from that promise. It's more than likely Williams became interested in Welsh nationalism post-1972. He was a young man then.'

'I wonder to what extent people in Wales were motivated to join nationalist movements when they saw what was happening in Northern Ireland?' said Bingham.

'Williams may have set up Bryn Glas 1402 for the specific job of targeting Holdaway. Who knows? He's had over forty years to plan his revenge. Margaret McDaid hadn't been keeping the best of health. Perhaps Williams knew her time was short. He's certainly been very clever in manipulating the other members of the group into targeting Holdaway. He had a perfect excuse with Holdaway buying a holiday home in Wales and bringing out his book. From what I'm also led to believe, Williams is a very charismatic leader who commands great respect and loyalty. He's also hard to refuse.'

'How about Dave Roberts?' asked Bingham. 'Glean anything from the parents? Did he have an interest in Welsh Nationalism? Could they confirm whether he was he a member of Bryn Glas 1402?'

'They admitted to their son's membership of the BNP. They see it as a legitimate party, which of course it is, however odious its politics. But they deny Roberts was involved with Bryn Glas 1402. However, they weren't convincing. And the Roberts family know or at least knew of the Williams family back in the day. We need to keep digging.'

'When Roberts joined the RAF, he would have been closely vetted,' said Bingham. 'If he did become a member of Bryn Glas, it must have been after he joined up. The vetting to get into Britain's armed forces is second to none. I'm reluctant to say this after your earlier carry on with McGhee, but good work, Jim. What are you going to do now?'

'I've got Holdaway in my office. We've got the CCTV through from the car park. We think it shows Roberts planting the bomb. I want to see if Holdaway can identify him as the man on the stairwell. It's looking pretty definite now that it was Roberts who planted the bomb. Apparently, before he joined the RAF, Roberts was in the bomb disposal unit of the Territorials.'

'Was he now? Perhaps that's why he was needed by Williams.'

'We've also got some photos to show Holdaway.'

'Right. While you do that, I'll fill McGhee in. His people have arrived from the south, so he's briefing them. Some of them have been liaising with the South Wales Police in Cardiff. We do need to find Williams as a priority. He's clearly dangerous.'

'Yes, but at least we now know he's only after Holdaway. The Scottish population's safe.'

'Let's not be complacent. He's a dangerous criminal, a terrorist. He's not stupid either. He'll know that we're closing in on him. Who knows how he'll respond when cornered. We need to catch him, Jim.'

'We will, sir.'

***

TUESDAY AFTERNOON, 5TH JUNE

'Professor. Have a seat.'

Carruthers didn't stand on ceremony, nor did he engage in small talk. There simply wasn't time. His stomach rumbled reminding him he hadn't eaten all day.

'We'd like to show you something,' said Carruthers. 'It's the CCTV footage from your departmental car park on the day of the explosion.' He gestured for Holdaway to take a seat in the meeting room.

The images on the large TV were grainy. For several seconds there was no movement among the cars.

'What am I supposed to be looking at?' the professor looked enquiringly at Carruthers.

'Be patient.' A few seconds went by. 'Right, here it is,' said Carruthers.

Out of the shadows, a figure emerged. Baseball cap on head, the figure was wearing jeans and a T-shirt. He glanced around, then, as if satisfied the coast was clear, furtively made his way to Holdaway's car crouching down out of view on the far side.

'We're pretty sure this is the moment when he was planting the bomb.' A little later the figure emerged. Carruthers froze the CCTV, as the figure looked up towards the camera. Despite the fact the man was wearing a baseball cap, it was still possible, through the grainy image, to see his face as he defiantly looked straight into the camera lens and smiled.

'Oh my God. He's looking straight at the CCTV camera,' Holdaway said aghast. 'He actually smiled. The nerve of him.'

'Is this the man you saw on the stairs? Could it be the same person?' urged Carruthers.

'Can I see it again?' asked Holdaway.

Carruthers rewound and ran it again.

'Yes, I think so. Same stocky build. Same square jaw. When I saw him he wasn't wearing the baseball cap, but I'm sure it's him. I can't get over the fact he's so cocky. The way he's looking at the CCTV camera.'

'Probably thought there was a tape in the camera and that it would be damaged beyond repair in the explosion. It's not far away from where your car was.'

'Who is he? A member of Bryn Glas 1402?'

'We believe he's this man, Dave Roberts, aircraftman, based at RAF Edenside. Do you recognise him from this photograph?' Carruthers passed over a photograph of Roberts that the RAF base had provided. It showed him in his uniform.

'He's in the RAF?' Holdaway asked incredulously. 'Is he Scottish?'

'No, he's Welsh, from Cardiff. And although he's a member of the BNP, he has no known association with any Welsh terrorist outfit.'

As Carruthers was talking the CCTV footage was still running. Out of the corner of his eye he saw something, some movement in the shadows.

'Hang on. What was that?' Carruthers played it again. He screwed his eyes up and watched intently. There was definitely the blurry image of another shadowy figure in the background. Carruthers froze the footage.

He turned to Holdaway. 'Do you see that, Professor? That second figure.'

Holdaway shook his head. 'No, I don't. I can't make anything out, but then my eyesight probably isn't as good as yours.'

'There's definitely a second person there when the bomb's being planted. Almost out of the picture. It's hard to see but it's there.'

Holdaway leant forward. 'I'm sorry. I can't see it.'

Carruthers picked up his mobile. 'Brown, it's Jim. Can you get hold of one of the techies for me? I've seen something on the CCTV. I want to see if we can enlarge it.'

'I don't understand,' said Holdaway, 'what would someone in the RAF be doing blowing up my car? Oh my God, you're not telling me the terrorists have infiltrated the military, are you? Do the Home Office know about this? Where is this man now? Have you managed to arrest him?'

'That would be difficult. He was found dead a couple of days ago.'

'Dead?' said Holdaway. 'Christ. None of this makes any sense. Can you please explain to me what is going on? How is the RAF involved? If this man, Roberts is– was a member of the BNP, what was he doing coming after me? And who killed him? If the man who was trying to kill me is dead, does this mean that I'm now safe? Perhaps it isn't Ewan Williams after all.'

Carruthers saw a glimmer of hope in Holdaway's eyes. He felt a wretch for being about to extinguish it. He didn't answer Holdaway, but rather opened a buff A4 envelope which he handed to him.

'We'd like you to look at some more photographs.' Carruthers brought out several photographs including those of the three known members of Bryn Glas. 'Do you recognise any of these men? Take your time.'

Holdaway studied each in turn. With each photograph he shook his head, until his gaze settled on the photo of Williams. Carruthers saw him hesitate. Holdaway picked the photograph up and brought it closer to his face.

'Do you recognise him?' said Carruthers.

'I've seen him recently.'

'How recently?'

'Maybe last week. In Castletown.'

'What was he doing?'

'Doing? Smoking a cigarette in a doorway. Across the road from the department. I walked past him. He looked up. I felt he recognised me, but I didn't recognise him. Yet even when I saw him I felt I knew him from somewhere.'

'So you do know him.'

'No, I don't, except… there's something familiar about his face.'

'So you *do* know him,' he urged.

'No, I've just said I didn't,' he snapped. 'It's just… there's a familiarity about him. I don't know him, but I feel certain I've seen him before. Before last week. I can't place where though.'

'When? When did you see him before?'

'The only feature I really recognise are the eyes. It's the eyes that are really familiar.'

'So, perhaps it's someone you met or saw a long time ago?' Carruthers knew he was asking leading questions of Holdaway but if he got the answer he wanted it would be worth it. 'The face has changed because it's aged. That's why you only recognise the eyes. People say that the eyes are the gateway to the soul, don't they? Imagine these eyes in the face of a much younger man. What would he look like? Where would he be?'

Just at that moment, there was a shout from the other side of the door. Harris, never a quiet man at the best of times, was barking some instruction to Brown. The shout seemed to unnerve Holdaway.

'It's OK, Professor. Just two of my officers. Take your time.'

This did little to calm Holdaway. If anything, he looked even more agitated.

'Was it the shout that bothered you?' Carruthers prompted, with a sudden brainwave. 'Was this man shouting when you saw him?'

Carruthers carefully brought out a fifth photograph and slid it towards Holdaway. The photograph was old. At least forty years old. It showed a young man with longish hair and a beard, wearing a plaid shirt with a wide collar. Carruthers waited for Holdaway's reaction, as he showed him a picture of Ewan Williams as he had looked in the mid-1970s.

'No, it can't be. It just can't be. It's not possible.'

'What isn't possible, Professor?

'I've seen this man before. I'm sure of it. He was shouting.'

'What was he shouting, Professor? What was he shouting?'

Professor Holdaway put his head in his hands and started crying. '"You've shot her. You've shot her, you English bastard." He was the man from the march.'

Carruthers gave Holdaway a few moments to compose himself before continuing, 'Look, there's no easy way of saying this. Before interviewing you, professor, I'd just come from interviewing Dave Roberts' parents. I found out they knew the Williams' family. Thing is, Ewan Williams' sister died a couple of months ago. We think her death has been the catalyst for the attacks on you.'

Holdaway put his head in his hands. He looked like a man whose past had finally caught up with him. He seemed to collapse back into his chair, his face the colour of parchment. 'I always dreaded this day coming. Somehow, deep down, I knew it would.'

Carruthers wondered how other soldiers who had been present on that day now felt. Did they still constantly look over their shoulders? Still check their cars for bombs? Feel guilt or regret now they knew what they did had been deemed unlawful? Or did they feel they'd simply been following orders?

'We're going to arrange for you to join your wife in Spain while we catch Williams. In the meantime we'll organise for you to stay somewhere safe until we can get a flight booked. How soon can you be ready to leave your house?'

'Tomorrow morning.'

'Why not later today?'

'I want one last night in my own home.'

'I wouldn't recommend that, but it's your decision.'

'It's what I want.'

'Fine, I can organise for one of my men to stay overnight with you.'

Holdaway shook his head. 'I'd sooner be on my own.'

'Look, we want to make sure you're safe. If you don't want anyone in the house we'll get someone to stay in a car outside your house.'

'If you think that's best.'

'I do. OK. We'll arrange for a car to pick you up tomorrow morning. I'll get DS Harris on to it.' Carruthers made a mental note to also get a man posted on the door.

Holdaway nodded mutely.

There was a rap on the door. Harris popped his head round. 'Can I have a word?'

Carruthers excused himself and left the room. They talked quietly in the corridor.

'I've just had a call from the lab,' said Harris. The results of the blood analysis on the T-shirt are back.'

***

The man sat in the kitchen of the farmhouse drinking a beer. The fridge door was standing open. An overflowing ashtray stood on the kitchen table, the air was thick with stale smoke. He'd been informed of the arrival of their captive. He knew she was in the barn. He'd told the boys no rough stuff and to look after her. He touched his bottom lip with a calloused finger. His mind wandered. Dave Roberts had defied his instructions. Had helped Holdaway stay alive.

The man didn't react well to being defied. He reached over and wrapped his hand round the handgun. He stood up. He wanted to talk to Mathews himself about how much she knew and what she'd said to the police. But first there was one more job to be done. And this time it was going to be done properly. Grabbing his cigarettes and car keys he left the farmhouse.

NINETEEN

Siobhan opened her eyes. It was pitch black. She was lying on a cold, hard surface. Rough scratchy rope bound her wrists and ankles. A foul-smelling cloth was tied around her eyes. Her head thumped. She felt woozy. And cold. Colder than she had ever felt in her life.

She lay perfectly still and listened. There was a stillness about the place. Outside she could hear birds. She breathed in through her nostrils, becoming aware of another smell. It was a strong familiar smell. Reminded her of cows. A farmyard. She had no idea how long she had been here. Time had no meaning. She tried to move. Her hands were tied tightly behind her back, so she felt on the ground with her fingers to see if they came into contact with anything. They didn't, but the rope dug into her flesh, making her wince. She fanned her fingers out best she could, feeling dry dirt and clumps of what she could only imagine was straw. Her lower back ached and there was a raw soreness between her legs. Her thighs felt bruised. Memories of the two men came flooding back to her. She was so frightened, she whimpered. She started feeling more woozy again. Within seconds she'd blacked out.

***

Carruthers stared at Harris. He found he was holding his breath. Finally the man spoke. 'The blood on the T-shirt matches that of Rhys Evans. We've also found Roberts' blood.'

At last. A breakthrough. If they could nail Dave Roberts for Rhys Evans' murder perhaps Siobhan Mathews would ultimately be able to get some closure. His mobile rang. He took it out of his breast pocket. 'DCI Jim Carruthers.'

'Jim, it's Ian Green from Ballistics. We've got the results on the bullet used to kill Dave Roberts.'

Carruthers looked at Harris. 'Dougie, you got a pen? Also some paper?'

Harris disappeared for a couple of seconds. Came back armed with both. Carruthers grabbed the pen. Cradled the mobile against his shoulder and accepted the spiral notebook from Harris.

'OK, said Carruthers. 'I'm ready.'

'Bullet came from a 9mm Browning handgun. That's all I've got at the moment.'

Carruthers thanked Green and finished the call. He looked over at Harris who was still hovering. 'Dougie, Holdaway's still in the meeting room. I'm popping back in to see him. But will you organise for someone to take him back to his home? I want someone to stay with him. Then in the morning he's to be taken to a safe house until we can organise a flight to Spain. When you're done getting this sorted, join us in the meeting. It's in Bingham's office.'

Gripping his notebook he walked back to Holdaway before heading to the next meeting.

***

The first thing she heard was birdsong. She had no idea how long she'd been unconscious. Her mouth was dry. She needed the toilet. She tried to break free from the rope around her wrists, but it was tied too tight. Tears of frustration pricked her eyes. She wondered if her rucksack was close by. If she could only get to it, her mobile was in the pocket in the front. But as she was blindfolded and she didn't have a clue where her rucksack was. She heard a noise. It sounded like a barn door being opened. Then footsteps growing louder. A voice echoed in the darkness.

'Don't be doing anything stupid. I've brought you some food.' The accent was Welsh.

She felt a rough hand on her shoulder. She was hauled into a seated position. The blindfold was torn away from her eyes, the gag taken out of her mouth. She was pushed down on to a chair. She blinked. Her captor loomed above her head, wearing a balaclava, dressed all in black. He crouched down beside her. She screamed. He put his hand against her mouth.

'Don't do that again,' he hissed. He kept his hand over her mouth. 'You won't, will you?'

She shook her head, wide eyes betraying her fear. Slowly he took his hand away and pushed a metal plate and cup in her direction.

'Eat.'

There was silence.

'I said, eat!'

'I can't whilst I'm tied.'

The captor knelt once more and untied her hands.

'I need the toilet.'

He took his time to make a decision. Finally he untied her ankles and hauled her to her feet. 'I'm coming with you. No funny business.'

He led her towards the back of the barn.

'I can't go in here,' she protested.

'You'll have to. You're not allowed out of the barn.'

'Why have you brought me here? I don't know anything.'

'The boss wants to speak to you.'

'I don't know anything. How long am I going to be kept here for? People will start missing me.'

'You'll stay here until the boss says otherwise. That's enough questions. Just behave yourself and you won't get hurt. You are going to behave yourself, aren't you?'

Siobhan nodded, swallowing down a sob.

***

'OK, gentlemen, we now know that the weapon that killed Roberts was a 9mm Browning handgun,' said Carruthers. He put his glasses back on the top of his head. He looked round the room. As he did he made eye contact with the three unsmiling faces of McGhee's men. He hadn't said more than a few words to them. He addressed his next comment to McGhee. 'Alistair, do you know anything about this particular handgun?'

'American,' said the tallest of McGhee's men.

Carruthers was trying to remember his name. Matt Rodgers. The tall man continued, rapping out his memorised facts. 'Used in the Second World War. Very desirable as a military issue pistol. It was reliable, accurate. Certainly had a lot of stopping power. Had a thirteen-round magazine capacity. Still in circulation today, although it's old. But it's also interesting because back in the 70s and 80s it was the IRA's weapon of choice.'

McGhee spoke. 'Matt is our resident firearms expert.'

There was a moment's silence.

'The gun's still at large,' said Carruthers. 'As are Williams and his accomplices. Professor Holdaway's flight to Malaga leaves at eleven tomorrow morning. He's been notified.'

'If we assume the gun belongs to Williams,' said Bingham, 'perhaps he was going to use it to take out Holdaway. Maybe he wanted to use a firearm that was as authentic to the time his sister got shot. Perhaps it was given to him by members of the IRA. However, with his criminal connections he would have no difficulty getting his hands on more recent weapons.'

Carruthers' thoughts turned to Holdaway. He felt increasingly uncomfortable letting Holdaway stay the extra night in his own home, even with a police guard. An image of a fairground came into his mind and of a man shooting a sitting duck.

The door opened and Harris joined the meeting. Carruthers addressed his next question to him. 'Everything organised for Holdaway?'

'Aye, boss. I've got one of the uniform's taking him back. And he'll have a guard overnight.'

Carruthers nodded his approval.

***

EARLY WEDNESDAY MORNING, 6TH JUNE

The man lit a cigarette, smoking it whilst keeping his eyes on the house on the top of the hill. He could see the police officer sitting in his car keeping watch. He knew the officer would need to answer the call of nature at some point. He would just have to sit tight until that time. He was fortunate that the professor lived somewhere isolated.

Several hours later he saw the door of the car open and the officer get out. The officer walked away from the car. The man felt for the bulky cold object in the pocket of his jacket. It was in place. He followed the officer keeping his distance. When the officer unzipped his trousers the man increased his pace. Hearing a noise the officer swung round. The man was ready. Before the officer had even cried out the man had smashed him in the face with the butt of the gun.

The man approached the front door of the house. Was just about to ring the doorbell when he realised the door was ajar. Wasn't sure whether this was unusual for the Fife countryside. He slipped on his leather gloves and slowly pushed the door open. There was no movement in the dimly lit interior but he could hear faint music. Something classical. He screwed his eyes up and could just make out a long hall with various doors off it and a spiral staircase at the end of it. Silently he went in the house and softly closed the door behind him.

He hesitated in the large hall. Cautiously he put his head round the room to the right and looked in. It was a living room. Unlit. And empty. He retreated. Light-footed, he walked down the corridor and opened the door to his left. It was a small bathroom. Next left he found he was in a large kitchen. Door to the drinks cabinet open; there was an empty Highland Park box on the table. He walked towards the back of the hall. The music became louder. Coming from behind a door to the left of the stairwell. No voices. Just music. He took his gun out. Gripped it tightly. Very slowly he turned the handle and walked into a huge dining area. The lights were blazing from a large crystal chandelier hung in the middle of the room. The long table beneath was set with silver service. A phone rang. The man slipped behind the door. Nobody answered, yet he felt the presence of someone in the house.

Keeping a tight grip on the gun, he went to the foot of the stairs. Ran his gloved hand up the polished wooden banister. Quietly climbed the stairs. Hesitated. At the top of the stairs was another bathroom. The door was ajar. The light was on.

The man stood at the threshold. Here the atmosphere was different. The air was warmer. Whisky scented the air. And something else. Something metallic. He frowned. Pushed open the door cautiously with the barrel of the gun. And after forty years finally came face to face with the man who had shot his sister.

***

Carruthers was processing the paperwork from the interview with Roberts' parents when Harris approached him at his desk. 'That Chinky girl's here to see you.'

'Chinky girl?' Carruthers had no idea what Harris was talking about.

'Flatmate of Evans' girlfriend.'

Carruthers frowned. 'She's Japanese, Harris. Put her in interview room one, will you? I'll be right along,' he said already standing. Alarm bells went off in his head. *Why was Tomoko here?* 'Bring us two coffees straight away.'

Dougie Harris sniffed. 'Do I look like the hired help?'

'To me you look like a DS who's already on thin ice for beating up a civilian, is apparently palming off his own duties to uniform and who could do worse than learn to listen to his superiors. So, two coffees. interview room one. Now.'

Carruthers knew that Tomoko would have been more comfortable in his office but he was too embarrassed to subject her to the pile of paperwork that was spilling out over his desk. Even if he had wanted to, he didn't have time to tidy it up.

***

'I'm so sorry for disturbing you,' said Tomoko, looking owlish in her round glasses.

'What is it Tomoko? Is Siobhan OK?'

'Well, that's just it. I haven't seen her for ages. I'm worried.'

Carruthers felt his stomach twist. With a sense of dread he asked, 'What do you mean? When did you last see her?'

'Just after she got back from the station. I was going to the library to study for the evening, so I ate early. She said she was going for a walk by the harbour to clear her head. She was pretty shaken by the interview and–'

'You mean you haven't seen her since Sunday?' said Carruthers.

'She was pretty upset with you. Said you had been tough on her. You don't really think she had anything to do with her own boyfriend's death, do you?'

Carruthers' sense of discomfort grew. He felt he'd been too hard on her. Now she had disappeared. He could kick himself. After all, she might be at university but that didn't necessarily prepare students for the real world. He looked at Tomoko. 'What were her plans that night? Was she going to go out for the evening after her walk?'

'No, she didn't have any. Told me she was going to eat a pizza in the flat, watch some TV, go to bed early.'

'Go on...' urged Carruthers.

'I came back from the library around 10pm.'

'What happened when you got home?'

'That's just it. Absolutely nothing. There was no sign of life in the flat. The lights were all off. I just assumed she'd gone to bed. The next day I got up early. Didn't have time for breakfast. Had to see some friends over in Edinburgh. I stayed over. By the time I got home the next day it was late. It was only when I got up this morning and went to open the door to the fridge to get the milk that I saw her pizza was still in the fridge.'

Carruthers felt his pulse quicken. 'OK, so what did you do next?'

'I knocked on her bedroom door. There was no answer but the door was unlocked.'

'Was this unusual?'

'No, sometimes we lock our doors, if we are going away for a few days. Mostly we leave them unlocked. Anyway, I knocked on the door. There was no answer. I went in. Her room was empty. Bed hadn't been slept in.'

'She could have changed her mind and gone out after all.'

'And not come back overnight – for three days?'

'Perhaps she met someone.' Even as Carruthers said this, he knew it wasn't true. He'd seen Siobhan as she left the interview room. She was horrified to learn of Roberts' death and angry she'd been accused of some involvement in her own boyfriend's death. She'd also been embarrassed about her one-night stand with the Welshman.

'She isn't like that, inspector. She wouldn't have gone home with someone else this close to Rhys' death. They haven't even had the funeral yet.'

'No, of course not. I'm sorry. Look, I'll–'

'Sir,' interrupted a striking auburn-haired police officer at the door, 'can I have a moment? It's important.'

Carruthers made his excuses to Tomoko and left the interview room.

'It's PC Waugh, sir. The man who was posted on the door guarding Holdaway. He's on the phone. You'd better get over to The Lodge, Strathburn.'

Carruthers felt his blood run cold. 'Why?'

'A body's been found. Waugh says it's Professor Nicholas Holdaway.'

'Christ.' Carruthers' mind was racing. 'Can you arrange for Tomoko to be taken back to Edgecliffe?'

The police constable nodded. Carruthers grabbed his car keys and mobile. 'Harris?' he bellowed. 'You're wanted over at the Lodge, Strathburn. Drop everything. I'll be right behind you. I'll meet you there.'

'Aye-aye, boss.'

He stuck his head back in the interview room. 'I'm sorry, Tomoko. I have to go. Urgent business. Try not to worry. I'm sure Siobhan will be OK. Maybe she's gone to her parents for a few days, eh? Have you got a number for them?'

Tomoko shook her head.

'See if you can find Siobhan's address book. Perhaps start ringing round her friends first? When she comes home, will you get in touch with me, please? If she's still missing by evening, then we'll get something organised.'

Tomoko looked less than reassured.

***

The recently painted navy blue front door to Holdaway's home was wide open. PC Waugh was standing none too steadily with his hand against the door frame. The man's face was caked with dried blood.

'For Christ's sake. What happened?' said Carruthers.

'I had to take a piss, sir. Didn't see him until he was on me.'

'Was it Ewan Williams?'

'I don't know. Aye. Mebbe.'

'When did you last check in on Holdaway and see him alive?'

PC Waugh looked at his watch and touched his head. 'It's all a bit hazy. About eleven last night. I saw the bathroom light go on at around one this morning, so he was still alive then.'

'Get yourself to hospital, man. Get that head looked at. Don't drive yourself. Get an ambulance.' The miserable-looking Waugh turned away.

With a heavy heart Carruthers walked into the house.

'Dougie, you here?' His voice echoed in the hall.

'Up here, boss,' called DS Dougie Harris from the length of the hall. 'I'm up the stair.'

Carruthers walked through the hall and took the polished wooden stairs two at a time. Harris was at the top of the stairwell. The DS jerked his head towards the open door at the top of the stairs. 'He's in there. Bathroom. I havenae been in. Didnae want to contaminate. Ye can see round the door. It's no' pleasant.'

There was an empty whisky bottle lying on the floor in a small pool of liquid. But Carruthers' eyes were drawn to the pattern on the wall in the shape of an arc. It took a moment to realise what it was. Blood splatter. The window was shut. Condensation ran down the mirror. Carruthers began to sweat. A naked man was lying in the copper bath. It was or had been Nicholas Holdaway. His hands were turned upwards towards the ceiling, as if pleading with his maker. His wrists were a mass of criss crosses and congealed blood. The bath water was copper-coloured.

'Jesus Christ,' Carruthers said. No need to enter the room. There was nothing he or anyone could do. The man was dead. He turned to Harris. 'Go downstairs. Search the house for any sign of disturbance. Don't touch anything. Wait for the SOCOs. I take it you've called them?'

'Aye, boss.'

'Oh, and Dougie, make sure PC Waugh gets to hospital.'

There is no dignity in death, thought Carruthers, looking from the broad retreating back of Harris, to the now immobile face of Holdaway.

***

Mackie straightened up and sighed. 'Looks like suicide.'

Carruthers frowned. 'Could it be murder made to look like suicide?'

'In my opinion it has all the hallmarks of suicide. See the marks across the wrists?' said Mackie. 'Deeper gashes are likely to have caused his death, but do you see the fainter gashes at the side? Looks like the poor bugger was building up courage. Used the whisky to calm his nerves. What a waste.' Dr Mackie shook his head, staring at the now near empty bottle of Highland Park on the bathroom floor.

Carruthers wasn't sure if Mackie meant the whisky or the Professor.

'Still, we mustn't jump to conclusions,' said Mackie. 'We'll conduct a full post mortem.'

As they came out of the bathroom, Harris appeared at the foot of the stairs, with his hand on the banister. 'Everything looks normal, boss. But it's weird. When I got here the lights were on in the dining room, dinner table set and classical music was playing. Creepy, eh?'

'Take your hand off the banister, you fool.' Dr Mackie's face appeared round the bathroom door, scowling at Harris. 'Next time, don't be so careless. In fact, just get him out of here.' He motioned to Carruthers, tutting and shaking his head. Harris and Mackie had crossed swords before, and Jim knew Mackie had little time for Harris, considering him nothing more than a thug in a police uniform.

'Can you give me a time of death? PC Waugh says the last time he looked in on him was around eleven last night; and he saw the bathroom light go on at 1am,' said Carruthers.

'We'll need the PM for that. Don't beat yourself up, laddie. Concentrate on the living now. There's nothing you can do for the dead. You're no use here. Best thing you can do is get yourself back to the station. I'll call you when I have some news.'

Carruthers nodded, choked. He guided Harris out of the house. 'I know I don't have to tell you, but don't touch the door on the way out, will you?'

'What do you think I am, some sort of numpty?'

Carruthers barely heard Harris' response. Mackie was right. There was nothing further he could do for Holdaway. His thoughts now turned to the living. Where was Siobhan Mathews? He brought out his mobile. Phoned her. It went to voicemail.

TWENTY

Siobhan had stopped trying to free herself from the rope. Struggling was futile. However hard she tried to loosen it, the rope just seemed to tighten. She could feel it digging into her wrists, cutting the circulation off to her hands. Her fingers were cold, starting to tingle. She wondered if she was going to die. The same man had periodically come in and given her food and water. She had seen him four or five times but she had no idea how long she'd been in the barn now. She was just vaguely aware of day turning into night and night turning into day.

'Get her up,' a Welsh accent commanded.

She felt herself roughly pulled to her feet. Placed in a chair. The strip of cloth covering her eyes was again untied; the gag loosened from her mouth. Her eyes adjusted slowly to the half-light. She had lost feeling in her left arm. She narrowed her eyes in an attempt to focus. She saw the silhouette of two men standing a few feet in front of her. Both wore balaclavas. One was the shape of the man who had been giving her food. But the other smaller man… she began to tremble.

'We're waiting for the boss. If you answer his questions, he won't hurt you,' said the taller of the two men. The man whose voice was familiar.

The door of the barn opened and a third figure entered. This man was large, his broad frame making him menacing.

'What do you want?' whispered Siobhan. Her throat felt scratchy, her mouth dry. She was trying not to give into a rising sense of panic, made more acute by the fact she couldn't see the men's faces. *Why are they wearing balaclavas? They can't want to kill me,* she rationalised. *They don't want me to identify them. If they were going to kill me, they wouldn't care. Whilst they keep the balaclavas on, I'm in with a chance of getting out of here alive.*

Knowing this gave her some strength. 'The rope is cutting into my wrists. It hurts.' Her voice came out as a whisper.

The tall man with the broad frame motioned for one of the other men to step forward. 'Loosen it,' he said, 'but keep her hands tied.' He sounded older than the other two.

The shorter man stepped forward, close enough to Siobhan for her to smell his pungent stale sweat. She cowered where she sat.

'Sorry about this,' the old man said. 'You'll feel a bit sick and have a headache for a while. I told them to go easy on you.'

There was something about being up close to this other shorter man. Memories came flooding back of rough arms, calloused hands, rank breath on her face and of her legs being forced apart. A man's body weight on hers, crushing her. The taste of saliva as he tried to kiss her. She couldn't breathe. Had he been the man in the back of the van with her? The smell was the same.

'Get him away,' she screamed.

'What's she talking about?' said the old man.

'Get him away.'

'Shit, Mal, you didn't touch her, did you? Is that what that noise was in the back of the van?'

The man called Mal begun stammering.

'You bloody fool,' said the second man. The man who had been giving Siobhan her food.

'I d-d-didn't rape her.'

Siobhan was still trying to wriggle free of the ropes.

'Nobody mentioned rape but you,' said the old man. 'I always know when you're lying. I said no violence, and especially no violence towards women. This isn't the first time you've let me down. You've become a liability.' He turned to the taller man. 'John, you know what to do.'

The taller man pulled a gun from the breast pocket of his jacket. Pointed it straight at the forehead of the stammering man.

Siobhan fell silent through shock. Found she was holding her breath. The shorter man tried to back away. The taller man pulled the trigger. A deafening noise. A smokey gunpowder smell. Mal fell backwards. Sprawled on the ground. Blood oozing from the single bullet wound to his head.

Siobhan could barely hear her scream over the ringing in her ears.

'What should I do with him?' asked the man.

'Christ. Why do I have to come up with all the answers. Shut up and let me think.'

***

'Any idea how he died?' asked Bingham. The Superintendent was sitting in his office behind his large mahogany desk. He cracked his knuckles. Once again Carruthers detected a faint whiff of cigarette smoke.

'Slashed wrists. Looks like a suicide. Can't rule out the possibility of murder, though. Mackie'll keep us informed. They're working as fast as they can. As soon as they have the official cause of death, they'll let us know. To be honest, I don't think it's in any doubt. Not for me, anyway. It all fits with him wanting to be on his own.'

'And why was he on his own, Carruthers? PC Waugh shouldn't have left his post.'

Carruthers felt a terrible pang of guilt before speaking. 'He was stationed in his car outside the house. Holdaway didn't want anyone inside. Waugh was answering a call of nature when he was jumped.'

'What a ruddy mess. We'll have to get someone who knows Holdaway to ID the body. Then, of course, his wife in Spain has to be notified, unless she flies home to do it herself. What else is going on at the moment?'

'I've had Siobhan Mathews' flatmate in, Tomoko Kawase. Says Mathews hasn't been seen since Sunday. She's worried about her.'

'Should we be?'

As he spoke Carruthers felt his chest tightening. 'I don't like the fact she doesn't seem to have gone back to the flat. Apparently, she was going to stay in and have an early night after her interview.' All his senses screamed to him that she was in trouble. He hoped to God that he was wrong.

'Last known movement?'

'Tomoko left her to take a walk on her own, down by the harbour at East Castle Beach after her interview. She was upset. I know that much.'

'Hasn't been seen since?'

'No, sir. And I can't raise her on the mobile.'

There was a knock on the door. Brown's grey head appeared.

'Reports have just come in of a gunshot over by a farm just outside Cupar.'

'Gunshot? Who reported it?'

'A birdwatcher. There's something else. Gunshot was followed by the sound of a woman screaming.'

'What do you think, Jim?' he asked.

'I don't know, could be just a local farmer scaring off pests or trespassers but I'll get it checked out. Might be nothing to do with Williams, but with a bunch of terrorists on the loose... They've got to be somewhere. A remote farmhouse would be perfect.'

'Brown, do we know who owns the farm?' said Bingham.

'Used to be old man Docherty's, before he sold it. I know it was on the market for a few months, but I don't know who bought it.'

'Wait a minute,' said Carruthers. He looked across at Bingham. 'Can I use your phone?'

Bingham gestured for him to go ahead.

Docherty had been a friend of Mairi's father. Carruthers had got on well with him though they hadn't been in contact since Jim's marital split. The memories of the times they'd gone fishing together were good ones.

He picked up the phone on Bingham's desk and dialled out. It was picked up on the third ring.

'Ronnie's garage. Ronnie Thomson speaking.'

'Ronnie, Jim Carruthers here. No, nothing wrong with the car. Just wanted to pick your brains about something. You know old man Docherty, don't you? Yes, that's right. Used to have the farm out by Cupar. Do you know who bought the property off him?'

Carruthers listened intently. 'Anything else you can tell me? OK, that's great, cheers. If you can think of anything else, you've got my number. No. Nothing wrong. Just routine enquiries for a case we're working on.' Carruthers laughed. 'Yes, you're right. We do always say that. Cheers, Ronnie.'

Bingham looked up as Carruthers replaced the phone. 'Farm's been rented out. Ronnie doesn't know anything other than it's a six-month rental. He lives pretty close to the farm. Says he's seen a couple of men go in and out. Said they didn't look much like farmers. Apparently, there's been increased activity there just in the last few days with a few more men arriving. Hasn't seen any women.'

'I don't know much about farms, but I would imagine a six-month rental's pretty unusual if you seriously want to farm anything,' said Bingham. 'This sounds suspicious. Like you said, it's a perfect hideout, of course. Remote, but still within easy reach of Castletown.'

'Bugger. I don't like the sound of the woman screaming. As you said, it might be nothing; on the other hand, we know we have terrorists in the area and a woman connected to the case is missing. Just to be on the safe side, I'm going to get a negotiator ready. If there's a potential hostage situation, we need to be ready. I'm going to put a call in just in case.'

Bingham stood up. Walked towards the office door, which Carruthers opened for him. They left together, talking as they went.

'I want you and McGhee to head over to the farm,' said Bingham. 'And for Christ's sake, try not to kill each other on the way. When you get there, keep your distance from the farm. If you feel it's safe to approach, do so with caution. We might be barking up the wrong tree, but if it is the terrorists up at the farm, and they do have Siobhan Mathews, we don't want this to turn nasty.'

Carruthers swallowed. He was starting to kick himself for not keeping a closer eye on her. 'I'll ask Dougie to find out who's leased the farm. We need to know. I'll get going and pick McGhee up as I go. We'll take my car.'

'Good. Unmarked is best. Don't do anything to draw attention to yourselves.'

'I've just had a thought,' said Carruthers. 'Might be worth taking some birdwatching gear with us. Binoculars, bird book, that sort of thing. The farm, if I remember rightly, sits right on the edge of a nature reserve.'

TWENTY-ONE

They drove inland on the A91. It was stiflingly hot in the car. Carruthers opened the driver's window to let in some much-needed fresh air. A warm breeze hit his face. 'Jesus, the weather's close,' he said, 'really muggy. Wonder if we'll have a storm?' He could smell static in the air. He was gripping the steering wheel tightly. His back was so tense it had started to ache.

The scent from the rape fields, once they'd left the golf course on the outskirts of Castletown, was overpowering. McGhee sneezed twice. 'Can you shut the window? It's setting off my allergies.'

Carruthers sighed but shut the window. The heat with the window closed was almost unbearable.

'Have you got any water?' asked McGhee.

'Jesus, you don't want much, do you?'

'Don't be so fucking tetchy.'

The two men lapsed into silence again.

'For Christ's sake are you going to keep this up the whole shitting drive?' McGhee demanded a few minutes later.

Carruthers ignored McGhee and kept driving. When he thought McGhee wasn't looking he sneaked a glance across at him. Jim could see the tension thrumming through McGhee, from the compressed lips to the bolt upright sitting position.

'Stop the car,' McGhee demanded.

'What?'

'You heard me. Pull over. Now.'

Carruthers pulled into the first safe place and with eyes blazing and mouth resolutely set he glared at McGhee. 'Now what?'

'Now we talk.'

'I don't think we have anything to talk about,' said Carruthers.

'Yes, we have. If this is a hostage situation and we go in the way we are now, we're more than likely to get ourselves killed.'

Carruthers looked straight ahead. He was aware of his shallow breathing.

'You'll more than likely get the hostage killed as well,' said McGhee.

Carruthers felt a twitch in his left eye. McGhee's words had hit home.

'Look Jim, whatever you think of me personally, we need to work as a unit. If we don't, we're done for. Terrorists don't piss about. This could be the most dangerous situation you've ever faced. I, for one, don't intend to get myself killed. And I'm certainly not intending to carry around a dead fucking weight, which is what you'll be if you don't put your personal feelings aside. Look, hate me all you like. But just not right now. Truce?'

Carruthers said nothing but weighed it up. He hated to admit it but McGhee was right. He looked sideways at the man and let out a long sigh that sounded like a pressure cooker letting off steam. 'OK, truce.'

McGhee nodded. 'Let's get going.'

Carruthers drove out of the lay-by. 'There's a bottle of water in the back seat of the car underneath that old rug. There's not much in it and it'll be warm,' he said.

'Thanks.' McGhee reached over to the back, moved the rug and grabbed the bottle. He opened it and took a swig, pulling a face.

'It's tepid.'

'Sorry.' Carruthers looked McGhee up and down. 'Have you ever been in a hostage situation before?'

'Couple of times.'

Carruthers looked at him questioningly.

'And before you ask,' said McGhee, 'they didn't end well. I'll tell you about it sometime. All you need to know is that lessons have been learnt. The same mistakes won't be repeated here. At least, not by me.'

Carruthers wanted to ask what those mistakes had been, but now wasn't the time.

'Let's hope this doesn't turn into a hostage situation but if it does, are you happy to follow my lead?'

'Yes,' said Carruthers. What else could he say? After all, what experience did he have of hostage situations? He looked up at the cloudy sky. There were some ominously dark clouds in it.

'Good,' said McGhee. 'Glad that's sorted.' As he said it there was a rumble of thunder. 'Think that storm you predicted is coming. How long until we reach the farm?'

'Not long. About seven minutes.'

They passed more fields of rape, the brightness at odds with the increasing darkness of the sky. The countryside was dotted with farms, ancient stone walls, and the occasional hedge.

'I never realised Fife was so beautiful,' said McGhee. 'Do you miss London?'

Carruthers shrugged. 'Sometimes. I miss the restaurants. And the football.' London had an undeniable buzz. Ironically, it had been Mairi who had been the one to be homesick first for Scotland, and who had wanted to move back. All the same, it had surprised him that he hadn't missed Scotland more. However, now he had returned north he was beginning to enjoy living in Fife.

'Do you like living in Hicksville, then? Always had you down as a big city boy,' said McGhee.

'Trust me, Hicksville has a certain charm. For one thing, you get clean air and beautiful skies. Although,' he looked out through the windscreen at the leaden sky, 'not today,' Carruthers broke suddenly as a pheasant flew across the road.

'Christ,' said McGhee. 'At least in the city you don't get fucking suicidal wildlife.'

Lightning slashed the sky to their right.

'I've always been fascinated by lightning,' said McGhee, 'although we could do with the storm holding off. Don't know too many bird watchers who would be out in the rain. Last thing we want is our cover blown. What caused the fire in Pinetum

Park Forest, do you know? It obviously wasn't a lightning strike. You were pretty lucky. Much damage done?'

'Not a huge amount,' said Carruthers. 'Hadn't long since started when the firefighters turned up. Caused by a disposable BBQ.' There was another rumble of thunder.

'Christ, people can be stupid.'

Carruthers swerved to avoid a pothole. 'Thank goodness nobody was injured. Fletcher was telling me there's a lot of cycle paths in the forest, I'm sure Michael wasn't the only cyclist in there when it started.'

'How's the eye?'

Carruthers absentmindedly touched it. 'Sore.'

'Well, you shouldn't have hit me. You were always going to come off worse. Don't think the nose is broken, thanks for asking though. I could give you a few pointers for a better punch, if you like?'

Carruthers didn't comment. They fell into silence. Finally, they drew close to the long dirt track that led to the farm. 'This is it,' said Carruthers. 'Old Man Docherty's farm. We should set off on foot from here.'

McGhee nodded.

They left the car behind, and walked cautiously up the track, all senses on high alert. Carruthers stumbled on some stones.

'Careful,' said McGhee.

At the first sight of the old farmhouse they stopped in their tracks. They were perhaps two hundred metres away from the farm. To the left was a copse of trees just beyond a field of wheat. To the right, a field of cattle and calves.

'Act normal,' said McGhee as he trained the binoculars on the property. 'After all, we're just a couple of RSPB members out for a day's birdwatching.' He lowered the binoculars. 'No sign of movement, apart from some cows.'

Carruthers gazed at the farm buildings. The old stone farmhouse had an air of dereliction, as did the green corrugated iron barn. A couple of white butterflies flitted low in and out of the grasses, and a swallow swooped over the barn.

McGhee handed the binoculars to Carruthers.

'Christ, it's humid.' Beads of perspiration were gathering on McGhee's top lip.

'Let's just enjoy it whilst it lasts,' said Carruthers, training the binoculars on the farmhouse. 'It's Scotland after all. How are you getting on being based down in the south, by the way?' There was a louder rumble of thunder.

'It's OK. Too full of English folk for my liking.'

'At least you get the chance to see some top-quality premiership games. Managed to get along to any?' Another rumble of thunder. This time much closer.

'Seen Chelsea a few times,' admitted McGhee.

That figures, thought Carruthers. *How typical of McGhee. Flashy and money-driven. Just like Chelsea.* 'I'm more a Gunners man myself. Andie's an Arsenal supporter. In fact, she's Arsenal mad.'

'You've moved on from Mairi already then.'

'If you want this working together to work, don't talk to me about my wife. She's off limits,' said Carruthers.

Carruthers lifted the binoculars to his eyes once again, and took in the wider vista, concentrating this time on the barn. The only movement was in the air. A dozen or so swallows claimed the sky as their own as they fought for supremacy. Suddenly, the sun appeared from behind the clouds, temporarily catching something behind the farmhouse and making it glint.

'Shit,' said Carruthers. 'There's a car parked round the back of the farmhouse. Why didn't I see that before? I'm going to move closer to get a better look. See if I can see the number plate.'

McGhee took the binoculars.

Just as Carruthers started moving, the door of the barn some hundred metres from the farmhouse, was thrown open. McGhee grabbed Carruthers' arm and pulled him back. A man dressed in black and wearing a balaclava came out and scanned the area. Satisfied that there was nobody else around, he disappeared back inside, only to emerge a few seconds later backwards this time, dragging something heavy across the ground.

'Jesus Christ. It's a body,' said McGhee.

Carruthers' heart leapt into his mouth, as he trained the binoculars he'd grabbed back off McGhee onto the figures by the barn. He found himself holding his breath, as he adjusted the lens to get a sharper look.

'Too large to be a woman,' said McGhee dispassionately. The lower half of the body was already out of the door, but not the upper half, which was still inside, partly obscured by the shade. The man left the body where it was. Went back inside. Carruthers strained over McGhee to get a better look.

'Easy tiger,' said McGhee.

Carruthers prayed that McGhee was right about it not being a woman – not being one woman in particular. Lightning lit up the whole sky. The man dragging the corpse suddenly reappeared, this time carrying a large shovel.

'Shit. He's going to bury it,' hissed McGhee. He grabbed the binoculars off Carruthers.

The man walked round the side of the barn disappearing from view. A minute later he reappeared without the shovel; strode purposefully back to the body. Glancing around as he went, he picked up the legs and dragged the rest of the body out of the barn.

Jim's eyes were dry from staring, but he didn't dare look away. What if it was Siobhan? Had he failed her this badly? The body came to view and the breath he didn't know he was holding rushed from his body as he saw a man. A man in a black balaclava. Were the terrorists turning on each other? There was a perceptible sigh when Carruthers saw the rest of the corpse. 'I'm going to call this one in,' he said. His hand trembled as he pulled his mobile from the top of his shirt pocket.

'Obviously something's gone wrong. If they're turning on each other, they're volatile and unpredictable, and from our point of view, more dangerous,' said McGhee as Carruthers called the station on his mobile.

'Still, makes our job a bit easier if it's one less,' said McGhee as Carruthers talked urgently into his mobile.

***

The barn was deathly quiet. Siobhan tried not to stare at the stain of blood on the dirt ground. She swallowed bile. The smell of sweat was strong in the air. And fear. Her own. She glanced at her captor who was pacing the barn. As he sighed, he ripped off his balaclava to reveal a red and sweaty face. Ran a hand over the stubbly grey of his crew cut. Siobhan watched the hard-set lined face, and shivered. Why had he taken the balaclava off? Because he was hot? Or because he was going to kill her? She no longer knew if she would live or die.

He put his hand in his trouser pocket. Brought out a packet of cigarettes. Opened the pack. Took out a fag. Placed it unlit in his mouth.

'Why did you kill Rhys?' she asked.

Silence.

The man drew a box of matches from his other pocket. Lit a cigarette and took a long drag. He exhaled slowly. Finally the man answered. 'He found out about my plans to kill Holdaway. He was going to turn Roberts in to the RAF. He had to be killed.' He started to pace the floor.

'I knew something was wrong,' said Siobhan. 'He wouldn't tell me what it was.'

'Probably didn't want to put you in harm's way.' The man grabbed a nearby bale of straw and straddled it. A clap of thunder made him look towards the barn roof. 'Do you know, I haven't been to confession for thirty years? Not much likelihood of finding a priest anytime soon round here either. I don't think they frequent farms very often.' Perhaps I should have made my headquarters a church,' he laughed mirthlessly. 'I need to get some stuff off my chest. In the absence of a priest you'll have to do.'

TWENTY-TWO

'When will the marksmen and negotiator get here?' Carruthers asked.

'Any time now. Don't go getting all nervous on me.' McGhee looked at his watch. 'Bryn Glas 1402 was never a big outfit. There can't be too many of them left.'

'What do they say? Just takes one,'

'Well, we've already got one,' said McGhee. 'What we want to know is, if there's more than one. I very much doubt our man with the shovel is the brains behind the organisation. He certainly won't be Ewan Williams. You don't get the top dog doing grave digging. They don't usually do their own dirty work.'

As he said this, Carruthers felt something wet land on his shoulder. There was another splat on the ground by his feet. The first drops of rain started to fall. He looked behind him to see a convoy of police and unmarked cars snaking their way quietly and very deliberately up the dirt track towards them.

'I hope they're not spotted,' said Carruthers, jerking his head towards the silent convoy.

'They're not amateurs. Any risk of that and they'd have left the cars at the top of the road. Lucky for us the farm sits in a bit of a valley. In any case, we still don't know if this is a hostage situation.'

'No, we don't. However, the terrorists haven't made contact with either the police or the media, as far as we know. If a woman is being held, for whatever reason, we don't want this to turn into a hostage situation. It's more likely to happen if they see this lot.' As he said it, McGhee turned round and waved his arms to caution those arriving.

'What's happened to the guy who disappeared behind the barn?' said Carruthers.

'Probably still digging his grave.'

Carruthers looked down at his hands. They had a fine sheen of sweat on them. He swallowed. His mouth felt dry.

He kept his eyes focused on the now still farmhouse, but was aware of the activity going on around him. He had a quick look to the dirt track behind them. He could see the marksmen. They had taken their weapons, and they were fanning out all around, stealthily taking up position. He calculated that there must be twenty or so individuals, all dressed in black, with Kevlar vests. All eyes were on the farmhouse and the barn, which suddenly seemed eerily quiet. The wait had begun.

***

'I never saw myself as a terrorist, although you probably do,' said Ewan. There was a loud hammering on the corrugated iron roof as the rain hit it. 'The Irish Republican Army didn't see themselves as terrorists, did they? They saw themselves as freedom fighters.'

'Is that what you are?'

'In a manner of speaking. It will be hard for you to understand, being English, but for centuries the Welsh, like the Irish and Scots, have been persecuted. Our customs, language, culture have all been under threat. We are a fierce and proud nation, us Welsh.'

'Is that why you turned to violence?'

'We all need a reason to get up in the morning. Something to believe in. Something to keep us going.'

'Most people have family and jobs for that.'

Ewan laughed. 'You've got spirit. I like that. And you remind me of someone. Someone close to me, before her life was blighted by being in the wrong place at the wrong time.' He stared at a point fixed somewhere behind Siobhan's head. 'Someone had to pay for that,' he continued. 'There are events from the past, my past, which you don't know about. Bringing you here was a mistake. I see that now. I'm sorry you got hurt.'

'Why did you bring me here? What did you think I might know?'

'It doesn't matter now. It's obvious you didn't know anything. All I know is that this is going to have a very different ending to the one I saw. Don't worry. I won't hurt you.'

Ewan fell silent. His eyes turned to the roof as rain started hard and unexpected. His eyes seemed infinitely sad as he looked back at Siobhan. 'I've seen and done many things in my time, Siobhan, but I've never hurt a woman. I've seen women hurt, though. One woman in particular. That changed my life as well as hers. She was my sister.' An image suddenly came into his head of his nineteen-year-old sister walking by his side wearing the paisley-patterned dress she always loved to wear. She looked so young, so beautiful, so full of hope. Full of promise of a future she would soon be denied.

'What happened to her?'

'She was shot by a soldier. Over in Northern Ireland. On a peace march.' He laughed but the laugh was hollow. 'Somewhat ironic, don't you think? I vowed revenge, but at the time she made me promise I wouldn't seek it.'

'She sounds like an incredible person.'

'She was.'

'What changed? What changed for you to go after him now, after all this time?'

'She died a couple of months ago. After her death, I didn't feel I had to keep my promise any longer.'

'If this happened in Northern Ireland, why are you up in Scotland?'

'I came after the man who shot her. He wrote a book and I recognised his photograph on the back of it – even after all these years. I think you call it serendipity.'

'Professor Holdaway? He shot your sister? The car bomb. That's why he was targeted? Did you mean to kill him? He was unhurt though. He wasn't in the car. He escaped.'

'He hasn't escaped, Siobhan. Neither one of us has escaped. We're both caught up in a dance to which there is no end. The past always catches us up. And all our actions have consequences. I've found that out. I'm older now. I regret a lot of what I've done. Perhaps my life would have been different had my sister not been shot. I often thought about the man who shot her. I hated him. That hate consumed me. I often wondered whether he regretted what he did.'

'Don't go after him,' Siobhan advised. 'I'm sure he'll have his own demons to deal with, if he is any sort of a decent human being.'

'If I have a job to do, I always finish it. I've waited so long to make Holdaway pay for what he did. In the end, I didn't get the opportunity.' He stood up. Walked towards her. 'I'm going to let you go, Siobhan. I'll–'

Gunfire peppered the air outside.

Siobhan screamed.

'Keep down,' shouted Ewan pulling her on to the floor. He grabbed an old blanket from the far side of the bale of straw and threw it over her.

He pulled out his gun and reloaded it.

'It's alright. I'm not going to use it on you,' he said. 'Keep your head down, keep quiet, and you won't get hurt.' Ewan pushed her head down hard.

Ewan crept to the front of the barn, opened the door a crack, just wide enough to look out. The rain was bouncing off the ground. Visibility was poor. He couldn't see anything except the dirt track leading up to the gate, to the left, the farmhouse. Beyond, the rolling fields of Fife were shrouded in low hanging cloud. He knew they had come for him, were outside. Time was short. He shut the door. Crouched with his back to it, cradling his gun to his chest.

***

Carruthers and McGhee crept forward. Carruthers trained the binoculars on the barn. He touched McGhee's arm to get his attention. 'That guy's back,' he hissed. 'No body or shovel though.'

259

As the man walked towards the barn, Carruthers saw a movement behind a fence. One of the marksmen. The terrorist jerked round, drew his gun. Fired.

There was a shout of pain. The marksman had been hit in the shoulder and went down. Suddenly there was a volley of shots from several different places, hidden shooters. The terrorist collapsed in a pool of his own blood.

A woman's shriek trilled from inside the barn.

'Shit, there is a woman in there after all.' Carruthers hoped against hope it wasn't Siobhan Mathews.

The rain was coming down in sheets now, making visibility even more difficult. His hair was plastered to his face. He was soaked to the skin, his clothes sticking to him. Even his feet were wet inside his trainers. There was a rumble of thunder. Lightning lit up the darkened sky. Outside the police marksmen held their positions, awaiting their next command.

***

Inside the barn, Ewan stood up and very carefully opened the barn door a fraction with his gun barrel and looked out. His eye took in the same view of the drive and the farmhouse. He opened the door a little further to widen his field of vision. This time he was rewarded. He caught sight of movement some way behind the gate. Police. He could smell them a mile off.

He knew the farm was most likely surrounded. There would be more than just two officers. Whatever else happened, he wasn't going to be taken alive. He wasn't a fool. Still, Holdaway was finally dead. He smiled, but it was a sad smile, as he kept his eye on the movement by the gate.

***

1972. He was with the marchers. It was cold but with a bright blue sky. He looked around him. The people he was with were purposeful but peaceful. He looked across at his sister wearing her favourite paisley-patterned dress embroidered with flowers. January. She wore her velvet cape over her dress. She took his hand and squeezed. He squeezed back. Her new husband was walking by her side. His friends beside him. Marching because they wanted peace. An end to the bloodshed. But then the first shots. People running. He grabbed his sister's hand and they began to run too. Found themselves down an alley separated from Meg's husband and his friends. He could hear people running behind him. A shot so loud it filled the air. Meg screamed. A second shot then a third. A moment later it was carnage. Shouts. Screaming. Gunshots. Terror. Saw the soldier on his knee in a firing position. Looked back at his sister. She fell as in slow motion. Pain and shock painted her face. Then he saw it. An ever-expanding pool of blood seeping from her body.

***

Ewan caught a movement as one of the two plain-clothes men adjusted his position, exposing his shoulder as he did so. He recognised the tall grey-haired cop. As Ewan drew his gun he saw the stockier man realise the danger and shove his colleague out of the way. Ewan pulled the trigger. Both men went down as the barn door was thrown open and the leader of Bryn Glas 1402 burst out shooting.

***

Ewan didn't make it ten yards before he was cut down by a hail of bullets. His death ended his forty-year search for the former soldier who had shot his sister.

He lay spreadeagled on his back with his eyes wide open and glassy, as if looking heavenward. No look of surprise was registered on his face, for he had already known his fate. A trickle of blood came out the side of his mouth and coursed down his neck.

TWENTY-THREE

Carruthers was winded by the weight of McGhee's body landing on top of him. He shifted to roll McGhee off him, as he struggled to sit up, squinting against the falling rain.

'McGhee?' No response. 'Alistair?' His growing urgency was revealed in his voice, as he realised that the man wasn't moving. It was then that he saw the pool of blood, which seemed to be spreading at an alarming rate.

'Christ, McGhee's been hit!'

One of the marksmen crawled over to them. 'Ambulances are on their way.'

McGhee's eyes flickered, as Carruthers crouched beside the prone form. He looked into the face of the man that he blamed for the breakup of his marriage. He realised he didn't want McGhee to die. They would never be bosom buddies, but here was a fellow police officer who'd been shot. It could so easily have been him. His voice was full of emotion as he spoke. 'You're going to be alright, Alistair. Ambulance is on its way.'

'Christ,' murmured McGhee. 'First names. I must be in a bad way.' His breath came out in ragged gasps.

'You'll be just fine,' Carruthers said with more conviction that he felt. Carruthers opened his rucksack and brought out his first aid box.

'Might have known you'd have a first aid box. Were you head boy at school as well?' McGhee groaned in pain.

'Boy Scouts. Keep quiet. I need to apply pressure.' He grabbed a bandage, threw the box on the ground. He applied firm pressure but within moments the blood was seeping through the bandage, even as the rain soaked it from above.

'Where the fuck is the ambulance?' shouted Carruthers.

As if in answer he heard sirens. Looked round to see a convoy of six ambulances snaking their way up the dirt track to the farm.

The marksmen had by now closed in on the farmhouse and barn, but seemed reluctant to enter.

'What's holding them back? There's a woman in there. She might be hurt.'

'Might be wired. Can't go in all guns blazing.' McGhee said through gritted teeth.

'Wired?' repeated Carruthers feeling stupid.

'Tripwire. Booby-trapped. And if there's one booby-trap device, there could be a second. Depends how much Semtex they managed to get hold of, and whether this was part of their plan. Ahh,' McGhee cried in pain as he shifted position.

Carruthers swallowed hard, worried about the sheen of sweat on McGhee's pale face. He did his best to stop the bleeding. His own shirt was covered in McGhee's blood, the rain spreading the stain. A quick image entered his head of the bloodied T-shirt found at Charlene Todd's. 'We need to get you to hospital.' When he had looked up again, the marksmen had now entered the barn. Again they heard a woman cry.

'Go and find out if it's her.' The words were slow and slurred. McGhee's breathing was becoming laboured.

'I'm not going to leave you. And stop talking. Save your energy.'

The paramedics had arrived and crouched on the other side of McGhee. They ripped his shirt and applied pressure to the wound with a large bandage. Then they gently laid him on a stretcher and hoisted the stretcher up.

McGhee's complexion had taken on a greyish look. He was trying to speak. Carruthers had to lean close to hear him.

'Go on, man. If it makes you feel better bring me a bunch of grapes in hospital.'

Carruthers hesitated, but knowing McGhee was now in safe hands, he grasped McGhee's uninjured shoulder and gave it a quick squeeze. There was nothing more he could do here. He then hurried over to the barn stepping over the spread-eagled body of Ewan Williams. One of the marksmen stopped him.

Carruthers grasped his arm. 'There's a woman in there. I think I know who it is.'

'You'll have to wait until the site is secure. When it is, I'll give you the go-ahead. OK?'

Carruthers waited. It seemed like an age. He saw the ambulance carrying McGhee snake its way back down the farmhouse track. He prayed the man would survive. He finally heard the words he wanted. 'Site's secured. You can go in now.'

Carruthers thanked him and stepped inside. His eyes took a while to adjust to the greater dark in the barn, before settling on a figure partially covered by a filthy blanket on the ground, surrounded by two of the marksmen one of whom who was kneeling beside it.

'We need another stretcher over here,' the marksman called.

Carruthers' heart missed a beat and with four long strides he was beside the huddled figure. He leant over the man and was shocked at what he saw. It was Siobhan Mathews. Her face and top were streaked with dirt and dried tears. There was a rip in her skirt. She was lying in a pool of what he could only guess was her own urine.

'Is he dead?' she whispered.

'Who?' asked Carruthers, having to draw down closer to her so that he could hear her faint whisper.

'That man?'

'I think so, yes. Oh my God, Siobhan.' She turned her head away from him. 'We need to get you to hospital.' He picked up one of Siobhan's hands in his. It was icy cold. He began to rub it.

'I want to see a female doctor. Can you arrange it?' She looked into his eyes as she spoke. Carruthers felt a lump in his throat, and could only manage a nod. 'You'll come with me?' Siobhan looked up at him.

'Of course I will.' He could call the station from the hospital, and at the same time check up on Alistair McGhee's progress. Just as he was heading out of the barn he noticed a rucksack in the corner and a dirt-streaked file on the ground. He bent over to pick them both up. Once they were safely in the ambulance Carruthers opened the file. It was the missing paperwork belonging to Rhys Evans.

TWENTY-FOUR

THURSDAY MORNING, 7TH JUNE

'Should you be back at work so soon, Andie?' asked Carruthers. He was leaning over her desk.

'I feel fine now, Jim. Just try to keep a good woman down. I'm just sorry I missed all the action though. What's the latest on Superintendent McGhee?'

'Bingham's seen him more recently than me,' said Carruthers, grabbing his coffee and notebook. 'Let's get to the debrief. He can fill us in.'

'Right, thanks for attending,' said Bingham a short while later in the meeting room. 'As you know, Ewan Williams has been killed. As has John Edwards.'

'How's Superintendent McGhee?' asked Brown.

'McGhee's undergone an operation to remove the bullet. He lost a lot of blood but should make a good recovery. He was lucky. Bullet missed all his major organs. He'll be in hospital for a while. There're transferring him to one closer to his home. I'm sure we all wish him well.'

There were general murmurs of agreement.

'I heard he was asking to stay up here in Scotland,' said Carruthers. 'Apparently he wants to have a break from the English.'

They all laughed.

'Dinnae blame him,' said Harris. 'I wouldnae want to be surrounded by the fucking English either.'

Fletcher scowled at him. 'If they had any sense they wouldn't let you cross the border.'

'OK, let's get serious,' said Bingham. He turned to Carruthers. 'What about Siobhan Mathews? How's she doing?'

Carruthers was thoughtful for a moment. 'I think she'll take longer to recover. It's more the psychological scars.'

Carruthers didn't tell the rest of the station about Mathews' rape, although he knew he would tell Bingham in private later. Siobhan had asked him to keep it quiet, and since the man who raped her was dead, he would respect her wishes without pushing. 'She's been really brave. I think Williams knew he wasn't going to get out of there alive. He used her as a confessor.'

'As we now know, Williams' real interest lay in paying Holdaway back for the maiming of his sister.' said Bingham.

'Why no' just pay for an assassin to kill him?' asked Harris.

'He would never have paid an assassin. Remember – this wasn't a business dealing gone wrong. It was personal. As the core members of the so-called terrorist group are now dead, we'll never really know for sure, so this is pure speculation. However, I think Williams wanted Holdaway to suffer. He literally wanted to terrorise him, to keep him awake at night fretting about why he was being targeted. That's why he sent the hate mail.'

'His writing a book on the failings of Welsh nationalism and buying a second home were opportunities just too good to miss, I suppose,' said Fletcher. 'With those facts, he was able to inspire and motivate the other members of Bryn Glas to go after a legitimate target.'

'Remember that had he not written that book, had it not been so ruddy popular and stocked in Waterstones, Williams would probably never been able to track Holdaway down,' commented Bingham.

Carruthers wondered if this were true. He remembered what Holdaway had said. Four hundred and fifty former soldiers were going to be re-interviewed about the events of Bloody Sunday.

'Why did Williams have Dave Roberts murdered? Was it because he knew too much? Outlasted his usefulness?' asked Harris.

'He'd definitely outlasted his usefulness. It was only a matter of time before the police picked him up. Perhaps Williams was worried Roberts would try to strike a deal with the police. Lesser sentence if he cooperated. He more than likely knew where Williams was hiding out. Could have blown his chances of getting to Holdaway. And remember, Roberts let Holdaway live. That in itself would have shown Williams that Roberts wasn't as committed as Williams thought he should be.'

Bingham cleared his throat. 'Right now, I don't know if any of you have seen the ridiculous headlines in one or two of the daily rags?' He picked up a newspaper and waved it around. 'Terrorists infiltrate Britain's armed forces,' he read out aloud. 'I would just like to make it clear for all of you that terrorists have not infiltrated our armed services. A press statement later today will be released to that effect. The MOD is not in the least bit happy about this.'

Harris, who had his own copy under his arm, hid the paper under an old copy of *Playboy*.

'The MOD have to find a way of getting that ruddy paper to issue an apology and retract the story before it sets off a general panic in the British public. It really is quite scandalous what these people think they can get away with. Freedom of the press has gone too bloody far, in my opinion. The RAF will be issuing their own statement about Dave Roberts being an active member of the BNP.'

Carruthers remembered some of the more unsavoury headlines of the gutter press about refugees, Muslims and terrorists, and had to agree with Bingham about freedom of the press.

'I thought you were allowed to be a member of the BNP if you were in the armed forces,' said Brown.

'My understanding is that, membership, whilst serving Queen and Country, is still legitimate, unless service personnel are actively recruiting. It looks as if Roberts certainly fell into the latter category.'

'What happened to all the BNP propaganda in Roberts' room, sir?' asked Fletcher.

'I've spoken to the RAF,' said Bingham. 'There'll be an internal investigation. Seems Dave Roberts, whilst unpopular on a lot of fronts, still had his friends at the base. It's likely one of his mates got rid of it for him, along with the poster, after he went missing. This is a mess for the RAF to clear up, but I wouldn't want to be in the shoes of the young man or woman who took those magazines. They'll be in a hell of a lot of trouble. The RAF police are taking this very seriously.'

'I feel sorry for Dave Roberts' parents,' said Fletcher. 'It will also probably open an investigation into the disappearance of that black apprentice at the garage where he worked.'

'Rest assured, if that man cannot be found, there'll be huge public pressure put upon the South Wales Police to open an investigation into his disappearance.'

'I blame Stephen Lawrence for all this,' remarked Harris.

'You can't blame somebody who got murdered by racist thugs. If you want to blame anyone, blame the murderers and the incompetence of the Met,' retorted Fletcher.

'Well, all this crap about institutional racism,' Harris threw back. 'And this drive that's been launched to recruit more ethnic minorities on to the Scottish Police Force. It's pish. I mean, how many black and Asian faces do you see in some parts of Scotland?'

'Ethnic minorities make up four per cent of the Scottish population,' said Fletcher, 'however they only make up one per cent of the police up here. I think having a drive to recruit more is reasonable.'

Harris snorted. 'All I can say is, thankfully, we already have our ethnic minority so we dinnae need to take anyone else on,' said Harris.

'Do we?' said Bingham looking confused.

'Aye, we do. We've got Andie. She's our ethnic minority on account of the fact that she's English.'

Fletcher gave Harris the finger.

'Right, that's enough,' said Bingham. 'Settle down. As I said, good job well done. That's it. Thank you for your time.' The room started to clear. 'Carruthers, can I see you in my office please? What I've got to say won't take long.'

Carruthers looked up, his heart sinking. He caught Fletcher's sympathetic eye. He glanced around the room and noticed Harris was smirking. He wanted to follow Fletcher's lead and give Harris the finger too.

Carruthers followed Bingham out of the room and into his office.

'Right, close the door.'

Carruthers did as he was bid.

'Take a seat.'

Carruthers looked at the proffered brown leather chair but continued to stand. He waited for Bingham to speak.

'Stand if you wish.' Bingham was silent as he scrutinised Carruthers.

Carruthers wondered if he was looking as careworn as he felt. He tried to hide the wariness and resentment he carried, but he could see Bingham looking at his swollen and partially closed left eye. Bingham let out an audible sigh.

'You and Fletcher did a good job with certain aspects of the investigation.' He paused and Carruthers could see that Bingham was deliberating how to continue. Carruthers' face was immobile but his heart was thudding. Bingham went on to speak his mind in his characteristically blunt fashion.

'However, you don't listen to orders. And when you do, you choose to ignore them anyway.' Bingham looked Carruthers in the eye. 'Then there's the matter of the fight between you and Alistair. Bad enough if it had happened outside the station. But here? Right under my nose? Where junior officers saw and have been talking about the incident. I can't let it go. I hope you understand that.'

Carruthers nodded.

'You will take an extended period of leave while I make a decision about your future.'

Carruthers made to speak but Bingham held his hand up.

'We'll discuss it when you get back. However, I should tell you that if you do remain at this station, it won't be as a DCI.

You'll be lucky to remain as inspector at all,' Bingham sighed. 'Dismissed.'

***

Carruthers walked out of Bingham' office. He closed the door carefully behind him, momentarily standing with his back to it allowing his head to rest against its coolness. He remained like that for a few seconds, then walked away back to his office.

'How did it go with Bingham?' asked Fletcher, putting her head round his door.

Carruthers couldn't bring himself to make eye contact with Fletcher. 'He's ordered me to take an extended period of leave in which time he's going to consider my future.' He didn't tell her about the demotion: that wasn't official yet.

'I'm sorry. That's tough. Do you want me to talk to him?'

Carruthers looked up fondly at Fletcher, knowing she couldn't do anything to help.

'No, it's OK.'

Fletcher was frowning. 'How long will you be off?'

'I don't know The details haven't been discussed yet.' He realised he hadn't asked Bingham. He swallowed down a lump that felt the size of a golf ball. 'At least I can take that camping trip I was planning on. You look as if you want to ask me something?'

'Whilst you're off, can we keep in touch?'

'Of course.'

Carruthers saw a look of relief pass over her face.

'There's something else,' she said. 'About the case. Do *you* think Holdaway had a right to get his book published?'

'That came out of left field, Andie.'

'I know. But, well, Bingham has just been talking about freedom of the press. I just wondered what you thought.'

'Of course he had a right to get it published. I guess the problem is he didn't think about the consequences.'

As he said it he thought about the satirical cartoonists over in France who had poked fun at Islam. Fully aware of the dangers, they had been determined to exercise their right to freedom of expression. And they paid the ultimate price.

'No, but, well, he wasn't to know that the brother of the girl he shot would have actually recognised his photograph on the back of the book forty years later and gone after him.' *However,* thought Carruthers, *how long would Holdaway have kept his anonymity for anyway? Would he have eventually been charged with attempted murder for the shooting of Holdaway's sister?* He didn't say any of this. Instead he said, 'I wonder if Holdaway would have committed suicide further down the line anyway? I guess we'll never know.'

'Has it been confirmed, Jim? Did Nicholas Holdaway commit suicide?'

'Mackie's pretty convinced. The injuries had all the hallmarks of suicide.'

'You wonder how the blokes who served in Northern Ireland and places like the Falklands actually coped afterwards.'

'Well, there was certainly less help for them than there is nowadays. At least post-traumatic stress disorder is now a recognised mental health problem.'

'I'm not sure that they're getting the help that they need,' said Fletcher. 'You and I both know that there's still a disproportionate number of service personnel who have mental health problems, end up homeless living on Britain's streets. I think the soldiers on that peace march were just as much victims as the people they shot. After all, they were young, scared, just following orders. It must be a terrible thing to have to live with afterwards.'

Carruthers thought the soldiers, like the marchers, would have been made up of a cross-section of society. There would have been good and bad people amongst them. 'The real victims were the people shot on the march and their families,' said Carruthers, remembering the details he'd read. He wondered how long it would be until he got the image of the man gently taking the shoes off the feet of his dead friend out of his head.

'What about Siobhan Mathews? Will she stay in Castletown?'
'Siobhan Mathews?' said Carruthers. 'I don't know. I'm not sure she'll be able to continue her studies. She may well have to take some time out. If she does leave Castletown, will she ever want to come back?' Carruthers thought if it was him he'd probably want a fresh start somewhere else. He thought about what Siobhan had said regarding Rhys Evans looking for his birth mother. A birth mother he would now never find, who would never know the baby she gave away. 'I found the folder by the way. At the farm. Evans had enough ammunition in it to bring down both Roberts and Williams. He'd also found his birth mother. I guess that's what he was on his way to tell Siobhan.'

'Oh my God, that's so sad. Are you going to tell Siobhan?'
'I think she'd like to know.'
'You never know what's going to happen in the future, boss.'
'No, you don't. Maybe that's a good thing. And talking about the future, Andie,' he said, 'tonight I want you to go home and talk to Mark about the pregnancy. You need to start making plans. Who's going to look after the baby when you're at work, for example?'
'Mark's family live close,' she said. 'I get on well with them.' She sighed. 'But you're right. We do need a proper chat.'
'That's a good start.'
But despite his positive words he remembered Mark's strange reaction to Fletcher being taken to hospital and a knot of anxiety gripped him. 'What about your own parents?'
'Telling them is going to be more difficult. They're old fashioned. They also live too far away to be of much help.' She looked across at him. 'You look as if you need a break,' she said. 'Especially after this business with McGhee. I hope you enjoy your time off. What are you going to do whilst you're off?'
'When I'm not exercising and drinking beer you mean? Hopefully lots of reading.' *And brooding.* He'd worked hard to become a DCI. Couldn't believe he'd thrown it away. 'Actually, that reminds me. Have you seen that bomb disposal thriller that's

been kicking around the station, *The Tick Tock Man?* Thought I might take it away with me, along with a couple of Bond books.'

'Bloody hell. Thought you'd have had more than enough of explosives and mayhem, Jim. Why don't you stick to fishing and hill walking?'

Carruthers looked over at Fletcher and smiled.

The End

ACKNOWLEDGMENTS

The encouragement and support I've had from family, friends and fellow crime writers has been huge, in particular, Sarah Ward and Alison Baillie who were my first readers. I would also like to thank Allan Guthrie who was very generous with his time.

Jacky Collins, Barry Forshaw, Kim Miller, Mike Linane and Rosy Barnes deserve a special mention for all their help and friendship in all things crime and writing.

Peter Robinson for his writing courses and DCI Banks series. It was the reading of 'In a Dry Summer,' that made me fall in love with crime fiction.

Tony Fyler and my wonderful and very talented former Editor, Gail Williams from Jefferson Franklin Editing Agency.

Avery Mathers, Kevin Blackley and Lester Knibb for police procedure although Avery was also a huge help in the writing department. Chris Wilson for advice on RAF procedure. Stewart Sutherland for obscure facts about Fife.

All at Bloodhound Books especially Betsy Reavley, Alexina Golding and Clare Law.

I am indebted to you all.

And finally, but most importantly, Ian Brown for encouraging me to board the flight that would take me to the University of Tallinn to study under Peter Robinson in the summer of 2011 at a time when my writing was faltering.

I would like to dedicate this novel to Brian McGrath, a thoroughly decent guy, who gave me huge encouragement to write this book. He sadly passed away before the novel was completed.

This is a work of fiction but based on certain real events. Those who know the East Neuk of Fife will recognise the fictional town of Castletown as being loosely modelled on St Andrews but any characters in the book are products of the author's imagination. Although this is a police procedural it is still a work of fiction and I hope I can be forgiven if I have stretched things a wee bit to suit the storyline. Any mistakes are my own.

Lightning Source UK Ltd.
Milton Keynes UK
UKOW03f0700100217
293882UK00011B/29/P